Mud

&

Horizons

Book 2 of Dust & Cannibals

I0549375

Bruce I Schindler

Copyright 2015, Bruce I. Schindler
All rights reserved.

ISBN: 0991462726
ISBN-13: 978-0-9914627-2-8

This is a work of fiction. All the characters and events portrayed in this book are fictional, and any resemblance to real people or incidents is purely coincidental.

By Bruce I. Schindler

The LaGrange Legacy

Dust & Cannibals

Touch Stones

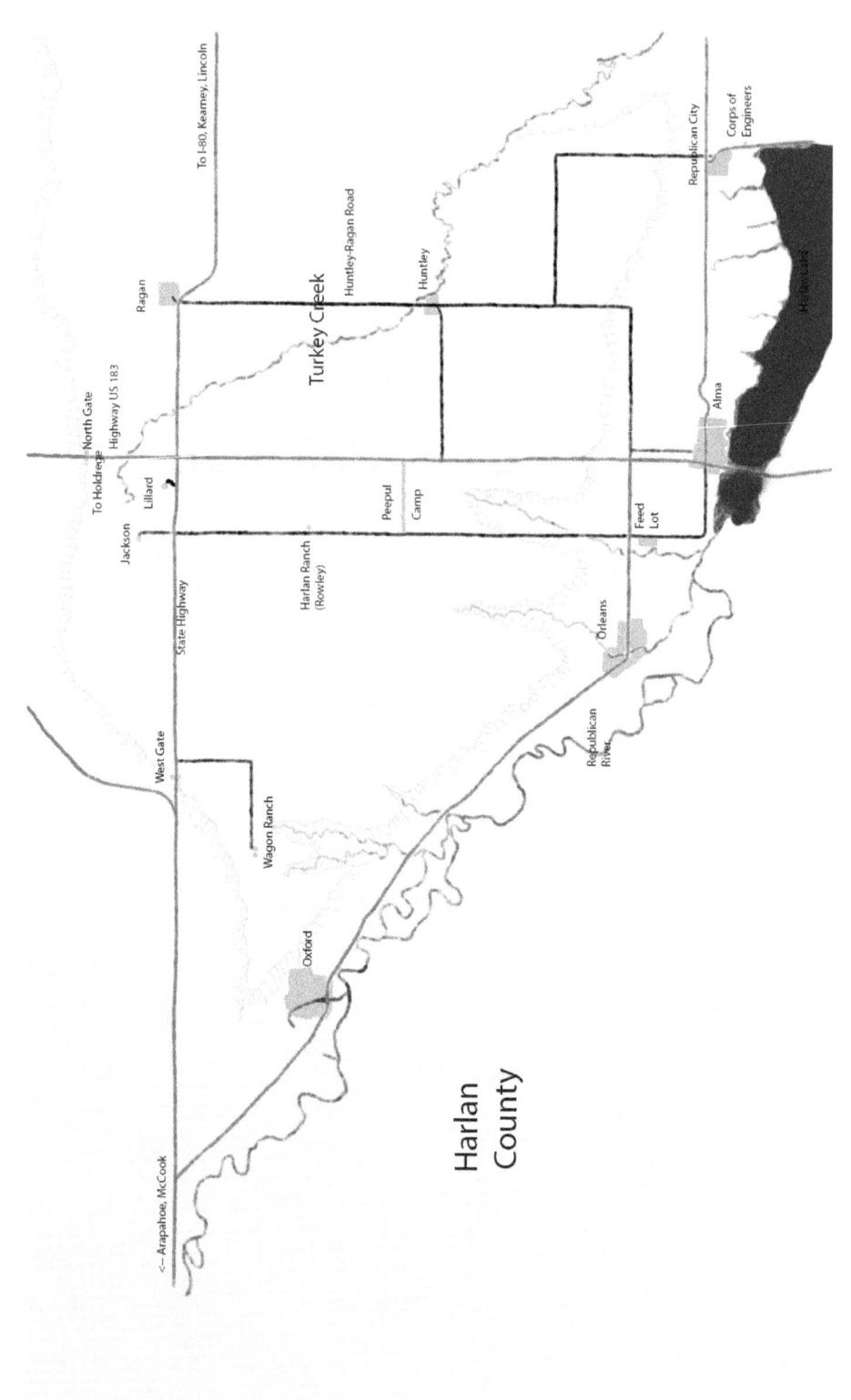

Chapter 1
Assisting Deputy Vince

The horizon called Mark like an old drinking buddy. Managing the Harlan Ranch and romancing Ellen usually kept his focus on taking care of current events. Now, with nothing else to do, he slipped back into the bad habit of comparing the nasty mud of the here and now to the clean lines of the horizon. He was only here because of Vince's mysterious request to help track bicycles, of all things.

He relaxed in the saddle, and left a loose rein so his palomino could crop the late summer grass beside the road. The filly now raised her head, and Mark looked around as Vince rode up, grinning at him.

"Ellen let you out of the house, I see."

"She couldn't get rid of me soon enough. On top of it, Kevin was strutting around, braying about how smooth he had everything going. Ellen pushed me out the door with ideas about fun things to install in the wedding house."

Vince laughed. "Did you tell her that they don't want you anywhere near there?"

"I tried, but she wanted me to pass the word along, if nothing else. Evidently, I'm supposed to peep, pry, and sneak around to figure out what they're doing. She'll give me the third degree about every possible detail, known or supposed."

"I've been there enough to give you a few things to tell her. It might make her think she knows what's going on. Maybe that can be your pay for helping me out."

Mark grinned. "That sounds like a deal. I still don't see what's so hard about following bike tracks. The bike tracks are never on the road. They are always off to the side. Where the bikes cross the road, the riders carry them to avoid leaving evidence. It sounds entertaining, but I can't see why you need me."

Vince grimaced. "We've looked at these damn tracks quite a while. Nobody has a clue whether they are friends or foes. We first found them when everybody went to Harlan Dam, and Mr. Lillard, Josh, and you had the shoot-out with that character calling himself Morgan Carr, who turned out to be a terrorist."

Mark was astonished. "How long have you been seeing these tracks?"

"That was the first time. I had the eastern side of the county. After you guys came back from getting the first solar buggy, it was all hands on deck to defend Harlan. Josh took care of western Harlan, and if he saw any tracks, he didn't tell me. When Josh and Alicia announced the wedding, I took over the whole county. Those damn tracks showed up again."

Mark thought he understood the situation. "Do you find fresh ones all the time?"

"They only show up now and then, like they're from somewhere else. If they were friendly, wouldn't they say hello?"

Mark scratched just above his temple. "Nobody in Harlan has a bike, at least nothing that works. The terrorists are the only other survivors, so this is major, whoever they are."

"That's what I think," Vince replied. "Maybe you can work with me to decipher this."

Mark considered a bit more. "Getting off the ranch to help you could be a challenge. Of course, Ellen thinks I should supervise the wedding house. She is really big on embarrassing the hell out of Alicia with what she calls a shivaree. That's even though Alicia is her best friend. The people rigging the place want me to stay away, thinking Ellen and I will be next."

Mark was astonished how that slipped out of his mouth. He quickly added, "Of course, some people's mouths run faster than any horse. Anyway, Kevin has the everyday stuff under control at the ranch, and Ellen neither wants nor needs my help inside. So, yeah, I'll take a look at these unidentified bicycle tracks of yours."

Vince chuckled. "You talk about other people's mouths. I should be happy to know somebody survived the Omega bug besides us and those terrorists. On the other hand, we don't have any idea who or what they are. You are the best tracker in Harlan, and I hope you can help us figure that out."

Mark grunted. "If there are other people, and they aren't dead set on trying to kill us, that's a good thing. Even if they aren't the terrorists, it doesn't make them our best buddies. We should keep this between as few people as possible for now. We sure don't need to mess up Josh and Alicia's wedding plans. This is the closest thing to a good time anyone in Harlan has had since the Omega dust went through. On the other hand, if there is a danger, we need to know as soon as possible. Where are these bike tracks of yours?"

Vince pointed to some nearby bushes. "There are some just behind that brush. We think our mystery people were checking out life in the mighty metropolis of Ragan."

Mark snorted. "Ragan had a population of fifty-eight before everything went to hell. With the refugees, it may have a couple hundred now. That had to be a major research project. Okay, lead on."

Dismounting and leading his horse, Mark carefully checked the tire tracks and other sign.

"There were two men," he said.

"Why do you think they were men?"

"If these tracks were made by women, they have very big feet. They spent some time here, and rode off in a westerly direction. They probably came from the Huntley area, from what you've already told me. Do we want to follow where they came from or where they went?"

"West is toward the Lillard place, so let's check that first. My people haven't had problems around Huntley."

The trail led behind a row of cedar trees forming a windbreak across the road from the Lillard Ranch, the de facto seat of government for Harlan. Mark nosed around the area in detail.

"They spent quite a bit of time here. They both slid under the tree branches to look at the Lillard house. They didn't leave trash behind, and it looks like they were here before. Mr. Lillard talks about the human race being an endangered species. Maybe this is the agency making a head count of the survivors."

"That is really cute, Mark. Did you learn all that from your father or mother?"

Mark's jaw tightened. "My parents died in a car accident when I was young. Neither the State people nor the endless chain of foster parents ever taught me squat about being cute."

"Oops, I do recall hearing about that. Write that off to a brain cramp coming from concern about these mysterious watchers."

"I suppose," Mark said softly. "Their trail leads south toward my place. They created their own trail. This isn't a game trail and none of us would use this way. We'd just ride down the road."

Vince blinked. "Does it say anything about their intentions?"

"It doesn't tell me a damn thing. Hell, Vince, you're the cop. What's your feel for it?"

"Uncomfortable," came a response through tight lips.

There were also signs of an area with a view of Mark's ranch, although no indication of more time spent there than at Ragan. At that point, the bike path led southeast. The destination was apparent.

"You know, Vince, I'm not pleased to go this way. There's only one place I know of in a line with this path."

Vince growled, "Yeah, we're headed for the old cannibal camp. I'm just glad they left."

"I'd swear there's still a smell to the place. I remember when Josh and I checked them out. I'm just glad they never saw us."

The bike path ran parallel to the camp, now just individual fire pits along an unused farm road. Then, it crossed US 183 where the cannibals had their ambush for unwary travelers. Looking across the highway, the continuation of the bike trail was evident. They followed it up a small bluff, into an obvious observation post.

"This hasn't been used recently, Vince. The great rain that took away the Omega dust also took any usable sign here. It took more than two people to man this, and was used for quite a while, maybe the same amount of time the cannibals were there. Josh and I both felt we were being watched. Whoever was here also watched us just over there."

Mark pointed at a shorter hill above where the head cannibal had his camp.

Vince looked at Mark. "If the cannibals had lookouts, they would have called out the tribe on you. Maybe they weren't part of the tribe. Did the cannibals have bicycles?"

"Their knives and stew pots were all I knew about. We know these folks are keeping an eye on us now, and they also watched the cannibals. How is your comfort level now, Vince?"

"My suspicions are running a figure-eight race. Where do we go from here? It looks like a well-worn trail heading east from here."

It was a short ride, ending at a former homestead. Efforts were made to weatherproof the place, and it was here the mystery men stayed. The stove was cold, but Mark found a few small live coals.

"They were here maybe three days ago," Mark decided.

Out back, there was a trench, used as a latrine and trash disposal site. An old smokehouse had been in use recently. Mark's nose gave him that information long before he got there. It was full of smoked meat.

Vince and Mark grinned at each other. "Beef and venison are good," Mark commented, "but pork is a good change."

Vince nodded. "It might distract Ellen from her shivaree kick if you bring home the bacon."

"That is an excellent idea. I need to head home anyway. If each of us rigs a travois, we could haul all of this. It must be a gift, right?"

"We use the contents of every place not currently occupied. This is in the public domain. Nobody lives here now, and those taken by the Omega Bug can't use it."

Behind the smokehouse, Vince made his own discovery. "Hey, Mark, does this look familiar?"

"Boy, howdy! Meals, Ready to Eat, better known as MRE. There are several cases of them. That brings back memories, mostly bad ones. I'll bet Ellen could create meals with this a soldier wouldn't even recognize."

"You can only hope, Mark," Vince laughed.

They found suitable long poles, which they put on either side of their saddles, letting one end drag on the ground. Their horses got nervous with the unfamiliar things trailing behind them but settled down after a bit. They then attached cross-braces onto the long poles, followed by smaller branches to form a platform. Since the sun was starting to get low in the sky, they hurried.

Mark mounted up. "I'll get this home and we'll meet here tomorrow morning. Does that sound like a plan?"

"It does indeed. Do you need me to go over the details about the wedding night house?"

"I got enough, I think. With all of this, it should work."

Mark and Vince exchanged grins the next morning.

"Was Ellen pleased with your day's work?"

"I had my excuses ready, but she took one look at the loot and yelled for Kevin to help haul stuff. They didn't even leave me with anything to do."

"That's how it was at my house, too, except that by the time I got to my house in Ragan, the entire town was with me. It was quite the parade. There were plenty of hands to help unload, and everybody hauled off some, so our pickings were slimmer than yours."

It was time to get to work. "We've seen everything at the old cabin. We might go through their garbage, but since they combined their trash dump with their latrine, I'm not inclined to dig."

"That might have been the point of it, and we need to find out where these jokers came from. In the old days, we could have done this more quickly. A couple of phone calls, and fifteen minutes in a car would have taken care of the situation."

"If we had electricity, gas, and all of that, we wouldn't worry about a couple of pilgrims on bicycles. All we have now is word of mouth and horses to ride."

Vince laughed. "I was just venting. After spending the better part of a year patrolling on foot, I'm grateful for horsepower and being able to talk to anybody, especially considering what the rest of humanity paid."

The trail followed just below the line of the ridge facing Alma and crossed the highway. Like at the old cannibal camp, they could see where the bikes were carried from one side to the field across from it. It was a curious procedure, but Mark and Vince agreed nobody saw these people.

The bikes stopped to observe the feed lot near Alma and another short stop above Orleans, now a ghost town. At last, the bike trail came to the end of the bluff that everyone called the prow of Lifeboat Harlan. This was where the dust, made up of all the human race the Omega Bug could eat, blew slowly past, only a few feet from the top. Only those lucky enough to be on top were around to consider their good fortune.

Vince was really moody, and Mark decided to clear that patch of air. "This is where Josh and I found you, isn't it?"

Vince stared down at the small town of Oxford below. "Yeah, and I've never been sure I did the right thing."

"What does your wife say about that? How about your kids? You chose life. Otherwise, you would have just been more dust for the rain to wash away."

"Yeah, that's what Mr. Lillard told me any number of times. Looking at my wife and kids tells me the same thing. Still, it seems like there's something I could have done. There's something I should have done."

Vince's voice faded away. It looked to Mark like the ghosts from that day, little more than a month ago, paraded in front of him.

Mark nodded. "We saw you sitting there, staring at the dust. The dust wasn't more than a foot or two from your boots. You'd been there so long, your horse just stood behind you, and I know horses don't like the Omega Bug worth beans. You weren't thinking of going into the dust, were you?"

"The thought occurred to me. There was nothing but that deadly damn dust. I was the only living person. It just seemed so pointless. If you and Josh hadn't shown up, I'm not sure what I might have done. You won't tell anyone, will you?"

Mark shook his head. "It's just between us, Vince. Whatever goblins you fight at night, I'm proud to be with you."

Vince sighed. "That helps, Mark. That helps a lot. Those bikes didn't go toward Oxford."

"No, they stopped here. You've got people manning the bridge, so there are people down there all the time now. The bicycle people thought that significant since they took this way on down the far side of the prow, away from Oxford."

"That trail goes straight to the highway to Arapahoe and McCook, Mark. There is no doubt they come from outside Harlan."

Mark studied the highway through his binoculars. "Where we found the first solar buggy was in Arapahoe. That's where the terrorists and cannibals ran into each other. The terrorists took out fifty cannibals and the cannibals got two terrorists. Doctor Dover said the dust didn't get quite as high as he forecast. That means a possibility of survivors in the hills outside McCook."

Vince nodded. "There is another consideration. If Josh didn't distract the second solar buggy, they might have come up through Arapahoe as well. These people could be survivors, cannibals, or terrorists. That gives us a one out of three chance of liking the people riding the bikes."

Mark grunted. "Even if they aren't cannibals or terrorists doesn't mean we're all good buddies."

Vince looked at Mark. "What do you think we should do?"

Mark shrugged now. "Keep somebody up here in case they come calling again. They want to be invisible, so maybe we should be invisible, too."

"I've been thinking about using mirrors as a signal. We could use them to signal both Oxford and the West Gate from here."

"Is that what you needed, Vince? We don't know any more than we knew before, and I have to get ready for this wedding, since I'm the best man."

Mark gritted his teeth as Kevin gave him a detailed update on everything he'd done around the property. At that moment, salvation in the form of Vince showed up. Vince gave Mark a significant glance the moment he saw Kevin, and Mark returned a facial expression warning him not to say too much.

Vince nodded slightly. "Hey, Mark, recall that little thing we talked about the other day?"

Mark nodded. "Did something more happen?"

"Yeah, with an extra wrinkle. Could you to get away for a minute?"

"I don't know why not. Kevin is showing me everything he's done. It's all better, faster, and finer than anything I could do. He may be getting ready to fire me. I should leave before he finds more shortcomings for his list."

Vince forced a chuckle. Kevin stood there preening. Mark already had his horse saddled, having intended to do something else when Kevin grabbed him. A moment later, Mark rode with Vince back the way he came, toward the shack and smokehouse.

"So what's up?"

"The bicycle people showed up. We found signs of two, right?"

Mark nodded.

"There are five now, live and in person. They came off the highway, and rolled up the path next to the prow like they owned the place. The lookout alerted Oxford and the West Gate. Then he led his horse down the hill toward Oxford. He hoped it was far enough so the bicycle people wouldn't hear anything."

Mark nodded. "That part went according to plan. There are five of them? Are they friend or foe?"

"Beats me. Maybe both, for all I know. The lookout crawled back up the hill to take a look. The group stopped at the top of the hill. There were three guys, a gal, and an old man."

"How old?"

"He might be as old as Mr. Rowley."

"Do the guys look like terrorists?"

"The younger men are all clean-shaven. They look and act military. They're peddling hard toward the Lillard place. They stopped briefly at the shack and looked in the smokehouse. Somebody stole their picnic."

"Well, now, that's just not right. They should report the theft to the authorities. That would be you."

"Yeah, well, since they aren't here, they can't lose anything."

Mark grinned. "We had a nice ham dinner last night, and there was bacon with our breakfast this morning."

When they caught up to the posse, the bicycle group already made a cold camp in the area they used to observe the Lillard place. Vince's group, all on horseback, formed a loose semi-circle around them out of sight. Mark took a look at these folks with his binoculars.

"The three guys are more than military. They are snipers. Each packs an M110 sniper rifle. The woman is a puzzle. She acts like a commander. All four of them play like the older fellow is an elder statesman. Looking at this bunch sends as many conflicting messages as we had looking at the tracks."

Vince nodded. "We will maintain a watch on these jokers. If they do anything to disrupt the wedding, my site commander authority to give an immediate green light. We have multiple weapons on each target. Speaking of stupid, why don't these military people keep better track of what's around them?"

Mark nodded. "We normally had at least one sniper with our unit. They were at the top of the food chain, protected by the troops they were supposed to support. The idea of anybody presuming to hunt them was completely outside their frame of reference. At least they set up their camp out of sight of the farm road. I need to get back to the ranch, but keep me posted."

Mark rode straight down the farm road. Kevin was just finishing the evening chores, so Mark let him work, and unsaddled his horse, and turned the filly out for water and feed. After hauling the saddle and equipment into the tack room, Mark was just coming out when Kevin hauled more gear inside. Kevin cleared his throat like he wanted to say something, leaving Mark just inside the door.

"You've been doing all these mysterious errands with the deputy," Kevin offered. "It wouldn't be connected with Josh's wedding night, would it?"

That jolted Mark's mind back to the big event for everybody else in Harlan. The M110 sniper rifles he'd seen still occupied a good chunk of his attention, even so. His response was slower than it might have been. Afterward, he considered it might have contained more judgment, as well.

"Oh, they'll have a memorable wedding. I don't know of much that Vince and I could plan that could hold a candle to a lifetime like that. The girl is hell on wheels."

Kevin just smirked. Behind Mark, Ellen purposely kicked the door. "You say Alicia is hell on wheels? If that's what you think of her, I wonder what you think of me."

Mark's mind worked furiously to head off disaster as he turned to face her. "I think you're somebody I'd better watch my P's and Q's around. Otherwise I'll be in more trouble than I can handle."

"Well, don't you forget it. Dinner's ready, and I came out to see if I could help you guys finish up." Ellen looked at their boots and wrinkled her nose. "If you two want to eat, those chore boots better not come into the house. By the way, you never have said what you and Vince have been up to."

"It's just minor stuff. Josh isn't available, and Vince didn't want to bother Mr. Lillard with stuff us peons can handle."

Mark didn't know if Ellen bought that, but it brought peace back to their situation.

As Mark and Ellen left for the wedding, Kevin was getting started with chores. It felt strange taking off like that, but Kevin said he had no problem missing Alicia's wedding, even though they grew up together. Mark told Kevin that he was in charge until they got back, which would be after dark.

As they rode, Mark sensed rather than saw Ellen glancing at him fairly often. The feeling ramped up until, as they were almost to the State highway, Mark felt she was bound to say something, ask him something, or require something from him. It didn't happen. Just when the tension became unbearable, Ellen saw Vince's people in the field just before the road, and stared at them.

She looked at Mark. "Is this the minor stuff you talked about the peons handling?"

"Yep," was all Mark said. This close, the bicycle people might hear him. It took everything to keep looking ahead as they went by. To keep from temptation, he looked the other way, toward the Lillard place.

"We're ahead of the Lillards," Mark finally commented, knowing when he said it just how lame it sounded.

"What did you think, Mark?" Ellen replied. "The last I heard, they planned to dress at home and go straight to the church. They won't leave for quite a while."

Mark and Ellen split up part way through Ragan. Mark's clothes were at a house where Josh was changing. Josh was already there, partially dressed and pacing back and forth to get his nerves under control. Mark had no words of wisdom, other than noting the tuxedo was a bigger pain than any military uniform. In addition, there was nothing practical about any of it. Josh agreed, observing they both had to get mentoring in how everything was supposed to be.

While getting dressed seemed to take the two men forever, Mark had little illusion about how long it would take Alicia and Ellen. They found themselves all dressed up, nowhere to go, and noticing the temperature was hot for this late in the season. Going outside in search of a breeze, Mark and Josh finally gave up and made the trek to the church. They went in the side door and a few minutes later, heard Lyle Lillard and his wife ride past. People continued flowing into the already packed church, which grew hotter by the minute.

Mark felt sweat dripping from every pore. Sometime later, Ellen walked down the aisle as maid of honor, her eyes fastened on him. Through the open door, the horizon called to him, just like when he was four years old. They told him to stand there in his muddy front yard, and wait for the lady coming to get him. Then, as now, he couldn't move … wasn't allowed to move.

Just after that, Lyle walked onto the platform. He was still sizing up the situation when Adeline, his wife, walked down the aisle, seating herself in front. Almost immediately, the music started playing. Mark watched Alicia and Dr. Dover do their march, and out of the corner of his eye, saw Ellen switch her gaze between Alicia and him.

As everybody turned around, Mark saw Lyle's hands unconsciously trying to grab something. Glancing toward the pulpit, which was slid to the back of the platform, he saw the corner of Lyle's notes peeking over the top. Lyle figured it out, and Mark wondered what he would do. Lyle stopped for the briefest moment, took a breath, and winged it. He kept it really short and to the point, soon pronounced them man and wife, and doing the kiss. Mark noticed Ellen's eyes continued flickering between the newlyweds and him.

The happy couple proceeded up the aisle and into the foyer. Mark offered Ellen his arm, which she grabbed possessively. Okay, Mark knew he was marrying Ellen, but it didn't prevent a twinge of regret that he didn't keep driving when he went to Lincoln to fetch Harry Dover. In the church's foyer, the women split off to freshen up. The men trooped back to the house to wipe the sweat off and prepare for old Mr. Kemp to photograph their merry group with his antique equipment.

After the pictures, everyone completed the procession, going out the front door of the church and around the side of the building. On the way, Ellen poked Mark and quietly asked, "Aren't those the same guys we saw in the field on our way here?"

On the far side of a field across from the church, Ellen looked at Vince and company. "It looks like it might be," Mark whispered back. He was glad she didn't pursue the subject.

The reception was designed to drag on, and a little before sunset, Ellen poked Mark. "Let's change back into our regular clothes while we still have light. Trying to do it in the dark doesn't appeal to me."

That made sense to Mark, so they made their excuses, and went to change. Mark went quickly so he could get the horses ready. He wasn't quite done when Ellen came out. They arrived as the newlyweds were forced into the carriage, which led a procession circling around Ragan, until they got to the "Wedding Night House."

After Josh and Alicia were well and duly locked inside, Mark and Ellen got a picnic bench with a great view of the bedroom of the place which had no curtains. As a shivaree, it was a total bust. Josh and Alicia went around the little house, taking a savage joy in making as much racket as possible. The wedding house bed was attached to a bell in the attic, and the two jumped on the bed like a trampoline, clanging the bell.

Mark leaned over to Ellen, and commented, "This new tradition may not last very long. Anyway, we should get going. We'll be feeding in the dark, but there's no sense in putting it off too long."

Kevin would have done chores long before, but the shivaree was a waste, and with his boss, Lyle Lillard, right behind them, Mark didn't want to miss an opportunity to score points. As they got up, Mark saw that Kevin's buddy from McCook, Conrad, was leaving too. Lyle always got Kevin and Conrad confused and might think they were together.

Chapter 2
Dealing With the Devil

Mark felt Ellen's disapproval coming in waves of broken glass. The heat associated with the feeling made him amend that to molten glass. About half a block later, Ellen shook her head.

"Are you so insecure, trying to score points with Lyle Lillard? You were so obvious, too."

Mark blurted, "It can't hurt. I never know when I might put my foot in it big time."

"There's nothing you could do to mess things up. After all, you're his designated successor."

"People say that," Mark admitted. "People say lots of things. They blow hot air, mostly. Kevin has been carrying on about how he can run the ranch so much better than I can. He may even be right."

That drew a growl from Ellen, making Mark shiver. At least she changed the subject. "The Wedding Night House turned out wrong. It just turned out all wrong. Why is that?"

Mark tried to be reasonable. "You and Alicia grew up together. She knows how you think. We did a hell of a job rousting the two of them after the rain. Did you think we could sneak up on them twice the same way?"

"It could have happened," Ellen insisted.

After a short pause, she added, "Alicia and Josh will be laying for us now."

"I've known Josh a long time. He talked retribution for the first time when we dressed this morning. Even if Alicia didn't egg him on, Josh has something in mind, with my total humiliation as the outcome."

"Make that our total humiliation. Speaking of which, Mark, what about us?"

Mark shuddered. She just broached the dreaded subject, and if it was possible to pucker his saddle leather, that would do it. The question took him back to their first big encounter during the great rain. "I guess we're going to be all personal right now?"

A voice came out of the early evening darkness. "Before the two of you two get all hot and heavy, making my innocent young ears red with embarrassment, I need a word with you."

Mark returned a mental thank you. "What do you need, Vince?"

"I need help from both of you," was the reply.

"What kind of help are we talking about?" Mark decided to play it straight.

"There's a situation at the old schoolhouse. I didn't want to interrupt the celebration."

Ellen's voice was sharp. "Were your people across the field from the church this afternoon?"

"Yes, ma'am, and I was, too. The bicycle bunch trailed the Lillards going to Ragan. They circled town and parked their bikes out of sight of the church. Then they quietly watched the church."

"This bicycle bunch is the small problem you two worked on these past several days, I'd imagine."

"That's right, Ellen," Mark responded. "Vince and his people saw their tracks around the county, and wanted my take on the situation."

"The pile of food you brought home was connected with them?"

"It appears so."

"That makes them more residents than visitors."

"It would, except they tried to make sure nobody saw them. They succeeded, too. The only shortcoming was forgetting our horses don't have bicycle wheels."

"They're checking us out? Are they more of these terrorists?"

Vince came in. "We don't know who or what they are. They aren't like the terrorists we dealt with. This bunch really has us scratching our heads."

Mark had a question at that point. "What happened at the church?"

"That was where we brought their expedition to a halt. Before I say any more, I need to know what you told Ellen about this."

"It should be evident I didn't tell Ellen anything. Still, I perceive the cop part of your brain requires a specific, declarative response. Okay, here it is: I told Ellen nothing. I'll probably bunk with the dog tonight, but that is the situation. Is that satisfactory?"

"It's nearly perfect. Oh, Ellen, please don't make Mark sleep with the dog. We've got enough trouble in the county without having Mark spend all his time scratching fleas. As it is, he smells more like horses than the horses."

"I'll think about it," Ellen snarled. "You said there's more to the story. So tell it already."

"I need you as an unbiased witness first and you will know soon enough. We're almost to the schoolhouse."

An abnormal number of lamps burned precious kerosene. That alone underlined strange things afoot. In addition there were quite a few horses.

"Doctor Dover and his bunch are upstairs," Vince commented as they entered the front door. "What we're interested in is downstairs."

Mark muttered, "I didn't know there was a downstairs to this place. What's down there?"

"There's a furnace room, and a couple of storerooms."

The three felt their way down the stairs carefully in the uncertain light. An old-style boiler took up most of the room. Mark wondered if they could convert it back to coal for winter. Of course, that would mean finding coal. Behind the furnace were a couple of doors, one of which was guarded.

"What did you do with the weapons?" Vince asked one of the guards.

He pointed back at the stairs. Vince nodded. "Mark, you identified them with binoculars. I think you should take another look, up close and personal. They are impressive."

"Sure, I can do that."

"Okay, Ellen, stand right here. We'll have these people walk slowly, one at a time. While they're between the doors, we'll make them face you. I don't think they'll be able to see you."

"What do I look for? Are they green? Do they have one eye in the middle of the forehead?"

Vince ignored it. "Mark, I'd like you to observe and witness."

"You haven't said what I'm supposed to look for."

"Ellen, I'm not entirely sure. We'll start with the lady."

A moment later, the woman Mark saw earlier was only fifteen feet away. Ellen was in front of Mark. Vince instructed the woman to take two steps toward a man holding a kerosene lamp, then to stop, and turn to her right, and give her name. She pivoted as though marching, took the prescribed steps, came to a halt, and executed a right face.

"My name is Samantha, or Sammie, Moore."

While she did that, Vince went beside Ellen. "Do you recognize her?" he asked softly.

Ellen shook her head. "I've never seen her before."

Mark saw Vince nod slightly. The deputy took a couple of strides toward the second storeroom door and the man with the lamp. "Please step in here," he instructed. Mark noted his polite phrasing, though it was obviously an order.

The woman, her posture like a member of the British Royal Family at an opera, moved into the room. The three guys with the sniper gear came out one at a time. Vince had each do the same thing. Mark forgot their names as fast as they said them. For each, Ellen declared she had no idea who they were. Mark was puzzled, with Vince insisting that Ellen identify them.

The bike trail headed west. McCook was one of many places down that road. Doctor Dover led a group of people, including Ellen and Alicia, from there to Harlan County, just ahead of the last and largest wave of dust caused by the Omega Bug. The Omega Bug ate only human DNA, and within seconds, turned a human being into a little pile of dust. Maybe the bicycle people said they were from McCook, and Vince was testing their story. If that was the case, Ellen clearly said they lied.

It was last chance time. The older fellow came out. He slowly walked forward, and Ellen stiffened. He faced the shadows, cleared his throat, and announced, "I am Alex Thomas."

Ellen shrieked, ran up, and gave him a hug. "Uncle Alex, you're alive! It's me, Ellen."

The hug went on and then Alex held her away from him, a hand on each shoulder as he stared fondly at her. "Ellen, baby girl, I saw my Alicia get married, and now I get to see you, too. It makes this old heart contented, I'll tell you."

Vince then moved everyone toward the stairway. "Mr. Thomas, I hate to impose on you at a time like this, but there are things we have to find out, and decisions we have to make. You're the only one who can help us. Can you tell us anything about these other folks?"

"Sure, I'd be glad to tell you anything at all. Well, I'll tell you what I know."

"That's all we're asking, sir."

"I appreciate the 'sir' stuff, but could you call me Alex, please?"

"I'd be pleased to, Alex. I'm Vince and this is Mark Tahner. He runs the ranch that is Harlan County, now. I heard Ellen call you uncle, so you'll want to know about Ellen and Mark. They're engaged."

Ellen spun toward Mark with a challenging glare. "Is that right, Mark? Are we engaged? I've wondered myself, and was about to ask you when Vince hijacked us."

Mark stood there, his mouth hanging open. He thought in terms of someday for marrying Ellen. Well, someday just arrived. He looked at Vince and then at Alex. Then, he looked in Ellen's eyes for what seemed like a long time. Finally, Mark went to one knee in front of Ellen.

"Ellen Markley, will you marry me?"

Ellen struck a pose. "Well," she said after the predictable pregnant pause, "I'm not sure. Can I think it over? I might need a while, like a day or two, or maybe a couple of years. Would that be all right? It took you this long to get around to asking. It's only right that I should get at least as long to think about it."

Mark struck out again. Kevin was hellbent to prove he could run the ranch better than Mark. Now, he was on the short end of the stick with Ellen, as well. He leaned forward with his knuckles on the floor. He went from nothing to pretty good since getting on with Lyle. Lately, he let himself believe things were going his way for the first time in his life. He should have known better.

He felt her hand on his cheek, and it slowly slid under his chin, lifting his face up.

"Hey, you big dummy, of course I'll marry you. Did you hear me? I said yes, I will marry you."

Vince laughed. "Okay, Alex. You heard it here first. How's that?"

"This has been a memorable day. I am truly blessed. If only Cordelia were here to see it."

"Aunt Cordelia? Didn't she make it?"

"She's fine, baby girl. She's fine. She just couldn't pedal a bicycle all the way here. Cordelia and I, along with a fair number of the neighbors got to the castle in time. We were saved from the dust and protected from the rain."

"Who are these others?" Ellen wanted to know.

"They claim to be Federal people, keeping track of a bunch of petty criminals so they don't get into any more trouble."

Mark had a thought. "Alex, were there any others who made it through the Omega bug and rain? I'm thinking about folks who just use knives."

Alex nodded. "Those are who these guys kept track of."

"Did you ever see their leader?"

"Yeah, he's a big fellow who calls himself Stanley Peepul. The rest adopted his last name. They call themselves the Peepul."

That was the cannibal tribe, Mark knew. "Had they been with this bunch a long time?"

"Ever since St. Louis, they said."

"What are they doing in McCook?"

Alex nodded. "Feral pigs were rooting up our fields but the Peepul pretty well cleared them out. They also bring in other game. They are becoming pretty good butchers and sausage makers. There's more pork than we can eat."

Mark, Vince, and Ellen stared at each other. Finding the cannibal tribe survived the Omega dust was not good news, especially after the tribe chased him to be part of their stew pots.

"Alex, could you excuse us for a moment?"

The three moved away, and Mark found his mind racing at full speed now. He turned to his housekeeper/fiancee.

"Ellen, is he really telling what he knows about the Peepul?"

"Yes, Mark, if he knew more about that bunch, he would have told us. He's just that way. From what you guys have said, I'm glad I never met this Peepul bunch."

Mark found that reassuring, and glancing at Vince to confirm his feeling, nodded to Ellen. "Take Alex outside. Talk about anything except the Peepul, and do not mention cannibalism. Our bicycle friends may have been trying to reform the tribe and make both themselves and the

Peepul socially acceptable. I don't know why these guys would throw in with the Peepul, but we just got a good lever to ensure they act polite."

Vince growled, "Taking the part of the Peepul only makes sense if they're part of the tribe. Have they partaken of the cannibal sacrament?"

"They admit to being with them since St. Louis. Who knows what they are?" Mark replied. "One thing is certain. They were separate from the tribe leaving Harlan. Nobody mentioned bicycles, and if anybody packed sniper rifles, Sheriff Crichton would have treated the situation differently."

Vince continued, "They had to know the tribe attacked Lyle Lillard. You guys never saw anybody else when you checked the tribe out, but I remember both you and Josh got a creepy feeling like somebody was watching you. We talked about it when we found the observation post by the cannibal camp."

"That's right," Mark responded, and came to a full stop.

"That bunch watched us the whole time. If the tribe discovered us, they would not have stepped in on our behalf. If they tried to help Lyle, he never knew about it."

Ellen emitted a low feral growl. "The Peepul bunch could have made both of you cannibal stew. That female, who acts like the queen of the universe, gives the orders, right?"

Mark nodded. "You're right on both counts."

"Give me five minutes with her. I'll rearrange her into something even the cannibals would think was unappetizing. If she had her way, I'd have never even met you. After all we've been through, and only now engaged, that is totally unacceptable."

"Turning you loose is tempting. Still, let's do it this other way for now? Her face will still be there later."

"Her face being there bothers me. Some people might think she was pretty. I know better."

Things close to getting out of hand. "Okay, this is show time. Ellen, you're playing a happy person, overjoyed because your best friend just got married, you got engaged, and your uncle Alex appeared. Go tell him about the wedding and our ranch?"

"We are engaged, aren't we? I like that. Yes, I can talk to Uncle Alex about our ranch." A smile suddenly appeared on her face, Ellen went over to Alex, and a moment later guided him up the stairs, chattering the whole way.

"How do we want to hit them?" Vince asked. "Do you want me to play bad cop to get their attention?"

"Why not? We have their undivided attention, but keep the guards close. Things could go south in one helluva rush."

"I fully intend to, Mark."

Three of Vince's guys went in, one carrying a lamp and two more just behind in the shadows with rifles at the ready. Mark and Vince followed them. The four people were told to sit against the far wall, and the lamp was placed on the floor close enough for Mark and Vince to see their faces. Mark saw irritation and defiance. It was time for some attitude adjustment.

Mark nodded to Vince.

"You had box seats for some entertainment July 4. An unmarked Harlan County sheriff's car drove north. Pilgrims calling themselves Peepul tried to stop the vehicle and invite its occupants to dinner. No, I misspoke. The car's occupants were to be their dinner. We declined their invitation. Yeah, I was in the car, and we didn't think it was funny. I'm even less amused to discover they had chaperones that could have stopped it. I believe you also knew of the attack on Lyle Lillard. He's in charge while we're under martial law. You're lucky he's not here now."

Mark noticed the four squirm a bit when Vince mentioned martial law.

"I am the ranking police officer in Harlan. Considering what you did, failed to do, and allowed to happen, I should create a chain gang. We need to clear a lot of ditches so we can irrigate next spring."

The woman spoke up. "We were under orders then. We only came to establish friendly relations on behalf of the people north of McCook."

Vince snorted. "You were under orders? What organization gave you the orders? Let me spell it out for you. Meet the gentleman with me. As far as you're concerned, he is the organization."

Mark thought that was his cue. "You didn't want us to connect you with the tribe of cannibals called Peepul. I think none of the McCook people know. You brought Alex Thomas after finding his daughter was alive. You came sneaking into Harlan, thinking we're idiots. Well, we're the idiots who grabbed three snipers and their commander. I believe you have a fourth sniper flying solo back in McCook. How long will the McCook farmers put up with you and your tribe once they find out who and what you are?"

Mark found pleasure watching the woman turn pale. It was visible even with the small amount of light. He hoped for just this reaction. If these people would ever agree to a deal, it would be right here and right now. Still, if he exposed too much of his position or expression, he could lose the advantage. Mark was happy to be in the shadow where they couldn't see him sweat.

"Okay," Sammie came up on the bait. "You have a deal or we wouldn't be going through all this."

"People establishing friendly relations come openly. Also, they bring tokens of welcome to their neighbors. I'm going out on a limb here. As the deputy mentioned, Lyle Lillard, who runs Harlan, doesn't know about this. He's the guy your tribe tried to take when he rode down the farm road. He didn't appreciate the invitation. If we can work this out, he doesn't have to know."

Mark let that soak in and then continued. "We will get you out of the county. You'll leave Alex Thomas to guarantee your good behavior. He will not be a prisoner but my personal guest. For the moment, we won't tell him about you. What's your cheer? 'We are Peepul. They are animals.'"

Mark stopped and forced himself to grin at them. "How do you like the cannibal sacrament of human flesh?"

That pushed Sammie completely off balance. "What? No, we never …" she stammered.

"Save your protests. When you ran out of human meat, feral pigs might be a decent substitute. At least, that's what I've read. Pedal hard for McCook. Bring back Mrs. Thomas and all the pork you can carry. Mr. Clock is not your friend. Come back through Oxford, the way the Peepul left Harlan. If you do it fast enough, we'll shake hands, Alicia will have a family reunion, and we send you home with beef."

"Okay," Sammie said woodenly. "What's the alternative?"

"If word gets out that Alex Thomas is in the county, all bets are off. Alicia will have a reunion with her father. We'll tell him what we know about the Peepul. We will also show him. Their camp still has a stench to it, but maybe that's just me. After that, we'll take Alex home and Alicia can visit her mother. We'll bring enough armed men to ensure the safety of our guest. What happens then is up to Alex and the others who call McCook home."

"Will we get our weapons back?"

"You can have your weapons back when we start moving you out of the county. You'll get your ammunition back at the county line. If any of you attempt to load your weapons while you're still in range, there will be no warning shots. We will operate on a one shot, one kill basis."

"You sound military," she replied, staring at the grimy floor.

Mark looked at her. "If being in the military is a problem, you'd better check a mirror. In any case, my past affiliations are not the subject. What happens to you is the deal. If you don't like my offer, there is Vince's chain gang. Guarding you would take people who should be doing something productive, so a chain gang would include you only getting to eat what we think your work is worth."

"You don't leave us any choice," returned a grumble.

"There's always a choice. Some alternatives might be more palatable."

She mumbled something under her breath.

Mark kept his cool. "I couldn't hear you."

"We'll take your deal."

"Very well. You will remain here. It wouldn't do for you to wander off, not that you'd get lost. You may know the county better than we do. You might accidentally get shot, though. While you're here, we'll get you something to eat. I don't know what we can find, but it will be at least as good as your cold camp last night."

With that, Mark backed away, and almost immediately, the three guards who stood silently behind them, moved forward to retrieve the lamp. Vince said a word at the door, which opened silently. Mark and Vince walked across the basement which seemed smaller now than when he arrived.

On the way out, Vince looked at Mark. "How do we sneak them out of here?"

"They can go out the way they came. Escort them straight east out of town. After you get clear of Ragan, turn south to that path they made going past the Lillard place. I think I can distract Lyle. That terrorist we took down in Kansas. Have you heard how he's doing?"

"He's well enough, I guess."

"Tomorrow morning, I'll tell Lyle the guy wants to talk. The trip to Huntley and back should take a good part of the day."

They walked upstairs, and found Doctor Dover waiting. "Excuse me, Mark, I should wait until tomorrow, but when could I see the vial?"

Mark considered good things were coming his way in bunches. The main thing bringing Dover to Ragan for the wedding was the chance to see the final vial. "We can do that tomorrow morning. First thing, grab Don Rowley, and get him to take you over to the Lillard place. I'll be there on other business. Lyle doesn't need to know we arranged it. Okay?"

Outside, it took Mark a few minutes to find Ellen and Alex. They wouldn't get Alex to the ranch until the next day. One of Vince's people offered Alex a place for the night. The bicycles were stashed behind the building, and Alex went to his evening's rest.

Mark had expectations as the two of them headed for home. Starting with an evening horseback ride with the woman who promised to marry him. There would be closeness, cuddling, and a steamy and passionate finale. Mark's luck had done well today. Granting this last wish was past its limit. Maybe it was past his luck's bed time.

Not far from town, the freight train of Ellen's focus obliterated the poor little subcompact representing Mark's romantic fantasy. "We have a lot to do. You need to help me move another bed into your room for Alex."

Mark sighed. "My alternative would be to stay in the bunkhouse. Sleeping on the couch is not an option. I remember when I relaxed there with my feet up."

"Living in the country doesn't mean we act uncivilized."

Mark made one last try for romance. "At least we're engaged now."

"We were, and everybody knew it. You just made it official. Now hush up while I concentrate on what I need to do."

After a long silence, Mark thought he found a worthwhile question. "Is Alex related on your father's side or your mother's side?"

Ellen never talked about her family. Alex, Alicia's father, was the first family she ever mentioned or acknowledged. Stranger, Ellen and Alicia always referred to each other as friends. He had never heard them talk about being cousins, which must be the case.

"We aren't related. Alex and Cordelia, his wife, are my godparents. They gave me a place to stay when Alicia and I came back from the city."

"What happened to your parents?"

"While Alicia and I were gone, Dad got a job offer near Seattle. We tried to get home before they left, but they left a week before we got back."

"Were they caught up in the earthquake, tsunami, and eruption of Rainier?"

"They headed out before all that. I got a letter from them around the time all that happened, dated late October. They were in Boise, Idaho. Their car ran out of gas. They had to walk ten miles into town. The folks in Boise couldn't help them, since there was no fuel or electrical power."

"Maybe they survived."

"Watching that hateful dust go by, knowing it contained just about the entire human race, it has been a real stretch to hope for anything."

"We made it here in Harlan. Maybe we could go to Boise sometime."

Ellen changed the subject. "You know how it is with Kevin. Anything that goes in his ears comes out of his mouth. How can we keep it quiet about Alex with Kevin around?"

Mark considered that and finally came up with a solution. "Don Rowley wants to grab the wagon place for his operation."

"Those are the two places that are back to back, right?"

Mark nodded. "Don has a point. It also makes sense for Harlan Ranch to expand there. I've noticed old Don will make no bones about wanting something. He'll try to get support. If that doesn't happen, he'll back off a while. Then, when nobody's looking, he marches in and takes it. I think he's getting ready to make a move on it."

"How do we stop him?"

"Kevin will be the head of our new division."

"If Harlan Ranch has a division, then that makes our house the ranch headquarters." Ellen sounded upbeat about that.

"Yep, and you, my lady Ellen, are the head of the headquarters."

The rest of the ride home was more comfortable, if unromantic. Kevin was already in bed in the bunkhouse and the lights out. Ellen waited while Mark took care of business. Remembering how Kevin got him in trouble the day before, Mark cheerfully rousted him.

"Kevin, you know how we planned to expand to the wagon place?"

Kevin's response was groggy and hostile. "Well, yeah. So what?"

"Old Don plans to move on the place tomorrow. It might be early. I need you over there tonight in order to stake our claim ahead of him. I'm giving it to you to run. It will be the Wagon Ranch division. You're chasing that girl, Susie, in Huntley. That might score you a few points that way, as well."

Kevin was wide awake now.

"You're making that a division of the ranch? You're putting me in charge? Boy, howdy! I'll grab my stuff and be on my way. Thank you, Mark."

"Don't thank me yet, Kevin. It will be a pain in the butt. Don't forget the mission against the terrorists in a couple of days. Maybe you can help supply the horses and cattle. I've seen how you shoot. Unless we're trying to waste ammunition, you'd help out more by training riders."

Chapter 3
Joy and Sorrow

Ellen came out to help with chores. Working with Ellen suited Mark very well, indeed.

"What will you do when the horses and students arrive?" she asked. "It could happen in the next couple of days."

"It should be the same as working with the sheriff's deputies. Kevin should be fine over there. Anyway, Rowley staking a claim is the kind of game he'd play. We'll get to see how our luck is holding."

"Our luck. I like that, Mr. Tahner. If this sneaking around backfires, you'll need all the luck you can get."

"We're going to need all the luck we can get in any case. It's like the joke about how many attaboys it takes to offset an awshit."

Ellen would take the farm wagon to get Alex while Mark distracted Lyle. After a quick breakfast, they were on their way.

At the Lillard driveway, Mark saw the carriage with Doctor Dover coming from Ragan. Mark quickly talked to Lyle about their prisoner in Huntley, recovering from heat stroke. Lyle was willing to go with Mark to interview him. Dover showed up wanting to see the vial. Lyle decided to use Dover on their prisoner, since there was an obvious connection. After all, it was the terrorists' promised attack that sent Dover and his buddies to Lincoln.

Mark suggested the main highway to Huntley. As they headed down the highway, Mark rode a little behind the others. He saw movement in a field that was away from the road to Ragan and mostly out of sight of the highway. Mark confirmed with second glance that Vince had the bicycle people moving.

He picked up the pace, so Lyle and Mark rode about even with Don Rowley with the carriage. Don had something on his mind, and finally looked at Lyle.

"I need the wagon place. I sent a guy to stake my claim this morning just before Dr. Dover showed up."

Lyle looked at Don and shook his head. "Now, Don, we agreed to talk about this. You know Harlan Ranch needs the space and facilities."

"Well, that's what I did," he growled.

Lyle looked over at Mark. "What will that do to you, with horse and rider training coming the next few days?"

Mark did his best to seem noncommittal. "We have to get by with the resources we find. Those coming later have to deal with it."

Lyle favored Mark with an appraising look and Don allowed himself a fast glance at Mark. Don obviously expected protests, but Mark let it ride, inwardly gloating.

Dr. Dover and Lyle soon got their captive to admit he was a terrorist. Not only that, but Harry was on their list of people they most wanted to despise. After leaving, Dover confessed that he was one of the Russian scientists who invented the Omega bug.

After seeing the vial and discussing what it would take to destroy the vial and the bugs in it, they headed back. At the intersection of the state road with the main highway, a guy waited.

Don growled, "What are you doing here? You're supposed to be guarding my interests."

"I would be, Mr. Rowley, but Kevin already moved in and said it was a division of Harlan Ranch."

Lyle laughed and slapped his leg so hard that it startled his stallion, Loup. "That's how it goes, Don. You jump the gun only to find out you weren't fast enough. It made more sense for the wagon place to be part of Harlan Ranch. You've got plenty of real estate already. You two still need to work together, you know."

Don growled and turned for Ragan. As they headed up the state road toward the Lillard place, Lyle looked over at Mark and nodded. "Was this what you worked on this week?"

Mark knew better than a complete lie. "No sir, it just came to me that I needed to do it then, so I sent Kevin after we got home."

Lyle waved and turned down his driveway while Mark headed for the Harlan Ranch headquarters. He found Vince was there, chatting with Alex and Ellen.

"Mark! You distracted the hell out of them. We watched you go by this morning."

"I saw you starting to move. It was pretty good timing. How did the bicycle brigade go?"

"They went like good little whipped mutts, with their tails between their legs. They connected the bike Alex rode to one of the others. We escorted them to the prow, and watched as they bumped down to the McCook highway. I'm certain they stopped to lock and load the second they got out of sight. Alex says they have trailers for those bikes. Can you imagine it? They'll install his wife, Cordelia, in a trailer for the ride back. Hopefully, they will also include plenty of pig."

Mark waved as Vince mounted up and left. It was a good day. On the other hand, his conversation with Ellen echoed, wondering just how much luck he'd need to offset what they were trying to do.

Mark had more on his mind than romance and the situation with the bicycle people. The really big news would come out of the council of war and they didn't invite Mark. It convened at the Lillard place a day after they sent the bike bunch home. Josh and he were the only two who were experienced warriors and young enough to be effective in the field.

Mark knew he'd be part of the spearhead, whatever they decided. Now engaged, it sucked even more than it would have in any case. The feeling at the Josh and Alicia Morgan household had to be the same. Presumably, Josh would speak for both of them.

Vince was the only person who came by that day. Mark met with him in the bunkhouse. He just let Mark know he put the lookout back at the prow to watch for the bikes. Vince also suggested Mark move the training to the wagon division. There were two houses plus paddocks and training areas.

Don showed up the next morning, driving a single wagon with three guys.

"Here are your students," Don growled.

Mark walked to the wagon after checking that Alex was not in sight.

"That's nice," Mark replied. "What are they supposed to ride?"

"The horses were okay to train yesterday."

Mark snorted. "Maybe the pheasants delivered the message and I didn't understand it. We'll train at the wagon place. I hope you don't mind taking them over there."

"Mind? Why the hell would I mind?"

"I'll ride along and let Kevin know the situation."

"Company's always welcome, even if it is you."

A few minutes later, Don commented, "You didn't hear about the horses, so did you hear about the plans to attack the terrorists?."

Mark nodded. "I just need know if we hit them sooner or later."

"They decided to call it off."

Mark stared at him. "How's that?"

Don managed a grin. "I kid you not. They decided anything we did would create more of a problem than we already had. Since the terrorists sent their last major weapon, that vial of Omega bugs, we'll get ready for winter instead of war."

"Warfare is back to a warm weather activity. That didn't take long." Mark thought for a moment and said, "You know, Don, Harlan Ranch could help with your stock, wagons, and equipment. If I ride along with you sometimes, I'd be in a better position to help with training and equipment."

One of the guys in the wagon looked over the side. "If you knew how old Rowley talked about you the whole way over here, you might not be so eager to make offers like that."

Don was back in full growl, casting an evil eye at the perpetrator. "You're just aching to walk, aren't you?"

Then he turned to Mark, suddenly more agreeable. "Lyle bent my ear yesterday saying sweet nothings that nearly burnt my brain. He went on about how you and I needed to work together. He said we're too small to have everybody snarling at each other. It sure sounded to me like he was snarling in my direction. Are you sure you haven't talked to Lyle?"

"I'm certain, Don. Whether a horse is for riding or for pulling, it's the same animal. Training is training. If we can work together and help Harlan survive, we should do it. Maybe we can leave each other alone where we don't agree."

"That almost sounds like a plan, Mark."

Another guy called, "Tomorrow. Did you know about tomorrow?"
Mark looked at Don. "What's tomorrow?"

"Oh, yeah, Lyle declared tomorrow a day off for almost everyone. We'll escort that vial of Omega bugs somewhere and dispose of it. After will be a barbecue at the park in Alma."

"Tomorrow, eh?" Mark looked at the trainees. "You guys won't start for another day. Kevin is chasing some girl in Huntley. If he doesn't slow down, she may catch him."

One of the guys in back chuckled. "That would be Susie Maguire. Yeah, she's reeling him in all right. From what I hear, Ellen's not only hooked you, she's landed you."

Mark just grinned and nodded. "Landed and on the scales. I hope she won't throw me back."

At the new division headquarters, Kevin acted astonished. It could have been having students before he had horses. Mark and Don on speaking terms may have boggled his imagination. Mark saw Kevin's distractibility set in as he contemplated having the next day off to pursue his dreams.

As Don drove off, Mark saw Vince ride in, apparently from the prow. He waited until Don went out of sight before approaching. The two rode off to the side, out of earshot of Kevin and the students.

"What do you think, Mark? Will our friends show up tomorrow?"

"They've had two days to get ready. When I saw you, I wondered if they showed up."

"No, but the lookout will signal Oxford and West Gate. Everyone knows to act surprised."

"One way or the other, Alicia will have a reunion tomorrow. Alex says Stanley Peepul refers to them as the dark lady and the four ghosts. I believe they've haunted my dreams enough. It's time for something likely to help us."

Other issues competed, but Mark wanted his romance to remain a contender. On the other hand, that element vanished after he proposed. With Alex as a house guest, Mark found a side of Ellen he didn't know existed. Before, she was the purebred country girl. Now, she was prim and proper, like she was a society doyen, with everything she did making the newspaper.

Their relationship abruptly became platonic. Mark wasn't sure it even qualified as platonic. Before long, Mark looked for any excuse not to be in the house.

The evening Alex arrived, Ellen came out to help with chores, but made it clear she intended to be as formal out there as inside. Mark soon suggested that he had the chores under control, and she might as well visit with Alex.

At supper, Mark's few forays into conversation were vain attempts. She vanquished them with either icy silence or a change of the subject. He reverted to his military training and behavior from foster homes where he spent most of his childhood. He sat at attention. His mouth remained closed, other than to insert a bit of food or sip a drink. As soon as his plate was mostly empty, Mark formally excused himself.

He wandered the place considering his lack of prospects with Ellen. He also saw Harlan Ranch as another prospect nearing its bitter end. The ranch was to train horses and riders, and Mark just gave it away. He leaned against the top rail of an enclosure and looked across the field. The tall grass rippled in the wind, beckoning him. The horizon was out there. Anything he had here was at an end. Wherever he went, he'd go like he came, on foot. The horses belonged to Harlan.

Ellen was chatting with Alex when Mark returned. Ellen did most of the chatting. The moment he came through the door, she declared it time to retire, and went into her room. Alex looked at both of them, but didn't say anything. Mark told him to go ahead to the bedroom, and he'd be along presently.

In the gathering gloom, Mark couldn't relax. He sat on the edge of the seat, back straight, hands clasping his knees, and wondered how things got to this point. His proposal ended their relationship, rather than taking it to the next level. War with the terrorists would have been an improvement. Maybe he should do that anyway, and go solo.

In the room, Alex got talkative. It might have been Ellen carrying on both sides of the conversation earlier. Was he after information? If Alex was after intelligence, he came up short, since Mark steered it back to McCook. Alex brought up the subject of Stanley Peepul a number of times.

Mark had to bite his tongue to keep from saying what he knew. The way Alex told it, Stanley Peepul underwent a drastic transformation since leaving Harlan County. The Peepul just started hunting feral pigs when they showed up in his area, mostly with switchblades and pocket knives. Only a few had spears.

Alex and his neighbors fabricated better spears, adding a crossbar above the spearhead. That would keep the pig from coming up the spear and attacking the hunter. Stanley was the best hunter, but a number of his people became adept after the dust and rain. All surviving the dust and rain did it at a place called the castle.

The place was built by a guy who came into a major fortune. His ideas apparently all came from the movies. One thing he'd been smart about was in making the place able to function off the grid. He ran out of money just when the place was finished. The monstrosity, complete with furniture, was the white elephant joke of the county.

Dr. Dover and his bunch showed up, flying into McCook. A place at the highest elevation was a requirement for them, and the castle fit the bill. Dover put out the word that waves of deadly dust were coming, and the only way to survive was to be above it.

Everybody living in the higher areas did fine as several waves of the dust went through. Suddenly, however, Dr. Dover put out that they would not survive the next and largest wave of dust. The key to survival was to move. He took a number of locals, including Alicia and Ellen, and headed for Harlan County.

A day after Dover departed, the dark lady and her four ghosts arrived, with Stanley Peepul and his tribe right behind. The dark lady moved into the castle, while Stanley moved his bunch into the combination stable and horse arena across from the castle. They never mentioned seeing Dr. Dover's group, so they must have come from another direction. How they got there from St. Louis was an open question.

Stanley, calling Sammie the dark lady, named her well. There were dark agendas all around her. Mark hoped her sniper bodyguard were better at putting rounds on target than on stealth. The dark lady took to living like royalty as though born to it.

Alex said the feral pigs multiplied like crazy when the economy went down the toilet. There wasn't enough ammunition to hunt the pigs, and nobody could afford the little ammo available. The pigs expanded their territory, rooting up gardens and small fields. The arrival of the Peepul was a sign from heaven. Their willingness to stay separate from the local population was welcome, too. Alex and his neighbors thought there was something unsavory about everyone in the so-called tribe.

The next day, Don Rowley and Vince gave Mark all the excuses he needed to be off Harlan Ranch, working with the change in training sites. It gave him something to say at supper, when they put together a plan. Alex was overjoyed at the prospect of reuniting with Alicia.

Mark would go solo with the procession. Ellen would not go with him, which suited Mark. It would have been too painful to be physically close, but light years apart. The official reason was to do the chores and ensure everything was okay at both Harlan Ranch and Wagon Ranch. Mark actually did the chores.

Ellen would take Alex and wait in what was now the ghost town of Orleans, halfway between Alma and Oxford. It would keep Alex out of sight and give him a degree of comfort. If the bikers showed up, Alex and Ellen would convoy with them to the barbecue. If nobody came, they would drive to the barbecue late in the afternoon. Ellen could surprise Alicia either way.

Mark hustled to catch the main group. The group would form in Alma and head east. Almost everyone was on foot, so the group went slowly. He started passing stragglers at Republican City, known locally as Rep City. Slowing, Mark maneuvered through the walkers. He caught up to Kevin in the middle of the group. Susie rode double with him. Mark touched the brim of his hat and grinned at them as he passed. Kevin got a little red in the face, but Susie was just enjoying it all. On his part, Mark felt old and out of touch, a feather blowing in the wind.

A solar buggy, carrying the vial of Omega bugs, led the procession. Dover and four of his associates were in the carriage right behind, with Don Rowley driving. Mark had gone to Lincoln so Dover could play father of the bride at Alicia's wedding. Dover's group walked, arriving in time for the wedding. They all wanted to see the end of the Omega bugs.

Lyle and Adeline Lillard rode on one side of the carriage. Josh and Alicia were just behind the carriage. When Mark came up on them, he congratulated them as sincerely as he could.

Both Josh and Alicia regarded him suspiciously. "Did Ellen send any surprises?" Alicia wanted to know.

"There's nothing up my sleeve, other than my arm," Mark swore. The surprise Ellen had might be amusing. Right now, the main surprise would be if Mark was still in Harlan a couple of days from now.

"Is she redecorating our house?" Josh queried.

"Not that I know of. Toilet paper is in short supply these days. Before you ask, I don't think she's adding any improvements or features, either."

Mark picked up his pace, and came up on the far side of the carriage.

Lyle looked over at Mark. "Glad you could make it."

"I'm glad to be here, sir. Ellen is taking care of things at Harlan. With Kevin in the procession, she may need to get up to the Wagon Ranch division, as well. She plans to get down for the barbecue."

Lyle nodded agreeably. "Don tells me that you two decided to bury the hatchet somewhere besides each other's head. He even claims you two have some kind of agreement about the wagon place and the horses."

"It's nothing formal. We just figured it made sense to cooperate where we could. I can help move things forward, training stock that has more aptitude for hauling than riding."

Lyle nodded. "I've also decided something to help things along. Sheriff Crichton told me to get and use all the horses for the good of the county. I'm going to follow his direction even though you'll squawk a bunch, Don."

"I'll squawk now and avoid the rush," Don grumped. "Why don't you give me some good news for a change?"

"You got Mark offering to train stock for you. Here is the deal. All horses are part of the Harlan remuda. At the same time, the horses you're using, Don, remain under your control. Mark, you're responsible for the rest. When you put people with horses, and the horse and rider don't match well, take back the horse and do it again."

"You're killing me, Lyle," Don growled. "How can I take care of my freight business without horses?"

Lyle shook his head. "One more time: the horses you have can stay. You will let Mark know how many of what breeds you have, and where you have them. Mark, keep me up to date on all horses, who has them, where they are, and their condition. You'll have to periodically go out and look at them. Back to you, Don, keeping the horses is conditional on you helping me. We have to keep everyone in the county fed and housed, even if they can't pay you. You said you owed me for saving you from the cannibals. Here's an opportunity to pay it forward."

Don gritted his teeth.

Later, Mark looked around. "There aren't many folks with us now. Where are we, anyway?"

"We're near Red Cloud," Don announced, still fuming.

"We've come that far?" Mark saw a mailbox that looked like the name "Peepul" may have been on it. "How's this for a place to dump the Omega bugs?"

The crowd stood in a semicircle upwind from the dry well shaft. Doctor Dover removed all the safety features from the vial, assuring it would shatter on impact. Then they watched the vial drop down the dry well shaft at the old Peepul place.

As far as anyone could tell, this was where the cannibal, Stanley Peepul, grew up. Foundation stones hinted where a small house had been. Bits of charred wood and building material spoke of a fire long ago. There were the ashes of what had been a fire in his heart, but Ellen had put that out, too.

Lyle softly slapped Mark's shoulder. "You look awfully pensive, my friend."

There was no way Mark would discuss his real thoughts. "Who thought we'd head out from Harlan with that stinking Omega bug, and dump it in the well of the cannibal who would have cheerfully eaten all of us?"

"Those odds are about the same as the chances that our merry little group would still be around when the rest of the human race was wiped out. Maybe long odds are what we do now. Probably we'll live regular boring lives now. Does that sound like a plan?"

Mark considered who waited in Harlan, and who might come. There was also the cannibal who survived the dust to become a mighty pig hunter. It took all his self-control not to snort. "Regular boring lives sound good. Even with that, simply surviving are long odds."

"I understand what you're saying, Mark. Try to keep the faith, though."

Lyle strolled off, leaving Mark to think about faith. The only faith he had at the moment was that the next few days would find him chasing the horizon.

Returning to Alma, they kept picking up people who turned back earlier. Kevin and Susie were still missing. Near Rep City, a horse came at a fast trot. It was the missing pair, still riding double. As they passed, it was clear they hadn't been on top of the horse all that time. There was straw in her hair and clothing put on in a hurry. They also had unnatural gleams in their eyes. Don and Lyle noticed as well.

Don spoke in a low voice, designed to be heard by Lyle and Mark. "I thought I knew the next couple to get married. I might have bet good money. That couple is just farting around instead of getting things done. Of course, I'm far too proper to mention names."

Lyle chuckled. "Don, I might mistake you for a crotchety old fart if I didn't know better. Your jibes are as subtle as your bets are a sure thing."

Arriving at the park in Alma, they were greeted with the smell of brisket and barbecue sauce. A line formed immediately. Everybody grabbed plates and settled around tables or sat in the grass. Mark didn't get anything, wondering he should wait for Ellen. His appetite got lost along the way.

Somebody yelled, "Would you take a look at that!"

Mark saw the Harlan ranch wagon, with Ellen holding the reins. Two people jammed in beside her on the seat, with a group of riders around the wagon. Five bicycles and riders, each towing a trailer, rolled in front. One trailer had an aluminum patio chair in it. The rest were piled high with meat.

Mark decided he needed to look like things were normal with Ellen. In addition, there was the play-acting he volunteered for. That in mind, he walked to the wagon, and gave Ellen a hand. They both helped the other two, an older couple, get down. It remained to be seen how this would play.

"Mark, this is Alex and Cordelia Thomas. They survived the Omega dust outside McCook. They came all this way to see us. Isn't that great?"

They were doing the act, so Mark continued, too. "I'm pleased to meet both of you. You're from McCook?"

Alex and Cordelia both nodded.

"Your last name is Thomas? You wouldn't know someone named Alicia, would you?"

Mark didn't know if that was too much, but it seemed to work. "Oh, my, yes," Cordelia said. "Our daughter is Alicia. We know Ellen, too. Do you know about Alicia?"

"We'd better take you to her. I think she has some news for you."

Mark and Ellen led them to the newlyweds, where an uproar ensued.

Mark turned to see the dark lady behind him. "Could I speak to whoever is in charge here, please?"

"Certainly, ma'am, I'd be glad to. What is your name?"

"Samantha Moore. I go by Sammie. We are from McCook. We heard there might be more survivors. We wanted to get together and see if we can help each other."

"With winter coming on, that could certainly be helpful. I'll take you to him."

Lyle was watching the Thomas reunion, but looked over as Mark came over with the delegation. "Mr. Lillard, this is Samantha, or Sammie Moore. They are with a group of survivors from McCook."

Lyle and Sammie shook hands. "Mr. Lillard, we've harvested a lot of feral pigs over in our area. We brought some meat, mostly ham and bacon. Is that okay?"

"I certainly think so. Would you care for some of our beef barbecue?"

"We'd love it. We could smell it as we came into town. This is a lovely park."

Mark slid off to the side. Lyle played a deep game, so it might be a while before he'd know if it all worked. Meanwhile, everything seemed positive. Their arrival coinciding with a celebration was a stroke of good luck. Hell, Lyle even gave him a new job, keeping track of all the horses in the county. Things were looking up on that front. Now, if there was some good news on the female front, it could be fantastic.

Chapter 4
A Different Outlook

The happy noises continued. The play, such as it was, seemed to be a hit. Now it was time to face the tag ends of his future. Mark took a deep breath, and went to find Ellen. She was on the outskirts of the Thomas group, listening to the conversation. He took a deep breath, knowing she might blow him off right now.

"Would you care for something to eat?" he asked quietly.

"I'd love to."

That was her most romantic response in nearly a week. Okay, she got emotional about food. They loaded up, and Ellen led the way, going to a somewhat secluded tree. Hope began to rekindle that he'd taken her words and action the wrong way. A moment later, Ellen dashed it.

"Did you see Kevin today?" she asked.

Mark sighed. "Kevin and Susie were with the group."

"Sure, but I want to know about them."

Mark was puzzled. "They rode double on Kevin's horse. I passed them going out. I didn't see them again until we got back to Rep City."

Ellen was not satisfied with his answer. "What were they doing all that time?"

The switch from no conversation while eating to her giving him the third degree confused Mark. How could he say it and stay within the prim and proper mode Ellen now espoused? The best he could do was to attribute descriptions elsewhere.

"There were observations they might not have acted properly."

Mark leaned over to take a bite of well-sauced brisket. Ellen's hand came under his chin, grabbing his jaw and turning his head so they were eye-to-eye. "Don't give me double talk. Give me the straight scoop."

Ellen withdrew her hand, now splattered with barbecue sauce, and cleaned it off with her tongue, keeping close eye contact with Mark.

Evidently, they were no longer doing the social scene. Prim and proper just left town. She asked for a direct answer, so that's what he would do, even though it would probably get his face slapped.

"Nobody saw them. They passed us on the way back. There was hay in her hair, and their clothes were askew. I was with Don Rowley and Lyle Lillard. Don made snide comments that they would be the next couple to get married, while some other couple he specifically didn't name just talked about it."

"What do you think?"

Mark didn't want to talk about it or think about it either. "I think the shivaree may not have gone well, but you put this one over Alicia."

"Damn right," was her response, "but that wasn't my question and you know it."

Maybe it was better to just get it over with. "Okay. The evening of the wedding, you nailed me with the question, 'What about us?' I thought the answer was that we would get married. At least, that's what you said. Ever since, your actions have been the opposite. The message has been to go away and stay away."

"Why would that be?" Ellen voiced it as a challenge.

Mark had suddenly had it with all the game playing. "When you came to Harlan, you figured to become the leading lady of the one and only ranch. Now I've turned into an also ran, so you're moving on to the leading candidate. Poor little Susie may have Kevin's eye now, but neither could have a clue about what is coming."

"You think I'm a really cold bitch, don't you?"

"You're whatever you need to be."

"Don't you think I have feelings for you?"

"I thought you might. It was my most fervent hope, in fact. You can call whatever you have as 'feelings.' I'm working on several career moves. Any of them will make your situation easier."

"They are feelings, deep ones. What career moves?"

"We now know of survivors at McCook, so there could be survivors elsewhere. Maybe I can find some of them. Also, we don't know how many terrorists still exist. In any case, that number needs to be pruned down to size. Size zero would be good. A third thing would be to hang with Doctor Dover. He invited me, but I don't know if he was serious."

Ellen looked at Mark, incredulous. "Your career move number one is suicide. Career move number two is near-term death, including a great deal of torture. With career move number three, you'd make coffee for the doctorates. With their survival skills, you will die badly."

"Any of them makes your situation a great deal easier. All I've done is piss off everyone. This will cure that, as well." Mark's appetite evaporated, and the sight of the plate sickened him. That was for the best, too. Soon, he'd no longer eat food that could keep somebody worthwhile alive.

Ellen suddenly picked up the dishes. She returned, empty-handed. "Come on, big dog. There's a table available."

She led him there, and sat him down. Ellen took Mark's hand and put her other hand on top. "How can I make you believe there's something going on besides what you think?"

Mark shrugged vaguely. "A great deal goes on I don't know about. Anything close to me will probably slap me alongside the head."

"Can't you believe there are people who want to help you?"

Mark chuckled bitterly. "Now you're talking about the state foster care system. That was their mission statement. Fat lot of good it did. The last family I was with did help me, but that was pure luck. I happened to have inclinations in the direction of their interests. Most kids would have found it nothing but torture."

Ellen cocked her head. "So I have to show you how some of your natural inclinations are in the same direction as my interests. Maybe I can also demonstrate how my natural inclinations go the same way as your interests."

Mark looked at her, mystified. "I suppose so. I can't imagine how that would be, though."

Ellen smiled knowingly as she dampened two fingers on her tongue. "Hold still. You've got barbecue sauce on your chin."

Mark obliged, as she dabbed on his face. Okay, he had an inclination to get sauce on his face. Ellen appeared to have an interest in removing those spots. Did that mean there was hope? She seemed to promote the notion. Mark didn't know why.

It was getting dark when people finished eating. It would take an hour to walk to Huntley, and many lived in Ragan, or even farther. That meant everyone looked for a place to sleep. That wasn't difficult since Alma was deserted, although Don Rowley had hauled off a lot of the furniture along with anything else he deemed valuable.

Mark sat backwards at the picnic table, his elbows on the table. This was already a major change, since Ellen would have never allowed such behavior at the house. Instead, she sat next to him in much the same posture he affected. Lyle led the bicycle people across the road to a motel.

"I see the dark lady and her ghosts will stay indoors tonight," he commented.

Ellen nodded, and pointed out other people. Some headed for that motel or one of the other two nearby motels. She was very interested that Alicia, Josh, Alex, and Cordelia took over a house facing the park. Mark's appetite finally returned, so they took it in like they were at an old-time drive-in movie, except they destroyed brisket instead of popcorn.

Mark suddenly remembered he never unhooked the horse from the farm wagon. In addition, his horse needed attention. He popped up with Ellen right behind him, and headed over to check it out. They found that others already took care of the situation. Mark could only shake his head, bewildered at others just doing it, as well as his own forgetfulness. He headed to the wagon for his bedroll, wondering where he would sleep.

In spite of her warming to him, Mark expected Ellen to join Josh, Alicia, and her family. She didn't have that in mind. His initial thought was to stay as far away as possible. Now, it was uncertain. He pulled out his bedroll, and handed Ellen hers. He opened his mouth to ask Ellen her intentions when he saw Lyle was out of the motel, striding toward the two of them. Not only that, he was motioning in their direction.

"Hey guys," Lyle said as he came up. "That was one hell of a show."

"I guess so," Mark replied carefully.

"I need to pick up our plates and help clean up," Ellen commented, starting to slide away.

"Oh, no, Ellen," came from Lyle. "I want you in this conversation."

Mark and Ellen exchanged glances in that last bit of daylight.

"I said it was a hell of a show and I meant it. It was well-scripted. The concept was brilliant. Everybody played their part convincingly. There were some glitches with the staging. I saw there was only one place for Alicia's parents to ride, and Alex looked too fresh to have straddled a pile of hams for fifty miles. In addition, Vince's posse was across the field in front of the church after the wedding. I don't believe Josh and Alicia knew anything about it. Mark, you and Vince have been thick as thieves. The Omega bugs are gone, we're not at war, and the wedding is a done deal. It is time you tell me what is going on."

Mark considered that was his life. If he picked up a dime, shining on the ground, he'd get blind-sided by a semi. He knew the whole thing was a long shot. Lyle had him dead to rights, and no amount of weasel-wording would make it better. He put his bedroll back in the wagon, scratched a late-season bug bite in the crook of his elbow, licked his lips, and told Lyle what he knew. Some was news to Ellen. Mark leaned forward, his elbows on the side of the wagon, awaiting his judgment.

Ellen surprised Mark by being the first to speak up. "Mr. Lillard, this isn't helping one bit. When I saw Mark earlier, he was ready to give up and leave Harlan. I no sooner got him calmed down and halfway on his feet, when you knock him down again. What he doesn't know is if he does this suicide mission against the terrorists, I'll be right beside him, keeping his magazines loaded."

Mark stared at her, his mouth hanging open.

After a minute, Lyle leaned on the wagon next to Mark. "Sammie Moore perceives a division in Harlan leadership. She wants to make that a complete split. Mark, I see no reason to disabuse her of her illusions. Tomorrow is September 11, and I think we should include her in a 9/11 memorial observance here at the veterans memorial. Maybe we can pry some of that agenda out of her then."

Mark was still in shock from Ellen's comment, but Lyle's comment did register. "You still want me to be part of this, after everything I did?"

"I certainly do. As for your other major issue, Mark, I saw how you looked at Kevin and Susie. I also noticed your reaction to Don Rowley's dirty old man routine. Normally, newly engaged folks dream about the future. Contemplating suicide is not part of that future. You, and I'm talking about both of you, are important to Harlan."

Ellen appeared reassured. Mark wasn't sure where anything stood. Lyle's proposal caught his interest, though. It would be interesting to get a handle on the dark lady and her ghosts. He raised his head and briefly nodded to Lyle. "Yes, sir, I can help with that," was all he came up with.

Lyle sighed. "The motel is packed, but I saved a pair of rooms. Come on, I'll show you where they are. The only rooms were adjoining."

Lyle led the way, not looking back. Mark and Ellen followed, bedrolls in hand. After everything that happened, Mark no longer had any ideas or plans. It was pitch black in the room. He felt his way around the walls until he came to the bed, where he collapsed. Mark lay there, using the bedroll as a pillow. His major conclusion was that he screwed things up, both with his job and with Ellen.

He lay there, wondering how he could have avoided all of this. He got no answers, other than remembering some wit who maintained it was easier to stay out of a hole than to climb out after you fell in. That was no comfort. Ellen talking like there was hope for them didn't mean any existed. Then there was thinking he could outwit Lyle. He should have known better.

Mark heard a soft knock. It didn't come from the direction of the room door. It was off to the side. He felt his way toward the knocking, finally finding a door. Was this the connecting door Lyle mentioned? After some effort, he got it open, feeling Ellen's breath only inches away.

"Lyle was right. There is a connecting door," she commented. "I didn't know if you would open it. May I come in?"

Mark was on uncertain footing once again. "Sure. Why not?"

The rooms were mirror images, so Ellen knew exactly where she was going. She held Mark's hand to show him he was going there, too. They sat, side by side, on the edge of the bed.

"What are you thinking about, Mark?"

"I'm meditating on how totally I screw things up."

"Are you worried about Lyle? You shouldn't be. Lady Samantha came, agenda in hand. Lyle was on to both her and her agenda instantly. You confirmed it for him several different ways. He is going to keep you running Harlan Ranch. Beyond that, you are part of his overall plans. You did good."

"I'm glad for your vote. I'm even happier that you're still talking to me."

"How's that?" Ellen actually sounded puzzled.

"Everything I said or did today ended with my foot in my mouth. That applies to this entire week. Everything just turned out wrong."

That got a moment of silence. Then her hand stroked his upper arm. "Oh, I get it. I wasn't all lovey-dovey, so you assumed it was your fault. I hate to break this to you, Mark, but you are not the cause of everything that happens around you. It's just how I was brought up. It was pounded into me from early on that I was to be a good girl around my elders. That training went double when the elders in question were my Uncle Alex and Aunt Cordelia. It's just part of who I am."

At this point, Mark distrusted his instincts, judgment, and anything else. He kept his response as neutral as possible. "Okay. I see what you're saying. I still don't get that comment, where you told Lyle that you would follow me into battle against the terrorists."

"Mr. Tahner, when I said I would marry you, I meant it. That means wherever you go, I'm going to be there too. If you do something stupid, you can count on hearing about it from me."

"On the other hand, if I make decent choices, you'll still be there. You might not include some of the commentary."

"You know what they say — happy wife, happy life. It almost sounds like you get the idea."

"There's no guarantee. I'm known for backsliding. Do you promise to give me good counseling when I need it?"

Mark thought he could feel her smile in the dark. She softly leaned against him. "That comes with the territory. Is there anything else I can help you improve?"

"I'd like to have more time with you like this. What do I have to do for that to happen?"

"Yes, it is nice, isn't it? Our interests and inclinations align well with each other in that regard. Do you suppose there are other areas where we might agree?"

Mark's mind was racing at this point, even while his body was reacting in another fashion. "Since we're engaged, perhaps we could explore possible consequences of it. Marriage might be a logical outcome."

"Are we in a race with Kevin and Susie?"

Mark snorted. "I don't care about anybody's love life or marital status other than ours. When it comes to getting married, Ellen Markley is the only person whose opinion counts."

"Still, Lyle Lillard said you had a look in your eye as they went past."

"That reflected how I would have liked to have been with you at that moment. It also reflected my certainty that any chance of it was zero."

"That's where I found you at this afternoon's festivities. What do you think of how you are with me now? Do you still envy Kevin?"

"I never envied Kevin, only his situation. He is the rising star. Seeing him with Susie punched my ticket for hell. It was another piece fitting the pattern of my life. On the other hand, what Lyle talked about earlier is on top of telling me to get an inventory of all the horses in Harlan, including those used by Don Rowley. Then there's this with you. I hardly know how to take second chances, Ellen."

Ellen stroked Mark's arm again. "You thought things were going sour, so it was time to bug out. Growing up in foster homes had to be tough. I thought I had it rough, and I had both parents. That was in addition to Alex and Cordelia as godparents. I guess you thought of the military as your family, except the military and the country didn't return the favor. I still can't believe they declared all of you guys killed in action, and then wouldn't admit you were alive when you were standing in front of them."

Mark grunted. This wasn't a direction he wanted to go. "The military quit us before we quit them." He paused for a moment to find a new subject. Finally, "How do I know the right thing to say and the right time to say it?"

Ellen sighed. "You put in a lot of time and effort learning about ranching and horses. Before that, you focused on being a soldier and warrior. You also spent beaucoup time learning how to track animals and things. Where would you be now if you'd spent that kind of time studying women?"

Mark nodded. "I probably wouldn't be working for Lyle, and I almost certainly wouldn't have found my way here to you."

Ellen giggled. "That's the smartest thing you said in a long time," she said as she put her hand against Mark's chest, pushing him down on the bed, and coming down on top of him.

A while later, she whispered, "Can you bear being without me for a moment?"

"Why?"

"I want to get my bedroll. I'll sleep here, if that's all right."

Was it all right? It was more than all right. At the same time, he didn't want to let go of her. Ellen read his internal conflict perfectly. Mark could only hope she felt the same way. It was quite some time before their lips separated, and longer still for their interlocked fingers to release.

It seemed only a moment before she returned. She left her bedroll by the door. That meant she intended this conclusion all along. What mattered wasn't her intent but the current actuality, which outstripped his wishful thinking.

When she tossed her bedroll to the side, he swiftly discovered she'd been busy, indeed. What he felt in his arms was all Ellen, and only Ellen. Her clothes somehow vanished along the way.

Ellen took Mark places even his fantasies never dared to venture. As he fell asleep, happily snared in her arms, Mark recalled his comment about not only being caught, but landed, on the scale, and hoping she didn't throw him back. He was being clever then, but discovered that statement came true big time.

Far too soon, a flash of light interrupted his dreams. Peering in the direction of the light, Mark saw Ellen's inviting silhouette between the curtains. The room faced the park. He got up on one elbow to enjoy the view, and decided he'd never tire of it. Ellen looked at him and shook her head.

"That looks suspiciously like a leer, Mr. Tahner. Somebody might get the impression that you're just a dirty old man."

"I should live so long. You'll wear me out first."

Ellen walked over to the bed and inspected him. "The only part I'm concerned with is reviving just fine. Your romantic life is doing fine. Now you need to pay attention to your professional life. The grills are hot and they have breakfast going in the park. One table is occupied by everyone who's anyone in Harlan. That's with one exception, whose butt is still in bed."

"Is the bicycle bunch there?"

"There is no sign of them. Come on, lazy bones. You'd already have the chores done at home."

"Right. You know, it's really hard to undress neatly in the dark."

"As I recall, there was no 'neatly' to it. Now get moving. I just got a whiff of bacon. It must have been some they brought from McCook. I want my share."

Ellen proved she was serious about breakfast. She was dressed and had her bedroll together, while Mark was still getting his boots on. He caught up to her in the hallway, and found she had her game face on.

She gave an appraising sideways look at him. "This is the time for movers and shakers, buddy boy. You're the tiger. They're your breakfast."

That brought a flashback of the cannibals, and Mark found he had no difficulty having a serious look. "Lyle said last night that he had a plan to separate the bicycle people from their agenda. Since I'm part of it, I'd better get moving."

Ellen nodded. "That's my boy."

They walked into the warm morning, answering waves from across the road as they strode across. Ellen's nose hadn't lied. Carrying their plates to the table, Mark saw Ellen missed a few movers and shakers.

"Where are Don Rowley and Harry Dover?" Mark asked idly.

Vince looked at him. "Doctor Dover wanted to get back to Ragan, so Don took him."

Mark sipped the coffee. It wasn't as good as what Ellen made. "Is he headed back to Lincoln already?"

There were shrugs all around, and the conversation changed to Josh, Alicia, and the surprise reunion the previous evening.

"That was a real stroke of luck that Alicia's parents survived. Not many families survived," Vince observed.

Ellen stopped eating in mid-bite, and stared at the table. Mark saw moisture in her eyes, and immediately stepped in. "Now we know about survivors at McCook, so it raises hope other groups out there survived. It would be nice to have more reunions. Maybe Ellen's folks made it, too."

Vince tried to cover his misstep. "My wife said we need to have you two over for dinner sometime."

"That would be nice," Ellen replied in a monotone.

"You know," Mark improvised, "this bacon is better than what we liberated from the abandoned cabin."

Ellen got up shakily, walking away from the table. Mark immediately got up with her. She was weeping, but no tears came. Mark had nothing he could say, so he just held her. It left Mark facing the table, so he saw Lyle look at the two of them, and then around the group. Everyone was in shock.

"Vince," Lyle said, "you put your foot in it big time. I didn't want to see political correctness carry over to our group. Everyone is entitled to their opinion, and can say what they want. Still, everybody lost friends and relations in that damn dust. It will be a sensitive subject for a long time. Think about it before you go rattling off, okay?"

Ellen finally got her emotions under control. She returned Mark's embrace, just leaning against his chest.

She whispered, "Thanks for standing in there for me. It wasn't what you said, so much as showing me your heart's in the right place."

"Anything between you and your bacon cannot be tolerated."

That got a small chuckle. "You got that right. Okay, let's go see what might still be fit to eat. I'm sure the eggs are stone cold."

Vince was quiet after that. Lyle's eyes constantly flicked from one person to another. Mark only now appreciated how the man constantly evaluated, measured, and contemplated. A person like that was not one to alienate, and Lyle supported him, even against Don Rowley. Maybe second chances did happen. Mark hoped he'd be smart enough to take advantage of them.

Lyle looked toward the motel. "Our guests don't keep our hours. We have things to do and long rides to get home."

He turned to Vince. "Do you know of any national flags around here?"

Vince was happy for the conversation any direction beside his faux pas. "There's one under the counter in the sheriff's office."

"Could you get it? We'll have a memorial ceremony. Also, ask Josh to join us."

Vince left, and Don's main driver walked up. "What do you want to do with the meat?"

"Divide it between the store in Huntley and the co-op in Ragan. Everybody gets a share."

As the driver turned to go, Mark asked, "Don't you usually drive the carriage, with Don on the freight wagon?"

He grunted. "Don said Doctor Dover was easier on him than you two. You didn't hear that here, though."

Mark blinked and Lyle nodded. "Not long ago, Don wanted to stomp you into the ground. Yesterday, it looked like your engagement was over. Yet, this morning, you are with Ellen, and Don ran instead of facing the results of his unsuccessful land grab. Your luck is still with you. With that being the case, let's go fetch our guests. You can come too, Ellen."

Mark and Ellen followed Lyle into the motel. When Lyle knocked, Sammie answered immediately.

Lyle gave her a professional smile. "Good morning, Ms. Moore. Mark says you and your cohort look and act military. I agree. In that vein, I have a question for you."

Mark saw Sammie brace herself.

After a pause, Lyle inquired, "Do you think of this as the United States of America?"

She stared at him. Finally, she blinked and shook her head. "I hadn't really thought about it, sir. I still think I am a USAF officer in spite of knowing there is no longer a national military force. This is the middle of what I always considered the United States. I can't consider myself anything but a citizen." She looked at Lyle questioningly.

Lyle nodded. "Two months ago, on July 4, we had an Independence Day parade here in Alma. That evening, I raised a glass, and proposed a toast. 'God bless the United States of America,' I said."

"That was a beautiful and appropriate thing to do," she said.

Lyle continued, "We knew there was no functioning government, but we were all Americans. After the barbecue last night, we talked about today being September 11, when terrorists attacked us. We are going to have a ceremony at the memorial across the road. Would you care to join us?"

"I'd love to," Sammie replied quickly. "My father was career National Guard. He died in Iraq."

"It will be an honor to include you, especially considering that."

The memorial was dedicated to Vietnam veterans, but seemed quite appropriate for the occasion. Vince was back with the flag, and Mark helped him check the flagpole.

When he finished, Lyle turned to Mark, "Why don't you, Josh, and these good McCook folks, form a line by the flagpole. Oh, all of you get your weapons. Ms. Moore will be along in a minute.

While most of yesterday's crowd were gone, quite a few stuck around for the memorial. It was a long time since Mark did anything like this. It looked like Sammie also had to wing it. As she centered herself on both the unit and the flagpole, Mark saw her silently mouth the procedure. He guessed she was trying to remember the sequence of orders.

Tom, the lead sniper and Josh exchanged glances. Tom gave Josh a high sign with his eyebrows, and Josh nodded. He quietly brought them to attention. Sammie clicked into gear, commanding parade rest, then doing an about face to face the flagpole. Lyle, carried the United States flag to the flagpole. Mark thought Lillard was marching. He attached the flag, then glanced at her. Sammie turned her head over her shoulder, commanded attention followed by present arms. She turned to the flag, and saluted as the flag went briskly to the top of the pole, then slowly to half-staff.

Afterward, Mark had no idea whether the ceremony was correct, but it satisfied everyone. After Lyle secured the line to the pole, Mark saw Sammie and Lyle momentarily regard one another. Suddenly, she snapped to attention and saluted him. Lyle returned the salute.

Lyle faced both the military group and the onlookers nearby. "Not long before the Omega dust came through, we felt compelled to toast our country's independence. We did that, knowing the country had no government. In effect, we toasted ourselves, because we were, and now are the country. While the Omega dust nearly ended humanity, it did not erase us or what we believe."

Lyle Lillard paused, and looked at the flag, not all that far above his head at half mast. "Now, we gather to mourn the losses inflicted on us this day in 2001. Sammie Moore lost her father, fighting that foe. She became an Air Force officer. Her four companions are also military. Josh and Mark fought our enemies in Afghanistan and again on the Mexican border. We still fight terrorists who make it clear they want all of us dead. Our goal is for them to always be disappointed. Finding more survivors is a matter of rejoicing. Let good fortune smile on us as we go forward. We will have a moment of silence for those taken from us since that awful day."

He bowed his head, as did everyone. Mark noticed Sammie wiping away tears. Ellen said he knew nothing about women. Mark thought Lyle knew a great deal, and found out something about her. Mark wasn't sure what, other than that Sammie wasn't a total iron lady or ice queen.

Chapter 5
Onion Agenda

Mark helped Lyle separate the McCook visitors. Lyle invited Alex and Cordelia to enjoy their time with their daughter and son-in-law. The rest of the group went back to the motel for a chat. Mark figured his part was to keep their visitors polite. After all, he could pull the plug on their scam.

The motel had a small meeting room, the entire center occupied by a fake mahogany table. Lyle took the head. Sammie was heading for the same place, but stopped next to Lyle. After a moment, Lyle had her sit on his right. Her four compatriots filled in down that side of the table. Mark had the other side to himself. Lyle put an elbow on each chair arm, and intertwined his fingers. Mark rested his chin on his fingers, the swivel chair aimed so Lyle and Sammie nearly faced him, and her sniper friends in his peripheral vision.

"It is good to get together," Lyle opened. "I think it's a priority for us to stay in contact. We need to get a feel for what we can offer one another. I propose you all stick around a few days so you can see what we have in Harlan County, or, as we've recently taken to calling it, simply Harlan. Mark will be your escort. He can show you whatever you like. We don't have any secrets here."

Lyle turned slightly toward Mark. "I should have asked you about this earlier. Will that be a problem?"

Mark shook his head. "No sir, Kevin has the day-to-day work under control at the ranch. Their bikes look beat up. Something could break if they run around the county much."

"That's a good point, Mark. The carriage is in use. How are we fixed for trained horses?"

Mark shrugged. "All the horses belong to Harlan. If you need me to pull some back, that's what I'll do."

Lyle leaned back. "We can get another horse or two for training. Then Kevin can demonstrate horse training while he teaches it."

"So you want to use Kevin's horse?"

"Yeah, why don't we? Put Ms. Moore on that horse. That way, there will be an extra bicycle if one breaks. We can keep everyone moving."

Sammie seemed stunned. Mark thought it was a good thing both Kevin and the horse were at Wagon Ranch. Recalling Ellen's reaction to Sammie, Mark thought it prudent to keep the two women as far apart as possible. His analysis might be off base. Mark considered how wrong he'd had things figured about Ellen just the night before and shuddered. It was a good thing Lyle didn't notice that part of his reaction.

Lyle then took off on a different tack. "You've got pretty good meat cutters, judging from what you brought."

"They are getting better. The hunters bring lots of hogs and game. The meat cutters get loads of practice."

"Some of our people will go back to McCook with you. In addition, we'll send beef as an exchange gift. The difference is that we'll send it on the hoof so you can decide how you want it handled. Are you up for that?"

"I think we can do it."

"Josh will want to see where his bride hails from. Josh, Alicia, and her parents can go in the carriage, to have a comfortable ride. Horses aren't as fast as your bikes. There will be an overnight stop at Arapahoe. Don Rowley will go, to start trade with your area. Oh, Mark, I want you to organize this. It will be quite a convoy to McCook."

"When should we do this?"

"There's no hurry. Oh, Ms. Moore, how much experience do you have riding horses?"

"I rode a horse a few times, a long time ago."

Lyle nodded genially. "That should not be a problem. Mark, it looks like you get to teach Ms Moore some basic horsemanship, too."

Mark took a deep breath. "Yes, sir, I can do that."

Lyle declared the meeting done and headed out, leaving Sammie and company in the board room. Outside, Lyle looked at Mark. "You got tense when I asked you to train the Moore girl. What was that about?"

"Ellen would like nothing more than to destroy the dark lady."

Lyle had to ponder that. "Does she see her as a threat?"

"Yes, but not like that. Ellen sees her very existence as a menace. There was too much chance that Stanley and his tribe might have feasted on bits of Mark while Lady Samantha and her ghosts looked on."

"Well, do the best you can. What did you think of the meeting?"

"I expected you to dig more than you did."

"It wouldn't have done any good. If we nailed them on a few things, they would just concoct other fairy tales. Now, consider what we just set up. Josh goes with his bride and her parents. With them go beef which have to be handled and processed by the Peepul. In addition, Don will peep and pry everywhere. You will be along for the ride. I'll have to think about whether Ellen should go."

"What possible purpose would that serve?"

Lyle grinned. "All of the social, business, and personal dynamics cause friction. Enough sparks flying can shed light. Everyone has to have to pay attention, though."

Mark nodded. "This is the Lyle Lillard show."

"You've got a ticket, my boy. Walk right in. Maybe there's a bearded lady. It will be entertaining. It might take your breath away."

"I'll pass on the part that takes my breath away. Now I'd better go see a man about a horse."

Ellen scowled at Mark from the farm wagon seat. Mark's horse was saddled and tied behind the wagon. Mark was almost to his horse when he heard Lyle.

"Hey, Mark, just a minute."

Mark sighed. "Yes, sir?"

"What do you make of our guest? The woman, that is."

"Isn't that what the Lyle Lillard show is supposed to discover?"

"No, I mean her military rank and affiliation."

"Oh, that. She already said that she's an Air Force officer. Alex heard one of the snipers call her Lieutenant. She's been around a while, so I'd guess her rank to be First Lieutenant."

"Okay, I agree with that. Now for the hard question. What is her specialty?"

"That beats the hell out of me. I'll guess Military Intelligence. She doesn't strike me as a human intelligence type. That leaves the technical end, like electronics."

"That agrees with my estimate, and I was in signal intelligence back in the day. What about the snipers?"

"They aren't Air Force. They've been together a long time, and act more like each other than any service. I'd vote against them being Army. That leaves the Marines."

"Those were my thoughts, too. Back to our previous conversation, I just decided to save you from breaking the news about the horse to Ellen. What do you think of that?"

Mark sent a note of mental thanks to whoever made that happen, and walked with Lyle to the wagon. Ellen was now puzzled rather than scowling.

"Ellen," Lyle opened, "do you remember Morgan Carr, who escaped from Rep City just as the dust hit? I disliked him the moment I laid eyes on him. It was a gut reaction. I'll grant nobody else in Harlan liked him either. I saw you had that reaction with the young lady from McCook and respect your instincts. However, we have to play nice for now, so I'm lending her a horse while she's here. Mark has to give her horsemanship training. That was not Mark's idea. I told him to do it."

Ellen stared at him. "Okay, Mr. Lillard. Thanks for telling me. You didn't owe me any explanation of what you do."

Lyle nodded agreeably. "I know that. Still, there are a number of things I want Mark to do. If you kill him, he will have a hard time doing them."

"You make it sound like I'm dangerous or something."

"There is a commonality between you and Alicia. One of you is just dangerous. The other one is flat deadly. I haven't figured out who's more likely to fill each role." Lyle then turned to Mark. "Head to the wagon place. On your way, pick up whatever horse Adeline says is ready to train. It just became time for Kevin to quit mooning and spooning, and concentrate on his job. Little Susie knows where he is."

Mark got aboard his horse, considering the fact that he could read the filly more easily than any of the human females in his life. On the other hand, Ellen gave him a far better feeling last night. If he'd studied women like he spent on all those other activities, he might have figured something out by now.

Just then, the four snipers walked out of the motel. Lyle yelled at them, "What branch are you guys?"

"Marines, sir!"

Lyle looked at Mark and nodded. As Mark started forward, he heard one yell back, "Is that a problem?"

"Not at all," Lyle came back. "I'm just glad we're on the same side, guys."

Mark was beside Ellen by then. He said quietly, "I also hope you and I are on the same side."

"You've done and said sensible things ever since last night.How long will that continue? Are you trying for a record?"

Mark shook his head and shrugged. "It's like a mine field. With every step, my life could go boom. Back to current events, Lyle gave me a long list to do. I'll be pushing it to get home before dark."

"Is there anything special you'd like for dinner?"

Mark stopped cold at that. Ellen served what she served. It always tasted good, and Mark always ate it. "When I get back with a horse bound for the dark lady, the likely menu is crow and humble pie."

Ellen favored him with a slight smile as they started moving forward. After a moment Ellen glanced at Mark. "Tomorrow, you get the honor of bringing the horse down here to teach her ladyship about horseback riding."

Mark nodded. "You could come down, too. You could translate my man-speak into something she understands."

Ellen's eyebrows arched high. "That is tempting, Mark. Oh, that is so tempting. Yes, I could tell her a lot, and she'd certainly understand. Still, Mr. Lillard said he wants us to play nice. That means clamping my jaws when I'm around her. At the ranch, I can scream without bothering anybody except the horses."

Mark nodded. "I'd better treat you with kid gloves. I'd hate for you to take out your frustrations on me. My chances of survival would be slim to nonexistent. Now that I think of it, I should just stay in the bunkhouse for the duration."

"Mr. Tahner, you will stay in the house and take your medicine like a man. I'd hate for you to be around that dark lady and forget there are better examples of women. That could be hard on you. I noticed that one sniper glancing her way like he wants to get up close and personal. I think they called him Tom."

The next morning, leading Kevin's horse to Alma, Mark felt much better for taking Ellen's medicine. He enjoyed it so much that if she hadn't pushed him out the door, he'd have stuck around for more of her cure.

In Alma, Sammie and her sniper buddies were outside. Mark was alert to something between Sammie and the sniper leader, Tom. That made him uncomfortably aware of Tom as he worked with Sammie. Usually, he adjusted the stirrups with the rider aboard since it was easier and faster. To avoid problems, Mark estimated the stirrups, and had her dismount. After that, he had Sammie practice mount and dismount a number of times. Afterward, they moved on to controlling the horse.

"We train our horses to react in specific ways. None of their training includes much on the reins. Mr. Lillard doesn't want them getting a hard mouth. Here are the leg cues you need to learn."

Before long, all four snipers headed behind the motel. Their declared purpose was to build a corral. Later, they would need to find feed. A scratchy feeling in his neck told Mark that Tom was keeping an eye on both him and the dark lady, whether he was visible or not.

Initially frustrated, Sammie slowly got into the swing of it. She finally started to enjoy the experience. Considering this was her first lesson, Mark considered she came a long way.

"Mark, could we ride outside the parking lot?"

"Sure, why not? Where do you want to go?"

"Over there by the lake, I think."

"That will be fine. Lead on."

As they left, Mark again felt the prickly sensation of a chaperone. Mark also knew Sammie had more on her mind than practicing her equine handling. It wasn't too long before Sammie stopped.

"Mark, I wanted to tell you how much I appreciate you honoring our agreement."

He was ready for that. "I told you Alicia would have a reunion with at least one of her parents. If it was only Alex, there would be questions about how Alex showed up in Harlan. You came, so we played it that way."

Sammie nodded. "I had no idea it would work out this way."

"We all winged it. Alex stayed with us, and from talking to him, I knew you had not told him about the Peepul. It wasn't up to me to say anything."

"The Peepul … Stanley, actually, figured out they had to change. They were eating roots and bugs when we contacted them. Seeing them starving, we showed them how hunting pigs could benefit them and the folks around them."

"When did this happen?"

"It was after the tribe left Harlan. We camped up on that pointy bluff above Oxford."

"The folks in Oxford were on their own?"

"No, when we reported the tribe started moving, we got orders to warn anybody in their path. We told the resident deputy in Oxford. We didn't say anything about their diet. The deputy said he called the sheriff. Afterward, he thanked us, and said they would handle it. We went back to our camp."

"From what I heard, the tribe's odor was more than enough warning. Still, thank you for warning them."

Mark paused and then, "Okay, what happened then?"

"They marched a short distance, but Stanley made them stop on a slight rise. Before long, a wave of the dust came through. After the dust cleared, Stanley led them toward Arapahoe. They were in a sorry shape by then. I decided to make contact. Stanley had been aware of us for quite some time, and thought of us as 'dark lady and four ghosts.' They'd have died about five miles from Arapahoe if we hadn't brought them a feral hog to eat."

"How did Stanley know about the dust?"

"He says he smells it. His warnings have been dead on."

"It only takes one miss to be dead. For that matter, it only takes one Omega bug to be dead."

Sammie didn't react. "When the tribe saw two people in Arapahoe, Stanley yelled at them to stay back, that they were dust people. They wore yellow environmental suits and opened an ice chest. Sure enough, there was the dust. The front runners were already on them, slicing their suits with their knives. Stanley lost fifty people. The stuff also got the two dust people. We went to McCook, and saw a group coming. Stanley said the leader was one of the dust people, so the tribe hid from them. Do you believe me?"

"You tell good stories, if nothing else. Let's get to the bottom line. What are you trying to do?"

"You have organization and people who can do things under these conditions. We're just limping along. We want to build trust, and find what we can supply that Harlan needs."

"Trust? Lady, you have no idea what trust is. So far, you have only demonstrated that you can act rationally. Let me tell you about trust. Say that you're in the boonies, and somebody's behind you with a locked and loaded weapon. Trust is when that's not only not a problem but a good thing."

"I didn't intend to get a philosophical discussion here."

"You're not having one. Let me put a face on the body behind you with a loaded weapon. How about my Ellen? You remember the gal at the schoolhouse?"

"I'd be really worried. I'd probably be dead. I heard what she said."

"I agree. Now the face belongs to Vince as he escorted you through Harlan."

"I'd be concerned. Okay, I was very concerned."

"Okay, now the face belongs to one of your snipers. Let's say the face belongs to Tom."

"There, I'd feel secure."

"I understand that. I think Tom wants you to feel that way." Mark turned to the source of the major prickles in his neck, and said loudly, "Don't you, Tom? Quit slithering around in the bushes and join us."

Tom appeared out of nowhere. Mark thanked that strange feeling for coming to his aid again.

Confused and irritated, Tom growled, "What did I leave visible? I blew something. I'm losing my edge."

Mark grinned. "I didn't see anything until you stood up. It's a feeling I get when a predator tracks me. It saved me any number of times."

Sammie was astonished at Tom appearing and shocked at Mark's comment. "Let me make sure I go this straight. There's no way someone could sense the dust or people associated with the dust. On the other hand, it's perfectly natural to sense when somebody's tracking you."

Mark considered that. "The group leaving McCook was with Doctor Dover. Ellen and Alicia were part of it. They were trying to escape the dust, not spread it."

"Yes, Alex and Cordelia told me," Sammie replied. "Still, Stanley insisted there were dust people. Maybe he was talking about somebody involved with it."

Mark grunted. "Dover and his associates were tracking the dust."

"I got the distinct impression that it was somebody involved with creating it. Stanley never gave a clear explanation even after I got him to learn enough so we could have a conversation."

Mark was shocked. Dover only divulged his real identity the day after the wedding when the terrorist prisoner recognized Dover. Later, Harry claimed to be one of the inventors of the Omega bugs. Was that a secret? Mark revised his plan of attack.

"Harry Dover is not his real name. He now claims he helped invent the Omega bug. We don't think it's the whole truth, but we destroyed the last vial, so it doesn't matter."

Sammie and Tom exchanged meaningful glances. Ellen was right. There was something between the two, even if they both denied it, even to themselves. Suddenly, it hit him.

"Sammie, Tom — I'm going to say something. I don't want to offend either of you, but when you two get close to each other, I swear I can see sparks or electricity or something."

Mark leaned forward onto the pommel of his saddle as they stared at him. "Yes, there is something going on. I remember the Air Force strictly enforced fraternization regulations. Officers and enlisted did not mix, and especially not female officers and enlisted. Sammie, you're an Air Force officer even though there's no longer an Air Force. How long has it been since an Air Force plane was actually in the air, anyhow?"

Sammie looked questioningly at Tom, who shrugged. "What the hell," Tom commented. "You might as well tell him. He already knows more than enough to mess us up."

Sammie hesitated. Finally, she licked her lips, which Mark associated with how a horse shows it is processing information. "The last plane took off just after New Year's, when the terrorists set off the nuke under Times Square, killing the Vice President among many others. The plane was Air Force One, carrying the President, Secret Service, and a bunch of Homeland Security goons. They flew to Offutt Air Force Base, Omaha."

Now Mark stared at them. "How do you know that?"

Tom released a side pocket of the pack he always carried. Mark had noticed the stubby antenna sticking up but ignored it except to wonder why he would carry dead weight. There were no functioning cell towers, and the satellite communications network was dead.

Tom pulled it out. "You know what this is, right?"

"It is, or used to be, a sat phone. With no functioning satellites, it's dead weight."

"As of New Year's, there were still functioning satellites. I don't know how they controlled the network. Our mutual boss called Sammie and me. The only name either of us had for him was Gutierrez. She knew him as a Major. I knew him otherwise. He ordered us to follow the Peepul tribe, but not to intervene in anything they did. We were to coordinate with Colonel Whitaker, commander of the Corps of Engineers at the dam outside Rep City. When we got there, the Colonel repeated what Gutierrez said, adding we could not contact the locals. Not to intervene. Not to warn."

Mark was disgusted. "You marionettes marched to the beat of the drum. You watched as they murdered people, chopped them into stew meat, and served them as holy sacrament by Willy the rat. I want to read the citation they write up for your medal of valor. Hell, maybe I'll write it. Are you sure you never got in line for Willy and Stanley to bless you? We are Peepul. They are animals. I bet you loved that cheer."

Both Tom and Sammie shuddered. Mark directed the sternest possible look at them. "Both of you are in charge. That means you are both responsible for everything that happens or fails to happen. That's everything, folks. The Nuremberg Defense, 'We only followed orders,' is a dog that won't hunt. I'm no judge, and you aren't on trial."

Mark continued after a moment. "I cannot control what Alex and Cordelia find out from Josh and Alicia. You need to decide more than what you want to do. You need to figure out why it needs to be done. Ms. Moore, I'll be back tomorrow to give you more riding lessons."

Mark touched the brim of his hat, wheeled his horse, and rode off without looking back. There was no doubt or hesitation about his next move. He reported everything to his boss. This time, Lyle wanted all the detail Mark could muster, and more besides. At last, Lyle was satisfied, as was his wife, Adeline, who listened, too.

"What's your impression, Mark?" Lyle wanted to know.

"We peeled another layer off the onion, but there's a lot more we need to know. Ignorance isn't bliss, and it can get us killed. How far we have to go to get to their real agenda remains an open question."

Adeline chuckled then. "If you peel all the layers off an onion, what do you find?"

Both men looked at her.

"There's nothing left. An onion is nothing but layers."

At home, Mark retold everything to Ellen. He had mixed feelings whether anything was accomplished. Ellen listened closely and when he was done, she nodded her head. Then she cocked her head as though listening to a far-off voice. Finally, she grinned and clapped her hands, startling Mark.

"You are incredible, Mark," she informed him. "I'd have loved to have seen it. First, you are Cupid, impaling the two of them with your little bow and arrow. I'll bet you looked cute flying around with nothing on."

Mark felt embarrassed, and wanted to move on. "I was just sitting in my saddle, actually."

"Then you turn into the lord high prosecutor, letting them know that you'll see them both hang."

"Yeah, but I said they were not on trial."

"That's the best part. Now they know they really are on trial. That was a master stroke. It was genius. I am in awe."

Mark blinked. "You tell it like I was far above my usual competence. If I did or said something decent, it must have been the medicine you administered."

"Oh, you devil, taking advantage of a poor innocent girl. Well, come here and slay me with your mighty sword, great warrior prince."

Mark stood there with his mouth agape, wondering where Ellen came up with that. He didn't wonder very long, since Ellen administered additional medicine for Mark.

The next morning, Ellen announced, "Who knows what great things you'll say today? I want to witness them. Oh, you never said how her ladyship is progressing in riding."

Teaching Sammie to ride had vanished from Mark's radar. "She's not a natural, but she pays attention and tries to do what I say. Maybe she tries a little too hard."

"Maybe I can help out."

"Will this be before or after you scratch her eyes out?"

"No, silly, just because I can't stand her doesn't mean I can't work with her."

Mark shook his head in bewilderment. "I'll try to act like that makes any sense."

"It's not hard. If you had a choice, would you have anything to do with Don Rowley?"

"I got it, now. It still doesn't make a damn bit of sense. I don't care who we're talking about, either."

Ellen fluttered her eyelashes at him. "It doesn't have to make sense. It just has to work."

In Alma, Ellen did help. Her observations were always on time. Ellen never interrupted Mark's training, but during breaks, Ellen suggested things to Sammie. At times, Mark couldn't communicate a concept, but Ellen got the point across, often with only a few words. The situation was sufficiently comfortable that Ellen offered to share the lunch she'd brought with everyone. Tom and Sammie took her up on the offer. The other members of the team elected to go elsewhere.

The conversation wandered in a bland vein, when Ellen looked at Tom and Sammie sitting fairly close together, and hurled a zinger.

"So, Tom," Ellen said innocently, "when did you know you wanted to be with Sammie? You know, as something more than just sergeant and officer."

After a bit, Sammie looked at Tom. "That's a good question. When did you decide you wanted to be more than a subordinate?"

Mark had flashbacks to Ellen hitting him with that kind of question, and was glad he wasn't in the crosshairs. Tom shrunk a bit and looked at Mark. Finally, Tom came up with an answer.

"It was when we followed the Peepul here from Missouri. We knew she was from Nebraska, and I thought she'd cheer up when we got across the Missouri River. Instead, she got really morose. We knew what route the Peepul had to take, and crossed the river bottom ahead of them. They were never supposed to see us and they were walking, so we had a day to sit in a little town on the bluff."

"Were you able to find out about the problem?" Ellen asked Tom gently. Sammie looked nervous.

"Yeah, she went to high school in Holdrege, just north of Harlan County. Her parents divorced. Sammie wanted to be with her father, but her mother got custody. When Sammie dared go to college where her father was stationed, her mother disowned her."

Sammie broke in. "I graduated from Holdrege High School. Dad was full-time with the National Guard. In the summer before my senior year, they transferred him to Lincoln. Mom liked Holdrege, and rather than move, she divorced him. I was to finish high school there so I wouldn't feel out of place. That was a joke. Most of the kids were from families who'd been in the area forever, and I was the perpetual outsider. After graduation, I went to the University of Nebraska at Lincoln. I needed the ROTC scholarship."

Mark and Tom exchanged glances.

Sammie continued. "Dad and I got pretty close. Mom didn't like it at all. Dad was mobilized for Afghanistan as I finished my sophomore year. They already accepted me for the advanced ROTC program. Three months after he got in country, Dad was killed. Momsie ranted and raved that Dad did it just to spite her, even though she divorced him. I accepted his flag at the funeral service. They took Momsie away because of the commotion she made."

Ellen leaned over and patted Sammie's hand. "Did you ever patch up things with your mother?"

"We didn't speak or communicate after the funeral. I invited her to my graduation and commissioning. She didn't come or even reply. Two National Guard Colonels, a man and a woman who worked with Dad, came to my commissioning, and pinned on my bars. I felt that made the service my new parents. Now I don't know who or what I am."

Ellen looked back at Tom. "And with that, your heart went out to her. That is so sweet."

Chapter 6
Circus Parade

Mark pronounced the riding lessons done soon after lunch. Sammie had enough basics that she could ride back to McCook. His next task was to organize the group going to McCook. As he and Ellen rode off, Mark saw Sammie and Tom having a close discussion. He couldn't tell what they were saying, and didn't think he wanted to know.

Mark looked at Ellen. "You claimed that I played cupid. I had a front row seat to see how a master does it. No, it is more than that. One of them is somebody you would rather not be near. That makes it even more astounding."

Ellen smiled innocently. "Aw, shucks. You're only saying it because it's true. I did help out explaining stuff about riding, didn't I?"

"Yes, you did. I am truly not worthy."

"I hope you remember your status."

Ellen stayed with him as he went by the feedlot, Mark told the owner about taking beef to McCook on the hoof, and needed a drovers. Most of the people would have to walk, especially while herding the cattle.

As they headed for home, Ellen got to domestic problems. "How is the firewood supply for this winter?"

"We've got a couple of cords of wood for the kitchen stove. There are three cords for the stove we use for heating. I'm glad we haven't had to fire it up yet. Now that you mention it, I need to take another look at the chimney. One thing we don't want is a flue fire. It's a good thing Kevin has the trainees. They can help chop wood for the place. I didn't see any wood there."

"If he runs out of wood, he's got little Susie to keep him warm."

Mark had a smart-ass reply, but a wave of good sense overwhelmed him. Anything he said would get him in trouble. Mark swallowed hard and changed the subject.

"When do you think those two mares might foal? They seem dead set on delivering after winter sets in. That could be a problem if it's a cold winter. I remember the stories Mrs. Lillard told about their situation in past years. The vet doesn't seem worried, but I don't think he ever went through winter with an unheated facility."

"With the trainees down the road, maybe we should convert the bunkhouse into a couple of heated stalls."

"That would be a major amount of labor. It's only me unless you know some more kids who want to come out."

"Everybody wants to work for you. Harlan Ranch is where the action is. The alternative is to slave for Don Rowley. Speaking of slaves, why did Sammie, Tom, and company follow the Peepul? The organization along with the people ordering them to do it no longer existed."

Mark nodded. "That is a special kind of insanity they preach in the military. They call it professionalism. In action, it is what you heard from Sammie and Tom. Hell, it's what happened to Josh and me. We barely survived Afghanistan. When we got back to the United States, they said we couldn't be there because they declared us dead."

"You could have just taken off then, right?"

"That would have been a rational response. Instead, professionals that we were, our bunch walked all the way from the Pentagon to El Paso, Texas to fight the drug cartels. We ended up in a firefight with al-Queda, or one of its branches. I can't talk about those five continuing a mission after doing it myself. I do wonder about snipers and an Air Force intelligence officer working for the same guy. They had a mission in St. Louis, and left under odd conditions."

"How's that?"

"Think about what a sniper does? This involved at least the Air Force and Marines. In addition, they have those satellite phones, which they claim functioned long after we had any satellites."

Ellen looked at Mark. "The snipers were in St. Louis to take out a target. It had to be a major target. The group left town right afterward. Whoever pulled the strings didn't want them having to answer stupid questions."

"That is a good summary. They still pack those satellite phones, so they think their boss might be alive and able to communicate. Offutt Air Force Base may have living, breathing people, as well as the President and his playmates. Congress kept enacting legislation, so the President may have issued Executive Orders all this time."

That caught Ellen off guard. She tried to laugh and snort at the same time, and ended up with a coughing fit. "So all this time, we've had a patriotic duty to catch radio transmissions from Omaha. I knew there was something I needed to do. Those power lines coming to the house. They're supposed to carry electricity. Right?"

"Yeah, I'd send a check, but the mailman hasn't picked anything up since I've been there. I could drive around and look, but there's no gas."

When people wanted to make jokes, the best bet was to talk about everything that was no longer available.

"By the way," Ellen added, "the grapes from Chile should be good now. Why don't you get a few bunches next time we're at the store?"

"Of course, the store's shelves are bare. What on Earth would I use to pay for it? Money isn't worth anything."

"The grapes are from Chile. Use pesos."

They laughed all the way home.

Mark now devoted himself to planning the upcoming trip, and went to sleep thinking about it. Ellen commented during chores the next morning that his mumbling kept her awake. He rode back to the feedlot, meeting twenty-five cattle starting for McCook. They would move the cattle fifteen miles a day. If they moved faster, it would run their weight off. The main group would leave in two days, catching the herd near McCook. Mark decided at least one sniper should ride with the cattle.

In Alma, he located Sammie and her bunch. He told them what he was thinking. Tom supported the idea.

"Stanley's hunters go as far as Arapahoe. They'd consider the cattle legitimate game even with your people there. They won't think that if one of our guys is along."

Tom immediately told one of his guys to get his stuff and hit the road.

Mark shook his head. "Tom, there isn't that much of a rush. The herd won't get much beyond Oxford today. Your bicycles could go tomorrow morning and be up to the herd by tomorrow afternoon."

Tom shook his head and told his guy to do it. Mark reflected that was the military he remembered.

At the same time, Mark saw Sammie and Tom were distracted. Every spare moment, the two of them were discussing things quietly. Mark guessed it was the conversation Ellen started yesterday. Their situation seemed the same as the day before. Mark didn't care, but Ellen would require a full report, so he paid more attention.

He didn't stay long. Protecting the herd was only one thing keeping him awake. The next item on his list meant a long ride up to Ragan. He had to be sure Don Rowley had somebody making the run. It turned out Don would make the run himself with his double-header, two freight wagons with his team of draft horses. He couldn't pass up an opportunity to sniff around an entire town. The carriage was also ready to go. Josh, Alicia, and her parents would ride in it.

"Hey Mark," Don called after him. "How long will we be there?"

"I figure about three days. Isn't that how long it takes for guests and dead fish to acquire a certain odor?"

"That sounds okay. It's enough time to check the main places that might have something worthwhile."

"You know, Don, if you share a list of things you were interested in, we could pass the word if we saw something."

Don looked at Mark like he was an alien on a UFO, and rubbed his cheek. "Yeah, I could do that. If it was really good, I could make it worth your while."

One last stop was to check with Josh and Alicia. Alicia chose the spot while the dust was still going by. She wanted a view of Harlan Lake and the Republican River. With the warmth this late in the year, there was a nice breeze. Josh was off to the side while Alicia and her parents talked, so Mark did not have a hard time getting him away.

"Did her parents talk about the folks who showed up in McCook?"

"Yeah, they did. It sounds like some of the Peepul tribe survived. Not only that, they now keep the feral hog population under control."

"Did you or Alicia tell them about the Peepul when they were over here?"

"No, I didn't say anything. Alicia doesn't know anything beyond the stories she's heard."

"I guess you noticed the bike riders."

"Yeah, sure. What about them?"

"It turns out they've kept an eye on the Peepul ever since St. Louis."

"Is that where they're from? That doesn't matter much now."

"The bike riders claim credit for turning the Peepul from their old nasty ways to their current hog hunting, pork processing situation. In addition, they only told the McCook locals that the Peepul were petty criminals and drug users."

"Alex and Cordelia said the Peepul keep to themselves. They agreed not to use the roads. There's nothing about them being friends, but they're being useful. I can't fault the taste of their pork."

"Lyle says that for the moment, we won't share what they used to do."

"Hey, Mark, these are my in-laws. I just met the people, and I like them. I won't volunteer that kind of information. On the other hand, I'm not going to lie, either. Do you hear what I'm saying?"

"Yeah, I hear. Oh, here is a memory test for you. In Afghanistan, our commander mentioned the name of the guy above him. Do you recall who that was?"

Josh stopped for a moment. "That's a wild question. It has been a long time. Oh, yeah, it was Gutierrez. Why?"

"The bike people are military. The gal is a lieutenant in Air Force intelligence. The other four are Marine snipers. They say they all worked for the same person, a fellow by the name of Gutierrez."

"No shit."

Mark and Ellen spent every minute getting ready. Lyle stopped by and let Ellen know he wanted her to go. Ellen took the news well. At least, Mark thought she did. They were too busy to discuss it and Mark saw little of Ellen the rest of the day. He was getting things set up to keep the horses going while they were away.

It included making sure Kevin knew he needed to take care of things. Kevin said he had enough people on hand to make it happen.

Ellen was quiet during dinner the evening before the trip. They sat together and held each other as darkness fell. Mark felt comfortable with her.

The next morning, after minimal chores, they moved out, traveling light. Everyone would meet at the Oxford gate. Mark and Ellen were the first ones there. Sammie and her snipers arrived next, which amazed Mark, knowing their disinclination to get up any sooner than they had to.

Maybe they were eager to get back to the castle everybody talked about. They'd all find out how great this place really was in a couple of days. It might also be that Sammie and Tom wanted to continue their conversation in more familiar surroundings. As Lyle pointed out, they had an agenda, and watched everything they said around anyone from Harlan. Lyle supposed they'd scripted everything before they had ever set out.

Don on his double-header showed up next, avarice leaking from every pore. It was astonishing just how fast the man had gone from down and out to being the wealthiest man in Harlan. He had warehouses full of things he'd grabbed from empty houses, stores, and everywhere else. Don had more people working for him than anyone else, and Don made sure they all put in a full day's work, too.

The carriage took a little longer. The driver had to circle around to Josh and Alicia's house before heading to the rendezvous. Mark glanced at the position of the sun as he saw the carriage coming, and figured they would make Arapahoe with no trouble. The cattle herd should be leaving Arapahoe, with their two-day head start.

All the Harlan people were upbeat about meeting and greeting their new neighbors. Alex and Cordelia looked pleased to head for home. Josh and Alicia were in the carriage, their horses on lead. Ellen seemed okay with it, but Mark wondered if Ellen might have refused to go if she could. She had no family there, and her only friend was in the carriage.

Mark suggested that Ellen ride next to the carriage alongside Alicia. He rode beside Josh. Soon, Ellen, Alicia, and Cordelia rattled on like they had never been apart a single day. There was scarcely a crack or crevice in the conversational slab for the men to slip a word in edgewise. Finally, Mark exercised his prerogative as leader of this circus parade, and rode ahead to see where Sammie's mind might be.

Conversation with her was the opposite of what he'd seen with the carriage. She said little, and seemed preoccupied. Mark's mind went back to Lyle's theory that all her lines were rehearsed. Maybe she was out of script. Mark gave up, and dropped back to Don Rowley.

"This will be a a long run for your rig, Don."

Don grunted. "Yeah, and all of it will be on pavement, too. I don't know how the iron rims on the wheels will handle it. I brought plenty of lube and a couple of extra wheels. I wanted more, but Clay can only do so much. He put my wheels ahead of several other jobs as it was. I hope our farrier and blacksmith can get an apprentice."

"How's that going with him putting new rims on your wheels?"

"He did several of the wheels I've got on now. You asked for a list of what I'm looking for. I jotted down a few things. If you see any of them, I'd appreciate you letting me know." Don pulled a piece of paper from his shirt pocket.

"We'll see what we can do," Mark said as he accepted the list. "By the way, did you consider what happens if McCook becomes a regular run?"

"I don't see too many runs right away. It won't be long before winter will make this pretty chancy. Naturally, if we can help each other, and that way needs a wagon, I'd be happy to do what I can."

Mark considered Don would be only too happy to collect his fee. For such a long run, he would tack on a notable freight bill. At the same time, his demands for additional draft horses would become urgent. One pair of draft horses could not take care of everything.

"Naturally," Mark finally commented.

Mark saw a highway sign showing Arapahoe was five miles ahead. He was feeling good about that when the entire group suddenly came to a halt. Riding forward, Sammie faced a large guy standing in the middle of the road with a spear. Other men with spears, stood behind him. The spears looked strange, with a crossbar under the spear head.

Mark saw no hostility on either side. Then Mark recalled Alex saying he and his neighbors made spears like that for the pig hunters. This must be the group of hog slayers and former cannibals. At least he hoped they were former cannibals.

Sammie glanced at Mark and turned back to the big man. "Stanley, this is Mark. Tell him what you told me, please."

He looked at Mark. "Thirteen dust people came into the area. They followed the river bottom, avoiding McCook. We followed them. After they left our hunting grounds my people and I took them. They are a mile back in the trees."

Sammie called him Stanley. Yeah, that was the name and he looked like the guy in the cannibal tribe they scouted. This guy was not talking about pigs. From what Sammie said, what he called dust people must be terrorists.

"How many dust people escaped?" Mark asked.

"None," Stanley answered. "We knew the dark lady and her ghosts went this way. We didn't want these creatures be a problem."

"What did you do with them?"

"We left them where they fell. With the dust people blood, our spears and knives are contaminated. We won't be able to use our weapons or harvest wild pigs near here for some time."

That was interesting. "Nothing associated with these dust people can be used, and animals eating them aren't any good. Is that what you're saying?"

"That is correct. Pigs feeding on the bodies will have a bad taste for a long time."

"How long ago did this happen?"

"Soon after we took them, my hunters saw the cattle on the highway. They also saw the ghost. He said to wait for you and to show you the hat several dust people wore. The ghost said you would know what we were talking about then."

Two hunters brought a twenty-foot sapling trunk, with something suspended in the center. Mark rode up to it, and pulled it off the branch. He opened it up to see what it could be, and nodded.

"Thank you, Stanley. The ghost was right. I know exactly what you're talking about. It also fits with what Sammie, who you know as the dark lady, told me."

Mark rode to the carriage, where Josh was getting out to see what was going on. "Look at what was heading our way, Josh. I haven't seen one of these since we left Afghanistan. Who would wear a Kandahar cap?"

Josh looked at it and breathed, "Terrorists. How many were there? How many escaped?"

"They say none of them. Stanley, their leader, is more concerned about their blood contaminating spears and knives. He is irritated about their carcasses polluting wildlife. The terrorists won't leave us alone."

"Maybe we should have marched against these jokers anyway," Josh replied, looking at the cap through narrowed eyes. "We'll need to tell Lyle when we get back. Do we need to send somebody right away?"

"I don't know. This size of group would more likely be doing damage assessment. The herders can take word back."

Mark wanted to say more, but with Alex and Cordelia there, squelched the urge. Soon, everyone got moving again, and Mark let Don know about the situation. Keeping his voice down, Mark told Don what he'd figured out about the hunters. The big question was whether Stanley and his hunters could be trusted.

Don had an observation. "During World War II, the United States, Great Britain, and France were looking for allies against the Germans, Italians, and Japanese. Russia wasn't just Russia in those days. It was the USSR, and run by a dictator as ruthless as Hitler. Hitler and Stalin may have been too much alike, since they ended up at war with each other. The United States thought anybody against Hitler was a friend of ours, so we became allies of convenience."

Mark recalled that history. "The moment the Germans and Japanese were out of the equation, the USSR became, not only our enemy, but one sworn to bury us."

"You've got it, Mark."

Mark thought about it. "Our buddy Stanley may support our cause, thinking of us being his seed corn, which he would rather see planted than cooked."

Don nodded. "That's how I see it."

"Stanley already took out more terrorists than everything we've done. Maybe we can accept his aid and his pork. I wonder how Sammie and the Marines figure into this?"

"Do you mean like if they're part of Stanley's little tribe?"

"That is part of it. Nothing I find out amounts to anything."

The conversation was never idle chatter, but Don gave Mark a very serious look. "Lyle will want to know what you think needs to be done. What you tell him will be a large part of what he decides to do."

"I'd rather just chase horses."

"Instead, you've got this heavy load. That's not to mention whatever you and Ellen finally decide."

"You already figured that out, Don."

"I thought I figured it out. Now, I'm not so sure. Well, we're coming into Arapahoe, and our McCook friends have selected a campsite. I'd better find a spot for the cook fire. All the food is right behind me."

Mark saw snipers waving at them. "It looks like they found a spot."

Seeing a line of clouds toward McCook, Mark rode to the carriage. Since the weather had been clear the last couple of weeks, that seemed strange. He pointed it out to Alex.

"That is our strange weather," Alex said. "It's been like this ever since the big rain. That weather is farther than it seems. Mid-afternoon every day, clouds and heavy rain roll through. It lasts until after dark."

"That's peculiar, all right. We haven't had anything strange about our weather."

Alex nodded. "We noticed that. The storms stop ten or fifteen miles west. Beyond, it's dry and the game all moved. That's why Stanley's tribe hunts this direction."

"Stanley mentioned Arapahoe was their limit."

"Sammie Moore told Stanley that was as far as he could go. From here on belongs to Harlan. All the pigs behind us are yours."

"On the weather, it is like you're under a curtain dividing a dry area west of you from the wetter area that we're in. Harlan got lucky several times, then."

Alex agreed. "The Republican River is dry west of us. The river starts at McCook, now."

"That makes me wonder about the Platte River then. It's sure flowing at Kearney."

Alex shrugged and shook his head.

Mark saw Sammie riding into a residential area. "What's up with that?"

"She's not one to be around people. She'll stay in one of the houses, I suppose."

"I'm surprised her military escort isn't with her."

"There's her and then there's them. The Peepul are another thing. A number of them were on drugs. We don't trust them. Sammie and her group make them go around our farms when they go between the castle and the river."

"Where is this castle?"

"It's at the top of the ridge north of McCook. Our farm is near it. The castle was high enough to escape the dust. We're thankful for that."

The next morning, breakfast was nearly done when Mark focused on the absence of the dark lady. Her merry little team of snipers were quietly talking and looking around, mostly in the direction she rode the previous evening. Finally, Mark saw her coming, barely hanging on as she rode.

Ellen checked her out. "Now there's an emotional train wreck."

Mark thought he should check it out, and got there the same time as Sammie.

"Would you guys mind a foreigner?" Mark inquired. No objections were raised, and Mark joined the circle.

Sammie looked around. "What do you think about Alex Thomas running the show? It seems like everything I've done or tried lately has been a disaster."

"Maybe I should go," Mark commented, and started to get up.

"No, that's okay," Sammie replied. "I'm not saying anything you don't already know."

Tom cleared his throat. "What happens when Mr. Thomas talks to Stanley?"

"There's no way to stop him. Josh knows, and Alicia probably does. After that, there's no way Alex won't know."

"True enough," Tom admitted.

"Alex can work with the Harlan County people. After all, Alicia is now married to one of the main men, so it's a guaranteed connection."

Tom considered that. "What if Alex decides he doesn't want Stanley and his tribe around? What if he considers us part of them?"

Sammie shook her head. "I have no answer for that or anything else." Then she glanced up. "You could take it, Tom."

Tom looked astounded. "I don't do people. Our team sticks together because nobody else will have us. What we do, we do pretty well. We handle people our superiors tell us desperately need our specialty. They use us to threaten the rest. Somebody thought we needed to chase a bunch of strung-out cannibals. Maybe they did it for giggles and grins. If you think what you've done is a disaster, turning it over to me would be a million times worse."

The conversation lapsed. Sammie wasn't eating. Tom looked at the lieutenant. "Let's walk," he said. Tom then glanced at the team and raised his eyebrows. "You guys clean up the site."

Then he looked at Mark. "Why don't you come with us? I may need a witness."

Mark went, but kept some space.

Tom looked at Sammie. "Okay, Lieutenant, if you want me to run the show, I'll do what I can. If I do something dumb, let me know. You'll always have veto power. Also, I'll get advice from both Alex and Stanley. Should I have both of them together?"

"Keep them apart," Sammie murmured. Mark strained to hear. It was good she was on Tom's left side. Mark noticed Tom's hearing deficiencies in his firing, or right ear. To judge from Tom's reaction, he barely heard her as it was.

After a pause, Sammie continued, "I stayed between them so they'd never deal with each other directly. Now it's all falling apart, and it's my fault."

"This is not about fault, Lieutenant," Tom responded. "Nobody can control everything all the time. I don't know why anyone would even want to."

"You never met my mother," was her reply, indistinct but hard-edged.

Mark glanced at Tom whose expression reflected he already heard about her mother. That made Tom's choice of follow-up conversation interesting.

"What would your mother think if you took me to meet her?"

There was silence. Sammie stopped, looking up at him. "She always talked about how Dad was a good-looking man. You are gorgeous by any standard. She'd have liked that a lot. Not only that, there's something commanding and dangerous about you. She'd have wanted to conquer that."

He smiled slightly. "I'm not commanding and dangerous. I might be deadly, like a weapon for somebody else to turn to their own purposes. Those purposes may not be what I was made to do. You can use a pistol to pound in a nail."

Chapter 7
Castle & Jimmy

Tom glanced at Mark, who wanted nothing more than to stay out of this conversation. Mark raised his eyebrows in a 'let's hurry this up' sort of signal.

Tom nodded. "We'd better mount up, ma'am."

They made good progress. As they approached McCook, Don looked for a lunch stop that wasn't right on top of the small herd of cattle. Mark didn't need more than a nose to know they were close to the herd.

Sammie rode over to him. "Can we talk privately, please?"

Mark brought his horse to a stop. "Don is looking for a lunch spot. It shouldn't be very far, so stopping briefly will not be a problem."

Sammie took a breath. "Mark, you have Harlan County going every direction at once, like a circus ringmaster. Yet you don't seem stressed. I'm trying to figure out what I could have done differently. I just feel like such a loser."

Mark considered recent events and nearly choked. "If that's what you think, you have no idea what's going on, either in Harlan or my head. You think I'm some kind of leader. I'm not. Lyle Lillard is the leader. I speak for him as best I can when I have to. So far, what I've done has been wrong as often as not. In the Army, I saw officers in charge. I also served with some commanders. A leader is beyond them, although that's not to say a commander is slacking or anything."

"I see what you're saying, but there had better be more than that."

Mark rubbed his chin, something he'd noticed Lyle do when he was thinking. "Okay, I guess your military career field was technical. You might not have had anybody under you."

She nodded. "I usually had a couple of clerks, but nothing like a command."

"You went into a tightly knit group of enlisted troops. They weren't even in your service. You were the officer in charge. Everybody knew it. Nobody wanted it or liked it."

"Yeah, that's how it was, all right. Maybe that's how it still is. How is a commander so different?"

"I was never more than a low ranking enlisted soldier, so this is just an opinion. The officers in charge mostly focused on pleasing the boss, and most seemed more interested in moving on than on the mission itself. Someone I would call a commander performed required missions, but a commander would also be just as concerned about the people working for him."

Sammie was on the brink of outrage. "You don't think I'm concerned about the guys I've got with me?"

Mark saw it, but plowed ahead. "Think about it. The military the five of you work for no longer exists. Say you were in a factory. Your group puts lug nuts on the right rear wheel of each vehicle on the line. No more cars come down the assembly line. The assembly line stopped and the roof blew off the factory, but your team is still there."

"That's an ugly comparison."

"After El Paso, my commander, and I do consider him a commander, decided something. We just fought a major battle long after the country declared us dead. We'd fought our way out of Afghanistan and caught a ride with the Navy back to the States, only to find we'd been written off. We walked from Washington, D. C. to El Paso with no help from anyone, and fought what turned out to be al-Queda in Ciudad Juarez across from El Paso. Our commander decided it was enough, and personally wrote us our separation papers."

"When we watched you and Josh come up on the Peepul camp, the guys commented you knew what you were doing. The proof came when you and the deputy caught on to us and designed a plan. That deputy and his people swept us up like it was nothing."

Mark waved off the compliment like it was a fly, and returned to his story. "Our commander saw no point to more nonexistent missions. It would just get his men killed. With Lyle Lillard, I think you see a leader. He figures out what needs to be done, and proceeds. If people share his vision, then he'll have company."

"I think I see your point."

Mark managed to survive with her so far, and decided not to stop. It was time to let Sammie know how far short of the mark she came. "I don't think you get it, though. Those following a leader don't spend their time playing politics. One thing: they never leave the leader in the dark about significant developments."

Sammie looked like she saw a ghost. "Are you saying what I think you're saying?"

"When you guys showed up, Lyle wasn't fooled for a moment. After you went to the motel, he called me on it, and I ended up briefing Lyle on everything. You tried to play us against each other, and Lyle decided to let you think you succeeded. The whole idea was to figure out your agenda. Since we still don't know squat about your agenda, we didn't succeed either."

Sammie was aghast. "What tipped him off?"

"There were several things. Lyle said he enjoyed the show, and thought it was well-scripted. He thought everyone played their part. Your question confirms that you still don't get it. You manipulate people to do things. For Lyle, the only winning game is to find like-minded people to do whatever needs done."

"If you're trying to make me not feel like a loser, you also failed big time."

Mark nodded. "When you stepped down this morning, I thought that was the act of a commander. Tom may now be in command, but you may be on your way to becoming a leader. Take that opinion for what it's worth."

As Sammie rode off, Mark wondered about what he said. It was like somebody smart took over his mouth.

The wagons set up for lunch on the next hill, well within sight. After starting after the main group, Sammie suddenly held up and waited for Mark.

"It's a good sign," she commented. "The clouds haven't started to build yet. We may get home before the storms."

Mark took it as a positive sign that she wasn't still hung up on their conversation. Don took them into a park on the south side of the road, where a soft breeze kept most of the smell of beef on the hoof away from them.

Sammie rejoined her group, and Tom had Dave Askren, one of the snipers, go with the herd as pathfinder and to get the herd in the corrals by the castle. Dave grabbed some chow before he set off.

Mark and Ellen ate with Alex, Cordelia, Josh, and Alicia. Over lunch, Alex commented, "Alicia, do you remember that boy who was so taken with you before you left for Harlan?"

Alicia was astonished. "Jimmy Bower? It seems like such a long time ago. Is he alive?"

"Yes, but he got strange. Nobody could put up with him up on the ridge, so he's wandering around McCook. Since we're be going through town, I thought I'd let you know."

Alicia considered that. "He was strange before I left. Getting away from him was a big part of me going. I was kind of scared of him. If you see that creep, let me know."

The group rolled through McCook. Mark was used to the towns around Harlan, but this place made him uncomfortable. Before long, Mark saw a guy who had to be Jimmy. He looked like too many miles of bad road, and reminded Mark of the druggies with the Peepul. The sole resident of McCook silently watched them go by.

Sammie saw him, and slowed her horse to let the carriage catch up. Ellen picked up on Jimmy soon after that, and let Alicia know. Mark saw a glint in Alicia's eyes. When the carriage got almost even with Jimmy, Ellen nodded and Alicia stuck her head around at him. "Hi, Jimmy!" she said cheerily.

Jimmy's face lit up with hope and anticipation. "I'm so glad to see you!"

By then, the carriage was even with Jimmy, and he could easily see Mr. and Mrs. Thomas, as well as Josh. Grinning from ear to ear, Alicia continued, "You said I was crazy to go off with Doctor Dover, and you were right. I am crazy. I'm crazy in love with Josh. We just got married."

With that, she grabbed Josh and laid a deep, passionate kiss on him.

Jimmy's expression flipped over to anger, and his face got red. Mark realized this was exactly what Alicia wanted. Josh could pound Jimmy senseless, assuming he was content to leave it at mere fists.

Mark gritted his teeth and waited for Alicia's drama to play itself out. All at once, Sammie brought her horse between the carriage and Jimmy. She directed a steely glare right at Jimmy, along with her index finger.

Jimmy stared at her, like a mouse suddenly aware of a hawk. Sammie pointed two fingers at her eyes, followed by stabbing her index finger at him. At the same time, she silently mouthed, "I'm watching you."

The man's expression changed again, this time to pallor and fear. He seemed to totally deflate. A moment later, he faded into the shadows of an alley.

Ellen and Sammie exchanged glances, and after a moment, Ellen nodded thoughtfully. Maybe the women could make peace. Mark now hoped they could reach a mutual understanding.

Clouds gathered as they turned north, heading up the ridge. There were a couple of positive aspects to the situation. First, they were almost to their destination. Second, if the promised storm started before they arrived, the wind and rain would be at their back.

The farms were all green. Moisture was good. Continual rain was a problem. It would be nearly impossible to get hay sufficiently cured. Mark didn't know how they would be able to feed animals for the winter.

The carriage turned off at a small place with the Thomas name on the mailbox. Not much later, Mark saw the place they called the castle. It looked like a Hollywood set. Their first stop was a stable and arena across from it. The situation could have gotten sticky, since Stanley's tribe lived there. Stanley somehow already returned. He organized his people, working side-by-side with Mark.

Mark and Ellen, Don Rowley, and a few others, were invited into the main house. The rest had to decide whether to stay in the arena or to camp on the floor in the main house. Either way, everyone would be dry.

Some of Stanley's tribe worked as domestic servants. Mark wasn't sure whether he was more uncomfortable with the idea of servants at all or knowing who they were. Outside, the storm seemed like a miniature version of the great rain.

Everyone stared at the evidence of abundant electricity. Lyle Lillard having electricity was amazing, but the extent of it in this mansion was beyond belief, even setting Don Rowley back. The abundance of what was now a miracle that used to be considered a necessity was the main topic of conversation during the meal. Sammie delighted in playing the condescending royal to the visiting rabble. All the same, Mark realized she was just as much a squatter in the place as they were.

After dinner, Sammie found her guests places to sleep. It was a big house, but there weren't nearly as many bedrooms as the size of the place suggested. Mark and Ellen were the last guests standing. Finally, Sammie took Ellen and Mark upstairs and down a corridor.

"Mark, this room is yours. Ellen, I realize you two are engaged but not married. I'll give you a choice. You can sleep here or I can come up with something else."

"What would something else be?"

Sammie looked at Ellen, her lips pressed together. "We're short on space, so you would have to bunk with me."

Mark's wondering whether they declared a truce might be answered in a minute. Whatever Ellen chose, Sammie could turn it to her own advantage, manipulative as she was. Rooming together might be more than either woman would tolerate, even so.

Ellen shook her head. "I watched them build this place. I dreamed of staying here, but never like this. Sammie, I appreciate you looking after my virtue but I'll stay with Mark."

Sammie seemed relieved. She nodded, and took a few steps toward the opposite wing. Then she turned and with a half-smile said, "Have a pleasant evening. Breakfast will be in the dining room when you get up."

Mark had a fit of good sense and didn't comment. He walked into the room with Ellen.

"Did you see how Sammie automatically took her seat at the head of the table, like she was the lady of the manor?"

Mark couldn't figure out what she was going for. "It looked like that's where she always sat. She looked at Tom after realizing the screw-up. We're in a high-class place, so maybe it was a faux pas. Whatever it was, he seemed to say not to worry about it. I thought he played the lord of the manor rather well."

Ellen wouldn't let go of her aggravation. "The nerve of the woman, telling me I could sleep in her room."

Mark's good sense kicked in. He clenched his jaws in order to keep from saying anything and walked over to the window. "The rain is letting up. I can't imagine a place with rains you can set a clock by."

Maybe he said something right, since Ellen started exploring the room. "Ooh. We have a private bathroom." In a moment, Mark heard the unfamiliar sound of a faucet. "There's running water here. They've even got hot water. Can you imagine that?"

"The last running water, other than at the Lillard place, was on the aircraft carrier coming back to the States. We had to stand in line for that. For a private room, electricity, and a bathroom with both hot and cold water, my memory and imagination fail me."

After a moment, Ellen called again, "I'm going to take a long bath." She looked from behind the bathroom door, showing enough for Mark to see she had nothing on. "It's a big tub. Would you care to join me?"

Sitting in opposite ends of the tub, Ellen grinned at Mark. "You know Sammie expects us to indulge in a great deal of hanky-panky. It's great, achieving my own desires and living down to others' expectations all at the same time."

Mark felt her foot slide into his groin. Ellen smiled. "We agree on that. However, we need to try again for the bath. Somebody turned this bath water all icky and brown. I'm all for getting all down and dirty, but I want to start out clean."

Later, he was exhausted from the day's ride but even more so from the night ride. The two lay side by side.

"Ellen?" Mark asked, "Do you still want to marry me?"

Ellen turned over and laid a finger on the tip of his nose. "Of course I do. What makes you ask such a silly question?"

"Oh, I don't know. I only hoped you weren't disappointed with my shortcomings."

"You have shortcomings? I don't know of any." Mark felt her hand go exploring. "Oh, that? It wasn't so short a little bit ago. I'll bet that with the help of the right woman, it wouldn't be a shortcoming."

"The right woman," Mark mused. "Maybe I should look around. You never know. There just might be someone."

Her hand suddenly grabbed and held with an iron grip. "Oh, you've done it now, Mr. Tahner. Maybe I'll just pull that sucker out by the roots and keep you from temptation. When you proposed to me, it became all mine."

She suddenly straddled Mark, who lay there weakly grinning. Before long before her prediction came true. It was no longer a shortcoming. Mark considered it was nearly a miracle. Of course, if this was nearly a miracle, keeping Ellen satisfied might take more than a miracle. Mark decided to devote his life to the attempt.

Later, they both lay together, spoon fashion, facing the window. They watched the moon through the breaking clouds. Falling asleep, Mark considered what a long, strange day it had been. He couldn't complain how it ended. He needed to figure out what was going on with Sammie, Tom, and that bunch. He also needed to figure out Stanley Peepul and his tribe. Right now, he was satisfied to be next to the woman he loved.

Mark and Ellen woke up together. It was later than usual, with half the solar disk already above the horizon. Ellen decided another bath was a necessity. With two baths last night, this was their third bath in two days. He tried to recall the last time he'd taken so many baths but drew a blank. Baths with such great company was beyond comprehension.

Downstairs, Mark didn't know if they were early or late, as nobody else was there. A girl came out to see what they wanted. She was quiet, shy and uncertain. Both Mark and Ellen went for the bacon, eggs, and biscuits.

Ellen looked at the perilously skinny girl. "What is your name?"

"Vickie, ma'am."

"Well, Vickie, did everybody else have breakfast already?"

"An older man was here at first light. They said his name was Rowley. The dark lady and four ghosts will come later."

Vickie became more agitated as she stood there, seeming glad to run into the kitchen. A few minutes later, when she brought their meals, she seemed calm, but being near them unsettled her.

Whatever Vickie's personal quirks might be, the breakfast tasted like a professional chef did it. That went with the atmosphere of the place. Beyond that, the Peepul had bacon curing down really well. Granted, it was only recently that he'd had any. Not having any for a long time might contribute to the taste.

Their hosts showed up as Mark and Ellen were finishing. Tom and Sammie stopped and looked at each other. Finally, Sammie gave Tom body language aiming him for the head of the table. After a moment, he gave in. Vickie took their orders. Then she filled all the coffee, including Mark's and Ellen's. Vickie seemed calm around Sammie and the Marines, but kept her time near Mark and Ellen to a minimum.

Mark nursed his coffee and watched them. An opportunity to see his hosts in their natural setting would be good. Tom and Sammie were not in a hurry, so Vickie was out several times. Every time she was calm until she got near Ellen and him. Then she got agitated. Mark was ready to leave, when a woman ran out of the kitchen, going to the head of the table.

"Ma'am, sir, Vickie got all peculiar this morning. Just a minute ago, she started muttering, 'Stanley says I should think for myself. I think I want to be satisfied and happy. What will make me satisfied and happy? I know what will make me satisfied and happy. Jimmy Bower will make me satisfied and happy.' Then she grabbed her switchblade, jammed it in the pocket of her dress, and ran out the door."

Sammie and Tom looked at each other. Mark saw a note of panic. "Thank you, Dora. We'll take care of it," Sammie said to the woman.

Tom looked at his team. "Come on, guys. We need to save a life."

Mark asked, "Jimmy was the guy in town, right? We'll saddle up, too. You say the Peepul have changed their ways. We'll see how it has gone."

Mark and Ellen were leading their horses out of the building when Stanley came out to check on the excitement. Mark relayed what Dora said, and Stanley thought for a moment. Then he looked at them and wrinkled his nose. "Did Vickie seem nervous when she got close to you two?"

That was a strange question. "Well, yes, she did. Why?"

"Both of you are throwing off clouds of pheromones. During the big rain, Jimmy Bower tried to get in her pants. She would have cut him into stew meat, but we saved him. I believe she's going to give Jimmy what he tried to take, but I'd better go in case I'm wrong." Stanley stood pensively for a moment. "Maybe I should be there in case I'm right, too," he added.

Mark shook his head. "You're awfully well spoken, Stanley. I saw a guy like you in Harlan on the minimum maintenance road. He didn't act like you, though."

Stanley looked at Mark thoughtfully. "You and another guy checked us out from the little bluff overlooking the road. I saw you, but Willy had his plan and ran things, so I kept quiet. Everybody thought I was a dummy or retard until the dark lady came and told me I had to take care of the tribe. That meant I had responsibility and a mind. She helped me remember how to use my mind. We need to go. I will give you this call three times when I find them," and Stanley gave an accurate mourning dove call.

Stanley headed toward a ravine on foot while Mark and Ellen headed down the road at a lope. Mark and Ellen looked at each other. "We're generating a cloud of pheromones?" Mark asked.

Ellen laughed. "Stanley can smell Omega dust. Why wouldn't he pick up on pheromones? They say everybody does. They just don't know what motivates them."

"So that's been my problem all this time."

"Believe me, that's the least of your problems."

"You are the best solution I've ever found."

"Mark, that's a mistake. I'm not your best solution. It's far more likely that I'm your biggest problem."

"Not from where I'm sitting. Thinking about Stanley, I've never heard of such a radical transformation in a human being. The way he talked, you'd suppose Sammie was a miracle worker."

"Don't press your luck, Mark. I felt pretty mellow until you had to bring up nasty subjects."

At the Thomas place, the carriage was disappearing down the ridge. Alicia and Josh were just mounting.

"We were going to see this castle everyone talks about when a herd of bikes raced downhill. Now here you are. What's up?" Josh wanted to know.

"You remember Jimmy? One of the Peepul women is going to find him. The jury is still out whether she intends to cut him or breed him."

Alicia laughed. "She'll eat him, one way or another. Either way, I just have to see this."

The carriage driver wasn't in a hurry, and the four caught up to it in a hurry. As they passed, Mark asked the driver. "Do you know if Don Rowley is in town?"

"That's my information," the man replied with a yawn.

Mark grinned briefly and touched the brim of his hat as they rode on.

"We're trying to keep a cannibal from cutting a low life. Now you're finding out whether Don's in the area. I don't get the connection," Josh commented.

"I had an idea," Mark replied.

Josh shook his head. "Mark Tahner and an idea are in the same place. Now we need to be terrified, folks."

They just reached the edge of town when Mark heard the three mourning dove calls. "That was Stanley's signal. How the hell did he get here so fast?"

The calls repeated, and they headed for them. Soon, they saw the bikes, and nearby their riders next to a wall. Tom strode up to them.

"Tie your horses back here," he instructed. "Dora was right. Vickie was hunting for Jimmy. She trapped him in this store. We can watch at both the front and the back."

Mark and Ellen headed to the front, where Tom and Sammie crouched under the window, along with Stanley. The remaining snipers went in back with Josh and Alicia. The store facing east, the morning sun lit the two inside like a spotlight. Vickie had Jerry in a corner of the store. Her knife was open, and she switched the blade from hand to hand, like the knife fighter she was. Jimmy, terrified, kept looking for a way out. She slowly approached, savoring the moment.

Mark whispered to Stanley, "Shouldn't we do something?"

Stanley shook his head. "If she was going to take him, she would have done it before now. The meat tastes rank with all that adrenalin. She's just playing with him."

Vickie was now up to Jimmy, her left forearm on his chest and her knife at his throat.

She stared in his eyes and chanted, "I am Peepul. Are you animal?"

Mark remembered that chant, except it was "I am Peepul. You are animal." Vickie made it a question, like Jimmy might prove he was not an animal.

Jimmy stammered, "You know who I am. I'm Jimmy Bower. I was nice to you. Remember?"

The only sound was Jimmy's sweat dripping on the floor. Maybe Mark just imagined the sound. Jimmy caught sight of them watching, and there was pleading in his eyes.

Vickie said, "I remember when you talked to me. You said nice words, but showed me you were an animal. I should cut you, but I just ate. Tell me, Jimmy Bower, what can you do to make me satisfied and happy?"

Mark had no idea what that was about. He glanced at Ellen for a hint. She appeared fascinated with how the whole thing was going and acted like Mark didn't exist.

Jimmy stuttered, "What would make you satisfied and happy?"

Vickie replied, "My mother always told me being good would make me satisfied and happy. Being good only made me lonely. Willy Jameson told me drugs would make me happy and satisfied. He didn't say the drugs would kill me. Willy told me I had to find money to give him after the drugs took over my life. I begged, borrowed, and stole what I could. Then money no longer existed, and there were no more drugs."

There was silence for a moment. Vickie scraped some whiskers from Jimmy's throat and continued. "Willy quit talking about being happy and satisfied. I had to cut people into little chunks to stay alive. Willy went away, and now there is food and a dry place to sleep. Stanley doesn't say a word about being satisfied and happy. He says I need to decide things. I've decided I want to be satisfied and happy."

Stanley whispered, "That's the longest speech I ever heard from her. Maybe this is a good thing."

Vickie slowly released her hold on Jimmy, and backed up a step even while slowly waving her switchblade in front of his face. She reached up with her free hand and unbuttoned the front of her dress. Then she let her dress drop. She had nothing on underneath. Jimmy gasped even while he stared.

Vickie continued, "Everyone says men and women can make each other satisfied and happy. Do you like what you see? Can you make me satisfied and happy, Jimmy Bower?"

She took half a step forward and unfastened his pants. Vickie pulled down his pants and underwear with one hand. Then she cocked her head to one side, critically considering what she had uncovered.

"Yes, you might be able to take care of my needs," Vickie murmured. "Remember, though, you have to keep me satisfied and happy. You also have to earn my trust, but it won't be right now. Lie on your back, Jimmy Bower."

Mark heard fidgeting during that. Whatever Jimmy thought about having sex in front of an audience, he obviously valued his life more.

Vickie dropped down on him with no foreplay. It might have been that the hunt scenario with confrontation was her idea of foreplay. Ellen grabbed Mark's hand. Pornography had come to their brave new world.

Having to crouch below the front window of the store made Mark's legs cramp. He turned around and sat on the sidewalk. Ellen turned and got Mark's attention. She nodded toward Sammie and Tom, who were both transfixed by the scene inside, and tight against each other, side by side. Ellen raised her eyebrows like that was significant. Mark decided there was no way to know what those two would do until it happened.

Looking at Stanley, Mark quietly asked, "Do you think she might let him impregnate her and then kill him?"

"A couple of women in the tribe might do that. I don't think Vickie is one of them. On the other hand, she surprised me today, so who knows? We need to make sure she doesn't do something like that."

Chapter 8
Jimmy & Vickie

Mark listened to the heavy breathing from the couple inside. There was heavy breathing from Sammie and Tom, too, though they were still clothed. Mark thought that was good, but he was hardly in a position to be prudish.

Ellen leaned over and whispered, "Would you like to be the couple inside?"

Mark, surprised, shook his head. "It would not be my preference, but a knife to my jugular could change my mind. Why? If that's something you want to do, I'll be more careful when you have a knife."

"That isn't anything I want to do. I was just curious."

The sounds inside stopped. Mark turned and saw Vickie was now beside Jimmy, her head propped up, looking at him.

"Jimmy Bower, you made me happy and satisfied. How long will you keep me satisfied and happy, Jimmy Bower?"

Vickie used Jimmy's full name each time, as though she was making up a new chant. At the same time, Jimmy's breath got ragged, like he had difficulty getting up the courage to answer the question.

"How long do I need to keep you satisfied and happy, Vickie?"

"The rest of my life," Vickie replied. "You need to keep me satisfied and happy for the rest of my life."

Mark saw another reason for Jimmy's ragged breathing. Vickie stroked Jimmy's chest with the side of her switchblade. Jimmy licked his lips, looking alternately at the knife and at Vickie.

"I can do that," Jimmy finally croaked. "Yeah, I can do that."

There was a sudden screech of iron wheels on bricks, with the heavy clop of draft horses coming around the corner. It shattered the moment between Vickie and Jimmy. Mark turned and saw Don Rowley.

"Hey, Mark," Don called. "My carriage driver said you asked about me. I figured you found something from the list I gave you."

Mark heard scuffling inside the store. Sammie and Tom turned around as well, so he stood up, dusting off the seat of his pants. "Good to see you, Don. We came to witness a prenuptial agreement."

"A what?" That protest came from Jimmy inside. "What the hell are you talking about?"

Sammie and Tom looked at Mark. Sammie turned red as she tried to keep from bursting into laughter. She got it under control and said, "A prenuptial agreement. Yes, that's what it sounded like to me."

Mark nodded. "Don, is your carriage still around?"

"Yeah, we didn't know what you guys were up to, and stuck around in case somebody needed a ride."

"That might be the case. What would you think about runs between here and Harlan if there was someplace at Arapahoe to stop? It would have a place for the driver and passengers to sleep, with facilities for horses and wagons."

"That would be good. Yes, I could handle that. Do you think we can do some trade?"

Mark nodded. "I think Lyle would buy anything benefiting both sides. There's already pork for beef."

Don nodded, gratified to be part of the scheme. Then he came to a stop. "Who would want to live at Arapahoe?"

"I have a couple in mind." Mark turned to Sammie and Tom. "You guys want trade. Would this be a start?"

"It does. Do we know the couple you are talking about?"

"Yes, you do." Mark looked at Stanley. "As leader of your tribe, you could conduct a wedding, especially if one of them was a member of your tribe. Isn't that correct?"

Stanley kept a straight face. "That would be the case, yes."

Mark rubbed his hands together. "That is splendid. We don't want to keep the eager couple waiting." Mark did an elaborate bow, bringing Stanley through the door. Stanley walked slowly to Jimmy and Vickie, now dressed and standing side by side, staring at the crowd.

Stanley went to Vickie. "We heard Jimmy pledge to keep you satisfied and happy for the rest of your life. It isn't a deal unless both sides get something. What do you pledge to Jimmy? He must get something from you to do this willingly."

Vickie stared at Stanley. "You said I should decide things for myself. I decided this was what I wanted to do. Now you tell me I can't have it."

"The only way Jimmy will keep you satisfied and happy is if you keep him satisfied and happy as well."

Vickie thought about it and turned to Jimmy. "Jimmy Bower, what can I do to keep you satisfied and happy?"

Alicia, Josh, and the three marines were inside, which completed the circle around the couple. Jimmy started to think he could get out of this without getting into even more trouble. With that last question from Vickie, he knew he was toast. He saw Alicia with an evil grin on her face, Jimmy quickly looked away.

"What we just did seemed good to me," he said finally. "I'd like it better without the knife."

"There you have it," Stanley proclaimed. "We heard them both pledge they will keep each other satisfied and happy. Also, they consummated their marriage before these witnesses. As leader of the Peepul, I declare you two are in fact man and wife. Jimmy Bower, you are an honorary member of the Peepul tribe. Vickie, we have to know what to call you. Will you take your husband's last name?"

Vickie paused for a moment to think about it. "Vickie Bower. Vickie Bower. Yes, I like that."

Mark told them. "I want to congratulate both of you, and for your honeymoon, I personally recommend the Arapahoe Inn. We don't know the location yet, but the managers are wonderful. You will be the first ones there."

Mark escorted them out the door. "Don, these are your passengers. They're going to start the Arapahoe Inn."

Don turned, waved his hat, and almost immediately, the carriage rolled up. Don looked at Mark and Ellen. He shook his head.

"You aren't the second couple married, so I lost my bet. Who'd have thought these two would be it?"

Sammie and Tom came outside, and Mark saw something chewing on Sammie. She looked at the carriage and shielded her eyes from the sun as she gazed toward Arapahoe.

"Mr. Rowley?" Sammie called up to Don. "Would you be able to load supplies for them?"

"Yes, ma'am, but it will be tomorrow before I could get it to them."

Sammie nodded. "They'll be there without a thing. That sucks."

Mark thought that odd language for the dark lady. She hesitated, and then whispered something to Tom. Tom's eyes got big, and he leaned back, staring at her.

Mark read his lips as he said, "Really?"

Sammie nodded her head emphatically.

"Okay," Tom mouthed. Sammie smiled and gave Tom a light kiss.

Sammie turned to everyone. "That's no way for newlyweds to spend their wedding night. I just figured how to give them a room at the castle tonight. Then you newlyweds and Mr. Rowley can head for Arapahoe, and do it right."

Ellen poked Mark in the ribs. Mark looked at her, remembering the housing crisis of the previous evening, and wondering what was going on. The only way Sammie could have an extra room was if she bunked with Tom. Ellen looked smug.

"I told you, Mark. Didn't I tell you?"

Mark nodded. Yeah, she told him. He still thought it could have gone either way.

Vickie stared at Sammie in disbelief. "Ma'am? You're saying I can stay in a guest room?"

"Yes, Vickie, that's what I said. Let's head up to the castle for lunch. The dining room table is wide enough to put the happy couple at the head of the table."

Sammie looked at Jimmy, now. "We're giving you another chance. Maybe you've turned over a new leaf."

One of the marines brought Sammie's bike, but something in the back axle screeched, caught, and finally let go altogether. Sammie glared at Mark. "Did you put a whammy on my bike?"

"It wasn't me. Be glad it didn't happen in the middle of nowhere."

Sammie nodded sadly. "Mr. Rowley, could I ride back to the castle with you?"

After a sniper manhandled the bike over the side, Sammie looked at them. "You guys boogie up to the castle as fast as you can, and have Dora start a nice luncheon."

The four marines headed out at full speed while the rest retrieved their horses. Don started the wagon rolling, letting the carriage go in front. Once the mounted contingent caught up, Mark slowed down wondering if Sammie would talk about Jimmy. Obviously, there was a great deal of history there. Ellen stuck around too, but Mark didn't know if it was to hear the story or to protect him. When Alicia heard Sammie start talking about Jimmy, she also slowed down.

Sammie organized her thoughts. Then, "We got the Peepul hunting feral pigs, and came into McCook. Stanley suddenly said he smelled more dust people. We took a look, but only saw ordinary people. Stanley pointed to an older guy. The others smelled like dead things, he said, but this guy smelled like death itself."

"You watched us leave town?" Alicia blurted.

Sammie nodded. "Exploring the town, this twerp came around a corner. It was hard to say who was most surprised. He looked us all over and finally stated we weren't with the professor, looking at Tom like that's who he needed to talk to. Tom didn't argue the point, and asked about the cross-country runners."

Ellen giggled. "We couldn't move fast enough for Doctor Dover, but he was the slowest one."

Sammie considered that. "The guy went on about how his girlfriend was with them, and he couldn't talk her out of going. He came into town hoping she'd get some sense and go back home."

Alicia cracked up. "That was Jimmy."

"Tom acted like Stanley hadn't said anything, and asked why there was such a rush. We heard a name as they were going by, someone called Dr. Dover. The twerp said that was the professor's name. He flew into town a while before and took a group into the hills north of town. He preached about dust that killed everybody it touched."

"Well," Mark observed, "that part agrees with Dover's story."

"Jimmy said they moved into the castle, and carried on how this dust was killing everyone on Earth. He also said the hills were among the few safe places. A cloud of dust went through, and after it cleared away, there was nobody in town."

"How did Dover come by this knowledge?" Mark wondered.

'The twerp said Dover worked for the government. After that wave of dust, he got a bunch of true believers, including his girlfriend, Alicia. Jimmy tried to tell her the so-called doctor was up to no good, but she went when he and his bunch announced another and final cloud of dust was coming, and according to their figures, this area wouldn't be safe."

Josh nodded. "That's what he said when he hit Harlan."

"It was only later we heard his name was Jimmy Bower. He suggested we could hang out at the castle since the professor moved out. He rattled on a while, but the important thing was that it was on the highest hill in the area."

"That sounded innocent enough," came from Ellen. "At least he gave you decent information."

Sammie nodded. "He wasn't anyone I wanted to know. Still, he gave us an idea about a place we could stay. Staying too close to the Peepul was a creepy thought, no matter how cooperative and helpful Stanley was being."

Mark thought it was interesting that Sammie defended being near them.

Sammie glanced in Mark's direction. "After we moved to the castle, Jimmy brought several local farmers who talked about a pig problem, and elaborated on what Jimmy said. The pigs rooted up what fields the farmers planted. The pigs also killed young livestock and rooted in front yards. Stanley had several people armed with spears, and could point to successful hunts."

"That's how you got into pork production," Don commented. "It is a welcome addition to our diet."

Sammie gave him a half-smile. "Stanley volunteered his people to take all the hogs they could find. The subject of trading for the meat came up, and the farmers agreed to barter the meat for other food and goods, and Stanley agreed."

Mark glanced at the carriage while Sammie caught her breath. He didn't hear anything.

Sammie continued her story. "To demonstrate he was serious and maybe to get some good will, Stanley immediately took hunters to chase hogs. After they left, one farmer observed he wouldn't have dealt with the Peepul. However, with Sammie and Tom vouching for them, he would give them a try. There were concerns about the Peepul hunting so close to their farms."

"The dust must have been close," Josh commented.

"Stanley warned us. He came back from a hunt, and told us he sensed the dust, and he knew it would be really bad. So, the afternoon of July 20, we invited everyone to the castle."

At that point, Sammie dropped into a trance, reliving the day:

"Do you guys run this bunch?" an older guy asked Tom and Sammie.

Sammie chuckled. "We were originally only observers. The tribe wasn't supposed to know we were around. Now, we're chaperones and sometimes mentors. Stanley, the big guy, leads them. Is there a problem, sir?"

"Jimmy Bower struts around like he's in charge. That isn't the case. Nobody contradicts him. He has a short fuse, and can get violent."

"We didn't get the benefit of that yet. Thanks for letting us know, Mister ...?"

"Thomas. Alex Thomas. He can be mister personality. He dated my daughter, Alicia. At first everything was great. Then his temper came out and she tried to get away from him. He decided she was his property. That was the real reason she went with Dr. Dover. We'd have gone too, but with my trick knee and back, well, hell, we couldn't keep up."

"He mentioned the name, Alicia, and said he hoped Alicia would turn around. He talked about how he tried to talk some sense into her."

"Is that what he called it? That explains her black eye and bruises. I hope they're right about there being a safe place. I think he said it was in Harlan County."

"We watched the last batch of dust go by. All of a sudden, there were no people other than us. Nasty stuff that dust."

"You saw it kill people?"

"All you can say is that it was fast. Does Jimmy Bower think this dust isn't real?"

"Who knows what he thinks? He talks out of both sides of his mouth. Speaking of the devil, he's on his way now."

Sammie switched to commentary. "As he came up, I got a glimmer of what Alex Thomas talked about, watching his facial expression and body language go from friendly to hostile and back, like he wanted to be both at the same time but didn't know how to do it. He finally ignored Alex in order to work on Tom and me."

Then she was back in character, now sounding like Jimmy. "Old man Thomas is bending your ear, I see. He's no doubt telling lies about me."

Tom smiled slightly. "He just told us you've got the best place around here. That makes you the most humble man I ever met."

Jimmy reddened and changed his approach. "What's this about killer dust coming?"

"In McCook, the only people were coming or going. What happened to the locals?"

"You're talking foolishness like the professor. Are you some of his believers?"

"We never met the man. We got close and personal with the dust and barely escaped. Since you don't think it's dangerous or else don't believe it has anything to do with you, why are you here?"

"I came to see if I could talk some sense into people."

"Like you talked sense into Alicia?" Alex growled.

Tom stepped between them. Turning to Jimmy, Tom smiled but it wasn't a friendly smile. "Mr. Bower, we let everyone know, and some chose not to come. That was their decision. Maybe nothing will happen. If Dr. Dover is right, what's coming might hit us here, in which case we're dead anyway. We see this as our best bet to survive. If you want to go home, good luck and God bless."

Sammie recalled her reaction. "I watched Tom in some awe. It wasn't what he said so much as the warrior aura he radiated. I had a sudden vision of him wearing a bearskin, with a massive two-handed sword. Jimmy felt it too. Jimmy could have physically handled the older man, but with Tom confronting him, Jimmy seemed to wilt. I saw something else. Jimmy wanted to hang around the castle in case it was safer, while laughing at everyone if the dust didn't come or wasn't dangerous."

Sammie blinked. "Jimmy turned away. After a couple of steps he stopped and turned his head. 'What happened to Alicia was an accident. She tripped and hit her head. You're a stupid old man.' He angrily scuffed the ground as he went, kicking some small pebbles. Alex was infuriated, but Tom held him back. I saw Jimmy abuse a fence post unfortunate enough to be near him."

Sammie's reliving of the event seemed to freeze.

Mark laughed. "Maybe Jimmy and Vickie will be a good pair. He's scared spitless around her and that knife. On the other hand, he can get nasty about everything else."

Don Rowley snorted, almost sounding like one of his horses. "You gave him an appropriate life sentence. He won't dare make Vickie mad at him. Making him run a hospitality operation was marvelous. He'll have to play nicely when he has guests. That idea was inspirational."

Mark shook his head. "Like Josh told me earlier, an idea and my head are a dangerous combination. The outcome is yet to be determined."

Mark turned to Sammie. "I got in the way of your story. You watched Jimmy head downhill while the dust was coming up to take care of his problem. That should have ended the story."

Sammie gathered her thoughts. After a moment, she summarized the next several weeks. The dust level came almost to the property line, but then retreated, day by day. A rain to end all rains came in before the dust withdrew very far. Stanley gave them warning about that, as well. The rain pushed everyone into the main house for shelter.

Then she fell back into the memory again, reenacting the various characters:

The first voice was Sammie, addressing the snipers. "We have to cut back on electricity. This rain has gone on for a week now. With the thick clouds and no wind, the solar panels and wind turbines can't recharge the batteries. We have to keep the refrigerators going, and we need to use the stoves, but the lights have to go off, unless you guys have a plan in hand."

Tom was increasingly depressed, along with the rest of the team. "Sounds like you've got the situation well in hand, ma'am," was all he said.

"I could get more response out of Stanley's tribe," Sammie snapped. "Hey, sorry guys. I don't need the 'ma'am' stuff, but we have shut down anything that doesn't have to be on. Okay?"

The team got moving, and turned off lights in the room. Sammie tried to lighten the mood, at least with Tom. "It's a good thing we charged everything. How's your satellite phone?"

"It's fully charged dead weight, like yours," Tom replied indifferently. "Are you expecting a call?"

Sammie ignored it and went to the back of the house while the rest went around to the farm families with the glad news. Stanley was in the study area.

"Stanley, we have to turn off all electrical devices except refrigerators. I hope you are at a stopping point in your studies."

"I am where absorbing and comprehending what I already studied is as valuable as reading more of it." Stanley immediately shut down the computer and turned off the lights. He looked at her. "Did you tell the Peepul?"

"No," she told him, "I thought it would be better coming from you."

Sammie blinked like she was putting her mental video recorder in fast forward. Then she frowned and blinked again.

"The area occupied by the Peepul centered on the kitchen. Stanley got them turning off lights and appliances. Others went everyplace they could check including out-buildings. Fortunately, there were enclosed passages from the main house. While they waited for the tribe's return, I asked, 'Will this rain last much longer? Could we go out in it now?'"

Sammie's commentary cut in. "I had visions of antennae coming out of Stanley's forehead, searching the cosmos. Finally, Stanley replied, 'There's less rain to come than has already been. I don't feel there's any dust in it or around here. The only real problem in going outside will be all that water.'"

She framed her thoughts a moment:

"Just then was a commotion as several Peepul carried in a body. They found him in a tool shed. It seemed incredible that they brought him in and didn't cut him up for stew meat. Stanley and I saw it was Jimmy Bower. He had a pulse. We let the farmers deal with him. I thought they'd be more charitable to him than he'd have been to them."

Mark saw Sammie fidget while she considered the story. "Three days after they found Jimmy, it was still raining, and everyone was three days more miserable. Jimmy was the worse for wear but as obnoxious as ever. I dropped by now and then. The farmers' wives cared for him because they cared for critters. They saw little difference between a runt pig, an orphan calf, or a runner-up in the 'look like a drowned rat' contest."

Sammie fell out of character. She said a few words and went back to approach it another way.

Mark reconstructed it as, "Jimmy didn't drown, but he was still a rat, and as full of himself as ever. I stayed away from him because of the creepy way he looked at me. There weren't many women anywhere near my age. Nobody wanted to be anywhere near the women with the Peepul. After a while, I asked Tom to stick close whenever I had to be around Mr. Bower."

Suddenly, Sammie was back into the story, relating how the drowned rat reverted to a form Alicia knew too well:

Jimmy focused on Tom. "She's with you most of the time," he sneered. "Is she your secretary? Does she get the lead out of your drawers?"

Tom bent his head down to get eye contact. Tom was nearly a foot taller than Jimmy, and Sammie got the impression of a school principle counseling a wise ass twelve-year-old. Sammie thought it appropriate, since that's how Jimmy acted.

"Mr. Bower, she is not my secretary. We only have one secretary in the military. That is the Secretary of Defense. I do not believe you were introduced. This is Lieutenant Moore. I am the senior noncommissioned officer of our team, and Lieutenant Moore is the commander. We are not in uniform, so you may refer to her as Ms. Moore."

"She's not in command of me," Jimmy sputtered.

"You should keep a civil tongue, Mr. Bower. The country has been under martial law for several months. We are in charge of this area. This is now a military facility. We invited you to stay here before the dust came. Your displeasure with our invitation was very clear. Right now, you are trespassing on a military facility. "

Jimmy now realized how bad his position was. He could fight if the opponent was weaker or run away any other time. Neither would work right now.

Tom saw his reaction, and let it soak in. "We had no requirement to give you an option, but we let you decide whether to stay or go. You stomped off in a cloud of righteous indignation, but didn't even leave the property. Lacking the strength of your own convictions, you hid like a rat in that tool shed. Lieutenant Moore can throw you out or subject you to any amount of military discipline. Do you understand, Mr. Bower?"

Sammie had to keep her expression noncommittal. Tom put her in the position of both chief executive and judge, so she needed to keep an appearance of even-handedness. Considering herself as representing governmental authority was novel. She thought the way Tom addressed Jimmy was a nice touch.

Sammie spoke evenly. "Mr. Bower, we won't go into why you acted as you did. Consider that a gift, since your motivations were not noble. We will require you to follow the rules and regulations. You've recovered, so your ration is the same as everyone else. There will be no lights or other electrical devices used until after this rain stops."

Jimmy pouted. Sammie wondered if his mother let him get by with that. "What if I don't like it?"

Tom took over. "You don't have to like it. Nobody has to like it. None of us do like it. You have to follow it like everybody else, including all of us."

"What if I don't follow it?"

Memories of wise-ass kids in high school flooded back to Sammie. She kept a judicial expression, and glanced at Tom. Luckily, he rode to her rescue.

"I will not predict Lieutenant Moore's decision. She could restrain you, which would mean locking you in a storeroom. Lieutenant Moore could also send you out the door. We would have to escort you past the property line. Since the team would not want to be out in that rain, we might not be gentle."

"I know my rights. I am going to appeal."

Sammie was amused, how Jimmy turned into a jailhouse lawyer.

"Appeal?" Tom fairly snorted. "There is no appeal for you. Later on, if government reappears, you could pursue redress of grievances. For now, however, Lieutenant Moore is in command. She is in charge if you want to look at it that way."

Tom now drew himself up to his full height, glowering down at Jimmy, who quaked in fear. "As her ranking noncommissioned officer, I speak for Lieutenant Moore, and she says you're very close to having more trouble than you want. The people who didn't join us before the dust came could tell you about it, but they're now dust themselves. Be thankful you're still alive. This way, you can annoy everyone with all that whining."

Sammie and Tom watched Jimmy slouch down the hall. Sammie shook her head. "He considered me a target for his romantic urges. You disabused him of that. My concern now is that he'll find some new and exciting way to be a pain in our collective butts. I'm voting for the rain to end sooner rather than later."

Tom nodded. "Didn't Stanley think we were getting to the end of the rain?"

"That's what he said three days ago. I can't tell any difference in the rain. Can we keep track of Brother Bower?"

"It's a big house, but we own upstairs and the Peepul control the back. It would give the team something to do."

Chapter 9
All About Jimmy

At the Thomas place, Alex and Cordelia both came outside. Alicia rode over to them with Josh right behind. The carriage kept moving, and Don halted the freight wagons.

"Jimmy just married one of the girls from the tribe," Alicia told her parents. "We're going to the castle for the reception. Do you want to come?"

"We'll pass," Cordelia said. "Give the bride and groom our best, though."

Mark saw Alex trying to maintain his composure through the short exchange. Alicia and Josh waved as they turned their horses to leave. Mark saw fury and hilarity crossing Alex's face in waves. That seemed to give Sammie's story some credibility. Of course, there was also Alicia's reaction to the whole thing.

After they got moving again, Sammie took up the story once more.

"The team and I kept the Peepul and farmers separated as much as possible. With Stanley, the need to be separate was never in doubt. In addition, the tribe knew the farmers would not understand them. The point was to enable the two groups to live side-by-side."

Sammie continued her defense. "Those reasons went even more for Jimmy Bower. With him, those reasons applied with exclamation points, underlines, and bold face. Even in the same room, they kept apart from one another. We actively promoted keeping it that way."

Ellen broke in. "Jimmy's clumsy move on you, Sammie, was rebuffed. All of us who knew him, treated him like a biblical leper. That left Jimmy with the women in the Peepul tribe. I see a bit of your dilemma."

Sammie nodded to Ellen, and Mark reflected on Ellen talking about not having to like somebody to work with them.

Sammie went on, "Jimmy ate with everyone else. He checked out who was most desirable, or more to the point, the least undesirable. It was obvious he thought the Peepul women looked better by the minute. I let Stanley know about the situation. It created a dilemma for Stanley. Part was whatever Jimmy tried to do. On the other hand, if he intervened after telling them to make up their own minds about personal affairs, it could make progress more difficult or even impossible."

"So Vickie became the target of Jimmy's amorous intentions," Don remarked absently.

Sammie nodded. "After dinner on August 12, Jimmy made his move. Vickie seemed incapable of anything besides following instructions. She would not and could not think or plan anything. Stanley should tell her what to do. He didn't, so Jimmy volunteered to be her new Willy. It was perfect. Here was a woman who had no ideas other than what he told her to have."

Alicia nodded. "All I had to be was empty-headed, and Jimmy would have been perfect for me. I'm glad it didn't turn out that way."

"When he went to her, she followed without any question. He took her to a private spot. We were close to Jimmy's little rendezvous location and listened to his attempts at conversation. Vickie didn't talk much, so the conversation stuttered and stopped more than flowed."

"What's your name?" was Jimmy's first question.

"Name? Do I have a name? A horse with no name."

"What does everyone call you? They don't just say, 'Hey, you!' They say, 'Hey, ... What comes next?"

"Nobody says anything to me. I go where the tribe goes. Name. Yeah, I had a name. Um, it was ..." She paused while she tried to remember. "Oh, yeah, it was Vickie. That's it, Vickie."

"Vickie is a very nice name," Jimmy sounded supportive.

"Where are you from?"

"The Peepul," was her response. The conversation would have been humorous if it wasn't so pitiful.

"No, I mean where did you live before you came here."

"Camps along a road. We knew it was our road. It had a big sign."

"What did the sign say?"

"I don't know. Oh, wait, it said, 'Minimum Maintenance.'"

"What city were you in before that?"

"Before that? I don't remember very well."

"Think about it. You lived in a place with lots of people and buildings and cars. You know where you used to live."

"Oh, yeah. City. Uh, St. Louis, maybe?"

"How did you go from St. Louis to that road with the Minimum Maintenance sign?"

"We walked."

"Did you find wild pigs as you walked from St. Louis?"

"No."

"What did you eat? Did you eat wild berries?"

"We are Peepul. They are animals. We eat animals."

"Pigs are animals. You ate other animals. That's good. What animals did you eat?"

"We are Peepul. They are animals. We eat animals." Vickie scrounged in her pocket, pulling out a switchblade knife which she opened, and started coming at Jimmy.

"We are Peepul. They are animals. We eat animals."

Jimmy began backing away from Vickie. "What are you saying? What are you doing? Put that knife away!"

Sammie sighed, "We all converged on the scene. Tom got the knife away from her, and two team members walked her over to Stanley. She didn't resist. Tom gave Stanley her knife as well. The rest of us backed Jimmy into the same corner where he chatted up Vickie. Stanley walked Vickie back toward the kitchen, and the privacy Jimmy wanted with Vickie worked to our advantage."

I told Jimmy, "There was a reason we kept the tribe separate from the rest of you. You just violated the hell out of that policy. We will hold you incommunicado until the rain stops."

"We debated the situation well into the night, and agreed the farmers had to get the story from us before Jimmy gave his version. Jimmy was more comfortable in that closet than he'd been in the shed. He was also more comfortable than nearly everyone else in that crowded house."

Mark shook his head. "At this point, the rain has gone on forever, too many people have lived too close to each other for too long, and you gave Jimmy time-out in a closet."

"Yes, that's about it, and I had no idea how long the rain was going to continue. Early the next morning, we still hadn't come to any other conclusions about Jimmy. All at once, we realized the background noise that had been with us for almost two weeks was no longer there. There was no longer any sound of rain. We all went to the windows and looked out. I guess it was around four in the morning. We couldn't see anything, but knew this unnatural storm had finally passed."

All the Harlan people nodded, remembering that morning.

"I cracked the window, and got nothing but sweet-smelling air, a welcome change from the hot, humid atmosphere. One ongoing debate was whether hot and humid air was better or worse than the dry, dusty air previously. I was about to find Stanley, and ask him whether the rain was really over, but Alex came in. He seemed quite agitated."

"I heard Jimmy ran afoul of you all," he told us. "Some thought the reason behind it might be personal. We all appreciate Jimmy being locked away for a while. It gives everyone room to breathe, but there was a thought you might be setting up to be dictators or something, you know?"

"Alex, I'm glad you came by. It saves us having to find you. Yes, we had to keep Jimmy away from everyone for a bit. We just noticed the rain stopped, so we may let him out sooner rather than later. We've tried to keep the folks we were following away from the local population. They were mostly drug addicts in St. Louis who lost their supply when the quakes hit. Unfortunately, they exchanged the drug habit for something even worse. We've worked to get them to stop. Jimmy chased after one of the girls, and messed everything up."

"Dare I ask what that habit is?"

"First, we'll talk about what Jimmy did. He got her off in what he thought was a private spot. He tried to bring the girl under his control. Instead, he let loose her private demon. She pulled a switchblade on him, intending to cut him as badly as possible. Jimmy's probably convinced she's a total head case."

Alex chuckled. "I would have loved to have seen that. Alicia should have carried protection like that. I understand you're saying these people were some sort of gang in St. Louis?"

"I went with the flow, and told him, 'In the chaos after the quakes, the group waylayed and murdered people. When the General got control over the area, he told them to leave town. He sent us to keep track of them. After local farmers captured the ringleader, Willy Jameson, they gave him an option of exile or death. He left the area, but from what we could tell, the dust got him. Stanley took over, and they're slowly getting their act together.'"

Mark came to conclusions of his own. Sammie was bragging about distorting the truth although what she said about Willy was true enough. Sammie concluding Alex wouldn't press that side of the issue confirmed his view of how she operated. Sammie defended herself by concluding the cannibalism issue wouldn't have a happy outcome for anybody. In any case, Stanley seemed to be moving his tribe away from all of that. At the same time, Mark wondered how the story would have changed if Alex and Cordelia were there.

Sammie continued her tale with Alex asking, "Was that big guy, Stanley, a drug addict, too?"

"No, he never was. Willy never wanted him on anything. Willy was a little twerp, and used Stanley as his big dumb enforcer. As it turned out, Stanley wasn't as dumb as Willy thought. With Willy gone, the group looked to Stanley for leadership. He knew there could be no peace where they were, so Stanley packed them up and they started walking. Stanley hopes there can be an arrangement here that can benefit everyone."

Alex's face hardened. "You just said they are bunch of murderers. How could we ever trust them?"

"They only do what Stanley says. Hunting for feral pigs and other game suits a number of them just fine. Learning to process the meat gives them something to eat and gives them a trade item. Stanley could take his tribe down to McCook. They can hunt pigs and other game. We could set up a spot where you and representatives from the tribe could meet to exchange goods."

"I'll talk it over with the others. What you say makes sense. I wonder what Jimmy made of the girl defending herself."

"I was desperate to keep the conversation as light as possible. So, I laughed and told him, 'That's hard to say. She had a really wild look in her eyes. Not only that, she continually muttered something while she waved the knife around. For all I know, he might think she wanted him for her dinner.'"

Alex thought that was hilarious. "That's a good one! Would it be all right if I passed that one around? Everyone will get a real charge out it."

"By all means. I have no idea where that idea came from anyway. We were about to talk with Stanley. He's got a real weather sense, and maybe he'll have some idea whether the rain is really over, or if something else is coming. Would you care to join us?"

"Don't mind if I do. It'd be awfully nice to get back home. Oh, you know, if Stanley's people were able to chase off the pigs that are rooting in our gardens, I think we could allow that, especially if we ended up eating the pigs instead of the pigs eating our gardens."

"It was almost sunrise before we found Stanley. He found a spot to sleep that even his tribe didn't know about. Once we got near him, he opened his eyes and looked at us. I asked him about the rain."

Stanley yawned, stretched, and stood up. "I believe we're back to whatever regular weather might be now. Everyone could go home in the morning. Since you got me up, I'll get the hunting parties ready to go. Will you excuse me, please?"

Alex, who stayed with us as we searched for Stanley, looked at me as we went back into the main part of the house. "When would you release Jimmy?"

"We'll wait until Stanley moves his tribe out, and give all of you at least an hour head start. He'll get an escort to the property line with an invitation to be scarce. Maybe he'll take the hint. Whatever happens, he knows we're keeping an eye on him. We'll secure the outbuildings better while we're at it."

Mark and Ellen looked at each other. Mark recalled that first glorious sunrise, and how they were all out there at first light, checking the area and getting horses saddled.

Sammie continued, "With sunrise came our first view of a cloudless, rainless sky in what seemed like forever. All of us went around opening windows and inhaling the fresh air. Several farm families were already outside. My next stop was to check the solar collectors. Even the early morning sunshine was charging the batteries at a good rate. The kitchen had a considerable movement toward cooking breakfast. There was no need to conserve now."

"Did Stanley find anything, or was he gone all day?" Mark wondered.

"Stanley and his hunters were back with fresh meat within an hour. He never said how they did it so fast. Maybe all that time of dust and rain gave the game a false sense of security. They were hauling a deer and a wild pig, which made all the omens positive. The farm families prepared to go home. In addition to hunting, Stanley also moved the tribe back to the arena. Stanley said they liked that because they could have open fires. Those still around were in the outbuilding used for meat processing."

"I bet that was a very happy breakfast," Alicia said.

"It was, and after breakfast, I asked Stanley to join in wishing the local farmers farewell and good luck. On impulse, I also asked for a moment of silence to honor those not surviving the deadly dust. I said something about how the rain washed away the pollution of the dust, as well as bringing welcome moisture to their gardens and fields. I hoped those who survived the dust found shelter from the rain, and that, with time, they would all find one another. I said that life would go on. It wouldn't be life as we knew it, but life nonetheless. Let us make it worthwhile."

Mark wondered if Sammie made that up after hearing Lyle at the memorial. It sounded a bit sappy to him. Looking around, it appeared the gals ate it up, though.

Sammie brushed back a stray hair with her fingertips. "I thought I was getting carried away with the whole thing, but than heard a number of voices saying, 'amen' when I finished. That's when I realized that while I hadn't meant giving a prayer, that's what it was. Everyone took off then. Alex Thomas and his wife were the last ones out, but it looked like he had something to say."

"You won't forget to let Jimmy out, will you?" Alex wanted to know.

"Alex, the last thing I want is to have to put up with him in any way, shape, or form. We'll give you at least an hour's head start, and send him on his way."

"Just hold off until high noon. None of us have clocks anymore."

"That sounds good. Out of curiosity, how far down the ridge does he live?"

"His trailer is not far before you drop off the hill going into town. It might not be in very good shape after all that rain."

"Would anyone let him stay with them?"

Alex shook his head. "That isn't likely. His best shot would be to find a house in town. Hell, if he did that, he could elect himself mayor."

"I hope your daughter, Alicia, made it through okay."

"That's the one thing we'd most like to know before we die, that Alicia survived all of this."

Stanley came up after Alex left. "I had a thought when the tribe moved out this morning," Stanley prefaced. "Processing the pork doesn't take many people. Also, the house took a beating with all those folks in it full-time. Could I bring some of them, and let them get the house cleaned up?"

"I appreciate your offering to do that. Vickie wouldn't be a candidate for that crew, would she?"

"She's definitely on it. I am concerned that Jimmy might come back after her. He might try to sneak into the arena, but I don't think he would invade the main house the way you guys took care of him."

"Okay, Stanley. Bring the cleaning crew. We're letting him out at noon. If you were in the area personally supervising, it might help him see the situation more clearly. After being up close and personal with her knife, maybe seeing her working in the house might send Jimmy on his way more rapidly. Say, do you think Vickie working around the house like that might encourage independent thinking?"

"I have to try everything, and hope something, somewhere makes a connection." He waved, and strode off toward the arena.

When the sun reached zenith, Sammie headed downstairs. Stanley was in the large entry hall, instructing a group of men and women. It sounded like he was training permanent staff, and I asked him about it.

"A lady needs her castle and retainers," Stanley told me. "A castle without staff is an empty, lonely place, don't you think?"

That didn't make any sense. We went to release Jimmy Bowen. Emerging from where we locked him, Jimmy was his usual obnoxious self. Close to the front door, Stanley turned and glowered at him, and Jimmy realized Vickie was just a few feet away. He suddenly became eager to cooperate, just to get out the door. We all escorted him to the property line, and Tom suggested if his trailer was too badly damaged, a place in town might be in order.

Sammie looked around and smelled the air, like she was once again smelling the freshness. "The next week was very quiet. Farm families showed up to make a case for how much meat they needed. Most of them brought vegetables for trade but spears came as well. Stanley moved to an apartment in the arena and stable complex, but would come over to the house to check out spears.

Josh was surprised. "It sounds as though they were really picking up hunting skills in a hurry."

Sammie nodded. "Stanley and his hunters now knew whether a spear would work for them. Further, Stanley could explain what they needed to make a better product. Meanwhile, they filled the meat locker and refrigerator to capacity."

"Was there anything more about Jimmy?" Mark wanted to know.

Sammie smiled then. "When the families came to trade, all of them had a 'Jimmy Story.' A common thread in the story was how Stanley's tribe were insane cannibals. Alex considered it a measure of Jimmy's own insanity that he even told him about it. The families laughed Jimmy out of the area. They said he moved down to McCook, where Vickie found him today."

Sammie finally ran out of story, which was good, since the castle just came into sight.

Mark nodded. "That's pretty slick, using the truth as a cover story. The cover story was more believable than the truth. Of course, you're stuck with it now. On the other hand, Stanley seems to be making a good-faith effort with his tribe. I don't know about anybody else, but I'm content to leave that sleeping dog lie."

Mark looked at Josh, who agreed with the difficulty of the situation. "The Peepul committed enough murders for the old-time media to have featured them for a month and a half. Hell, they'd have murdered us if they could have."

Josh stared at the approaching complex and added, "At first, I'd have packed them all into body bags. By the time they left Harlan, I didn't know where I stood. For moral turpitude, Lady Samantha, you take the cake. But it is your heart and conscience that has to live with it."

Alicia chimed in, "There is enough guilt to last a lifetime. None of us will ever believe the Peepul tribe couldn't relapse into their old ways.

Who knows what any of us might do under those circumstances? By the way, Ellen, with your love of traditional rituals, did you notice how Mark engineered a return to the old ways today?"

Ellen looked at Alicia, puzzled. "What are you talking about?"

Alicia grinned. "It's the ancient and honorable tradition of a shotgun wedding. That's what I'm talking about."

By that time, they arrived and Alicia turned to stare at the castle. "I came here a lot when they were building this place. It's straight from a fantasy. Those turrets make you think of knights and ladies."

Don chuckled as he stopped the wagon. "Jimmy's ears should be burning. Nobody talked about anything but him the whole bloody way. In any case, this is everyone's stop. All of you riding, tie your horses on the back of the wagon, and I'll take care of them. I'll see you all inside."

Inside, Dora was in a frenzy. Sammie walked around with her, back to her regal self, assigning seating and talking about what to serve. The lady Samantha also noted Stanley was not there, and sent one of the Peepul to fetch him.

Vickie, the blushing bride, had no idea what she should to do or how to act. A few hours earlier, she was serving the important people in the dining room, and now she was the honored guest. She was not only at the table, it was the head of the table. Oh, and somehow she'd become married.

When Stanley showed up, the wedding party was seated. Jimmy knew he was there on sufferance. The morning's events gave him such a case of jitters that his hand wouldn't stop shaking. Now, they seated Vickie and him at the head of the table. Tom sat just to Jimmy's right, and Sammie sat the other side of Tom. The plan, it appeared, was to separate him from Sammie, and let Tom pound Jimmy if the need arose.

On the other side were Josh and Alicia. Mark concluded the seating arrangement was not accidental, placing Jimmy where he had to look at all the women in his life. Whether that arrangement was a reward or a punishment depended on the individual's outlook. Jimmy's opinion was evident as he sat there squirming. Mark sat next to Alicia, who found it hilarious. Having officiated the wedding ceremony, Stanley sat next to Sammie, with the three marines beyond him. On Mark's side, Ellen was next, followed by Don Rowley.

Bottles of champagne appeared, and everyone toasted the shiny new couple. Jimmy sipped his gingerly. However much he consumed, it didn't loosen him up at all. Mark didn't think Jimmy would relax for a long time, knowing his bride sat there with a switchblade.

The food came out, and after the meal, Dora showed she could make magic happen by bringing a small wedding cake. After that, everybody went in separate directions. Mark decided to catch up to Stanley, which was no easy task, as the man could really move.

"Stanley, those dust people you and your people took out, how many were there?"

"Fifteen."

"We took a prisoner, who claimed the dust people have fifty fighters and six hundred slaves. The lady says you have read a large number of military commentators. Would you send a quarter of your fighters down the Republican River?"

"I wouldn't need any military experts to answer that. Nobody would do that. The slaves would be gone very quickly, I think."

"Now, if you had six hundred fighters and hardly any slaves, would reconnaissance make sense? This is especially if you've sworn to wipe out the people along the Republican River, and made several attempts to take them out with the dust."

"It would make perfect sense. You'd do damage assessment."

"Thanks, Stanley. That's what I thought."

Don Rowley walked by. He gazed at Mark with bleary eyes and shook his head. "I've got to get moving, but all that champagne got to me. My wife would kill me if she saw how much I drank. Now I have to go find the notes I made about where I saw everything. I've got a lot to do so the two newlyweds can set up housekeeping in Arapahoe. Oof!"

He stumbled out the front door and Stanley turned back to Mark. "The tribe will move to Arapahoe instead of McCook. The stopping place there should be that place on the eastern edge of town that sold agricultural machinery. The offices can be guest rooms. The retail area would be the dining room and lounge. The parts department can be the kitchen and manager's apartment. The wagons and animals would stay in the garage area."

"That makes sense. Where would your tribe stay?"

"My people could use the machine shop to field clean game."

Mark nodded. "You've thought about this. It puts you a long way from here, though."

"It's all connected to something else. I'd like to expand the tribe's hunting area, and you need to buy off on the idea."

Mark stood there, astonished. "Why do you think I need to approve anything?"

Stanley paused a moment. "My idea is to hunt the river bottom all the way to Harlan Lake. My people will get the pigs and you get meat and fewer problems. Also, we could give Harlan County a first line of defense from the dust people."

Mark considered that and sighed. "Right now, I have a feeling for what Jimmy's going through. A lot is happening really fast. You make sense, but I can't give you an answer. Lyle Lillard is going to have to make the decision."

"I understand that. The first step is for you to support it."

Mark thought about it for a moment. "I'm okay with it, but I don't know if I can push it very hard. Nobody in Harlan has seen what I'm looking at."

Stanley nodded. "At least you're not just blowing me off. I told the lady about it, and she wished me luck. One reason is to keep an eye on Jimmy Bower. I'm gratified Vickie actually made a decision. I'm not sure we should have handled it in such a steamroller fashion. Still, it's done. We'll just work with it."

Stanley went on out, then. Mark turned around and he saw Vickie and Jimmy at the top of the stairs. Mark wondered what they heard. Stanley had been looking their direction, so he couldn't have thought it mattered. Vickie was as wide-eyed as ever and Jimmy stood next to her, looking nervous.

Ellen leaned over the railing beside the newlyweds. "Hey, dummy, get up here. There's something we need to discuss."

Mark couldn't think what she could be talking about, but duty called using his fiancee's voice. Not only that, he was getting accustomed to obeying. Upstairs, Ellen grabbed his hand and towed him into their room. Inside, she shoved him toward the center of the room and threw the privacy lock on the door.

Mark suddenly knew what Ellen wanted to discuss but decided to play dumb. "Okay. So what do we need to talk about?"

"We had a good conversation going last night. I thought we should take up where we left off."

He felt an overwhelming impulse to be clever. "It seems like forever since last night, with everything that has happened. Maybe you need to refresh my memory. I vaguely recall three baths. There was something about brown water."

"We make beautiful poetry together and all you remember is the punctuation. I'll bet I know how to improve your concentration. Maybe I can borrow Vickie's switchblade. How did that go? My left forearm goes against your chest and the blade against your throat. That seems easy enough."

Mark grinned. "There's also the technique Sammie could use on Tom."

"What would that be, pray tell?" Ellen suddenly looked like she was about to embark on another mad, just hearing the name.

"She outranks him. All she has to do is call him to attention."

Ellen blinked, shook her head, and giggled. "You're impossible."

"I exist, so I can't be impossible. Now, I might buy being extremely improbable. Yeah, I'll admit to that."

"I have a problem with your solution."

"What's that?"

"If I call you to attention, I won't know if you're following my order if you're dressed. If you don't have any clothes on, then you will be out of uniform. That's a real predicament."

Mark rubbed his chin, trying to look thoughtful. "I see your point. The real requirement for being uniform is that everyone is dressed the same. That means then that if neither of us had clothes on, than we would be dressed, or undressed, in a uniform manner, and therefore in uniform."

"Mr. Tahner, you are burning daylight when we have to work off a bunch of lunch. It isn't that long until dinner. I suspect we're the only couple not doing something worthwhile right now. So strip, already!"

Chapter 10
Diplomacy and Inn

Ellen ensured that Mark worked off the luncheon. No drill sergeant managed to exhaust him like that. Worse, she was more energetic at the end than at the beginning. He never thought such a thing was possible.

The break came when they heard a soft knock on their door. A timid voice advised that dinner would be served in half an hour. There wouldn't be time for another bath, so they cleaned up somewhat and dressed.

They got to the top of the stairway when Vickie and Jimmy did. The newlyweds seemed a bit more comfortable together now. Mark got the impression that Jimmy didn't like the situation. On the other hand, being with Vickie might be a good thing. Sammie and Tom then joined the foursome, and they all went down together. That was only appropriate since they'd almost certainly spent the afternoon going down separately.

In the dining room, Mark saw that Sammie worked on more than cohabitation. She had Tom at the head of the table and stood behind the chair to his right. Sammie had Ellen sit across from her, with Mark in the next chair. Jimmy got the honor of sitting next to Sammie. Josh and Alicia went back to the Thomas house after the luncheon, so the boy-girl pattern broke down. Don Rowley sat next to Mark, and one marine sat beside Don while the other two were next to Vickie. Mark considered that Sammie guaranteed the seating made nobody happy.

Sammie attempted to get things social. She looked across at Don. "Were you able to find enough equipment, furniture, and provisions to get Vickie and Jimmy started in Arapahoe?"

Don shrugged. "There is enough for a beginning. While I was out, I saw about half of Vickie's Peepul tribe is headed that way. It looks like our honeymooners will have company."

Jimmy gulped, became pale, and beads of sweat popped out of his forehead. Mark thought it was to his credit that he stayed seated, at least. Sammie seemed not to notice, and pursued the subject.

"Will you be coming back here after that, Don?"

"I thought about it, but after I unload, I'll see what's in Arapahoe. I'll head back to Harlan after that. I have a pretty good idea what I can get in McCook."

"Do you plan on runs between Harlan and here?"

"I certainly plan on it. There's a demand for beef here, and Harlan wants pork. For other needs, I have some miscellaneous items I can look through."

Mark chuckled. "What he is saying is that he has warehouses full of equipment, furniture, and other goods. Absolutely nothing could be called miscellaneous. Every single item is inventoried, checked, and cross-checked. Put in your order, and he'll bring it, for a price, of course." Don glared at him when he said it.

Tom took over then. "So, Mark, you don't object to trade between us?"

"I don't mind, and I can't imagine Mr. Lillard having an objection. What he said before we left leads me to believe he's completely for it. Don Rowley's business is his own to pursue. In addition, we need a way to communicate. Your bikes would be ideal since they can go the whole way in a day. The trouble is that they're not going to hold up. Maybe some kind of express rider system would work."

"You've got the horses," Tom observed. "What would it take?"

"It would take a group of trained riders. We're working on that right now. Then we need all the horses we have and any more we can find. That would include any horses you can contribute. A message in one day with a relay would be possible. The road's good enough, we could even have people ride overnight, if necessary."

"That's impressive, Mark," Sammie commented. "How long will you and Ellen stay?"

"I'm sure some of you think I've already done more than enough damage," Mark said, looking at Jimmy and Vickie. "Staying in a civilized house is a real delight, but we should head back tomorrow as well. The sooner I see Mr. Lillard, the faster decisions can happen."

Ellen looked at Mark thoughtfully. Mark could see the question in her eyes of, "What's the matter with you Mark? Can't we just hang around here a while longer?"

After a pause, Mark decided to add, "If you don't mind, some of us could come periodically for some R & R. That's rest and recuperation for those not familiar with the military slang."

Tom nodded, and Sammie smiled. "That would be wonderful."

Something occurred to Mark then, and after hesitating, "You realize there's a down side to being friends with us. The terrorists swore they'd wipe us out. They might lump you in with us on that. Stanley's Peepul taking out the bunch near Arapahoe may have attracted their attention to this larger area, especially if there were terrorists not with the main group."

That got Tom thoughtful. "Are you proposing a mutual defense pact, too?"

"That's where I'm at, yes."

"How many terrorists are there?"

"We don't know. Our initial idea was to return the last vial of Omega bugs to them with our compliments. The problem was that we had no way to be sure we got them all. That meant we could make the situation worse rather than better. We think around six hundred of them are near Colorado Springs."

Tom chewed on that for a minute. "On our side, there's Stanley's Peepul, with about one hundred fifty. McCook is maybe that number again. What do you have in Harlan?"

"I'd guess three hundred or so. You guys probably have a better count than we do."

Tom got embarrassed, but continued, "Stanley improved the odds, getting rid of the scouting party. Of course, the scouting party had no idea they had chaperones, so we don't know their real fighting skills. Overall, we are outclassed as fighters. That is on top of trying to defend an impossibly large area."

"We thought that as well. Welcome to our world. Does that tell you why we got concerned about strange bicycle tracks all over Harlan?"

After dinner, Jimmy slid around the table, obviously intending to intercept them. Mark and Ellen exchanged glances as to what this might be all about.

Jimmy seemed both timid and worried at the moment. "Could I tell you something, sir? Could I tell it to you someplace private, please?"

After the story Sammie told, Mark had reservations about anything he might say. Ellen confirmed some of the generalities about Jimmy's personality. "Anything you tell me includes Ellen."

Jimmy led the way to an alcove, wringing his hands. "You talked about terrorists in there. Well, I may have seen some a month ago."

Jimmy had Mark's attention now. "What did you see, exactly?"

"After the rain quit, they threw me out of the castle. The rain wrecked my trailer. Mud came down, tipped it on its side and then crushed it, so I moved into McCook. It was a week after that. I found a place where I could get out of the afternoon rains, and made a mark for each day. The people at the castle were big on knowing the date, and letting everyone else know, too. They had sent me on my way about mid-day. Everyone else already left."

Ellen was frowning, and Mark was out of patience. "When are we going to get to the point?"

"I'm at the point, sir. I woke up at first light and made my mark, so it was August 20. I went to the main road, thinking I'd look for food. At the intersection where the highway comes up from the south, I saw some guys. I'd never seen them before in my life."

"Describe them."

"I counted thirteen. Some wore funny-looking caps, and they talked in a foreign language. They motioned me over. They all had rifles, so I thought I'd better see what they wanted. They looked like pictures from the Middle East I saw on television."

"Did they all carry the same kind of rifle?"

Jimmy nodded, somewhat fearfully. "Yes, sir, they were all the same."

"Okay, did they have wooden stocks?"

"Yeah, and they weren't hunting rifles. There were big banana clips in them. The fellow in charge didn't speak English. He said gibberish to another guy. After a bit, the other guy nodded, and then looked at me and asked how I survived the dust."

Mark thought that would have been a reasonable question if they were terrorists. "What did you tell them?"

"I was still mad at how everybody treated me, so I told them maybe I was just smarter than those who died. That got a grin from everybody in the group when the guy translated it."

"So you didn't tell them about the castle and all of that."

Jimmy shook his head. "They didn't tell me how they survived. Why should I tell them? The next question was if I'd seen anybody who knew more about the dust than a person could know. I knew who they had to be talking about. He'd taken Alicia away from me, so I had no reason to protect his ass."

Mark nodded. He could appreciate the sentiment even if nothing else. "I take you actually gave them that information."

"I did. I told them I'd seen somebody like that. Everybody called him the professor, and he talked crazy. He got people believing they'd have to go somewhere else to be safe. The guy with the group acted sad when he heard that. He said they came to give him his reward."

Mark had a pretty good idea of what they were there for, but he played dumb. "Give him his reward? Were they talking about money or a one-way trip to the promised land?"

"They didn't say, but I could tell that bunch wasn't from Publishers Clearing House. The guy with the group asked if I was the only survivor in the area. I had to say something, so I told them there were survivors. I added that nobody would want to get anywhere close to them. The guy asked why, and I said they were cannibals and escaped lunatics."

Mark smiled slightly. Jimmy nailed the situation better than he would ever know. "That should have derailed their train of thought."

"I guess it did, because after more talk with his leader, the guy asked a really off the wall question. They wanted to know if I was a Christian."

"They are religious fanatics. That's something they'd ask."

It didn't make an impact on Jimmy. "I knew folks around town. They claimed to be the only ones who could call themselves Christian. I wasn't one of them, so I shrugged and told them if they needed to go to church, there were plenty close by. I didn't go myself, so I couldn't tell them one from another."

"Was there any more talk?"

"Everybody got really friendly, like I was their buddy or brother or something. They asked if the professor said where he was going. I told them that I didn't know, but hoped it was a really long way. I also told them I figured the professor was likely part of that dust he knew so much about."

Mark considered Jimmy did good. "That wasn't too bad."

Jimmy grimaced then. "If I had shut my mouth then, maybe it would have been okay. I added that if they wanted to follow him, the professor and his bunch headed east, and I pointed on down the road."

"If they came after him, we'd have seen them. Maybe there wasn't all that much damage done."

"I guess they believed me, since the guy said I could join them. If I did, all I had to do was to say their oath or magic phrase, and I'd be in. They looked nasty and smelled bad even to me, so I told them they could do what they wanted, and maybe I'd talk to them if they came back through. Then I boogied up a nearby alley."

"Did they stick around?"

"They chattered for a while, and then went south. I think they just came from that way. I followed them for a couple of miles. They were pretty intent on making tracks. Nobody looked back, or even looked around."

That fit the terrorists' pattern. As soon as the way was clear, they sent people to Harry Dover's last known location. They established he was no longer there. That bunch hadn't gotten all the way back before the solar buggy was dispatched toward Harlan County.

Ellen's passion cooled off noticeably that night. Mark thought it probably started with him declaring they would go home the next day. The time spent with Jimmy didn't help either. At the same time, there were no feelings of hostility, and if the physical passion was less, the cuddling went on quite a bit longer. Mark could certainly handle that.

At first light, he saddled up and rode to the Thomas place. He needed to let Josh and Alicia know they were heading back.

"Do you need us to convoy with you?" was Josh's question.

"There's no need. From what I can tell, the road seems safe enough to go back individually. Don is hauling furniture and supplies to Arapahoe. He'll stay an extra day to scrounge there. I need to get back to Harlan and update Lyle. I don't know if you heard, but the Peepul will headquarter at Arapahoe."

"Why would he want to do that?"

"Stanley wants to keep an eye on Jimmy, for one thing. He also talked about wanting to hunt on east along the river. After what he did with the terrorists, it makes sense to have him as a first line of defense."

Josh chuckled. "You appreciate them volunteering to be the first ones to get wiped out if the terrorists show up en masse."

"There is that. Stanley with a pig sticker was an impressive sight. He is somebody I'd prefer with me than to have to fight against. Anyway, I need to get back up the hill if I want breakfast."

Josh snorted. "From the sound of it, those people will cook you just about anything at any time."

"It feels like being in a luxury hotel. I haven't heard of room service. Come to think of it, they'd probably do that, too, if I asked nicely."

Mark grinned and waved as he turned his horse and headed back to the castle. Even with everything he'd done, including putting his horse away, Sammie and Tom were just coming downstairs when he walked into the castle. He went into the dining room with them. Ellen and Don Rowley were already there.

"Hey, Don, you're getting a late start today."

"Why bother? I'd end up waiting for everyone else anyway," Don grumbled.

Ellen was talking to Don, so Mark took the next chair. The three marines wandered in next, followed almost immediately by Vickie and Jimmy. Soon, everyone was fully engaged with eating, except for Don and Ellen, who were now done. Don suddenly had an idea.

"If you two would share the space, we could carry some additional pork in the carriage, and leave it at Arapahoe" Don commented, looking at Vickie and Jimmy.

"That will be okay," Jimmy replied between bites.

"I packed what food I could around and between everything that's unloading in Arapahoe."

Vickie looked at Don. "What would we need to feed you and your people when you come through? For that matter, how will we know when you're coming?"

Don had to think about it. "That is a tough question. If you kept a pot of stew going, that would help. We can bring canned and bottled fruits and vegetables. Keeping you supplied will be like what we're doing in Harlan, only more so and farther away."

Mark suddenly remembered what kind of stew the Peepul kept on their campfires, and suddenly found himself a whole lot less enthused about the project, knowing Arapahoe would be the Peepul headquarters.

All at once, he came up with part of a solution. "Don, whenever you head from Harlan to McCook, why not take some beef with you? Folks don't want to eat pig all the time."

Don realized where Mark was coming from, and raised his eyebrows as he agreed whole-heartedly. Glancing around, nobody else picked up on it. They just seemed gratified at having more variety in the food at Arapahoe. Ellen didn't react, but she never had the pleasure of smelling the cooking pots of the Peepul when they were in Harlan.

After a few moments, Jimmy looked at Mark. "Sir, was that helpful, what I told you yesterday?"

Mark nodded. "It helped fill in the picture I have of the situation." That statement was true enough. His opinion of the situation along with the people remained the same. For a positive note, he added, "I believe you and Vickie are going to do just fine in the hospitality business."

"I hope I don't disappoint anybody," Jimmy replied, deciding to pay attention to his food.

"How do you plan to do this move?" Tom finally inquired.

Mark glanced at Don before answering. "We'll get to Arapahoe, and unload. It'll be rough tonight. With any luck Stanley's tribe can help us do things tomorrow. Ellen and I will get back to Harlan. I imagine Don will replace what he drops off in Arapahoe with what he finds in the town. I'd guess he'll head back to Harlan the next day."

Tom nodded. "When will Mr. Lillard make a decision?"

"I don't know. We'll get word to you as soon as we can."

"We appreciate that," he said, with a glance at Sammie. "I understand what Mr. Rowley does is separate from what Harlan might do."

Mark looked over at Don. "Mr. Rowley is his own man. Arapahoe is its own subject. Stanley and his tribe constitute their own situation. Still, all of us are connected, and I'm hopeful we can all get along together."

Don took the lead with the carriage following close behind. Those on horseback rode wherever they wanted. The drovers already departed the previous day. The name of the game was to be as far as possible before the rains started about mid-afternoon. With the temperatures dropping, riding in the rain would be miserable.

For miserable, Mark wondered if the cold rain and wind might be the better choice, since his alternative was to get wisdom from the chief executive of Rowley Freight. Don complained the entire run how this was not why he volunteered to go and how his retirement was rotting in McCook while he wasn't getting any younger. Don's song of sorrow was clearly heard, no matter where Mark rode in the group.

Other than Don's whine, served without cheese and crackers, the run was uneventful. Mark glanced at the sun as they approached Arapahoe, and estimated they still had several hours of daylight. A line of clouds back toward McCook reminded them of the afternoon storms, but the sky there was clear and the winds calm.

Stanley sent a couple of his people on through Arapahoe, to guide them. They jogged beside the group, and had no problem keeping up with the horses. It was such a strange sight that Don even shut up. At last, there stood Stanley in the road, spear in hand just like when he had stopped them going the other way.

Stanley's description was right on the money. The place had been an agricultural implement dealer before equines returned to being the major source of horsepower. It had a large parking area in front together with a large maintenance area in the rear. The front, glassed in area, had been a retail display area, with a parts counter to one side. The parts room was a good size. Facing the retail area was a row of offices. Stanley thought those could be guest rooms. Looking at them, Mark couldn't argue.

Stanley's tribe had done a great deal, considering the time they had. The offices, parts room, and retail area were all empty. A few pieces of equipment in the garage were too large or heavy to move. Don's draft horses plus the Peepul made short work of them. Then, the Peepul moved the wood-burning cook stove and two beds into the building. One bed went into the back of the parts room for Vickie and Jimmy.

Don's double-header held the furniture and equipment. His attitude was another matter. He had to leave nearly all the treasures he'd located behind. It took a real toll on his attitude. Mark noted how Don's shirt pocket bulged from notes he'd made about where he cached everything. It was possible the paperwork also contained curses for anyone daring to trespass on Don's stash.

At the same time, Mark thought it was a testament to Don's loading expertise to get so much pork in and around everything else. A major item was a wood-burning cookstove. Such items had gone from being an antique curiosity to a necessity. Members of the Peepul tribe found and rigged a smokestack from the stove to carry the smoke outside. They also came up with a fair amount of fire wood, and soon had the stove checked out.

While everyone played furniture mover, it was funny how Vickie and Jimmy stood staring at everything in total confusion. A change occurred when they got the stove going. Vickie went into action and organized pots and pans that came in the door. Tables, chairs, and dishes also arrived. All at once, Vickie was cooking up a storm. Before sunset, food came across the parts counter on dishes gathered from surrounding houses.

Vickie choreographed everything, including serving. Mark could see Jimmy was no closer to having a clue about any of it than before. That wasn't quite right. When Vickie handed him food, Jimmy figured out what needed to happen with it in a hurry. The two squatted together behind the counter where Vickie could see if anyone needed more of anything.

In spite of what he told Jimmy earlier, Mark knew it would be a long time before this could be acceptable as an inn. On the other hand, Jimmy was the best hotel manager around. As usual, it was because he was the only one. That made this place, dubbed the Arapahoe Inn, a five-star establishment.

They were next door to Arapahoe's previous motel. Stanley checked it out, and decided that rooms going outside made no sense with winter coming on. In addition, there was nowhere people could eat. For the moment, any overflow could go to the old motel. Maybe they'd want to go there anyway tonight.

After dinner, Mark was amazed when Ellen and he got the one guest room with a bed. There were no linens or privacy, so it was a case of throwing their bedrolls on the mattress. Unless the two of them changed their minds about privacy during love-making, they'd have to be content with simple closeness. It wasn't the castle, but Mark didn't think it was bad. Everybody else picked a spot and spread their bed rolls.

Outside, everyone contributed lariats and built picket lines for the horses in areas with grass. Containers were scrounged and the Peepul helped bring water. The horses were just like they'd have been without the Inn. Stanley was willing to discuss corrals or shelters for the horses, but everyone was too tired to pursue the point. It was dark, and had been a long day.

They lay facing one another on the bare mattress, noses nearly touching. Mark decided to try and get the situation off his chest.

"Did I accomplish what Lyle wanted, Ellen?"

"I don't know, Mark. You went above and beyond on a couple of things, like this situation right here. If you told me everything that Lyle said he wanted, I'd be reasonably optimistic that he will be pleased."

Sunlight bounced off the aluminum trim on the display windows, and found Mark's eyes in the less-than-private room. Everyone else was up and if the light hadn't awakened him the noise would have. They served lots of bacon and eggs. Don managed to get both in the carriage, on the opposite seat from the honeymooners to prevent their arriving broken. With no refrigeration, it was a case of use them or lose them.

Jimmy looked busy. It would have been more impressive if he found something else to do with his hands than wring them. After breakfast, Don announced he would stay in Arapahoe and work the town one day. He already proclaimed success, sorting through the pile pulled out of the Arapahoe Inn. Don was certain many more treasures awaited him.

The carriage, running empty and two horses pulling, set a pace as fast as Mark and Ellen cared to ride alongside. They all agreed to get home sooner rather than later. With a large breakfast, nobody felt hunger at noon. They weren't far from Oxford anyway. That got them home not much after mid-afternoon. Kevin and a trainee were at Harlan Ranch and clearly didn't expect them this soon. Ellen took both bedrolls and headed for the house.

"Welcome home, Mark. What do you want us to do this afternoon, boss?" Kevin inquired. "I'd be glad to fill you in on everything."

Ellen looked over her shoulder with what Mark interpreted as an invitation to keep his mind on important subjects.

"Kevin, taking care of the horses would be great. After that, just keep on doing what you've been doing. I'm sure it is all wonderful."

After the castle, Mark wondered what Ellen would do. For now, there was little to do but to get his butt over to the house as fast as he could. Ellen got in the door ahead of him, and was putting the bedrolls away when he walked in. She was now remarkably close-mouthed. That didn't help him figure out what might be going on. She just passed by without a sign or a word and headed into the kitchen.

"I need to see what we can do for supper," she called back to Mark. "Whatever Kevin has done, I'm certain he helped himself to whatever he wanted without replacing anything."

Mark would have been fine without eating. Nonetheless, Ellen fixed what she termed a nice light supper, and Mark reminded himself to not only enjoy it, but be certain to tell her it was the best food he'd had since they'd left the ranch. The comment went over well.

Ellen cleaned the kitchen just after eating, like religion. This time, the kitchen cleaning didn't happen. Instead, Ellen went into the living room. Mark recalled the old days, when meals were likely to be preempted by a television show. Mark heard a door open.

"Come here, Mark," he heard Ellen order.

She stood at the doorway to his bedroom. Since Ellen arrived, the rule was that all bedroom doors had to stay shut unless someone was physically going through.

"Is this the master bedroom?"

Mark again flashed back to the day she showed up. Along with the closed door rule, Ellen immediately declared what each room would be called. "That's what you called it, yes."

"This is where the master of the house sleeps."

Mark didn't feel very much like the master of anything, especially not at this moment, but went with the flow. "It seems like that, yes."

"Would the master's lady sleep here too?"

Now the light began to shine on Mark. "She could, if she desired."

"Am I your lady?"

That was a question he had no trouble answering. "There is no doubt about it. Yes, you are. Absolutely."

"Why don't I sleep here?"

"You can certainly sleep here if you want. We can't do anything about the past, but you are more than welcome now."

"Thank you, sir. I accept your gracious offer."

She immediately moved personal things into the so-called master bedroom. While that was going on, Mark checked outside. It appeared the chores were done. The apprentice was still working, but Mark didn't see Kevin or his horse.

It wasn't long before Ellen showed Mark once more how going along with the Ellen program had substantial and tangible rewards. Electricity, private baths, and hot water helped the ambiance but weren't necessities when it came to enjoying the moment.

Chapter 11
Mark's Ass and Lyle

Outside, Kevin and his apprentice were already halfway through chores. Kevin gave some instructions to the apprentice, and headed to Mark.

"Mr. Lillard said he wanted me to let him know the minute you got in. The apprentice did the chores, so I got on my way. When I saw Mr. Lillard, he said to give you a message."

Everything just turned upside down. "What message was that, Kevin?"

"He said you should stay home, and not wander off. Mr. Lillard said the chores were mine and your ass was his."

"He told it to you that way, did he?"

Mark appreciated that Kevin relayed the message with a straight face. "Yes, sir, he looked straight at me. He didn't blink. He didn't stutter. He didn't smile."

Mark took a deep breath. "Well, then, I should thank you for the message while I can. I need to find a silver platter suitable for presenting my ass to Mr. Lillard."

Mark walked back to the house. Ellen had both bedroom doors open. She was rearranging the master bedroom, and adding feminine touches.

"Company is coming, Ellen. Mr. Lillard is eager for my report."

She glanced at him. "Coffee is perking. Do you want breakfast before he gets here?"

Mark shook his head and shrugged. "I don't know what to tell you about that."

Just then, they heard a rider, and Ellen peered out the window. "I can't imagine he already had breakfast. I'll make some for all of us."

She hurried into the kitchen without closing either bedroom door. Mark walked to the front door. By that time, Lyle was already off his horse and handing the reins to Kevin. There was nothing to do but invite him in. Lyle glanced at the open master bedroom, but whatever he saw didn't show on his face. Ellen was right about him not having eaten, and soon they were all at the table.

Mark told his impressions of everything, without going into detail about the events leading up to the wedding of Vickie and Jimmy Bower. Ellen added a few comments.

Lyle considered the situation for a moment. "This place you call the Arapahoe Inn — is it ready for guests?"

"When we left yesterday morning, they could feed people, and there's an area to tie the horses. It's rude and crude."

Lyle nodded. "Stanley Peepul wants to hunt pigs down to Harlan Lake. He showed his good faith by taking out fifteen or so terrorists, you say?"

"That's what it amounts to. They showed me a Kalahari cap, worn by one of the bunch. I discovered later, that isn't the only unit the terrorists sent. Jimmy Bower told me of an earlier unit in McCook just before the last solar buggy. They were looking for Harry Dover. They tried to get Jimmy to convert, but he didn't go for it."

"Jimmy made a decent decision. I appreciate Harry Dover's concern about the terrorists more now. It sounds like Stanley stopped the tribe's cannibalism and offers things we need. All he asks is the freedom to do it. I can't leave that deal on the table for a minute longer than necessary. Mark, you and I need to ride to Arapahoe right now and take care of business. Ellen, could you ask your man out there to tell my wife we'll be gone for a day or so?"

Mark figured Ellen was planning domestic bliss, but she bit her lip. After a moment, she said brightly, "I'll get after it right away, Mr. Lillard. I'll also have Kevin saddle your horse, Mark. Be sure to take a bedroll. Speaking of bedrolls, there's an extra one you could use, sir."

As Ellen disappeared out the door, Mark walked into his room to grab his bedroll. Lyle looked in the door. "Ellen's redecorating, I see," he remarked.

"She's owned the inside of the house ever since she showed up. She also tells me what to do outside."

"That sounds more like a married man than an engaged one."

"I wouldn't know, sir."

Lyle laughed. "We're burning daylight. We need to get moving if we're going to get to Arapahoe."

They headed down the farm road until, near the old cannibal camp, they turned across the field where the Peepul marched when they left Harlan. Dropping off the high ground, they headed into Oxford. Riding past the guard post, Lyle told the guards that they'd return the next day. One of the guards commented, "This is looking more like a through-way than a gate."

Lyle replied, "That's exactly how we want it, too."

Down the road, Mark asked, "Will this work, with the Peepul so close?"

"With any luck, it should work just fine."

There were several subjects Mark hoped would not come up, and he was trying to figure out what to say if they did. Lyle's next question caught him completely off guard.

"How do you think things would be if all this hadn't happened?" Lyle wanted to know.

"You mean, if the dust hadn't come through?"

"No, I'm talking about all the disasters, both natural and man-made."

Mark considered that. "Josh and I were part of a man-made disaster in Afghanistan. If that hadn't gone to hell, our unit still wouldn't have seen Stateside duty. Every time they needed to do some nation-building, the geniuses in charge would send us there first for the initial tear-down."

"You were okay with that?"

"I believed it was my patriotic duty. When the Afghanistan mission imploded, I got a reality check. Standing in front of the Pentagon and hearing that I was dead set me on course for Harlan County."

"If that didn't happen, you'd still be in some exotic place, tracking bad guys?"

"The unit would be, certainly. It was starting to wear on me. I don't know if I could have made a career out of it. How would things have gone if the dust hadn't come through, and you were still training horses for Sheriff Crichton?"

Lyle thought about that. "There would still be people in Holdrege. Willy might still be a nuisance. We'd be a lot thinner for supplies since we couldn't help ourselves to everything around here. On the other hand, we were developing some commerce. This coming winter would be a major test either way."

They met Don Rowley on the road. Don looked a lot more pleased with life than two days earlier. Both wagons being full of treasures had a lot to do with it, along with the knowledge that more awaited him in McCook.

"Is everything okay in Arapahoe, Don?" Lyle wanted to know.

"Things are as good as they can be," Don allowed. "They can cook, serve food, and wash dishes. There's a bed for the hosts and one bed so far for the guests. Staying there is better than camping, but not a lot. Since you left, Mark, they installed a small water tank in the kitchen. That has improved the situation for cooking and cleaning. Now, if you'll excuse me, I've got important stuff to do."

On that note, Don rolled for Harlan. It didn't seem long before they arrived. Everything was eerily quiet. Mark had visions of Stanley's tribe turning on Jimmy.

"Hello?"

Mark's voice echoed. He heard a noise behind the counter where they set up Jimmy and Vickie. They strolled up to the counter, getting there the same time as Jimmy, who was still fastening his clothes.

"Yes sir. Welcome back," Jimmy said breathlessly. There wasn't much welcome in his voice.

Lyle took over. "We're sorry to drop in unannounced. I would have gotten reservations, but couldn't find your number."

Jimmy responded in kind. "Our number is unlisted. We only handle A-list people, you know."

Lyle just smiled, and Mark thought he'd better get things on track.

"We saw Don Rowley on the road. Are you doing okay with Stanley?"

"Stanley doesn't come to this side unless there's work. He keeps the tribe out and says this area is only for those traveling between Harlan and McCook."

Vickie was now dressed, and joined them at the counter. Jimmy glanced at her and back to Mark. "We just have one bed available."

Rather than get into formal introductions, Mark simply nodded. "Lyle, why don't you take the bed? Is Stanley around?"

Jimmy nodded. "He was here earlier, helping Mr. Rowley secure the cargo in his wagons. I'll be glad to check if he's still in back. Do you want me to let him know you are here?"

"If you could, please."

"I'll do that right now."

Vickie turned to get the fire going in the stove, and Jimmy headed to Stanley's place behind the service area. Mark followed at a distance, but was close enough to hear the exchange.

"Mark just showed up with an older fellow he called Lyle. They want to see you."

Stanley's voice returned. "That would be Lyle Lillard. I rated the two big guns in Harlan County. Were they in a good mood?"

"They attempted a little humor when they came."

"That is better than a snarl, certainly."

Mark rejoined Lyle, and Vickie seated them. She was pouring coffee when Jimmy came in with Stanley. When Lyle invited Stanley to join them, Jimmy remembered he needed to be elsewhere. With a nod, Lyle quietly directed Mark to reel in both of them.

"Can you and Vickie break away for a few minutes?" he asked.

Jimmy looked at Vickie. She nodded, so they followed Mark to the table. Jimmy grabbed a chair for Vickie. Mark wondered if it related to Stanley's instructions and concerns for Vickie's health.

Looking at the two, Lyle smiled "We weren't introduced earlier. I'm Lyle Lillard. People tell me I'm in charge in Harlan. Mark gave me his impression of things. After chatting with Stanley, I'm inclined to go along with what he would like to happen."

Lyle looked meaningfully at Mark, who licked his lips. Evidently, he was just made chief of protocol after his recent and extensive experience as a diplomat. "Lyle and I represent Harlan here. Stanley, you and Vickie represent the Peepul. Jimmy, you're the official disinterested witness."

Jimmy's eyes went wide. It was clear that Jimmy never thought of himself that way. He briefly nodded to Mark that he understood. Mark wondered if he had visions of trying to settle anything between these two groups.

Lyle took it again. "Stanley, you and your people did a real service for all of us, stopping that group of men. We know them as terrorists. You call them dust people. We agree they are not people either of us want here."

"Stopping the dust people is personal. They owe me. I'm happy it benefitted you, as well."

Lyle smiled agreeably. "Your tribe is also the source of the pork we're eating, and we like it. I'll offer you the river bottom to the downstream side of Harlan dam. That's more than your request. In addition, part of the town of Oxford is in Furnas County. A meat processing plant is in that part of the town. I'm offering you that, as well."

Stanley leaned back. "I'd have to split the tribe. I would get more than twice the area I now have for hunting. I would trade pork for beef or other items. In addition, you'd like us to resolve any stray dust people wandering through."

"That is the idea. In addition, your people can use the buildings on the Furnas side of Oxford for shelter. We'd require your people not to go beyond the Oxford town limits. Other than Oxford, you would stay in the area toward the river from the highway. You and your people would not interrupt anybody traveling the highway except if there are terrorists or dust people in the area."

Stanley nodded. "That's like the agreement we have with the people of McCook. The area and the facilities are beyond anything I could hope for. I am happy to accept your offer, sir."

"Jimmy," Lyle inquired, "did you follow what I offered? Did it make sense?"

Jimmy scratched his head. "I'm not familiar with the area, but it makes sense to me."

"The dam is south of Republican City, or Rep City. Oxford is on both sides of the Republican River. We have people where a bridge goes over the river. At that point, the river is also the county line."

After thinking about it, Jimmy nodded.

Mark perked up. Maybe he could contribute to the cause along with being able to put another notch in his coup stick. "There may be times that we need to cross the Republican River. We would need free passage if that happens."

Stanley showed no concern. "Anybody traveling on the highway goes through, unless they are dust people. In addition, we will alert you if we find any sign of dust people."

Lyle looked at Stanley and nodded. "I believe we have an agreement. Do you believe in shaking hands to seal an agreement?"

Both men stood up, and extended their hands to one another. Lyle then asked, "Would you break bread with us?"

Stanley hesitated but replied, "Certainly, Mr. Lillard. It would be my pleasure."

Vickie stood up and headed for the kitchen with Jimmy right behind. Lyle and Stanley both took their seats after they left. It didn't take long for dinner, such as it was. The supply of bacon and eggs was long gone, and the three men got the total remaining menu. It consisted of stew, skillet cornbread, and coffee. The food arrived in mismatched crockery, which, Mark reflected, went along with the place.

For all of his hesitation to stay in the public area any longer than required, Stanley quickly settled in. Lyle seemed fascinated with how Stanley related events. Never speaking in a monotone, he nonetheless stripped descriptions of all emotional content. Most people would dramatize the situation, so Stanley's approach made for a droll approach to the news. That didn't bother Mark. After all, everything Stanley said supported what Mark already reported.

Lyle guided Stanley, changing the subject whenever something piqued his interest. As it went on, the story line of Stanley was on led directly to subjects Mark vastly preferred stay buried. Mark got beyond uncomfortable and the more embarrassed he became, the harder Lyle pushed for information on the subject from Stanley.

Suddenly, Lyle slapped the table, exclaiming, "You're kidding!"

Stanley softly replied with a straight face, "It's true."

Lyle turned toward the kitchen, finally catching Jimmy's eye. "Come on out here, Jimmy. Just you."

Jimmy arrived while Lyle was still laughing. Mark was squirming in his chair and red in the face. Stanley leaned back with a bemused look, surveying Lyle, Mark, and now Jimmy, too. Stanley's nonreactive posture made Mark even more uncomfortable, and he realized his throat had become dry, too.

Lyle looked at Jimmy. "When Mark gave me his trip report, what he said sounded complete and comprehensive. It seems he left out a few details. It seems Mark and Ellen were the reasons Vickie wanted to have a romantic rendezvous with you."

"How's that?" Jimmy was mystified.

Lyle nodded to Stanley. "Tell him. He deserves to know."

Mark thought Stanley's story was awful the first time. The retelling was a hundred times worse. The trouble was that Mark couldn't detect a single change in what Stanley said.

"That morning, I saw Mark and Ellen at the stable. They were going to help chase Vickie. I saw, smelled, and felt the cloud of pheromones surrounding them. I told them that's what happened. I'd guess they are a few days less than nine months from being parents. I saw Dora, the housekeeper, later, and she described what happened. Vickie served Mark and Ellen at breakfast. Just getting close to them got her so worked up that she went out hunting for you."

Jimmy was aghast and turned toward Mark. "Knowing that, you two roared down the hill and stuck around to gawk while she had a knife to my throat. Did you want to watch me die badly?"

Mark wanted to be anywhere else right then. He had no reply.

Stanley shook his head. "She did not want to kill you. The knife play wasn't serious. If she intended to cut you, she would have done it long before she cornered you in that store. There was no way we could stop her from being with you."

"The knife play wasn't serious? It felt serious to me. I saw some of you while she massaged my throat with that blade. There were a number of looks but I didn't see anything like concern." Jimmy was a strange sight, nearly screaming while keeping his volume at a whisper to keep Vickie from hearing.

Lyle was the only innocent one in the room. He now looked at the participants in this little drama. Jimmy was the victim. Stanley took care of things the best he knew how.

Stanley continued. "Everyone knew you were starving there. Mark had the idea of establishing a stopping place here at Arapahoe. It seemed to be the best way to resolve a bad deal."

Mark glanced at Lyle, and saw he bought Stanley's story. There was nothing Mark could say in defense since it was true. Being a parent in nine months pushed it. Mark knew something else was a fact. Taking advantage of the situation just turned around and bit him in the butt. It was far worse than Ellen's attempt at a shivaree with Josh and Alicia.

Jimmy rose to the occasion. "I heard somebody describe what we had as a shotgun wedding. It seems to me that one of those was in order, but the couple should have been Mark and Ellen instead of Vickie and me."

Mark felt his face get redder, but didn't say anything.

"What do you think about this, Jimmy?" Lyle asked.

"It is nothing I could have imagined a week ago. This is better than anything I've seen in a long time. There's decent food available, where I used to spend all day trying to find anything. Keeping Vickie happy, satisfied, and healthy appeals to me right now."

Lyle looked at Jimmy with respect. "You could have played victim and walked away. Instead, you stood up like a man. You are making the most of the situation, and I admire that."

Mark didn't feel like a big man just then, and walking away suddenly looked good. The horizon's call just got a great deal more attractive and Ellen's charms suddenly seemed far less magnetic. Maybe the iron in him just turned to lead. Lyle forgave him when he tried to do the end run with the dark lady and the sniper team. For this, Lyle might send him on his way.

Lyle took a bite of cornbread and gazed out the window. Mark could only brace himself and wait for what came next. It was only a case of whether or not it would be with extreme prejudice. Should the criminal be executed with a sharp axe or a dull one?

Lyle finally turned to Mark, as though they were the only ones in the room. "You do a lot of things really well. Still, your impulse control seems nonexistent. If Stanley wasn't such a steady hand, it could have screwed things up big time. Do you understand what I'm saying?"

Mark understood too well. "Yes, sir."

However Lyle acted, Stanley was still there, impassive as a Buddha. At the same time, there wasn't a nuance or bead of sweat that he missed. Jimmy still stood there, looking as uncomfortable as Mark felt, shifting his weight from one leg to the other.

After a moment, Lyle continued. "I have no idea how you could make things right with Jimmy. Maybe that luck of yours will come to the rescue. Jimmy may someday decide you did him a favor. What you do for damage repair with me is another subject altogether."

That got Mark's attention. Could he repair this? Was it possible?

Lyle saw his reaction. "Our first concern is to make this place a going concern. I want both Stanley and Jimmy to know Harlan's intentions are good and our actions are substantive and timely. Mark, we'll go back to Harlan tomorrow. Gather up Kevin, the trainees, and your farm wagon. Have Ellen load all the produce and canned goods you can part with in your wagon. Then, have her to go to my place and we'll put more in. She should go to Ragan next, and Huntley if she needs to. She is to fill that wagon."

Mark blinked. "Yes, sir, I understand."

"While she gets the food, she will spread the word. Anyone coming to Arapahoe brings additional food and supplies. After getting all the food she can, construction materials are to load on top, because when you all get here, the construction materials will come off first."

Mark stared at Lyle. "Did you say construction materials?"

The look he got back was exasperation. "That's exactly what I said. You and your people will build a wall between the kitchen and their bedroom. Our hosts need privacy in their own house. I want the bunch of you back here the day after tomorrow, including the wagon full of supplies. While here, scour the town for beds and decent mattresses to fill all the rooms. "

This wasn't the coup de gras Mark was braced for. It wasn't anything he'd have volunteered for, either. "We can do that."

Mark could see Lyle planning as he talked. "You won't be the only one involved. Adeline told me several times about a group of ladies in Ragan who are talented with the old treadle sewing machines. We will bring them in the carriage, and the sewing machines they use will be in Don's wagons. They will make curtains for the guest rooms, and maybe for the front windows, as well."

All Mark could come up with was, "Okay."

The whole thing had thrown him into shock. Lyle was going crazy with this.

Lyle suddenly stopped with a loud harumph, and said, "I'll hunt down Don Rowley. That pressing business he mentioned is to prowl every place he turned into a personal warehouse. I don't begrudge him his retirement account, but we first have to figure out how to stay alive. His butt will be back here on that double-header of his, full of things to make this place function. If it makes a dent in his inventory, so be it."

Mark was licked his psychic wounds as he absorbed the situation. Jimmy just joined the Lyle Lillard fan club, and why not? Lyle was doing everything to make sure Jimmy and Vickie could survive in Arapahoe. Stanley nodded and headed out with his tribe.

Growing up in foster homes, Mark had two basic reactions to these situations. What he called chasing the horizon took another name when the authorities decided he failed once again to connect socially with the people. When he became old enough and got a high school diploma, he went into the Army. The Army didn't forsake him, but the country did, falling apart at home while he fought for it overseas.

His alternative to the horizon was to do something not identified in the punishment or torture. For Mark, this occasion meant corrals and wagon storage, plus a location for hay. He soon went into the service area to lay out corrals, leaving room for wagons and teams to pull in under cover. Another reason was to keep out of Lillard's sight. Maybe he could avoid additional punishment coming in the guise of projects invented on the fly.

In the service area, Mark's mind started clicking. He could see the biggest problem was securing the fencing, since they would have to punch holes through the concrete floor. Fence posts should be black iron pipe with the largest planks they could find between them. Horses were awfully hard on fences. It wasn't that horses purposely tried to destroy fences. It was just that when horses got into disagreements, trivialities like fences were hardly ever on their minds.

Ellen came back to haunt him. What if she was pregnant? It was all crazy. It was also a problem which defied resolution. Mark knew of any number of guys who left town when they had to deal with a girlfriend's pregnancy. He did have feelings for Ellen and there was nothing on the horizon to cure either a baby or a life he left behind.

Trying to think of himself as a father put his mind into a spin. He'd never thought of himself as the father type. Traipsing off after a whisp at the edge of the wild blue yonder, or anything else he thought he could do well, like tracking critters and bad guys, would not relieve him of any of the responsibility of having a family. Ellen wouldn't let him forget it, either, assuming Stanley had it right. If the man could smell Omega dust a long way off, the elements causing a pregnancy would be easy.

Sleeping by the front window, the first rays of the sun woke Mark. A night's sleep didn't change his mind about staying away from Lyle. Dressing amounted to pulling on his boots. Then it was the outhouse followed by the hand pump to get some water, which he splashed on his face and hands. Shaving would wait until he got home.

Lyle, the object of his avoidance strategy, approached the pump. Mark stuck around to work the handle and give his boss however much water he wanted. Lyle was no more enthused about cold water than Mark. A brisk feel to the air testified that all the unnatural warmth was draining away. They both hustled back to the Inn. Jimmy was in the kitchen. He had fired up the cook stove, coffee was starting to perk, and a pan of cornbread was ready to go into the oven.

Lyle glanced at Mark, "I believe it'll be warmer at the counter. Let's pull a couple of stools."

Mark's avoidance strategy was now out the window. He pulled a stool over next to Lyle at the counter. Coffee and stew presently appeared with a fresh pan of cornbread not far behind. It wasn't an inspirational way to break their fast, but it was hot and filling. Lyle didn't bring up yesterday's harangue, and Mark wouldn't volunteer the subject.

They saddled up and headed back toward Harlan. Mark long since ran out of small talk, and settled on not saying anything. As a way to keep him out of trouble, it sucked big time, and he knew it. Lyle finally looked at Mark.

"What are your intentions with Ellen?"

Mark was not about to share his current feelings. "I asked her to marry me. That is still my intention."

"Do you want to marry her sooner or later?"

"I want to get married sooner. The sooner the better, as far as I'm concerned."

"What does Ellen want?"

Whatever Mark said, he was putting words in Ellen's mouth. Saying he didn't have a clue would lead to questions about how serious they were. He couldn't think of anything to say that wouldn't display either ignorance or disinterest.

"She's terrified Alicia and Josh will ruin her day. Ellen even talked about having you come over whenever the mares foal, and have a brief ceremony in the barn. Ellen doesn't think they could ruin that."

Lyle's eyebrows rose. "Is that really what she wants?"

Mark gave up trying to invent words and intentions for Ellen. "Beats me, sir."

"Are we back to me being a 'sir' again? I thought we were beyond the military pseudo-polite stuff. I think you're still stewing over what I said yesterday. That's the deal, isn't it?"

Mark grimaced, but didn't reply.

Lyle nodded. "Let me ease your pain. As long as you don't quit me, I won't quit you. You are my ranch manager. On the other hand, you still have a lot to learn."

That sounded positive but might not be. What qualified as quitting? It could be coming up short on anything or for any reason. Maybe he should clear the air a bit.

"When the situation calls for a sir, I use it. I still wonder where I am. If I'm your ranch manager, why does Kevin report to you and give orders to me? Also, everyone in Harlan except me knew Ellen's agenda when she signed up as my housekeeper. That made me the brunt of a joke. Then, when I got close to her, everyone wanted to step on my head."

Lyle didn't reply for quite some time. He finally pinched the sides of his nose.

"Okay, your man Kevin got the wrong impression. We needed to know what you found out as soon as possible. I'll grant these new tasks aren't directly connected to ranch management. Maybe I'm grooming you for a larger role in Harlan."

That fit in with Ellen's comment the night of the wedding. "Yeah, Ellen told me I'm your designated successor. I find that hard to believe, especially now."

"What did you tell her when she said that?"

"I told her people say lots of things, and they're usually blowing hot air."

That got a nod of approval. "Did she believe you?"

"Not that I could tell. She already made up her mind, so mere facts no longer mattered."

"Some guys go through a lot of marriage without ever getting that point. You're off to a good start that way. That also goes for the other thing you were talking about. Your take on Ellen's situation is that you lose whatever you do."

"Yeah, that is pretty much it. What's the solution?"

Lyle favored Mark with a rueful shake of his head. "Discretion would be the usual advice. With your situation, that won't be either simple or easy."

Mark nodded. "There may not be a way to get there from here."

"If Ellen is in a family way, like Stanley thinks, you may be on a long and winding road, indeed."

Mark wanted to clear the air. His situation appeared just as murky as it was before he opened his mouth. Maybe he could get real information about something, anyway.

"I have to load the farm wagon. Then, I'm to bring Kevin along with the apprentices. One apprentice has to take care of the stock. Just to be certain, Kevin is to go?"

"Yes, Kevin goes. As for who stays, I'll leave that to you. Also, if you can locate guys who know construction, plumbing, electrical work, and any other trades, get them on board."

That was Lyle in operational mode. Mark liked working with him on that level. On the other hand, he had no real assurance that he'd be working with Lyle on any level whatsoever.

Meanwhile, Lyle added a postscript. "I'll round up Don Rowley. I'll have him look for people in the trades as well."

"When do you want me back in Arapahoe?"

"You have this afternoon. Your lady will collect supplies and you gather people. Take as many construction supplies as possible. You'd rather build corrals, but we need to get the interior of the place habitable first. That wall between the kitchen and their bedroom needs shelves on the kitchen side for a pantry. Take plenty of heavy-duty plastic to seal off the construction area. We don't want to eat stew with a gypsum flavor. Everyone heads for Arapahoe tomorrow morning," Lyle finished.

Chapter 12
Arapahoe Raid

There was no reason to put off what he could start right away, so Mark's search for talent started with the bridge guards, asking about people with construction experience. He was on the same page as Lyle in that regard, since his boss asked where Don Rowley might be. Lyle got a helpful reply, and was off to Alma. Mark went around Oxford, finally recruiting a couple of people.

Then Mark made a bee-line for the ranch. It came to him that Ellen had two aspects. One was a hard worker and eager lover. The other was a fomenter of and precursor to catastrophe. Recent examples showed her focus on giving pain. What happened with Jimmy and Vickie wasn't a conscious thing. Mark thought he cobbled together the instant marriage, but now thought he somehow got it from Ellen.

Mark concluded there was no way he could or would have come up with that silly ass scheme. He spent his whole life avoiding pain, not causing it. Okay, there was the military and terrorists. His life was falling into place until Ellen arrived into his life. Her agendas and manipulation went beyond the dark lady's wildest dreams. By the time he got to the house, he concluded Ellen was the real problem. What to do about it was beyond him.

Ellen came out as he rode in. She evidently expected him to jump off his horse and take her in his arms. Mark made no move to dismount, and Ellen stiffened and crossed her arms. Mark regarded her just as he thought Lyle would look at a subordinate who got away with too much for too long. In other words, like Lyle looked at Mark since Arapahoe.

"Mr. Lillard wants everybody to make Arapahoe a going concern."

"This smells like blow-back from something we did in McCook." It was not a question. "What did you tell him?"

"Everything he got from me, he learned before we left. You were there the whole time. Everything else he got from Stanley and Jimmy. When they were done, he didn't need to connect any dots. They brought out things I didn't even know. The worst part is that Mr. Lillard made me sit there through the whole thing."

"So it's Mr. Lillard now?"

"It's Mr. Lillard, sir. He gave both of us assignments. You need to hook up the wagon and load it with all the food we can spare. Then go to the Lillard place and Ragan. Get as much as you can. Pack carefully, since construction material needs to ride on top of all of it. Mr. Lillard says we have to head for Arapahoe first thing tomorrow."

"Am I the lady of the manor or the drudge?"

"You're the lady who will do it. I'm just relaying it from Mr. Lillard."

"You said it's Mr. Lillard, sir."

"That is exactly right. Now I need to spread some joy on Kevin's head."

Ellen glared at him. "Well, bully for Kevin. If you have any doubt, Mr. Tahner, we will discuss this further, and at great length."

Mark didn't respond. He touched the brim of his battered straw hat and headed out at a canter, not looking back. Mark was already working on Kevin's comeuppance. One thing was certain. Ellen could do her job or she would be out of a job. Playing lady of the manor might be more tenuous than she thought.

Mark had to give Kevin credit. He was working with the apprentices, and it appeared he was making substantial progress with both his new horse and the apprentices.

"Kevin, we need to talk right now."

"Okay. What's up?"

"All hands are going to Arapahoe, but somebody has to handle things here and at the ranch headquarters."

"That would be me."

Mark shook his head. "That person can be anybody but you or me. That is direct from Mr. Lillard. Which apprentice would be best for the job?"

"This wouldn't have anything to do with the message I relayed to you, would it?"

"It's the same story, but a new chapter. Now, choose somebody. How is your new horse progressing?"

"It's a work in progress. There's no way I'd ride it to Arapahoe. I liked the one you gave away. Why?"

"The new horse should get you to the ranch headquarters. You'll drive the farm wagon. It will be loaded with supplies and construction materials, as well as a pile of passengers. I want you there at first light tomorrow, bedroll in hand."

Kevin looked at Mark doubtfully, so Mark took it one step further. "As a matter of fact, grab your bedroll. You're coming now. We need to find people to help with construction. You know all the people from McCook. We need anyone and everyone."

Kevin and Mark found people in both Ragan and Huntley. Those without horses grabbed bedrolls, and started walking toward the ranch headquarters. Mark promised he would find everyone a ride.

At the ranch, Kevin went to the bunkhouse just as Ellen completed her rounds. She was not happy with having to load the wagon with food under the construction materials. She found everything they needed to get the job done, including the tools.

"Did you see Don Rowley?" she wanted to know.

"I didn't even smell him. That was Mr. Lillard's project."

Mark took advantage of being home to clean up and shave. It would be several days before he'd get the opportunity again. Ellen, meanwhile, showed him what was available at home, if he made the right choices. At the same time, she made it clear that until he made those right choices, she could be an ice queen.

Mark decided to ignore both the promises and the threats. Ellen did her assignment, so she had a job. That was all. The game play moved from the kitchen to the living room, and finally into the bedroom. Yes, Ellen had every intention of sleeping in the master's bed.

Mark blew out the kerosene lamp and climbed into bed, where Ellen waited, arms crossed and legs closed. He didn't look her direction or say anything. He lay on his side, facing away from her, and went to sleep. If he snored, Mark supposed he would hear all about it.

Waking during the night, Mark realized something. Ellen insisted on moving into Mark's room, and the next day, she could hardly tolerate either the room or him. Lyle subjecting him to a dose of reality helped Mark's focus a great deal. The absence of warm snuggly moments was not a good time, but since he was doing a job for Lyle Lillard, he could start the next day being well-rested.

It was before sunrise when Ellen singlehandedly put out breakfast for everyone. She had additional supplies for this occasion as well as for filling the wagon. Conversation between them was nonexistent. Each did their job, and silently took part in tasks best done by both of them. The lack of conversation caught the attention of several of those around the area, but nobody said anything.

They got underway soon after first light. The wagon went slowly and carefully since the wagon was full of breakable items as well as people. Mark rode double with a worker, and everyone else with a horse did the same. Kevin squeezed as many as he could on the seat of the farm wagon and sat astride the horse pulling the wagon. It was uncomfortable for everyone, but they got to Arapahoe early in the afternoon.

Mark knew he imagined it, but it sounded like the horses sighed in relief as they got rid of the unfamiliar loads. It wasn't until they got there and were unsaddling that Mark realized he hadn't seen Ellen the entire time. She must have ridden a bit behind. He took the lead, and didn't even know how many people he had. It seemed like a crowd but there were twelve. Still, that was nearly a tenth of the population of Harlan. Who knew how many more would show up?

Jimmy walked out, doing his impersonation of the good innkeeper. He even acted like he was happy to see them. "We got our first frost this morning. I'm glad it warmed up."

Mark just grunted in Jimmy's direction, and directed Kevin where to put the wagon. Everyone else began unloading. There was no time to waste. What would Mr. Lillard regard as quitting? Anyway, with Lyle and

Jimmy being each other's heroes, Mark couldn't afford to be anything other than focused.

Behind him, Mark heard Ellen taking care of the social angle. Maybe she thought there was some benefit from buttering up Jimmy.

"Yes, indeed, it made for a pretty nice ride," she said brightly.

Mark led the troops inside, plowing by Vickie in the kitchen. They immediately moved Jimmy's and Vickie's bed out into the main room. Then they hauled in rolls of clear plastic, and lumber and set to work, erecting a temporary wall just beyond the stove and tank. They even taped the plastic to the walls.

Mark was gratified how that put Jimmy off his game, not that it took much effort. Mark thought he should give Jimmy a bit of a heads up about what was coming.

"Jimmy, you'll need to cook a lot of food. The people you here are just the first part of what is coming. There will be another six or eight in the carriage. Don Rowley is coming, and will have additional people. I don't know how many."

"Okay, Mark. I'd better head into town to take care of that. There are a couple of restaurants that might have large pots."

"That is a good idea, Jimmy." Mark saw Ellen give him a hateful look, while maintaining her icy demeanor. With that, he made a concession to polite conversation. "Like you said, it is good we warmed up after that frost."

"Yeah, it's a little early, though. Don't you think?" Jimmy asked.

Mark remained focused on the task, but also noted Jimmy's actions. Before long, Jimmy drug back a large stock pot from the center of town. At the same time, the carriage pulled up, Don Rowley's regular driver had the reins. A local lady was on the seat with him, and four sat facing each other behind him. All talked non-stop. It didn't look like the driver enjoyed the experience.

"Where should I take these ladies?" was the driver's question, but Mark got the impression the driver had another term than 'ladies' in mind when he said it.

"Take them to the old motel," Jimmy told him. "Get yourself a room, too. We took the locks off the doors, so you can get in. Use the privacy lock inside the room."

Inside, his people were framing a wall. Vickie approved the arrival of the stock pot when Jimmy hauled it in. After cleaning it, Jimmy put the stock pot on a low stool, and helped Vickie pour the stew in it. Then they teamed up to get it onto the stove.

Just then, the ladies from the carriage stormed into the place and invaded the kitchen. Mark didn't know whether they came to help or just supervise and kibitz but it was suddenly one Jimmy and six bosses. Before long, Jimmy decided to fill the water tank and find more coffee pots. Mark hoped the ladies actually did something.

The sun was low in the sky when Mark noticed Jimmy pushing a wheelbarrow full of treasures toward the Inn. At the same time came a rumble from the other direction. It was Don Rowley coming in, and it sounded like a heavy load. Don's wife was beside him. Two guys were on the seat of the second wagon of the double-header, plus four more riding horseback.

Jimmy pushed his wheelbarrow up to Mark, wiping sweat off his brow. They both stared at the incoming traffic.

"There aren't be enough rooms for this mob, even using the motel. Some will have to stay in houses around here."

"I told you there would be a lot of people coming, Jimmy."

Jimmy shook his head. "When you Harlan people do something, it's not just halfway. I have to wonder why Mr. Lillard is doing all this. He said I did the decent thing. That doesn't connect to what I'm seeing here."

Mark nodded. "I've been asking myself the same thing. Lyle has made lots of right decisions. Those decisions have kept us alive and well. Usually, the reasons are clearer than this. Maybe he'll tell us sometime."

At that point, Mark thought being nice to somebody Lyle obviously liked might be a good thing. "By the way, I'm pretty impressed how well you took hold here."

"I'm not doing that well. At the moment, I see many buckets of water and arm loads of firewood in my future."

"If I see anybody between jobs, I'll send them to help you. Do you see anything on Rowley's wagons that you ordered? It is too dark to see clearly, but the shapes I see don't add up to anything I'd connect with upgrading this place."

"I'm amazed at what's already been done. Now, Mr. Rowley's brought a ton of stuff plus guys to take care of it. I only hope we've got enough food to feed everybody."

"There are supplies in the farm wagon. They'll come off the wagon after all the construction materials find a new home. Keep your chin up. If you can get through tonight, you'll be just fine. I'd better get back to work. Like I said, anybody sitting on their thumbs will be working for you."

"Thank you, sir. I really appreciate it."

Inside, the wall separating the bedroom and kitchen was fully framed, and they had drywall up on the kitchen side. To Mark's eye, the work showed a fair amount of skill. One of the guys with Don Rowley was checking on the situation, and asked Mark's crew not to drywall the bedroom side until he installed a few things. That stopped the project, and Mark's people began cleaning up.

Mark went back outside to look at the equine equivalent to Jimmy's sleeping room dilemma. Dealing with all the stock and wagons was not going to be easy. In the waning light, he had the apprentices and Kevin take the horses to the river for water and to graze. Mark only hoped Stanley's bunch would leave them alone. Horse meat in the stew would not do anything for making friends.

Inside, his guys had volunteered for some of the grunt work, getting water and wood. At the same time, the visiting ladies, now augmented by Mrs. Rowley and Ellen, took over cooking duties from Vickie. There were so many, they did a tag team operation. Ellen ignored Mark. Mrs. Rowley noticed it, but if she said anything, Mark didn't hear it.

The women did not stay in the old motel, but came back to the Inn and took the more private areas that would become guest rooms. The men spread bedrolls, becoming a wall-to-wall floor covering of people in the public area. Mark took his bedroll into the service area, hoping to find peace, quiet, and some protection from the weather. The prospect of waking up with frost on his face didn't impress him. Then again, if he had to hit the road, he'd get very familiar with it.

Mark had become accustomed to no more than a few people within a mile. Just having this mob nearby would have made it a very short, unsettling night. A considerable number followed Mark into the service bay. The result was a night filled with hacking, coughing, and mumbling. In addition, there was a cold wisp of wind every time somebody went to the outhouse. Mark didn't think anybody got a decent night's sleep out of the deal.

Trying to get some sleep, Mark's thoughts went back to Ellen. Was she pregnant? What was she telling the other women about him? Mark considered it a given she was giving many dirty details of how he was an ungrateful bastard. With her proclivity to spread hate and discontent, she would spread it on thick. Letting himself think about Ellen got him into all this trouble in the first place.

To get out of trouble, he needed to keep his focus on the project. It had to be a product that could not be criticized. His group already took care of what Lyle assigned. It seemed clear that Don was about to take it to a whole new dimension with no help from him at all.

What job could Mr. Lillard possibly groom him for? What did he say? Oh, yeah, he said a larger role. What did that mean in a group as small as Harlan? Lyle Lillard ran it. Don Rowley was the resident tycoon. Josh and Vince took care of security. Mark only got involved with the bicycle tracks because Josh wasn't available. Josh would have handled the lady and her ghosts far better than Mark did.

Harry Dover played a number of roles. He was at the same time, the super-villain, mad scientist, and weather forecaster. The only position with a help wanted sign was that of apprentice to Clay Williams, the farrier and blacksmith. Mark was in decent shape but couldn't imagine doing that on a full-time basis. Still, the farrier and blacksmith jobs were necessary. Maybe he could try it.

If Ellen was pregnant, Mark was responsible and would continue to be until the child was of age. Heading for the horizon would prove him every bit the louse she thought he was. If he didn't marry her, he was still responsible for the child unless somebody else stood up to do it. Who would that be? The only candidates were the three unattached Marine snipers.

Mark had no doubt the periods of sleep he got were as filled with mumbling and groans as anybody else there.

He awoke stiff, cramping, and a nasty taste in his mouth. In the main area, their host was getting after his kitchen duties. The ladies were back again, as well. Coffee was perking and pans were going into the oven. It was not possible to know the time of day from the food being served.

He was in no hurry for breakfast since it was more of the same. That persuaded Mark to take his morning constitutional through the frost to the outhouse. From there, he made a quick stop at the hand-pump for a splash of water. If personal hygiene went quickly the morning he tried unsuccessfully to avoid Lyle, it went double quick now. The effect of cold water with the temperature below freezing had to be experienced to be appreciated.

Back inside, the temperature was more to his taste. Stew, cornbread, and coffee were on the counter. Mark heard snide comments about breakfast being leftovers from dinner. Since there was no alternative, everyone took what was offered, ate for a few minutes, and picked up where they left off. With his guys done with their job, they now helped anywhere they could.

With nothing to do, Mark went outside. The strange cargo in Don's double-header turned out to be solar panels and other gadgets. Even with the frost, Don's people were hauling the solar panels onto the roof. A couple of other guys were inside, stringing low-voltage wire. Mark now realized the point to not finishing the walls.

Two of Don's people were at a well head next to the building. They stopped Jimmy, and asked how deep the well was. Jimmy told them the hand pump couldn't be more than fifty feet. They commented their pump was limited to no more than two hundred feet deep. Mark watched the two tag along with Jimmy to the hand pump. One worked the pump enough to fill a bucket. The idea was to verify the depth.

Later that morning, workers and cooks were on top of each other while lunch was being prepared. The solar panel guys were hooking up a control panel, and debating where to place batteries. Meanwhile, the two guys who were dealing with the well, wanted to pull the wellhead. Still others were debating layouts for things that Mark couldn't quite hear.

The well people then went to Mark, saying they needed people for a few minutes. Mark gathered most of his old crew and led them around to the wellhead. They soon had the pump out, and another guy came over to let them know the place was on a septic system after all. Mark got the impression this was a high-end operation, indeed.

Meanwhile, a high-efficiency wood burning stove arrived in the public area. There was no time to enjoy it because everyone was forming a line. The shelves on the outside of the bedroom wall were ready, and it was all hands on deck to bring in the cans and mason jars full of food.

Mark got in line. Jimmy was a couple of places in front of him. Inside, Vickie supervised the ladies, organizing everything. Ellen was with that group, and she studiously ignored Mark.

Jimmy and Vickie decided that having drywall only on the kitchen side was fine. Jimmy thought he could put storage places between the two by fours. Mark looked in Jimmy's bedroom just as an electrician flipped a switch. Mark thought it was astonishing as a light came on. The guy nodded, more to himself than to Mark, and turned the light off again. Mark got nervous. Everybody he brought now worked for Don Rowley, and he was standing around.

Teams hauled in refrigerators which ran on twelve volts and were super-insulated. Strange-looking round outlets were on the wall, where they already plugged in one of the refrigerators. He stopped to listen to it quietly humming. On the other side of the room, a trench in the floor ran under the wall. A pipe in the bottom of the trench was even now being connected to a faucet.

"Once we check for leaks, we'll hook a hose and run it outside until it runs clear and tastes good," one guy bragged. "After that, we'll attach everything so they can fill the tank. When everything is working as it should, we'll cover all this up. Does that sound right?"

Mark was astonished that somebody asked his opinion. Knowing nothing about plumbing, he found no fault with it. Jimmy wandered through then.

"What was this about a septic system?" Jimmy wanted to know.

Mark did know about that. "This was never on the city sewer, so the bathroom should work. The challenge is to get water everywhere. Even if we haul buckets of water to refill the toilet, it is better than going to the outhouse in the cold."

Jimmy shook his head in amazement. Just then, Vickie tapped on his shoulder. "Isn't this something?" she whispered in awe. "Could you make another trip and get a can opener? Who would have thought we'd ever need such a thing?"

"Yeah," Jimmy told her, "and refrigerators, too. There's even running water. I didn't know it at the time, but you coming after me was the best thing that's ever happened to me."

Vickie gave Jimmy a shy smile followed by a warm kiss that lingered longer than it might have. Jimmy grinned foolishly. "One can opener, coming up."

Mark found a sour taste in his mouth, and left the scene of domestic bliss. Outside, he helped unload bed frames. Everyone hurried since the temperature fell as fast as the sun. The afternoon storm clouds toward McCook looked more like snow. Mark made a mental note to put on his jacket the next time he got near his ditty bag.

The electricians declared the batteries sufficiently charged to turn on some lights. Everyone was still gawking at the miracle of light when the plumbers announced the bathroom was functional, too. A line formed at the bathroom door. The sound of the toilet flushing for the first time set off an exchange of excited grins and scattered applause. The door opened, and the next person went in with a bucket of water. The one coming out handed an empty bucket to the next in line, who headed for the kitchen faucet.

Jimmy returned, handing two can openers to Vickie who had cans lined up. The contents swiftly joined the amplified stew. The ladies joined everyone else in the dining room, taking bowls of stew with them.

After eating, they ceremoniously carried the honeymoon bed into a real bedroom. The two had been in a guest room during construction, and looked delighted.

Each worker now competed for the empty guest room. There was no grand prize winner. The price of a soft mattress was sleeping with several other bodies. There was an entire town full of beds, and no people. In spite of it, everyone was crammed together in a former farm implement dealership, called the Arapahoe Inn.

Mark might have claimed the room, but it would only have been if he was with Ellen. He didn't need to be with her. It was evident she decided Mark was not where she was going, either. At the moment, that suited him well enough. He went out to the service area and grabbed his bedroll. As he decided whether to sleep in the public area where it was warm, or in the service bay where it might be quiet, Kevin came up to him.

"Mr. Lillard gave me another message. He sent it by Don Rowley. Mr. Lillard wants both you and Ellen back in Harlan. There's cargo that had to wait, since it needs refrigeration. Also, anyone not needed here and without horses can go in the farm wagon."

Mark cocked his head. "I saw you and Don in the corner. I'm quite certain there's more to the message."

Kevin got nervous at that point. "Well, yeah, there is. Mr. Lillard said there was something he wanted me to do personally. The thing is, I'll need your horse and tack to do it."

"Mr. Lillard didn't say any horse. He specifically said my horse?"

"That's how the message went, Mark. I feel bad having to tell you anything like this. I really do."

A wave of resignation swept over Mark. It didn't matter what he'd done or failed to do. Lillard fired him and took the horse, as well.

Mark finally shrugged. "If that's what he said, that's how it will be."

Kevin licked his lips nervously. "Mr. Lillard said Ellen had to go too. I don't see her. Could you tell her?"

Kevin could relay his happy little messages all day, but that went over the line. Mark just looked at Kevin through narrowed eyes. "It's your message. You deliver it."

Kevin gulped, backed up a step, turned hurriedly, and returned to the public area. Mark knew any other contents of that message were not to him. Kevin was now the golden boy. This special project looked more like gopher work. Some places used unpaid interns for it in the old days.

As for sleeping in the public area with the warmth, the exchange with Kevin made the deciding vote. The chill factor from Ellen's cold shoulder made being in the same room just too much. Going back to Harlan on the farm wagon with her would be bad enough. Then again, since she still had a horse, he wouldn't even see her. How did Ellen figure into any of this? That puzzled him. Being with her was the problem, but they forced them together … sort of, anyway.

Enough guys slept in the service bay, they kept the door to the public area open. Mark laid out his bedroll. Things were simple. Mark wasn't in charge of anything. Was Ellen pregnant? It didn't matter. She wanted nothing to do with him. His moral debate of the previous night was over. Any baby would only be hers. It would never be his.

Half asleep, Mark went back to the possibility of working for Clay Williams, learning about the farrier and blacksmith trade. It would be hard work, but it would be mostly next to a furnace. Spending the winter next to a fire was not a bad thing. Maybe he could help Clay this winter and then chase the horizon. He still had alternatives.

Pieces began to fit together. Lillard decided to get rid of him before this fool's errand ever started. Mark should have known he was done when Lillard talked about not quitting. There was no way Lyle could quit Mark in the future, because he had already done it. Mark's last function was to haul supplies and workers. Lyle figured Don Rowley might need them. It was Don's deal the whole time.

It was a joke, and like Ellen signing on as housekeeper, Mark was too dim to know he was the brunt of it. Sure, Lyle was grooming him for a larger role. There was Harlan, and the larger world outside Harlan. His promotion was to that larger world. Even with the possibility that other survivors were out there somewhere, it became clear there was no place Mark would ever call his own.

He would eat and drink when he could. He would sleep whenever the opportunity arose. Whatever he saw and wherever he went, only he would know or care. When he died, it would be the pointless end to a futile existence. Mark Tahner survived so much to ultimately live and die for no reason. At least the terrorists, insane as they were, had what they considered a righteous cause.

Oddly, he slept fairly well that night.

Chapter 13
Reacting Badly

Waking, Mark saw Kevin checking the tack Mark had considered his own. Last night's reflections and this morning's reality looked the same. Mark shivered in the early morning chill, realizing it might be just cold reality. His bedroll and the clothes on his back were all he owned.

In the public area, Mark carefully stepped over and around sleeping forms. Just as he got to the counter, Jimmy wandered out of his room. The electricians put a light close to the stove, and Jimmy fumbled a bit before he found the switch. It wasn't long before the stove was hot, and coffee started to perk.

Lacking anything better to do, Mark asked Jimmy about the perking beverage. Jimmy told Mark a secret. They called it coffee. If they were lucky, the odd coffee bean might even be in it. Most of it came from roots, along with combinations of grain. Roasted and ground, there was no confusing it with the coffee of the old world, but it was hot and more or less filled the void.

Mark, Kevin and a couple other guys were at the counter when the first cups came out. Ellen wandered up, rubbing her eyes. Mark was at one end, so she went to the far end. Mark concentrated on the beverage in front of him. Jimmy reported the stew was hot but it would be a few minutes until the cornbread was done.

Ellen went into the kitchen, closely checking the refrigerators. She told Jimmy the units were marvelous. Her ability to sound perky one moment and spiteful the next was beyond belief. She also said they were going back for more stuff in Harlan, and would return the following day. Kevin delivered his message, bless his pointy little head. Her being there at all was the main indicator, of course.

The cornbread came out, and Kevin ate in a hurry. After muttering an excuse, he headed to the service area. Before long, the service door rattled open, and Kevin headed west at a good pace, ignoring the frost. The door came down quickly, most likely courtesy of the guys sleeping out there who didn't care for the gust of cold air.

The two guys at the counter were the only ones needing a ride. They were both trained to drive the wagon, and seemed excited to do it. Mark shrugged and told them to get it ready to go. Mark looked it over after they were done, and decided they could drive it. Mark found a place in the cargo box, and hung on as they bounced over the ramp going out. He didn't see Ellen and didn't expect to. The instructions were to present themselves at the Lillard place. They would not, of course, be together.

On the highway, Mark looked toward the Republican River bottom. He wondered if Stanley Peepul moved into his new realm. It was still a question whether Stanley's hunting parties inside the tree line made him feel more or less secure. Then again, it was no longer his concern.

Less than an hour out, Mark saw Ellen coming, and turned to sit with his back against the side of the wagon, concentrating on the view across the river. She passed the wagon behind Mark and said a few words to the guys driving. Her interest in Mark couldn't have been less if the wagon was hauling manure.

Later, he turned to look at the hills on the other side. In some places, the dirt bluffs were quite close to the road. Closer to Harlan, the high country disappeared. It wasn't long before the massive dirt bluff called the prow came into view and the road split. One followed the lowlands toward Holdrege, while his route took him to Oxford.

In the Furnas side of Oxford, Stanley already had his people at the meat packing facility. Some were crossing the road, and hurried to clear the road for the wagon. They were honoring that, at least.

Nobody knew what to think of Stanley's bunch being so close. Mark couldn't help them out, other than to tell them the tribe took out a group of terrorists because they didn't like their smell.

"What do they think of our smell? I remember how they smelled when they left here. Nobody cared for their odor, either."

"They don't smell that way now, do they? You aren't wearing one of their hog stickers, so that should tell you something. Like they say, be courteous to everyone and friendly to no one."

The two guys got off in Oxford, and Mark took over the wagon. His instructions were to report with Ellen. Neither knowing nor caring where she might be, he headed to the Lillard place.

"Where's Ellen?" Lyle wanted to know.

"I don't know, sir. She passed the wagon a short way out of Arapahoe. I haven't seen her since then."

Lyle considered that. "We'll figure it out. Right now, get over to Don's warehouse in Ragan. Your load is ready."

At the warehouse, he saw they had solar power, and inside, long lines of refrigerators hummed. Don's workers filled the wagon with ice chests. The foreman specified the ice chests were not to be opened until he got to Arapahoe.

Mark didn't know where to go then. He no longer had the ranch house, but there was the bunkhouse. It was more comfortable than the concrete floor at the Arapahoe Inn. It would put him near the wagon, and he could hit the road for Arapahoe first thing tomorrow.

An apprentice was doing chores when Mark got there. Ellen's horse was in the corral, answering one question. The apprentice took the horse and wagon, so Mark grabbed his bedroll and headed into the bunkhouse. The apprentice looked at him strangely, but didn't say anything.

Mark just nodded. "When you get done, you might as well head back to Wagon Ranch."

"I'll do that. Thanks," came the reply.

Toward sunset, there was a knock on the bunkhouse door. It was strange the apprentice was back, but when he opened the door, there was Ellen.

Her eyes were red. Whatever caused that, Ellen was now in full fight stance, her feet shoulder width apart and her hands tightly clasped into fists on her hips. "I thought we had something in common. What the hell happened? What did Lyle Lillard do to you?"

It was not cold, but the breeze felt like the middle of winter. At the same time, he felt incapable of laying the blame on her. Well, he could blame her, but there was no way to say that directly.

"I lost the ranch. I lost my horse. I lost you. End of story."

"What are you talking about?"

"Mr. Lillard put me in charge of all horses. Then he gave Kevin's horse to the McCook woman. This morning Kevin took my horse and tack. This special project in Arapahoe he supposedly gave me belonged to Don Rowley the whole time. I transported the grunt labor. What brings you out to speak to the has-been anyway?"

"The way you ignored me, I knew it was over. I moved out of the master bedroom. There was no action there. You can have it back, all to yourself. I promise not to bother you."

Mark shook his head. "You're waiting for somebody to occupy either the master bedroom or house. That would be Kevin. He took off toward McCook, so you'll have to wait a couple of days for the new boss. I'll be out of here before sun-up. My final job is to deliver a load of ice chests to Arapahoe. Somebody there can drive it back."

"You make it sound like you're not coming back."

Mark looked at her bleakly. "What would be the point?"

"What about our mutual interests and inclinations?"

"Those were the pheromones Stanley mentioned. For someone we thought a retard, he spoke about it both graphically and with clinical detachment."

A look of disappointment swept across Ellen's face. "What about my determination to be with you whatever and wherever you are. Don't you remember that?"

Mark found himself at another parting of the ways. This time, his choice didn't matter. After all was said and done, both roads led to hell. "I can't stop you. I advise against it. All I see is a meaningless life and a useless death."

Ellen shook her head and sighed. "You shouldn't start such a journey on an empty stomach. Dinner is ready. I don't deliver. There's a place at the table. I promise not to rape you if you don't provoke me. For that matter, I might not touch you or say anything if you prefer."

With that, she spun on her heel and headed off through the gloom toward the main house. It never failed. Every time his life choices were simplified and clear, something complicated it again. After a moment, he followed Ellen to the house. Inside, Mark did not look through the open bedroom door as Ellen marched into the kitchen. She pointed to the chair he usually occupied.

It was surreal, sitting where he always sat, in a house he'd come to consider his own. None of it was his. It had never been his, and would always belong to somebody else. He felt like a ghost. Then Ellen put food in front of him like he was quite substantial. She served it, placing the plates without getting close, and in absolute silence.

If this was back to that game they played with the dark lady, where the first to speak lost, Ellen won. Mark couldn't stand it any longer.

"What is the point of all this?"

Ellen turned and gave him a smug look and nodded. "I still matter to you. Whether you like it or not, I have an impact on you."

Mark had to agree. His eyebrows furrowed, he nodded slightly.

Ellen continued, "That's a good thing, because you still matter to me, damn it. Whether I like it or not, all of the weird things you do impact me."

Mark was now completely perplexed. If he wandered off to some fatal destination, was he was sentencing her to the same doom? That prospect was absolutely unacceptable, which only proved she was right in the first place. Ellen really did matter to him, whether he liked it or not; whether he wanted it or not.

Ellen turned her back, walking to a sideboard on the other side of the kitchen. At the same time, she left him to stew about what she said. She turned around with two desserts. One was for him. She sat opposite him at the table with the other.

"You thought this through. Where does it all go? Oh, the meal was delicious, by the way."

"Thank you for the compliment, and yes, I did think about it some more. Whatever one of us might do, both of us can do three times as much. If we try something smart, it can become something brilliant."

Mark got the drift. "If we do something off the wall, it can become a catastrophe. What does that say for tomorrow?"

"Tomorrow has to fend for itself. What happens tonight?"

Ellen was deadly serious. Mark just stared at her. After a moment, Ellen stamped her foot.

"You're a war hero and a horse trainer. What you've done would have killed twenty other men. In spite of that, you don't know your own mind.

I'll tell you how it will be. So you won't hate yourself in the morning, don't stay with me. Go sleep in the bunkhouse. The only personal items here are your Army backpack and rifle. I'll have them by the door. Be here for breakfast. Go now."

Mark was starting to visualize the night in Ellen's arms until she said that. Would he feel bad about that? That had been the case lately. Ellen would have things her way again. Mark shuffled out the door in defeat, and found his way to the bunkhouse. The little potbelly stove still had enough live coals for him to start it again quickly. That was more than he could say about Ellen. It was a thoroughly miserable and confusing night.

Mark, not knowing what to expect, knocked timidly on the front door. Ellen answered immediately and professionally. There was little conversation during breakfast, and that was about getting ready to go to Arapahoe. It was still dark when they were ready to go. His pack, bedroll, and weapon were beside the front door. He picked them up as they left.

It suited the situation, saddling and harnessing fresh horses in the dark and cold. Mark put his gear just behind the wagon seat, on top of the ice chests. They passed Oxford just as the sun was coming up. Mark might have gone faster, but in addition to telling him the ice chests had to remain closed, the guys at Don's warehouse also specified the contents were fragile. Keeping that in mind, he gave the load as smooth a ride as he could.

The guards at the bridge watched Peepul tribal members beyond the bridge. They knew Lillard gave permission, but it didn't make them less nervous. Not many saw the tribe leave Harlan and also survived the dust. Those who had, made everybody else aware of the situation. A few things Mark heard stretched the truth a long way. A couple comments were flat out fabrications. It sounded like standard war stories.

They made good time. Mark had nothing to say. Anything Ellen had to say would not be to him. They were almost in sight of Arapahoe when Mark became aware of riders coming. The turned out to be Lillard and his wife, Adeline. Lyle nodded to Mark as he came up beside the wagon.

Lyle was almost jovial. "What do you think of your cargo, Mark?"

Mark blinked. "I think I'm giving it the smoothest ride possible."

"Didn't you look at it?"

"No sir, the ice chests were to stay sealed for the run and I needed to handle it carefully. I followed their directions as best I could."

Lyle glanced into the wagon, and pursed his lips. "You've packed for a trip."

Mark didn't understand Lyle's cavalier attitude. "I have no reason to stay."

Lyle looked puzzled. Mark saw Ellen and Adeline both focus on the conversation. "What are you talking about? Don't you remember our conversation a few days ago?"

"Yes, sir, I remember it very well. You said as long as I didn't quit you, that you wouldn't quit me. As of yesterday morning, I neither had a horse, nor any say in the matter. Actually, that was the evening before. Kevin already does the training, and now he has the remuda. That leaves me with this one last task."

"And then?"

"Then I have no function, and makes me more of a burden to Harlan than that terrorist, or whatever he is, that we are holding as a prisoner. It is time to go."

Lyle looked disappointed. "I also talked about your poor impulse control. I did not see fit to share some things with you. There were other things I could have told you but didn't. For those, I'll apologize up front. Mark, you're making major decisions based on less than a tenth of the information you need. In any case, you still have the place you stayed last night."

Now that was funny. "You'd let me stay in the bunkhouse. It might get crowded sometimes, but I appreciate that."

Lyle looked astounded. "You stayed in the bunkhouse? Where was Ellen?"

"I wasn't in the house. You'll have to ask her or go check yourself. It is your ranch."

Lyle and Adeline looked at Ellen, who returned a steady gaze. Lyle turned back to Mark. "I thought there was more to the chill than the temperature. It's also more than the icy reception we got a minute ago. Mark, you think you no longer work for me. I disagree, but could you do me a personal favor?"

Mark cocked his head slightly. "It depends on the favor."

Mark wondered if Lyle would take offense at that comment, but Lyle accepted it at face value. "The favor I'm asking is to curb your impulses for a day or so. We have something planned. Once you have seen what it is, maybe you'll have enough information to decide what you want to do."

Ellen tied her fate to his. He couldn't rush when it added the burden of her death to his own. For that matter, he had no idea whether Ellen would make good on what she said. He glanced at Ellen, whose steady gaze rested on him. He could not read her face or the situation.

"I can do that," Mark finally said in a monotone. "I will put off doing anything for a day or two."

Lyle nodded. "Is it much farther to Arapahoe?"

"We're almost there." A slim column of smoke rose into the sky. "That is the Inn."

After a few minutes, Lyle looked back over at Mark.

"You know, Mark, I spent most of my military time as a low-level enlisted. Soldiers do things to keep their butts from undue aggravation. Not all those reactions are useful when you are in a position needing a level of responsibility."

Mark stared at Lyle. "I don't know what you're talking about. I have no authority, and trying to levy responsibility when there is no authority is bogus."

"That is true. Let me use an example. There's that woman, Sammie Moore. Stanley calls her the dark lady. Think about your conclusions and their factual bases. Compare that to how Ms. Moore conducts herself. You were so exasperated with her actions that you confronted her about it. You even related it to me in detail."

Ellen, Adeline, and Lyle all looked at him the same way.

Lyle spoke again, "I don't expect an answer right now. You said you'd cool your rockets for a day or so, and I will take your word for it. Still, think about this while everything else is going on. As a matter of fact, I don't want an answer at all. You need the answer. Be accountable to the face in the mirror."

Lyle let it drop then. The Arapahoe Inn slowly grew closer. People were outside working. The great project Mark was supposed to run was doing fine without him. In fact, neither the work nor the people doing it had missed him at all.

Mark carefully backed the wagon to the door. He wouldn't take a chance on breaking whatever he'd been hauling this late in the game. A line formed to unload the containers. Mark pulled his personal gear up on the seat with him while keeping a foot on the brake and control over the horse. The load disappeared far more rapidly than it loaded, and Mark still had no idea what he brought. It must have been good, the way everybody talked about it.

Pulling the empty wagon around to the side, Mark was astonished. Corrals were in place. He had a close and personal acquaintance with the work that went into planting posts like those. Where did they find the manpower? The changes continued as he drove into the building. A large water tank now perched above the public area. Pipes led to stock tanks. Getting it up there took an enormous effort. However they did it, there was running water for animals as well as humans.

The solution for the manpower appeared. Stanley's tribe had pitched in. Just then, a couple of tribal members told Mark they'd take care of the wagon and horses. Mark shook his head in wonder, climbed down, and handed them the reins. After grabbing his gear, Mark watched them. The two knew what they were doing.

Inside, Mark saw Jimmy and Lyle. Lyle looked pleased with himself, saying, "I believe you'll like what's in the refrigerators. Since you got into cooking, you'll have to expand your repertoire. Breakfast will no longer be what you had for dinner the night before. I don't know if I should say any more. What do you think, Adeline?"

"Tell him what we brought, dear," she replied. "There's no way for him to get near the refrigerators with everybody gawking right now."

"You're right, as always." Turning back to Jimmy, "There's a good supply of eggs, milk, and white flour. People can have pancakes, if they want. That's not the whole reason why we came, but we'll keep a little back for later." Lyle turned back to Adeline with a chuckle.

Mark considered it was a worthwhile load, and his job was done. He promised to cool his rockets, using Mr. Lillard's quaint term. He looked at the mob in the public area. Members of the Peepul tribe were a large part. They were in small clumps, but their presence really struck Mark. The guards in Oxford would really go crazy.

Everyone was covered in sweat-soaked dust. The eau de working man was obviously from punching the post holes for the corrals out back.

Breaking a sweat together created a feeling of fraternity. Mark identified that feeling from his time in the Army.

Then, Mark saw Ellen drag Lyle and Adeline off to a corner. She was making a point. In fact, she was making an emphatic point. It was too quiet for him to hear. It made him flash back to Jimmy screaming almost silently as he found out the details about Vickie coming after him.

Lyle and Adeline both disagreed with whatever she said, and tried to calm her down. It wasn't working. If they succeeded, Mark would have felt obligated to find out how they did it. It felt like Lyle and Adeline were on his side at the moment. The tableau was interrupted by Jimmy announcing lunch was available. Everyone knew the menu, and stood aside to let the tribal members get their stew, cornbread, and coffee.

Mark was in no rush. The only reason he was still there was because Lyle asked and he promised. Lyle, Adeline, and Ellen were still in the corner. They didn't look at him, but he felt their focus on him. He felt extremely uncomfortable and moved away from the direct laser focus of Ellen's weaponry.

Before long, there were bowls of stew on the counter, and no takers. He wandered over and got one. Among other things, having it gave him an excuse to haul it out of the public area. He sat on the floor in the service area, with his back against the wall, not far from where he slept the last night he was there. He became conscious of somebody standing there, and wasn't surprised it was Ellen. She wasn't by herself. Lyle and Adeline were right behind her. He lost what little appetite he had, put the food aside and stood up.

"I want to break off our engagement," Ellen spat at Mark. She glanced over her shoulder at her two companions. "I want to, but Adeline and Lyle insist I shouldn't."

Mark felt they'd just had this same conversation, except now their positions were reversed. If nothing else, she was now going in a direction that would keep him from being the cause of her death. That was a relief, of sorts.

"I couldn't argue with you before. I won't argue with you now. I can't stop you from following me. I wouldn't make you go with me."

Mark felt an involuntary tear in the corner of his right eye. Along with being a relief, it was also the worst damn news in the world. He looked at Lyle. "Is this what I needed to know?"

Lyle shook his head sadly. "You need to know. However, this isn't the information I talked about. This is nearly the opposite of what we expected to deal with. Our planning, such as it was, dealt with how we could keep you two separated by any means necessary, including whips and pry bars."

Mark shook his head. "When Miss Ellen Markley makes up her mind, whips have no impact. There's no pry bar big enough to make her change course. The only course is to do whatever the hell she wants and try to be happy with the outcome."

Ellen stared at Mark. "It sounds like you're on my side."

Mark shook his head. "I'm cooling my rockets for a day or so, at Mr. Lillard's request, trying to get information for an intelligent decision. Hopefully, I can make a decision that matters."

Adeline smiled. "Mark, in horse training, you know the objective is to get the horse using the thinking side of its brain instead of just react. Well, you're on the thinking side of your brain. I have to congratulate you. Now stay there."

Lyle and Adeline went back into the Inn, leaving Mark and Ellen facing each other.

"Did you mean what you said? Was that a real tear?" she asked him.

"I meant every word. Yes, it was real."

Mark didn't want her see any more, so he turned around and picked up his dishes. It was too bad he couldn't show proper gratitude for the meal. At least he could leave the place clean.

Returning his cup and bowl to the counter, he saw that Vickie was showing Jimmy all their new treasures. Mark tried to absorb all of the transformation, both of the building and the people running it. Jimmy seemed hugely changed. An example occurred just then. Jimmy seemed to hear an inaudible call to action, and headed past Mark.

"With all of the people, we use a lot more wood," Jimmy told Mark as he went by. "Larger pieces for the high-efficiency stove. We're going through piles of split wood for the cook stove. The wood pile shrinks at one hell of a rate."

Mark decided that cooling his rockets didn't require him to be a drone. "Why don't I help you?"

The two of them headed to the back of the building, and gathered saws, axes, and splitting wedges. The question of where to find wood was not trivial. The river bottom was Stanley's hunting ground. The next place was anywhere and everywhere else for branches downed by storms. They drug some back to the Inn.

That was when Mark realized Josh was back, strolling around the corner with Lyle. Mark kept with Jimmy as they drug the wood around the building. Jimmy set up to start sawing, but the blisters on his hands made him have second thoughts about the project, and Jimmy went back inside. Mark thought about the difference between good intentions and meaningful results, and started chunking the pieces of wood. It was nothing new. He split piles of it in Harlan and was hardened to that kind of work. Maybe he could feel like he was earning his keep.

Attempting to work for his supper didn't last long. Mark was barely warmed up with the wood cutting when Lyle and Josh showed up.

"Mark, I sent you here on a job. Josh and I are looking at all of it. You should join us."

Nothing other than the wall inside had anything to do with him. Still, he promised to be getting facts. That appeared to mean that if Lyle wanted him someplace, he should go.

Inside, Jimmy was between the group of ladies who had taken over the kitchen and a new career as wood cutter, even while the blisters on his hands disagreed.

"Hey, Jimmy," Lyle commented, "are you still doing okay with Vickie and living here?"

Jimmy looked around. "Are you kidding? Everything is better than I could imagine. Yesterday, I tried to help with the corrals, and got a bunch of blisters and a sore back. Vickie put me on limited labor today. I only hope she's happy and satisfied. I still have to figure out how to get enough firewood."

Lyle nodded. "Mark and Don did everything I asked. They did more than I asked. We'll soon start keeping horses here. That way, if we need to get messages to McCook, we can do an express ride."

Jimmy looked concerned. "I remember you talking about that. I don't know much about horses, so somebody else will have to take care of the saddles and stuff. I could check the water and feed, though."

"Stanley said his people can handle that end. By the way, did any of the McCook people come through?"

"No, sir, and it's just as well. With so many people from Harlan, I couldn't have handled McCook as well."

"I'm glad to know that. I'll catch you guys later," Lyle said, and he walked off.

Jimmy looked at Josh and Mark. "Mark, thanks for helping me bring wood up. Mr. Lillard said there was another reason he came. I can't complain about all the surprises, but do you know what he was talking about? This question about McCook sounds like it might be connected."

Josh and Mark looked at each other. "I never heard anything," Josh said, shaking his head. "Lyle made no bones about it when he sent Kevin to fetch us. We never saw the folks at the castle. Lyle didn't ask me about anything, either. Did you hear anything, Mark?"

"Nope, nothing at all." Mark was about to launch a pity party for himself, but squelched it. Another way to get the same place occurred to him. "Say, Josh, I seem to have a little extra time. Do you need any extra help on your border patrol?"

Josh shook his head. "We've always been a team, Mark. I see Lyle's conferring with Kevin again. Whatever's going on, I'd rather get my horses from you than from Kevin. That's in case you needed a vote. I have to find Alicia. I'll catch you later."

Now, Lyle was coming back over to Mark and Jimmy. He was looking at Jimmy.

"Getting wood is a challenge," Lyle observed.

"Yeah, it is sure getting to be one."

"Wouldn't it be easier to get your wood from the river bottom?"

"I don't want to mess with Stanley's hunting area."

Stanley joined their group then. "If my people aren't hauling pigs out of the woods, they could bring wood for your pile."

"That would be great, Stanley," Jimmy answered.

"What I'm thinking, Jimmy," Lyle continued, with a nod of thanks to Stanley, "is when Harlan people come, they could bring wood as well as food. Would that help you out?"

"Yes, sir, it certainly would. Thank you so much."

Lyle then peeled Mark off to the side. "Walk with me." He phrased it like a request, but the voice was all command. They headed for a less public area where Adeline had Ellen corralled.

"Both of you need to be at breakfast tomorrow. You not only need to be there, you need to hang around. Don't wander off. As you heard, Mark, we've got the wood chopping covered."

"This evidently connects with the information you say I need to know. Would you give any hint about the content?"

"This is all you get until tomorrow."

Ellen decided defiance was in order, glaring at the people Mark now considered his former employers. "I do not do command performances," she said under her breath.

Adeline stepped forward and patted Ellen's hand. "You'll do this little thing, won't you dear?"

Ellen stomped off somewhere, and Mark wondered whether she was going to have to find someplace else to work. Then he thought he'd better catch up with his personal possessions. The most important item was his bedroll. It turned out Jimmy stashed them behind the counter.

Chapter 14
Sentenced to Marriage

Tribal members entering the Inn woke Mark before daylight. Lyle didn't hint what information Mark needed to have. That meant anything out of the ordinary needed attention. The sight of Peepul in the public area certainly qualified as out of the ordinary. Inside, Lyle and Adeline directed the Peepul in rearranging the tables and chairs, with particular attention to those closest to the counter. Mark scratched his head, and went back to get his bedroll.

Being early got Mark a short line for the bathroom. There was no hot water. Still, not having to trek out into the cold air and a pipe full of water felt like luxury. That was information he should consider. Leaving Harlan meant leaving comforts and luxuries like these. It was strange how people used to think of them as essential services.

His hygiene done, Mark saw Ellen. She took wood-burning stoves and no electricity in stride. If he left and she followed, how would she handle sleeping under the stars and waking up with frost on her nose? She kept her distance, and from what she said yesterday, following him was not going to happen anyway.

Mark would have let others go first. For that matter, he would have cheerfully skipped the whole breakfast event if it meant he could avoid Ellen. That didn't happen. Lyle and Adeline pushed Ellen into line first, and Mark right after her. Then came Alicia and Josh, which increased Mark's concern. For what it was worth, Adeline and Lyle were next.

The ladies from Harlan did all the cooking. Lyle beckoned Vickie and Jimmy from behind the counter and into line just after Alicia and Josh, but ahead of Adeline and Lyle. Mark couldn't imagine what it meant and didn't have time to think about it since they were already at the counter.

The ladies cooked the eggs for Ellen and Mark at the same time. Then, Adeline directed them to the center table where the only chairs faced the counter. That made them the centerpiece of the meal. Ellen glanced at him as they moved sat down. It was clear that she didn't care for the arrangement either.

Mark's stomach was knotted up. Several people made it clear that cold eggs would not be tolerated, so he ate them. He noticed Ellen spent more time stirring her eggs than putting anything in her mouth. Then it occurred to him this might be the last hot meal he'd ever see. With that, he decided to savor every bite. Who knew how long the memory of this meal would have to last?

Even with him eating slowly and Ellen playing with her food, both were done long before the last of the people in line were served. One of the ladies made the rounds with a coffee pot, ensuring nobody had an empty cup, or even a half-empty one. Another lady came around and picked up their plates. There was nothing to do but stare at his coffee and feel the tension in his body rise to unbearable levels.

The last person finally got through the line, and the ladies doing the cooking brought their breakfasts at almost the same time. Lyle waited a few moments and then got up and walked over to the counter.

He pounded on the metal counter with his fist and turned to the room. "Your attention, everyone," he announced loudly.

Okay, Mark thought, this was the main attraction. Lillard did well as the ring master. That made Mark one of the lesser clowns. He'd have been more comfortable behind a thick layer of grease paint.

Lyle began, "After the dust and the rain, I had the vain notion to remake society so everybody could just get along. Our friends in the Peepul tribe challenged that before the dust even came. Afterward, the terrorists showed up, saying the only way we could get along was if we were dead."

That bought a few chuckles around the room. That wasn't news, so Mark waited for Lyle to say something he could use.

"I still harbor the happy fantasy that we can tone down the hate and discontent," Lyle continued. "To reduce some of the major situations we need to reinstate a few lesser evils. One will be personnel rules, for lack of a more polite term. These are not Harlan rules. These are my rules. Don Rowley has his own rules. Those of you working for him know what those are."

Everyone knew Don was a micromanager of the first water. Lyle's comment drew a few more chuckles, and some of the laughter sounded a bit nervous. At the same time, he relaxed a bit, even as he wondered where Lyle was going and why he chose to bring it up now.

Lyle leaned against the counter in an apparently casual fashion, glancing at Adeline before continuing. "I hoped what I'm about to say is obvious, but recent events prove that's not the case. If you do your job as well as you know how, we'll be fine. That's even if everybody doesn't have the same approach. The first Lyle Lillard personnel rule is this: If I fire someone, I will do it in person. The person I fire will have no doubt. They won't have to rely on rumor, innuendo, perceived snubs, or esoteric vibrations through the grapevine."

Lyle swept his gaze around the room with no more attention in Mark's direction than any other. Ellen looked at Mark very hard. Lyle made that point, and Mark got it loud and clear. Lyle certainly didn't stutter when he said it. Still, what Lyle said might not be the case all the time. Lyle might unconsciously contradict his official policy.

There was stated policy and there was business practice. If actual conduct followed official policy now and then, that was good enough for the owners and managers. If a peon transgressed official or unofficial policy in the slightest, it was too bad. It didn't matter whether the peon even knew the policy existed.

Lyle interrupted Mark's reflections after a pregnant pause. "The only way you will know whether this is real or me just blowing hot air is when things happen how I described. More than that, they have to happen that way all the time."

It was as though Lyle was reading his thoughts just then. Still, there were a lot of pieces to the puzzle, and none of them fit.

Lyle took a breath while Mark tried to figure out where all this was going. He went back to the circus analogy. Lyle was ringmaster and Mark was the clown. Ellen had a strange feral look about her. Mark now had a vision of the clown in the cage with the lion. That didn't seem funny.

Lyle suddenly clapped his hands, interrupting his flight of fantasy and circus of horror.

"That is not what I came up here to do," Lyle then said. "In fact, my plan changed quite a lot since yesterday."

He looked at Adeline, and sighed. Then he looked at the adjoining table. "Josh and Alicia, could you come up here with me, please?" They were surprised, but stood beside Lyle.

Lyle changed his gaze. "Jimmy and Vickie, could you stand with me as well?" They nervously went up beside Josh and Alicia. Both couples looked at each other. Mark saw Josh raise his eyebrows questioningly. Jimmy mouthed, "I have no idea."

Lyle continued, "The Omega dust will be a raw memory for a long time. It cleared away most of mankind. The endless rain cleared away the dust. We knew survivors were on the elevator in Alma before the rain, but couldn't get to them. When the rain quit, we raised a rescue party."

Looking at Josh and Alicia, Lyle shook his head apologetically. "Somebody thought we should roust Josh and Alicia, so they could join the party. They were not ready for our arrival, and particularly not ready for the noisemakers carried for the occasion. While Adeline and I were there, we were no more ready for the wake-up call than Josh and Alicia."

There were whoops around the room. Mark swallowed. This could mean a nasty time, but it was common knowledge. Ellen stared at Josh and Alicia. At the same time, Mark realized Lyle and Adeline Lillard did everything possible to keep him together with Ellen the last several days. Was this part of that? It was an awfully strange way to go about it.

"Later," Lyle continued, "when they tied the knot, somebody wanted them to have a memorable wedding night. It was certainly memorable, but nothing like what anyone thought would happen."

Now, Josh and Alicia stared right back at Mark and Ellen. Mark squirmed. Ellen looked like she wanted to be anywhere else.

Lyle continued, "At the wedding ceremony, I commented that Josh and Alicia were already married, and it was our task as a community to accept that fact. The statement seemed in keeping with the situation.

However, some have stretched that statement far beyond what I talked about."

Until then, everything pointed at Ellen. Mark felt he should do or say something to defend Ellen. With that last sentence, however, Mark felt the implicit accusation switching back to him. There was no defense for what he did, so he cringed, waiting for the axe to fall.

"More recently was another event. Some here did more than just witness it. This time, somebody expanded my statement to include the idea that a couple having carnal knowledge of each another should be considered married."

Jimmy looked nervous, while Vickie didn't react. Mark felt Lyle's spotlight on him. The blow was coming, and it sounded like he intended to make it as painful as possible.

"So," Lyle went on, "we have had two weddings. The first included acceptance of an ongoing relationship. The second was motivated by convenience and opportunity. Beyond that, the two who took advantage of the situation caused the second situation."

Lyle nodded almost imperceptibly toward the side of the room. Mark saw Kevin slide quietly out to the corral. Every eye in the room was now focused on him, making Mark too nervous to imagine what the mission might be. He only wished he were doing it instead.

Lyle now looked and pointed at Mark and Ellen. "Fun and games are over. I'm talking about you two. Now it is time for you to stand up and be counted, one way or the other."

Mark braced his hands on the table, about to get up, but Ellen's hand slammed his forearm, keeping him down. He looked at her, but she was glaring at Lyle.

"It was never fun and games, Mr. Lillard," Ellen said quietly. "You turned this into a courtroom and made yourself both prosecutor and judge. For all I know, you are the executioner, as well."

Mark agreed with that. It sure felt that way to him, even though Ellen saying something he agreed with scared him. Look at what happened before when they agreed. They did what Lyle was talking about right now.

Lyle shook his head. "I'm making observations. Any trials are in your mind. My intention in coming out here was to join two young lovers in matrimony. Instead, Mark thinks he needs to head for the hills. Ellen hasn't decided whether make Mark's life a living hell by being with him, or make him suffer more by not being near him. Her slamming his arm onto the table a moment ago was as intimate as they've been lately."

Ellen's hand suddenly withdrew from Mark's arm. Mark shivered when she did that. He was surprised at how good her hand felt. Still, Lyle's observations needed a response.

"You told me to get information and not jump to conclusions. Just before you invited us to join the happy couples standing beside you, Kevin embarked on another mission at your nod. Whatever you're doing will happen whatever Ellen or I say or do. Am I reacting again?"

Lyle smiled slightly. "When I announced the purpose of our little get-together, you didn't scream and run. It appears you're thinking. As for your comment about this being predetermined, it started that way." Lyle paused and took a breath. "For now, let's just say the situation is provisional. Whether you stand up is beside the point. The only fun and games going on are between you two, and that has to stop. As for the courtroom drama, there are issues of simple justice to discuss."

Mark thought it was a good thing Ellen wasn't a viper. Her response came out as pure venom. "What issues of simple justice? We've done nothing wrong."

Lyle favored Ellen with a sad smile. Mark reflected on the advice about thinking instead of simply reacting.

"Does nothing wrong include personal entertainment at the expense of others?" Lyle inquired. "Rousting Josh and Alicia had its moment. Saving the two guys on the Alma grain elevator was our mission, and knocking on Alicia's front door would have been faster. The shivaree didn't work. They didn't do it much in the old days. Josh and Alicia's reaction should tell you why. It also makes them feel justified in getting back at you, and you never know when it's coming, or what form it will take."

Alicia looked at Ellen. Mark couldn't remember such an evil glare. "Remember that, Ellen. I will get you, and it will be memorable, too."

Lyle nodded. "Just keep it between you, and don't get carried away with it. With our small population, and the scarcity of couples of child-bearing age, anything that reduces the number of such couples is unacceptable. All of you do realize that humans are now an endangered species."

That got a snort from Josh. "Mark, you old stallion, I just realized the new career that Lyle has for you. He's putting you out to stud."

There were snickers, much to Mark's dismay. Ellen growled, "I am no damned brood mare."

Her comment resulted in guffaws. Lyle raised his hands to get quiet.

"Mark, you're the ranch manager. I said that as long as you didn't quit me, I wouldn't quit you. It looks like you did just that. This is not the time or place to discuss what you may be in the future. Ellen, I heard how you forced Mark to propose. I also heard about the nights that Alex stayed with you. You were so prim and proper on one hand, and Mark was so frustrated on the other. Alex told me he was certain neither of you had propriety on your minds."

That drew some chuckles around the room.

Lyle looked at Jimmy and Vickie and then turned back to Mark and Ellen. "Ellen, Mark said, you contemplated me dropping by the ranch while your mares were foaling, to say some magic words and declare you two married. That would have been long after the two of you took up cohabitation as a way of life. The fact that you were only ones on the ranch made the rounds, and was the talk of Harlan."

That occurred to Mark, but he never looked at it like that. At the beginning, Kevin and Conrad lived in the house. When Conrad went to the feed lot and Kevin moved into the bunkhouse, there wasn't much reaction. There was a lot of reaction after Kevin left and Alex went home. Was this as a public shaming of him and Ellen? Mark recalled reading that was far more common than the shivaree.

Lyle seemed to specify they should stay. This public shaming, if that's what it was, meant the man was serious about them staying in Harlan. Otherwise, Mark thought, he'd have just thrown them out, like he did with Willy.

"The loose talk was nothing but rumors," Lyle continued. "Then at the barbecue after we got rid of the last vial of Omega bugs. Mark and Ellen became a couple and the subject of speculation again. I sent them to McCook to collect information. They found out a few things, but also caused disruption."

Lyle looked at Jimmy. "Stanley described the events leading up to your marriage to Vickie. Should that be how we conduct nuptials?"

Jimmy nearly choked. "I didn't want it for myself. I wouldn't want to even hear about such a thing."

"Still, you don't mind the outcome."

"That was only because Vickie and I figured out how we could be together. My problem with it was how, when Vickie and I were in the store, we were surrounded by a bunch of uninvited folks gawking at us. Maybe some people like being stared at like that. I don't even want to know such a person."

Lyle managed a leer. "What about taking down the curtains in one of the guest rooms? Then, we would keep Mark and Ellen in there until they give us a performance. That's what they did to you."

Mark glanced at Ellen, horrified. She returned the look. Then they both looked back at Lyle and Jimmy.

Jimmy shook his head emphatically. "No, I meant it. If you did that, I'd leave. All of the comfort here would not be worth it."

Jimmy glanced nervously at Mark and Ellen, and then back at Lyle. "As a matter of simple justice, they deserve it. In spite of that, it's not how we should go. Everybody would run around trying to get back at others."

Lyle grinned and nodded. "You're a man after my own heart, Jimmy."

He turned to Josh and Alicia. "Jimmy doesn't want to go along with my suggestion."

Alicia snorted, "I didn't know the way to Jimmy's heart was with a switchblade and the promise to have his liver for lunch. It might have made life far less painful for me. I'm glad I held out for Josh. I was there. It was the grossest form of entertainment imaginable. I plan retribution for what Ellen did, but not even she deserves that."

Mark glanced at Ellen, who still stared at Alicia. Emotions flashed across her face. He saw immense relief along with a little thankfulness, immediately followed by worry about what Alicia might have in mind.

Lyle looked at Adeline. They locked gazes and Lyle finally nodded. Mark got the impression of psychic communication between them. Lyle scanned the room, finally returning to Mark and Ellen.

"Ellen, you said this felt like a court of law. I disagreed, but this went like a hearing. The people you hurt don't want to push the issue. That leaves me to uphold the welfare of Harlan. Looking at the two of you, 'happily married' is the first oxymoron after Omega. However, for the sake of Harlan, I sentence you to live as man and wife for the rest of your natural lives. May God have mercy on all of us. Mark, you can kiss the bride, or she can scratch your eyes out."

Mark couldn't believe what happened. He didn't try to kiss Ellen, the declared bride. He suddenly realized that he might have gotten away with it since Ellen appeared to be in shock. As it was, no presumptuous groom got their eyes scratched out.

Lyle looked at them. "Mark, when I asked your intentions, you said you wanted to marry Ellen, sooner rather than later. Ellen, you wanted to avoid a shivaree. You both got your wishes. In addition, you're still working for me. That's another wish granted. It must feel like Christmas."

Josh came up and slapped Mark on the back. "I'm not sure whether to offer congratulations or commiserations. It's like they say, old buddy. Be careful what you wish for. You might get it."

Ellen suddenly shook her head, and went after Lyle. It reminded Mark of a small dog barking and snapping at a stranger. The only saving grace was the fact that her attack stopped short of being physical. Mark's reconstruction of her monosyllabic screeches went, "What gives you the power to make us married, anyway? You don't have any power."

Lyle just nodded. "You're right. I don't. Sheriff Crichton made me an honorary deputy and later, an honorary under-sheriff so I could be in charge of deputies. Vince should be in charge. He's the only surviving government official, but he wants no part of it. I'm the de facto authority for now. When Josh and Alicia asked me to officiate at their wedding, I had no power to marry them. I didn't with you, either. I just said how things were. Jimmy and Vickie are another case, but Stanley handled that."

Ellen spat, "What if I say I'm not married?"

Lyle remained calm. "That would be a lie. That you and Mark aren't entwined around each other right now is irrelevant. The fact is that you are married. You are married to Mark. You have been married to him for a couple of weeks, at least."

"What if I refuse to go along with this ... this travesty?"

Lyle scratched his chin and pursed his lips. Mark thought he saw a slight sparkle in Lyle's eyes. "Mark is still your boss and he still works for me. Mark is no longer the ranch manager. I haven't decided what he is. Cooperation with the Lyle Lillard program is your best bet to ensure I spend an adequate amount of time considering his fate. Whether you consider yourself married, Mark's fate is your fate. You will either be his wife or his employee. If you are his employee, he will decide what tasks best suit you. If Mark mucks stalls, then you will work for the stall mucker."

Someone called out, "The carriage is here."

Lyle's smile had a forced quality to it. "That is your ride to the castle at McCook for three days. Consider it either a honeymoon or an office retreat."

After a moment, Lyle added, "See what you can find about the bunch running the castle. We will leave the ranch wagon in Arapahoe. The horse you use, Ellen, is another matter. Don't count on it being here when you get back. Mark, your gear stays here. Neither of you need a bedroll. Oh, try not to cause additional turmoil."

By the time Mark and Ellen grudgingly pushed back their chairs and stood up, Jimmy and Vicky were by the door, holding Mark's and Ellen's coats. Mark figured Ellen decided on a trial separation even before Lyle said the words condemning them to a life together. That went along with what he figured out after Stanley filled Lyle in on everything in McCook.

This would have been called a 'marriage of convenience' in the old days. That was another old custom back to haunt them. Most of those old customs were good for a giggle, a grin, or a knowing shake of the head if you were not personally involved. Otherwise, they were just a pain and aggravation. As to being employer-employee, the interpersonal dynamic made the marriage of convenience look quite good. Both of them sucked big time.

Even the smart alecks shut up. Their walk out the door resembled a wake more than a wedding. This was state-sponsored matrimonial homicide. Ellen shrugged into her coat and stomped out to the carriage. Mark gave her as much lead as possible. She scrunched as far into the corner of the seat as possible. It didn't take a body language expert to know she didn't want him anywhere near.

As he climbed in, she favored him with a poisonous glare in case he hadn't picked up on all the other communication. It was also in case he had any hallucination about closeness. Like any sensible clown locked in the lion's cage, Mark sat as close to the near side as he could and still close the door.

The carriage was barely onto the road when Ellen opened up. Mark read about the Civil War. If he was Fort Sumter and Ellen was South Carolina, the initial barrage alone would have leveled the place. People would have heard the bombardment all the way across the country in San Francisco. There was no wind, and Mark knew they heard it loud and clear at the Arapahoe Inn. Again, her mouth went faster than his mind could comprehend. He got general impressions.

"You didn't stand up for yourself," was how he understood the gist of her argument. "You didn't defend me. What kind of man are you, anyway?"

It was a non-stop, full-volume screech. Mark thought back to other times. There was no closeness in this endless harangue. It was a harpy attack, and Mark could only hope to survive the tearing beak and vicious talons. Somehow, in the middle of it, Mark heard Lyle calling for his horse to be saddled.

His first defense against Ellen's attack was to tune her out. He was good at it. Several of his foster families screamed as a matter of course. Mark considered a life of mucking stalls, and found he was indifferent to the possibility. The problem was having Ellen as an assistant, the rest of his life would be like this. She was right, estimating she could triple his misery. Merely tripling it may have understated the situation. He looked at her directly, bringing her tirade to a momentary halt.

"Why are you looking at me that way?" Ellen almost immediately found a new angle for attack. "Why aren't you saying anything? Don't you have any pride? That nasty old man cannot decide we're married. We're supposed to be chaste until a wedding, and passionate ever after. I'm not married to you or any other damned loser."

That answered Mark's first question. Ellen would be his wife or his employee, and she just declared how it would be. He nodded his head, stood in the open carriage, leaning forward for balance. Using the rear-facing seat as a step, he grabbed the back of the driver's seat and pulled himself around.

"What are you doing? Are you afraid to face me? You can't do that," Ellen screeched.

The driver slid over and Mark settled in next to him. He caught movement out of the corner of his eye. Turning, he wasn't surprised to see two riders coming after them.

He turned to the driver. "Dave, why don't we pull off the road? There's some pretty nice grass."

Ellen's continuing diatribe was reduced a bit by distance, elevation, and continuity. The noise now resembled bad static on an old radio. He could communicate through it.

He looked at Dave and kept his voice as level as possible. "We'll be stopped for a few minutes. How do you like working for Don Rowley?"

"He's okay. I'd rather work for you and the ranch, though."

Mark smiled and shook his head. "No situation is forever."

That was more for himself than wisdom for the driver. It was a wish, and a prayer rather than a statement of fact. The carriage rolled to a stop. The harangue from the back continued.

"We'll wait for the oncoming riders, Dave. I know who they are. In any case, I want a witness. While we wait, I'm going to stretch my legs."

The subject matter from Ellen changed, but the noise was ongoing. Mark, now on the ground, walked around beside the carriage and was about ten feet from Ellen, where she was coiled up like a rattlesnake, ready to strike. Mark adopted an aggressive stance like he would use in horse training. It was sometimes necessary, especially with untrained stock, to take extra measures to get the horse's attention.

"You," he told Ellen, his arm and hand extended. "Employee. Hush up. Now."

Ellen sat with her mouth still open for a moment. She slowly closed her mouth and pressed her lips tight together. Lyle arrived just then, clearly evaluating the situation. He nodded like Mark did something right. Adeline was there a moment later.

Mark nodded to them. "Mr. Lillard, ma'am, I've been gathering facts. Ms. Markley has let everyone know how unjust the world is. I want to address a couple of things. She said, 'That nasty old man cannot decide whether we're married.' She followed that with, 'I'm not married to any damn loser.'"

Ellen gasped. "I never said that. I wouldn't say that."

Dave turned around. "That's what she said, Mr. Lillard. That's exactly what she said. Mark climbed onto the driver's seat with me just after that."

Mark nodded. "Thank you, Dave."

Lyle cut in, "Dave, why don't you take a stroll down toward the river. Then, when Don Rowley and everybody else asks you what happened, you can honestly say you don't know."

After Dave got out of earshot, Mark continued. "You said Ellen would be my wife or my employee, and she made her choice. In the beginning, I was the only person unaware that Ms. Markley aimed to be the ranch duchess when she signed on as my housekeeper. Her strategy was to marry the ranch manager. When the ranch manager had performance problems, he was no longer the road to her destination."

Lyle nodded his head very slightly. Adeline listened closely.

"I appreciate you keeping me on, sir. If you have me muck stalls, I'll do the best job I can. I cannot make Ellen be married to me. At the same time, she would never do a minute's work for me. Ms. Markley can go where she wants, but I recommend you take back the horse she uses. The reason for her preferential treatment no longer applies."

Ellen stammered, "How will I get around?"

Mark glanced at her. "You can catch a ride on a wagon or walk."

Mark turned to Lyle. "Am I handling this properly? I'm talking about the horses, now."

Lyle thought about it, and glanced at Adeline. "I'm fine about taking back the horse. The question is whether the horse stays at Arapahoe as the foundation for the express riders. However, she's still your employee."

Mark nodded. "It will be difficult while listening to continuous abuse. She would be the worst employee possible, causing more problems than productivity."

"I thought about that, Mark, and I have part of a solution. Ellen does not want to be married, but I have put you together. There has to be an exchange of services, if you will. You have to protect, feed, and cloth her. She has to do what you require. I should think some respect should enter into it."

To Mark, it sounded like the old deal with employees who would not work and could not be fired. Respect had nothing to do with any of it.

Chapter 15
Un-Honeymoon

Mark knew he was just a clown in Lyle's show. Ellen being chained to him would ensure he never became anything more.

"That might be okay for me," Mark replied, "but I don't believe Ms. Markley cares for anything we say right now. Even if you got her to agree with something, the estimable lady would consider it under duress, and ignore it. Where she appeared to consent at the Inn would be the first example. Productivity would be the second example."

Lyle thought about that. He sighed and looked over at Adeline for support. It didn't appearAdeline could help him, one way or the other.

He finally said, "With marriage, we need two willing parties. Before, you were both willing and eager to get married. Now, neither wants it. It was a mistake to join together those who should be very far apart. However, I have to consider that you two generated a child. Children are vital to our long-term survival, and I do not want single parents in our present situation. Winter will be bad enough without people split apart unnecessarily."

Mark stared at the range of hills on the north side of the road and suddenly found his mouth working without his conscious volition.

"My parents died when I was young. My memories only include them yelling at each other and fighting. I'm sure there must have been something positive between them, but I don't recall any of it. After that, spending my life with one foster family after another was the pits. Most of them screamed at each other or me. After it got too bad, I tended to run away. Ellen's tirade brought that back far too vividly for my personal comfort."

Adeline nodded. "I heard about your parents dying. Many thought it was no accident, and that one or the other steered their car in front of that semi loaded with grain. You already heard how Lyle has ideas of what an improved society would be like. I know that things have to change for us to even survive. We cannot have another generation go through this."

Ellen suddenly gasped. Mark's attention was so much on what the Lillards were saying, that he was startled by anything coming from that direction.

"Ohmigod! Ohmigod!" she cried, bailing out of the far side of the carriage. A moment later he heard her choking and vomiting. Adeline dismounted, handing Lyle her reins. She hurried around the carriage. Lyle raised his eyebrows and looked at Mark.

Mark understood the communication, and knew the discussion was not over. Before that, Adeline would share women's wisdom with his one-time lover, employee, and momentary wife. Her role as one-time lover crashed. Ellen as an employee would never work. Being married never got off the ground. Then something else occurred to him.

Mark looked back at Lyle. "She wouldn't make herself throw up just to make it look like something else, would she?"

Lyle shook his head. "Only Ellen knows the answer to that. Adeline probably has some idea. I'm the wrong Indian to ask about that."

Several minutes later, Adeline helped Ellen around the carriage, and let her sit on the carriage step. Adeline either heard Mark's question or knew what it had to be. She got to the point. "If she's putting on a show, it's a better job than anyone I've ever known. We're back to the question of keeping them together for the sake of the baby."

Mark blinked. When Lyle brought up the possibility of a pregnancy, he hadn't taken it seriously. "I didn't know that was a question. How did that even come up?"

Lyle shook his head. "No other question was worth bothering about. Where's King Solomon? I need wisdom, and nothing appeals to me."

He stopped and stared at Ellen, who appeared too miserable to care what they decided. Then he looked back at Mark. Finally, he cocked his head and looked at Adeline, who shook her head almost imperceptibly. Lyle turned back to Mark.

"You two may end up being the death of me. A while ago, I sent you on a three-day excursion to the castle. The original idea was for it to be a honeymoon. I gave you the option of considering it a company retreat. You're still going. Try to work out an arrangement. We'll get together again at the Inn in three days. I'll take time off from preparing for winter. That's how important this is. We'll meet there for a little privacy."

Lyle turned to Ellen. "Could you please keep the screeching under control? At least give my wife and me a chance to get out of ear shot."

Ellen looked up. "Yes, sir, I'm sorry for what I said about you earlier."

"I accept that. Still, remember that calling people names may not be helpful if you ever need a favor."

Lyle looked back at Mark. "It is admirable that you decided to do something about your situation. The fact that we didn't go that way had nothing to do with how you thought through the situation."

Mark sighed, lifted his hat slightly, scratching his hairline. "Do you have any advice what I can do now?"

Lyle looked astounded, and shifted in his saddle. "You ask that with Ellen sitting here?"

Mark gave a very tired shrug. "If she wanted to know, she'd find out about it anyway."

"Okay, decide what you want to happen. Define it as right. Anything else is wrong. Then, ensure the right things are easy and the wrong things are hard."

"Why does that sound like training horses?"

"That's all I've learned about working with people. It works with horses. With people, it may work or it may not. You can ask Adeline how successful she's been with me."

Adeline shook her head in mock exasperation. "That was supposed to be a super-secret technique. You're right, though. It works except for when it doesn't. Mark, if you love her at all, follow your heart. She may not be as cold-hearted and calculating as you think. There may be a lost little girl looking for something to depend on."

Ellen did resemble a lost little girl at the moment. On the other hand, Mark recalled encountering another creature recently with far different characteristics, and forced a chuckle.

"I'll keep that in mind. I hope you understand, though, when I stay away from those claws, fangs, and any deadly weapons close by."

Adeline shook her head. "As a sign of your new relationship, why don't you help her into the carriage? The day is warming, but her session left her chilled. Perhaps you could put a blanket over her."

Mark wrapped her as best he could in spite of how reluctant he was to be anywhere near her. Lyle and Adeline wished them luck, and headed back. Dave got back to the carriage soon after Lyle and Adeline left. He got the carriage rolling at a good clip. The afternoon storms at McCook didn't give a flip about their personal problems.

Mark wondered what tale Kevin would take to Harlan after seeing them. At the same time, Kevin couldn't tell them anything the rest of the mob at Arapahoe wouldn't have already passed along. Also, what Kevin said or did was of no concern.

Lyle was emphatic that the main thing was the possibility of a child. That was a very strange thing to think about. He didn't know how to be a father. He had the impulse to avoid pain. Recently, his impulses caused pain for himself and everybody around him.

Lyle was right on another count. An avoidance strategy never really worked either in the military or in training and riding horses. On the other hand, Lyle never said what Mark should do instead, unless being accountable to the face in the mirror counted.

Lyle had the makings of a good politician, if there was such a thing. When in doubt, kick the can. It worked in Mark's favor. He had three days to find a solution. If it didn't include Harlan, Mark had a two day head start on any pursuit. Being a good tracker, he could hide a trail as well as follow one. The face in the mirror would not bug him if there was no mirror.

At the castle, the dark lady would put them in the honeymoon suite. This couple wanted nothing to do with each other, but would be trapped there together for the night. He needed a solution sooner rather than later. No ideas came beyond the visceral need to chase the horizon.

Ellen finally unwound herself from the blanket. Mark, watched her out of the corner of his eye, while staring into the distance. The distance was where he needed to be.

"Mr. Tahner, might I ask a question?"

Mark didn't reply, but turned his head slightly to focus on her, his eyebrows raised questioningly.

"If I am now Ms. Markley, I should address you the same way. My question is how to rate things being easy? What are the right things, Mr. Tahner?"

That question got to the core of the issue. "People whip wise sayings on me. They all sound profound. Sometimes, people even add success stories. It's putting those sayings into practice where I find the snake in the garden. There is always at least one impossible aspect."

He paused, considering. "Here, it is the notion that horse training resembles our situation. It seems so straightforward. Everyone knows a trained horse carries riders or pulls wagons. Nobody has a clue what an acceptable outcome looks like with us, much less a good one. Adeline at least admitted her advice doesn't always work."

Ellen seemed to go along with Mark on that. She did not bring up the second piece of advice. Maybe she could not cope with the notion of real love between them. Mark wouldn't know it anyway. Lust was not love. He knew about lust, but that caused this baby business.

She finally asked, "What can we accomplish in three days?"

"We can keep things from turning into confrontations."

There was a look of understanding in Ellen's eyes now. "You don't want what you remember of your parents."

Mark pronounced himself amazed. She was listening. "I can't forget it. It hurts to talk about it. I will avoid the actions connected with it, no matter what. One thing I will not do is raise my hand against you."

"I'll try not to nag like when we left the Inn."

"Thank you. I thought it went far beyond nagging, but I'll take your definition for now."

Dave cut in. "This is the strangest newlywed conversation I ever heard. Josh and Alicia did the starry-eyed thing, where the future was theirs. Jimmy and Vickie didn't say much. I think they were just trying to figure out what happened. You guys had your first fight right out of the gate. Mr. And Mrs. Lillard intervened. Now you sound more like ambassadors than newlyweds."

Mark chuckled. "You might be right, Dave. What countries do we represent?"

"It beats the hell out of me. I only hope your countries don't have nuclear weapons."

"There are nukes all around the country. We could go on a tour and collect them."

"Not with me driving, you aren't. If you start that, I'm going the other way. Would the terrorists have a vacancy for a carriage driver?"

"Considering the way that Stanley and his pig pokers make short work of those sons of Allah, your life expectancy might be better chasing wayward nukes."

Ellen managed a giggle. It wasn't a very convincing giggle, but it was welcome. Mark appreciated the way Dave improved the atmosphere. Nobody got happy, but there were no frowns the rest of the ride. No answers to Mark's problems came, other than a continuing invitation from the hills on either side. They cleared McCook before the afternoon clouds rolled in. Maybe that was a good sign. Dave might care for the carriage and team, and get into the castle before the rain.

Mark never knew about Dave's success in beating the storm. Ellen and he were the celebrities of the hour, and everyone greeted them at the front door. That included Kevin, staying overnight before riding back. Sammie and Tom played the perfect hosts, but it clearly set them back to see Ellen and Mark weren't the inseparable mooning couple.

Mark knew Kevin blabbed everything he knew, suspected, or thought. Whatever Kevin said would have been no more than a briefing. Mark gave Ellen his hand as she stepped out of the carriage. In turn, she managed to not show revulsion as they went arm-in-arm through the door. It was perfectly polite, and totally in control, like two royals attending the opera.

Nobody brought up their marital status. Talking about it would have been odd if they really were the happily wedded honeymooners. In any case, Tom and Sammie only needed to compare their own experience with the two with the current reality. They wouldn't need a briefing from Kevin to see things changed.

Whatever Kevin thought, he kept to himself. Mark considered that a major news item. We have breaking news. Kevin is suddenly keeping watch over his tongue. Film at ten. That part suited Mark perfectly. He dreaded Kevin's incessant chatter. Maybe he already said it three times, and was advised to keep his yap shut. Such counsel from Tom would make a major impact, as Jimmy Bower could testify.

Everyone encouraged the presumably happy couple to retire early. To maintain their vows of civility, Mark and Ellen did that. It felt stiff and unnatural to both curb his tongue and keep smiling. It would not be appropriate for either of them to accidentally get nasty.

In the room, Mark told Ellen to take advantage of the bathtub and hot water. They left Arapahoe with only what they were wearing, Mark waited, fully dressed, by the bathroom door. When Ellen came out, he turned off the bedroom light and carefully turned his head to preserve her privacy. It wasn't like he'd see anything new, but it was appropriate.

Ellen quietly advised Mark that she would take the far side of the bed. After his bath, Mark found his way across the room to his side of the bed. The memory of crossing the motel room in Alma flashed in his mind. It wasn't quite as dark here. Anyway, the feeling was completely different, so he quickly squelched that vision.

Ellen stayed on the far side of the king bed, and Mark was careful to stay next to the edge on his side. He also tried to make sure he didn't take any of the covers. The comparison with them being like this at Harlan Ranch occurred to him. There, Ellen was trying to make a point. Now, the whole exercise was pointless.

Staring at the dark ceiling, he tried to figure which way was out. He needed to think and not just react. The best he'd get from Ellen was armed neutrality. Lyle decreed they were bound together for the rest of their lives. There was the issue of Ellen being pregnant, but sticking around would not change that at all. Pregnant or not, she deserved a better chance at a future than what he could give her.

"Okay, Lyle," Mark thought. "Here is where my reactions and the facts come together. I can do nothing to benefit Ellen, any child she might have, or Harlan. It won't do a hell of a lot for me, either. Whatever happens, there's nothing that'll come my way. You did everything you could, and I appreciate it, Lyle. The time has come for Mark Tahner to fade away."

Mark faded off to sleep, planning how to disappear without a big ugly scene. That, he knew, would help nobody. Clearly, he'd have to wing it, but with the intent crystallized, there was no doubt or hesitation about which way he was going and what he had to do.

It was not quite first light when he awoke. He dressed quietly and headed out, carrying his coat. Ellen was still asleep or at least pretended to be. Either way, he didn't intend to bother her. If she was pretending, she was voting for him to do this, too. What he did would lighten her load. At least, it would keep her from having to be with somebody she couldn't stand. He softly closed the door behind him.

Downstairs, Dora was working both the kitchen and dining room. It didn't look as though she'd been up very long. She handled his breakfast request without comment. Mark couldn't tell whether she remembered him from last night or from when they'd been there previously. His breakfast had not yet come out when Mark heard boots in the anteroom outside the dining room.

Kevin strode in, focused on his mission. He had little to say, other than to observe that it was a long ride, and he was happy to know he could stay at Arapahoe for the evening. Kevin's control of his tongue extended through the meal. He didn't talk about anything besides the breakfast.

Kevin's timing fit in with Mark's plans. After breakfast, Mark went with Kevin to the stable. They got his horse saddled in short order. Mark also got to work with the horse he'd come to think of as his own. It made for a goodbye of sorts, although Mark got a lump in his throat as Kevin rode off.

After Kevin disappeared down the road, Mark went to look at the horse Kevin should have ridden. Lyle gave it to Sammie. Mark could tell Sammie didn't ride the horse enough. Somebody else needed work with it. What horses learned would eventually go away if not refreshed periodically.

Outside the stable, frost sparkled on the grass. Bare areas were still muddy from the previous day's storms. It was a good a day to die. It was hard to say how long he'd continue breathing. Still, for all intents and purposes, he was already a dead man.

Mark went out into the frosty morning, squishing through the mud. Behind the barn and arena, he leaned against a fence, watching the last bit of sunrise. One boot rested on the first rail. In a moment, his other boot would be on the third rail, and he'd be over the fence. Death didn't seem a big thing, but there was no particular rush to it, either.

Mark paused, feeling that scratchy feeling in his neck. Something … no, someone was hunting him. The feeling was so specific that Mark didn't bother to look. A pair of boots quietly stopped next to him. The body wearing them jumped slightly and twisted to sit on the top rail, facing away from the rising sun. It was Tom.

"I've seen that look before. Usually the face wearing it was on a new recruit. If immediate action wasn't taken that look would take the recruit to a whole new category. Most of the time, it was AWOL. Sometimes, it was desertion. Either way, that recruit's problems got ten times worse."

Mark scuffed the mud, his gaze now downward. "That happened in the Army, too. In my experience, the recruit was usually trying to fix something."

"So, what are you trying to fix? You're standing there, a boot heel in the mud, and your eye on the horizon. That horizon looks clean from here, but there is just as much mud as you've got here. You won't find a solution there, Mark. You'll only find bigger problems."

"I know that, Tom. When I go over that fence, I'm just a dead man."

"That is not a normal sentiment for a newlywed."

"We aren't newlyweds. Lyle sentenced us to be together for the rest of our lives. Lyle says we could do it as a married couple. If not, Ellen could be my employee or we could figure out something else. Ellen rejected marriage. I guess I did, too. Nothing else has a chance in hell of working. Over this fence, I'm dead, and Ellen has her freedom. I'll grant freedom has a limited meaning at the moment."

"Damn. The last time you were here, we couldn't pry you apart. Then you showed up yesterday, just barely polite to each other."

Mark considered that was putting it mildly. "At least I can live up to my name and leave a mark in the world. By the way, good morning to you, too. Should I remark on the absence of Lady Samantha?"

"Since you just told me that you're a dead man, it shouldn't be any concern. That would include your formerly inseparable companion or what she is doing. How did you rate such strange treatment from Mr. Lillard, anyway?"

"He decided I went too far with Jimmy and Vickie, in spite of them seeming pleased both with the Arapahoe Inn and each other."

"You got the ball and chain minus the happily married designation. That takes talent."

Mark squinted sideways at Tom. "Do you ever wish you were back in the military?"

Tom snorted. "Are you talking about the garrison military, with spit shines and bullshit details? That is a big negative. Now, where we took care of business and our brothers, yeah, I could use more of that. Are you looking for a recruiter?"

"Josh and I went to the Pentagon to sign up. They said we were dead, and corpses couldn't pass the physical. We walked to El Paso and raised hell with the same bad guys we fought in Afghanistan. Other than a handshake or two, the only sensible idea came from our commander, who declared us retired and sent us on our way."

Tom laughed. "You want to go back to that?"

"No, but I could use some more knowing everyone watched each other's back, like in the war zone. We had no choice about leaving. It wasn't like we were an elite unit or anything."

"In spite of all that, your little bunch of mutts and mongrels was the closest thing to family you ever knew."

"Yeah, it was." Mark stopped and stared at Tom. "We never had a name, except one time from sharpshooters. They never came into camp. They stayed a couple hundred meters outside. We heard that's what they called us."

Tom favored Mark with a far-off smile. "That was us. Gutierrez ran both units by remote. He thought it was funny. You guys came up with a return name for us. We didn't think it was so funny."

"Assassins 'R' Us." Mark mumbled it across the fence.

"Yeah, that was it. Gutierrez got such a kick out of it, he made you guys the 31st M&M Brigade. We became the 12th ARU. We always said the 'U' stood for 'unit.' The 'A' and 'R' depended on who we were talking to and how clever we felt."

Mark nodded. "Our bunch was never at company strength, much less a brigade. The M&M brigades one through thirty were unknown. The same could be said of the first through eleventh ARU."

Tom chuckled. "We thought Gutierrez was playing a Dungeons and Dragons game when he formed your bunch. He managed to gather the strangest abilities he could find. It must have worked. I never heard of you guys suffering any fatalities."

"We had one. Unfortunately, he was one of my best friends, and was standing next to me when he bought it. Everyone thought Josh attracted good luck. There was also his marksmanship. When he did a bad guy, the round always went in the eye and out the ear, or in the ear and out the eye."

"I heard about him. I also heard about you. Gutierrez said you could track a snowflake in a blizzard, and if you shot a bad guy, there was no way he'd get up again until resurrection day."

"They always said that one bullet equals one kill. I just tried to meet the standard."

"You did better than nearly everyone else. The standard was only an ideal. You talk about Josh being lucky, but you have a sixth sense telling you when somebody comes up on you. I got acquainted with that when you gave Sammie riding lessons. When I walked up here a minute ago is another."

"About that standard, they would just say the next two-legged target I saw was to cease moving. My only tool was the weapon they issued. You've got a point about that scratchy feeling. The first I knew about it was when I was hunting deer and a mountain lion was hunting me. The game wardens said it couldn't be a mountain lion, but they couldn't deny the carcass. I shot it as it jumped me."

"I'd like to have that talent. What feeling do you get when women check you out, thinking you'd be a tasty morsel?"

Mark shook his head. "I couldn't tell you. It's never happened."

"I personally know of a couple of times. The first was when they brought me to Harlan Ranch, and I saw you working on the fence with your shirt off. Another time is right now."

Mark stiffened in surprise and turned around. Ellen was ten feet away, with Sammie a couple of feet farther. That's why Tom didn't want to talk about her. Ellen standing behind him was the last thing he could have imagined.

"I'm wearing a shirt and jacket this morning. I can't believe it can be arousing to listen to a couple of guys swap lies about when they were overseas."

Ellen shook her head. "It was none of the above. I have it on good authority you just described war stories. War stories always feature the teller as a far larger hero than he could have been. What I heard was someone acting like heroism was no big deal."

Mark shrugged. "I might have been decent in the kind of war we had. Stanley and his hunters have far more talent for the war we have with the terrorists now. I might be a passable horse trainer. Kevin can both train horses and the people who will ride them. That is a larger thing. I could help patrol Harlan. Josh is more interested in the freight business anyway. You need and deserve a life that I can never deliver."

Sammie took a few strides, landing midway between them. That put her five feet away, but turning toward him, it felt like she was only a few inches from Mark's face.

"Aren't you noble? You're stepping out of the way so Ellen can do what, exactly? Where is the army of suitors trying to get her attention? Nobody can give Ellen the life she needs and deserves. That life no longer exists. It wasn't available even before the stupid dust came through. You are so bloody honorable. It was the wedding night every girl dreams of, sleeping back to back, as far from each other as possible."

Sammie stayed centered between Mark and Ellen, but half a step back. It was far enough for Mark and Ellen to look at each other. Tom moved behind Sammie, putting his arms around her. She leaned into him and purred before getting back to business.

"We're playing a game, and it has already begun. Tom or I will say something about the problem here. Then the guilty party will take a step forward. I don't mean a baby step, either. Mark, that was your name, so do your part. Take a step directly toward Ellen. Do it now."

Mark nervously took the required step. The distance between them was now eight feet.

Tom took it then. "You guys like news, so here you go. Sammie and I decided to get married, and we want to do it soon. Kevin showed up with news that you tied the knot and would have your honeymoon with us. We thought that was great, seeing how tight you were ten days ago."

Tom looked at both of them. "Then Kevin saw fit to fill in some more information. We couldn't believe it, but when you got here, it was not only true but fell short of the mark. That made a big problem for us. Both of you take a step."

After a long moment of hesitation, Mark and Ellen both made the required movement. Only four feet separated them.

Sammie looked at Ellen. "You didn't get the wedding of your dreams. Still, you have to admit it was far more than you gave Jimmy and Vickie. Did you address your grievances to Mr. Lillard? No, you not only didn't take your problems back to their source, you took out your anger and frustration on your fellow victim."

Mark once again tried to figure out how to defend Ellen, but had no more idea how he could proceed now than when Lyle confronted them the previous day at Arapahoe. Ellen's lip quivered as Sammie glared at her.

"As a final slap in the face to Mark, you later had the gall to turn around and apologize to Mr. Lillard. Don't deny it, because all of that information came directly from you, and, lady, it is bad form, indeed. Take a step toward Mark."

Tom looked back and forth at Mark and Ellen. "You have nearly run out of room. Each took the same number of steps, so you're equally at fault. Sammie and I have been greatly inconvenienced, so both of you take a small step forward. Stop before you actually touch."

Tom gave Sammie a squeeze while that happened, and Mark now wondered what they had in mind. Mark involuntarily licked his lips, which felt abnormally dry.

Sammie finally said, "Okay, look in each other's eyes. We can tell if you're doing it or looking to the side."

Mark saw a hint of moisture in Ellen's eyes, and suddenly felt very sorry for things coming to this. Maybe the point of the so-called game was to get them back to square one. Mark felt Tom grasp his wrist and propel his hand forward. A few inches later, his hand encountered Ellen's at an odd angle. They changed the angle of their hands to a hold.

"That's it, guys. Try holding hands for a while. You can do it on the other side, too. See how it feels," was from Tom.

Mark thought it felt good, and didn't mind it at all. His earlier thoughts about chasing the horizon were now fading. The look in Ellen's eyes seemed more hopeful. At least he wanted to think so. Her hands felt good in his, too. Mark smiled a little, and he felt Ellen give one hand a small squeeze.

"Okay, kids," Sammie said softly. "Now it is time for you to try a kiss."

The kiss began very soft and gentle, like they had the rest of their lives to finish it. At least that was how Mark thought of it just then. He hoped Ellen didn't disagree too violently. If this was their last kiss ever, Mark wanted to make it worth remembering the rest of his life. Ellen seemed track his thoughts perfectly. The kiss became wider and deeper. Their arms left off hand-holding, and encircled one another. When they came up for air, Tom and Sammie were gone.

Chapter 16
Double Mate

"Wow! That was some game. Who won?"

"We both did, lover." Ellen glanced around and added, "I think we all did."

He suddenly had a thought. "Am I a lover again? Is there another step to this game?"

"We have to discuss the lover part, but I'm open to the idea right now. As for your other question, we could get closer," Ellen informed him, "but it's not going to happen in a corral."

"The stallions and mares don't have a problem with it."

Ellen shook her head. "The stallion gets the mare in a corner. She doesn't have any say in it."

Mark grinned. "The mare has more to say about it than you think. Where would you prefer we consummate our marriage, my love?"

"A little less horse and cow manure would help the ambiance." Ellen abruptly grinned at Mark. "Okay, if you can corral this filly, you can have your way with her."

Ellen suddenly broke loose, spun and sprinted through a side door into the arena. Mark chased her, but lost her in the stables. He knew where she must be going, but in the spirit of the game they just played, Mark decided to play this one, too. He looked in every stall, calling her name. He came out of the arena to see the front door of the castle closing.

Mark broke into a sprint, getting to the door a moment later. Inside, he saw Ellen's jacket disappear around the corner upstairs. Ellen was making sure Mark didn't get lost. There wasn't much chance of that now as he vaulted up the steps, three at a time, just as she disappeared into the room. Behind him, Sammie and Tom stood arm-in-arm.

"Tom, our newlyweds showed up for their honeymoon. I began to wonder if they would ever get here. They look so happy, don't you think?"

"Yes, they do. It gives me a good feeling about getting married."

Mark heard their comments, but concentrated on Ellen's waiting arms. Quickly closing the door, he took up their embrace where he left off behind the barn. There wasn't as much clothing involved this time. Mark's original idea was to throw her on the bed and have at it, but at the moment, it felt perfectly satisfying to simply hold her.

It didn't seem long before a soft knock came on their door. "Dark lady says the meal is ready if you want to join them."

Ellen pulled back a bit and looked at Mark closely. "How does this compare with being dead?"

Mark kept a gentle hold of her shoulders as he looked at her. He thought about the question. He finally nodded. "It was close enough for me to appreciate this moment. The voice at the door spoke of a meal. Speaking of things pertaining to life, are you hungry?"

"I'm famished. Unlike you, I didn't get breakfast."

"Much as I hate to let go of you, maybe we should get dressed and partake of whatever they've got."

When they opened the bedroom door, several of the Peepul waited with clothing. "Mr. Tom and the dark lady thought you'd like something clean to wear. They thought these might fit."

Everything fit well enough, and the Peepul waited outside for their old clothing. Ellen was delighted, and looked at Mark for a reaction.

Mark informed her, "I'm starting a borrowed life with borrowed clothing. Did I borrow you, beautiful lady?"

"Yes, you borrowed me from a guy who ran away from his problems. I hope you aren't that kind of person."

"I just found it doesn't matter which way I go, if every step I take is toward you."

Ellen approved and extended her arm. Mark took it in something like a gallant fashion. They strolled to the dining room, and discovered Dora had not been idle. The table had all kinds of food. A wedding cake was on a side table, and somebody even decorated the room a bit.

Mark thought of Jimmy and Vickie not that many days before. There was, of course, a much longer guest list. Mark couldn't argue about the quantity or quality of the food. Like Jimmy and Vickie, Mark and Ellen sat at the head of the table. Sammie was next to Mark and Tom was next to Ellen. The other team members filled in on both sides.

Part way through the meal, Tom looked at Mark. "Do you think you'll stick around? This will work a lot better if we don't have to put a leash on you?"

"I'll stay for now. Just out of curiosity, why did you come after me?"

Sammie looked at Mark. "Tom took one look and knew what you would do. We put out the word, and Dora sent one of her people the second she saw you. We grabbed Ellen, and concocted a plan as we went. Tom can tell you why."

Tom nodded and looked at Mark. "I'll give you one thing. You thought it through. You just didn't think far enough or wide enough."

"How's that?" Mark was puzzled now.

"You are the crown prince of Harlan. What is the result if you go missing here? Nobody in Harlan trusts us or Stanley Peepul and his tribe. Did my team take you out? Did Stanley or members of his tribe revert and you ended up in a cannibal cooking pot? Your disappearance would make relations with Harlan impossible."

Tom was right. Mark hadn't considered that. There were other things, too. "You make me sound important. I'd argue the point, but I see what you're saying."

Just then, Mark felt intense pain in his ankle. Ellen had kicked him hard, and was not pleased. "Can we talk about something else, please?"

Mark got the point. "Yes, dear."

Sammie brightened. "Ellen, I understand you like old traditions. How about what we did today for a new tradition?"

That perked Ellen up. "That is a good idea. Maybe we should see if this had enough glue to keep everything together."

Tom laughed. "If you two could stay together at least until Sammie and I do the deed, it would be really nice."

They were just finishing as the storms came in, rain beating against the house in sheets. As Mark and Ellen stood at the window, Mark saw snow in the rain. The snow got more predominant for a while and turned back to rain. Sammie and Tom were still there. The other members of Tom's team had taken off.

"What causes this strip of weather?" Mark wondered.

Tom shook his head. "You see how it comes in. What happens if it all turns to snow?"

Mark nodded. "This rain could make a foot of snow every day. That would cover your solar power array and be a real problem."

"That's what we think, too" Tom replied, nodding. "Losing power would be inconvenient. The roofs of some farmhouses might not stand up to the snow load. Would Harlan take some of the farm families for the winter?"

That was a bolt out of the blue. "I'll pass the word. It's not mine to say, Tom. I couldn't even say my supporting it would be a good thing. I'd be glad to take the request, at least."

"That's all we ask." Tom pointed at window. "It all turned to snow, now. Today's storm should end soon. With any luck, it will warm up tomorrow."

In their room, Mark ventured onto thin ice with Ellen. "I noticed you weren't as conversational as usual."

Ellen nodded. "When Sammie cornered me this morning, I said too much. She accumulates information like other women buy shoes. It's likely to come back to haunt me. Maybe I should make that coming back to haunt us."

Mark agreed. "She's an intelligence officer by training and a snoop by inclination. Did I say anything out of bounds?"

"You only said what they already knew. When Tom asked about evacuating locals to Harlan, you were spot on. If you guaranteed his idea going through, it would have flown in the face of what you said and did this morning. It was just about right."

Mark took a deep breath. This was as good a time as any to unburden his soul. "Do you know why I was behind the stable this morning?"

Ellen's face tightened, and she gave a small nod. "Sammie and I were right behind Tom the whole time. I heard everything. I saw more than I heard. Your foot was on that fence rail and your gaze over the horizon.

You could have been over the fence in a moment. Then, you would have been gone forever, wandering until your story ended with no one to see, know, or care."

Mark exhaled. "You read me completely."

"When Tom and Sammie came for me, I didn't want to go. It was a long night. I may have rested some, I didn't sleep. I saw you leave, and knew you wouldn't be back. I thought it was the best thing for both of us."

"I wondered if you were awake when I left. It didn't matter either way. If you were asleep, whether I stayed or went didn't matter that much. If you were awake, you were giving me permission to leave."

Ellen nodded. "You learned that much, at least. It is true. I did give you permission. You would be the knight-errant, slaying dragons and saving fair maidens. I'd go back to Harlan, and let everyone comfort me. Then I would be Alicia's friend and confidante, and everything would be lovely."

"Something happened between when they came for you and when we were behind the barn. What did Tom and Sammie say? What did they do?"

She waved off his question. "They told me what they told you. They were taking me with them whether I wanted to or not. What got me was a feeling of concern bordering on panic from them. They couldn't make that up. In addition, I thought it would be good to see you leave. Then I would know, and not just think it probably happened."

"Something happened after that. You said it was more what you saw than what you heard."

"As we chased after you, in my mind's eye, I saw you leaping over the fence and scampering to freedom. When I was a girl, my family saved a fawn. We turned it loose after it regained its health and could take care of itself."

Mark saw Ellen didn't give that part of the story willingly. "That's not what you saw when you got there."

"We cared for that fawn because the doe got badly tangled in barbed wire. When we found the doe, she was nearly dead, and too weak to fight any more. Her eyes were filled with pain and glazing over. That's what I saw when we came around the corner of the arena. You looked beaten, and about to drag yourself off to someplace private to get it over with."

"I didn't think I looked that bad," Mark replied.

Ellen looked at Mark significantly. "I realized something else while we stood there."

She had Mark's complete attention now.

"What everyone said was true, including what you said when we stopped with the Lillards outside Arapahoe. My goal was to be the lady in charge of the ranch. You were the road to my goal. Your fortunes rose, so I kept close and hung on tight. Of course I wanted a great, glorious wedding as the princess of Harlan."

Ellen stopped for a moment, and then continued. "That went with the status I wanted. Seeing you at the fence, I realized things had changed. Being close to you was more important than all the other stuff I craved. I didn't know until I saw you, poised to jump off into nothingness."

Mark started to nod but then shook his head emphatically. "Still, I didn't leave."

"You didn't leave then. That is no comfort to me. You might leave tomorrow. You could leave any time. I have to be happy with whatever time I have with you. That nonsense in Arapahoe wasn't a wedding. The step game was closer to one. At least everybody is willing to consider us married. Lyle and Adeline may need convincing. It doesn't matter if you do sentry duty or muck out pens at the feed lot. At least I could be with you. Mark, please stick around so I can be with you."

"What Tom said makes sense now. I was willing to give my life for a country and government. Most of the country, not to mention the entire government, didn't give a rat's ass about my sacrifice, no matter if it was real or potential. We found out the government's view at the Pentagon."

Mark looked deeply into Ellen's eyes. "Now, I have a reason to live. The reason is you, Ellen. The game Tom and Sammie did was more of a wedding ceremony than I could have imagined. We joked about getting married in the barn, but we got married behind it. That doesn't matter now. You're here, and you say you want to be here. I want to be here. I'm not too smart, but I'm won't mess up the best thing that ever happened to me."

Ellen moved to Mark, laying her head on his chest. "What you just said sounded pretty smart to me."

They stayed there for a few minutes. Ellen raised her head. "The rain stopped. Maybe we should have a look."

Mark walked over to the window. "You're right. I don't hear the rain. It's strange. The storms didn't stop like this before. It's so dark all I can see is the reflection of the light off the glass."

"Let's turn the light off so we can tell what's going on."

Ellen walked quickly over to the light switch while Mark peered through the window.

"I still can't see anything. There's no moon, and the clouds are not clearing off. They always clear off just after the rain quits. Something is really different this time."

"Look harder. Your eyes aren't dark-adapted yet," was Ellen's reply.

The whole weather situation seemed really spooky. Then, he felt her hands softly land on his shoulders, and slide around to his shirt buttons.

"I know what's wrong. You are wearing a shirt," she whispered.

Mark turned to face her, mapping her features with his fingers. As his hands slipped down her neck and onto her shoulders, he found she was right. He was the only one wearing a shirt. Exploring further, he was the only one wearing anything at all. Ellen didn't need any light to cure that situation.

The second night of their life sentence and the first night of their marriage, Mark and Ellen faced each other in the middle of the bed. Mark knew this was how he wanted to spend the rest of his life. A bug in the back of his head reminded him how both events and his tendency to go off half-cocked conspired against such resolutions. Still, the moment was now, and he immersed himself in it.

They were fully involved with each other into the night. Mark fell asleep, exhausted. All at once, he came to, listening. That's what was wrong. The wind always blew up the ridge. There was no wind now. He padded over to the window. It was difficult to make out anything. Still, there was enough light to see the wind turbines were motionless.

"Why are you up?"

"There's no wind," Mark told her.

That drew a growl. "You're the big, strong war hero and master of horses, but you can't handle calm air? Come back to bed. I grew up here. There are lots of times this area has no wind."

"Things are not the same since the Omega dust and the big rain. Things have gotten weird," Mark grumbled.

Ellen sounded fully awake and there was an edge to her voice. "Are you in charge of the weather? You won't be able to tell anything about the weather until it gets light. A storm is brewing right here in this bed. You are responsible for this storm, and only you can take care of it. You'd best get after it."

Mark knew Ellen was once again right, and shuffled back to the bed and his bride. At the same time, a corner of his brain which must have been in charge of worrying about uncontrollable situations continued to focus on the weather.

They woke with the dawn, but Ellen's plans for Mark had nothing to do with the weather. Later, Mark considered the problem was with the sky and a certain feeling in the air. Later, Mark guessed some of Ellen's actions last night and this morning.

"It's far better going to breakfast this way, than alone."

Ellen nodded knowingly. "It beats the hell out of chasing after you. I like that you appreciate the effort."

At breakfast, everyone talked about the weather change, and what direction it might take. The feeling was ominous.

Tom wondered, "Do you think you should start back today?"

Mark and Ellen looked at each other. Neither was in a rush to face Lyle and the inevitable questions and challenges. Finally, he replied, "I am in no rush. We'll take our day here. If the weather slows us, we'll make the best of it."

Tom nodded. "Sammie and I will tag along, if you don't mind. The rest of the team can be an honor guard."

"What's the occasion?"

"I told you about us getting married. It wouldn't be right to declare it ourselves. From what we've heard, Jimmy has become the mayor of Arapahoe. That gives him as much official standing as anyone."

"The honor guard will be for you more than us, but thanks for putting it that way. I take it you're not considering having Lyle Lillard officiate."

Sammie joined the conversation. "I understand your reluctance to go back. When we get near Harlan, everybody questions our motives and methods. I'll not get married anywhere near Harlan if I can avoid it."

"If you guys want to go with us to Arapahoe, I don't mind. Do you, Ellen?"

Ellen looked around. "We'll have a little parade. Hopefully, the weather will give us a break."

Nothing happened the rest of the morning. There weren't any clouds. There also wasn't any blue sky. There was only a strange haze giving a greenish cast to the sky. Mid-afternoon, when the storms usually began, there was still nothing. The situation was now beyond ominous. He went with Ellen on a tour of the barn. The horses were nervous. The cattle didn't act normal either. Mark questioned his decision to stay the extra day. Everyone around the castle was on edge, as well. Everyone agreed on an early start for Arapahoe.

The household staff was moving well before dawn. Mark and Ellen managed to indulge in newlywed activity before the staff let them know things were ready. There was nothing to pack and the clothes they came in were now clean.

Downstairs, Sammie, Tom, and the team demonstrated they could get up and get going when they wanted to. Everyone had a fast breakfast and headed out into a cold wind, now blowing down the ridge instead of up it. Sunrise was only diffuse light showing a deck of sullen clouds. Snow started falling before they got to the Thomas place.

Back in the carriage, Mark and Ellen tried to keep warm cuddling together.

"Is this better than wandering around in the woods somewhere?" Ellen asked.

"This is better than just about anything. I guess better weather would help, but I'm not going to argue about what we have here."

"Personally, I'd like it more if we had our bedrolls. Lyle messed up there."

"That is the truth. One thing I'm not doing this time is sitting up by Dave, on the exposed driver's seat. The snow is getting heavier every minute."

Sammie made good headway on her horse. It was a pity the horse first spent all that time in the stable and then had to do what amounted to extreme work. The guys, on bicycles, started in front of the carriage, but got in trouble as the snow first stuck to the road and then got deeper. Closer to McCook, the bike riders had to travel in the tracks left by the carriage.

Dave knew a place stocked with blankets and comforters that Don Rowley hadn't grabbed earlier. The group spent more time there than they intended, trying to warm up before setting out again.

The nature of the weather had changed, but the bad weather still centered on McCook. It wasn't as though conditions became good as they headed toward Arapahoe. Still, the going became easier. The wind was back with a vengeance, though, and it never got any warmer. Temperatures stayed below freezing. After a few miles, the snow accumulation almost disappeared, and they made better time.

Mark always liked his nose in the fresh air, even if the rest of him was covered. Ellen disagreed, insisting they totally cover themselves with the comforters. He didn't know if Ellen planned it, but they soon got frisky in their cocoon. It made for a very short trip. It also made for exchanges of knowing glances between everyone else when they finally emerged.

Ellen looked at Mark. "This is the second morning in a row where you aren't trying to take off for Timbuktu. I've decided being apart is wrong, and being together is right. How am I doing so far?"

"If this is training, I'm all in favor of it. Should we train some more?"

"Not right now. I think we're about to Arapahoe."

Mark looked around. The sun was low in the sky, and they were on the outskirts of Arapahoe. At the Inn, the doors to the service area were closed. Somebody yelled as they approached. Jimmy was right there, opening the overhead door. Mark thought that was a nice touch.

First through the door was an outbound rider who turned toward Harlan. The rider was wrapped for the weather. Mark wasn't sure who it was. He recognized the horse, though. The filly used to be his, so the rider must be Kevin. He picked up speed passing them, and there was no salutation. That was even stranger. He was back in the world of strange tests and actions associated with Lyle Lillard.

The garage area felt good after that ride. Jimmy came over to help Mark and Ellen out of the carriage while several of Stanley's tribe busied themselves, taking care of animals, tack, carriage, and bicycles. Mark did not see Lyle's horse, so Kevin was taking a message to Lyle. There would be no meeting at Arapahoe. Everyone headed into the public area.

"We're keeping the service room door open," Jimmy commented. "We don't want the big water tank to freeze."

"That makes sense," Mark agreed.

"There are more of you than we expected," Jimmy continued. "The three ladies are still here, so we only have two rooms." He looked at Tom and the team. "You guys will have to sleep on the floor. It's too cold for the motel."

Sammie spoke up. "Tom's with me. I'm sorry there's no place for the rest of you guys."

The three team members were all fine with it. "I don't mind, as long as I can get up close and personal with that heating stove," one said.

"That," Jimmy assured, "is no problem. The stove gets really hot. You might not want to get too close. It's your choice, of course."

Jimmy gave Mark and Ellen a room, with sheets and blankets on the bed. Jimmy had upgraded the place even in the few days they were gone. Sammie and Tom got the last room. The three team members found out about with the stove. Jimmy went into the kitchen, returning with an envelope addressed to Mark.

"They said to be very sure to give it to you. I got the idea you might want to look at it privately."

Mark and Ellen looked at each other. "That's a good purpose for our room, Jimmy. I guess we'll go there, then."

In the room, they sat side by side on the bed while Mark opened it. As expected, it was from Lyle.

"When Kevin came back from McCook, he said Tom and Sammie planned to resolve your situation. Adeline and I agreed there was no point waiting in Arapahoe with so much to do in Harlan. Kevin will let us know of your arrival. Vince will escort you from Oxford. He has instructions. Lyle."

"We go back to Harlan, but not home," Ellen blurted.

"I get that," Mark replied somberly. "Whatever happens won't be at the ranch."

"He's not telling us to get lost. He may have something good in mind."

"I'm picturing myself at the stock yard, hauling cow manure, one shovel at a time."

"We could live in Alma next to the lake," Ellen suggested brightly. "That would be all right."

"Ah, yes, that's the sunny side. Thank you, my love."

She gave him a wifely peck on the cheek. "It's either look at the sunny side or scream and destroy things. I promised that I would be calm and lady-like. Let's grab some of their famous stew and get some sleep. I'm exhausted."

Mark could not have slept in even if he wanted. The odor of bacon and eggs permeated the place. Ellen woke up as well, and they paused, looking at each other.

"Can you stand another day of me, Ellen? There's no telling where we'll wind up tonight."

Ellen laughed. "When I followed Dr. Dover, I didn't know where I was going. The trip hasn't been that awful. Parts of the journey have been pretty good."

"Then there were the parts where you were stuck with me." Mark grinned so she wouldn't take it wrong.

Ellen didn't. Her eyes sparkled as she gave him a kiss. "Yes, there were those times. Let's get breakfast. Any meal I don't cook or clean up after has to taste great."

Mark was surprised to see Sammie and Tom already up. Not only that, they had four tables shoved together, and a pair of chairs on each of three sides. Sammie waved them over.

"We want an occasion with all the couples sitting together. Why don't you sit here?"

Mark considered Sammie played the lady of the manor, wherever she was. Mark nervously glanced at Ellen, but she had no problem with the situation. The third couple was Vickie and Jimmy. The ladies got a kick out of it, and shooed them out of the kitchen.

After eating, Sammie opened with, "At Josh and Alicia's wedding, Mr. Lillard said they were already married in their own hearts and minds. The real purpose of the wedding ceremony was for the community to acknowledge that couple's status."

Mark and Ellen both agreed that was what Lyle said. Mark glanced at Jimmy, and saw he had a knowing look in his eye. Vickie seemed puzzled by it all.

Sammie then looked at Jimmy and Vickie. "Mark basically said the same thing about you two, although circumstances didn't add up to the conclusion. In spite of it, you have managed for a couple of weeks. That's a long way from your golden anniversary, but it's something, at least."

Mark couldn't deny his part in the fiasco, and tried to keep the most neutral possible expression on his face. Not being a poker player, it was not easy. Everyone's attention was on Jimmy anyway. Had it been two weeks?

Jimmy leaned back in his chair. "It's hard to know what to say to that. However it started, everyone has been awfully concerned with our health and how well we're getting along. I can only speak for myself, but living conditions are better than I can remember. For the record, Vickie and I are getting along just fine, thank you. She may tell me otherwise presently, but that's my impression at the moment."

Sammie nodded. After a moment, she looked at Mark and Ellen. "Mr. Lillard evidently wanted to go the same way with you. He finally just said the two of you would be together for life, and let you choose the status."

Ellen sighed. "That was the basic situation. My problem had more to do with how it was addressed. Mr. Lillard turned it into a cross between a courtroom and a circus."

Mark nodded, remembering his own reaction about it being a circus. He found it amazing that Ellen used the same term in thinking about it.

Sammie did not say anything about Ellen's observation. Obviously, she had something else on her mind, not that it was any great secret. "So, the idea is that two people live together as a married couple. Everyone acknowledges it, and treats them as married. That makes them married. Is that it?"

Mark and Ellen both looked at Jimmy and Vickie. Mark suddenly realized that of the three couples, they'd been married the longest. That was very strange.

Jimmy put it together, finally. "You two want to be married. Do you need to declare it sooner rather than later? In other words, next spring might not be appropriate?"

Sammie reddened slightly. "That is a distinct possibility."

Mark was amazed to see the iron lady and shield maiden blushing. Jimmy asked, "What do you want to happen here?"

"Sammie and I are the closest thing to a government at McCook," Tom said flatly. "We need somebody else to say the words. You're in charge here in Arapahoe."

"Stanley has far more to say about everything than me, but he left this morning. You could go to Harlan. Mr. Lillard already performed a marriage, plus whatever he did to Ellen and Mark."

Sammie shook her head. "We won't have a ceremony with him, or there."

Jimmy sighed and stood up. "Everybody gather by the wood stove. I need to put another log in it anyway."

Putting a log only took a moment, but that was far more time than it took for the group to come together. Jimmy looked at Tom and Sammie and then at everyone else, including Vickie, who stood just behind him.

Jimmy began, "Everyone thinks the tradition of marriage should continue in order to promote the future of our endangered race. It's strange, having so many marriages in such a small group. Could it be that a marriage bug got released just after the Omega bug?"

That got a few chuckles.

"There is one thing we don't have, besides the population. That would be divorce. There is no government, so there are no judges or lawyers. There are no churches. Marriage is now a one-way street. There is no way for you to get unmarried. When things get bad, you won't be able to walk away from it. Have you thought about that?"

Tom and Sammie looked at each other for a long moment. Mark and Ellen looked at each other, reflecting on their own situation. Jimmy then glanced at Vickie, who just grinned. Tom cleared his throat, pulling Mark's attention back to the couple of the hour.

"I'm fine with that," he said in a rough voice.

"Yes, I am, too," Sammie added. She suddenly sounded almost timid. Jimmy nodded and looked around the room.

"Here is the big moment. Tom and Sammie live as though they are married. They want us to acknowledge that fact. What do we say?"

Everyone laughed and agreed. The three Marines yelled oorah!

"So, Tom … What is your last name? Okay, Grimes. We agree that Tom and Sammie Grimes are married. So kiss, already."

After an extended deep kiss, Jimmy added, "Your room is right over there. You have the honeymoon special."

As the door closed, the ladies tittered, and the three Marines offered bawdy advice more notable for biological impossibility than the humor they attempted.

Chapter 17
Mark on Assignment

The ladies chatted for a few minutes, and then went to get ready to go home. With everyone checking out, each Marine could have a private room. How long they'd stay, only the weather conditions in McCook could say. Mark and Ellen checked the horse and farm wagon as they prepared to go.

A supply of hay would become a major issue if they started to keep stock in Arapahoe. Mark Lyle talked about this being a pony express stop. Then he made himself stop thinking about it. That project would be for another day, and for all he knew, for someone else to sweat. He also had to wonder why they were in such a hurry to face Lyle's music.

Dave was still checking the carriage when Mark and Ellen headed out, and stopped to open the overhead door for them. The small crust of snow crunched under hooves and wagon wheels. It wasn't long after they got on the road before the snow simply vanished. There was a cold breeze, and Mark knew the wind was much stronger on the high ground.

The realization hit him about this early snow. The trees still had leaves, so they were lucky not to run into large fallen branches due to the snow load.

Ellen interrupted his reverie. "Sammie and Tom's wedding made our step game look pretty decent. Their having the reception ahead of the ceremony didn't seem right. It was Sammie and Tom's call, though. What was that business about divorce, anyway?"

"It was on Jimmy's mind and came out his mouth. He knows what happened to him and he knew some of our situation. How he decided divorce was no longer possible is beyond me."

"You proposed a version of divorce, and it looked suspiciously like your foot hitting the fence rail. I planned to train with you this morning, but the smell of the bacon was just too powerful."

"The training you did yesterday is still holding. The horizon has no attraction now. I was just talking in general."

Ellen looked doubtful. "You talk like a different man from three days ago. You've been in business three days, and you are trying to give me a lifetime guarantee. I can't buy it. What does Mr. Lillard believe?"

Mark felt like he had come a long way in a short amount of time. On the other hand, he couldn't deny that absolute certainties one day had a bad habit of reversing themselves a day later. His decision to wander off into nothingness might have ended with him crawling back to Harlan with his tail between his legs.

"The Lillards will agree with you," he finally said. "Your problem was with how Lyle tried to put us together more than the fact of it. That's not an excuse for what I did. Nobody will believe what I say. It will be a long time for anyone even begins to trust the situation. I'm with you today. We'll see what happens tomorrow."

That seemed a satisfactory answer to Ellen. If she wasn't satisfied, she let the subject drop, and the ride felt peaceful. Mark finally pulled Lyle's message from his pocket and read it several more times. It was burned into his brain, but he continued trying to tease additional information from it. Nothing came of the effort. Lyle said what he said.

An hour later, the carriage passed them, its team high-stepping while their horse was just at a walk. Dave and the ladies wanted to get back to their homes and families. They all waved as they went past. Mark was not at all eager to find out what Lyle might have planned for his future. That supposed he had a future.

At the Oxford bridge, the guard force had increased to three. On seeing them, one guard immediately turned and jogged back toward the center of town. The remaining two stepped into the road, barring their way. They came to a stop in the middle of the Republican River bridge. From this point, even turning around would have been hard.

"We got orders not to let you across until Vince gets here," the one guard informed Mark.

Mark commented sourly, "Our management badges are revoked. We must use visitor passes. Higher authority must be with us everywhere, including the restroom."

"Geez, we're sorry. This wasn't our doing."

Mark saw a rider head straight up the hill toward the prow. He would be headed for the Lillard place.

Vince got to the bridge soon after. "We have to go a prescribed route. Follow closely and don't get cute."

"At least we're not in handcuffs."

"That's another thing. There will be no conversation. Keep your eyes on the road and the reins in your hands."

Mark and Ellen glanced at each other, and nodded assent. The rider would reach the Lillard ranch long before they did. Lyle and Adeline would have plenty of warning.

Their horse plodded along, making the trip to the Lillard ranch from Oxford longer than the run from Arapahoe. As they drove up, Mark saw Lyle waiting on the verandah. As they stopped, an apprentice came around the corner of the house.

"Dismount, and give the man the reins. Grab your bedrolls," Lyle ordered.

Mark remembered being certain the drive to Arapahoe was the last he'd see of the farm wagon. Ellen and Mark stood side by side. Mark felt nervous, and maybe Ellen felt that way too, since she grabbed his hand. Lyle stood at the top of the three steps, looking at them. Finally, Lyle broke the silence.

"The two of you came back. That is a positive point. You came back together, which is even more promising. Come into the house. We have some things to talk about."

Adeline joined them in the parlor. It felt like a living room to Mark. He usually avoided the situation by not calling it anything at all.

"During the endless rain," Lyle began, "I mourned the loss of the human race. I also thought about all the ways we could do it better. It all ran into the same brick wall, known as human nature. At one end are the terrorists, who want us dead. There's Harry Dover, who says he was involved with inventing the Omega bug. We have you two. What you might do next, nobody knows, including you. We'll start with your trip report, guys."

Mark glanced at Ellen, hoping for a signal. The only signal he got was discomfort, which made something else they agreed about. Mark gulped involuntarily and launched forth. He began his narrative just after the Lillard intervention. Lyle let Mark simply spin the tale. When he got to the scene behind the stable, however, Mark faltered, not sure what to say or how to say it. Ellen took up the story.

"Tom and Sammie were very worried what Mark might do. They knew Mark went downstairs and outside without me. They grabbed me, and we followed him behind the barn. Tom used their common military background to change both his intentions and train of thought. Then Sammie nudged me to say something. She and I were only a few feet behind Mark, but he didn't know we were there until I spoke up."

"Sammie and Tom got you two back together, obviously."

Mark nodded. "They gave examples to show us how the two of us having problems made things worse for everybody around us. With each example, they made us step toward each other. When we couldn't get any closer, we looked each other in the eye, held hands, and finally kissed. When we finished kissing, Sammie and Tom had gone back to the house."

"Just like that, you were inseparable again," Adeline commented, sounding very doubtful.

"We didn't become inseparable, exactly," Ellen told her. "We decided we were better off together than apart. The situation is one day at a time, and maybe an hour at a time. It was good enough for Sammie and Tom to go ahead with their marriage. Jimmy did the honors this morning before we left."

"Jimmy Bower has become a man of many talents," Lyle said.

"He has, indeed," Mark told him. "His biggest contribution to the event was when he commented how marriage continues in our brave new world, but divorce is now impossible. It remains to be seen how that will work out."

"You are certainly testing Jimmy's theory. How did you find things in McCook?"

"If the snow we saw three days ago, and drove through two days ago, is any indicator, I don't think very many people could survive the winter. Tom asked about moving some McCook people to Harlan."

"What did you tell him?"

"I said I'd pass along the request. So now I've done it." Mark carefully kept a neutral expression.

"It's not like Harlan is crowded. Trying to supply people in Harlan alone is certainly easier on everybody than dispatching supplies on a two-day run to McCook. Don Rowley wouldn't do it without goods coming back. By the way, Mark, that makes two things you handled just right. You told Tom that you would relay the request. You also specified that Don Rowley's business was his own to conduct."

Mark and Ellen sat in straight back chairs, their bedrolls beside them. Mark had nothing more to say. He'd been uncomfortable anyway. Now the silence was killing him. It was Adeline who finally spoke.

"I think you two should take your bedrolls to the guest bedroom. You are staying here tonight, so get cleaned up. Dinner is in a half hour. Before you ask, Ellen, I don't need any help."

Conversation during dinner was about the health of all the horses, and the progress made by those being nursed back to health. There was nothing about why Mark and Ellen were summoned in the first place. Mark wondered if that might not be appropriate dinner conversation.

Adeline served a pork roast. Mark guessed it was one of those brought to Alma the day of the procession and barbecue. Don Rowley might have brought some back. Such a dish was a rarity in Harlan. The combination of an up-scale meal with the certainty that they were being punished created further questions for Mark.

He needed a private chat with Ellen, but that wasn't going to happen. After dinner, Mark and Ellen were invited back into the parlor. Now, it almost felt cordial. In addition, Lyle gave them more comfortable seats than the hard wood chairs. Adeline came in just after them, carrying a tray of coffee.

"You are worried what will happen. It is a matter of great concern to both of you," Lyle began. "Frankly, we're making this up as we go. The conclusion will be as much a surprise to me as to you. We'll get one thing out of the way to clear the air. Mark, I'm removing you as ranch manager, effective immediately."

Mark expected that, and was braced for it. Hell, Lyle told him that earlier. It hurt anyway. "I understand, sir," he finally croaked.

Lyle held up one hand like a traffic stop. "Before you say any more, you did everything I asked and a lot more besides. You trained Kevin exceptionally well. You can't be ranch manager any more because you won't have time. I don't have a title for what you will do. Your first task is to set up an express rider system to McCook. The horse Ellen rode will be the first mount assigned. That horse goes to Arapahoe. When Kevin trains another horse, it will go to Arapahoe, and the horse in Arapahoe goes to the castle."

Mark's mind was now processing at top speed. "There isn't enough hay at either Arapahoe or the castle."

Lyle nodded. "You're working the situation. That is excellent. Use the farm wagon, and transport hay, first to Arapahoe, and then to the castle. We need to keep contact with them."

"Yes, sir, I'll do the best I can. Will I have any riders assigned?"

"For the moment, you are the rider assigned. You might not find the next part as palatable. I want you to pay attention to the job, so Ellen, you'll stay here for now. We'll develop more permanent solutions later. Making this even more temporary is my perception that Ellen may get you to see things I might not communicate quite as well or at all."

Mark understood something just then. Ellen was a hostage to ensure he completed the work.

"Take the night off. Tomorrow, gather supplies and get ready. If you could both gather them and get to Arapahoe tomorrow, that would be best."

Ellen helped Mark get the farm wagon ready to go. Not long after first light, they shared a lingering kiss before Mark climbed onto the wagon seat. It was now a thoroughly miserable place to be. Ellen's horse, the first contribution to the express rider system was on lead behind the wagon, the tack tucked under the wagon seat. The Lillards had brought it back with them from Arapahoe.

Taking back the horse was his final act as ranch manager. At the time, it seemed the thing to do. It did get Ellen's attention. It backfired, just like everything else he'd done. Ellen didn't say anything about it, one way or the other.

He drove to Harlan Ranch, the place he had come to consider home. Somewhere along the line, Mark had forgotten or ignored the fact that having a home was not a thing he ever had. Who knew where he'd end up? These last few days with Ellen kept him from thinking that he should have kept going when he hit the fence behind the castle's arena.

His mind returned to last night, and Ellen. After a seemingly endless session, he lay back and just enjoyed looking at her.

"Wow," was the only word he could think of.

Ellen smiled, but her eyes were deadly serious. "Did you find that memorable, Mark?"

"I hope to shout."

She nodded somberly. "Well, just remember that when your foot is on the fence and you're staring at the horizon. You just remember that."

"I will have no trouble remembering that, Ellen."

She appeared to consider his remark as Mark looked at her some more. "Do you know what flashed through my mind when Mr. Lillard said you had to stay here?"

Ellen looked at him quizzically. "I guess I don't."

"I thought he was holding you as a hostage."

"How would I be a hostage? What would it guarantee?"

"It would be for my good performance. I just reacted to the situation. The trouble is, thinking through the situation did not let me dismiss it. I argued with myself at length, but all I could do was to consider it highly unlikely. It wasn't persuasive."

"If they consider me a hostage, they think I'm valuable to you. It also means they want something from you. They want you to do what they want. They're also counting on you wanting be with me."

Mark was amazed. "You just made sure I want nothing but you."

Ellen looked at Mark closely. "Do you really value me? Will you say that when everything falls apart? Your instincts haven't evaporated. When everything you dread happens, every fiber of your soul will want to boogie over the hill."

She had him there. The only thing Mark could do was smile, shake his head, and repeat, "We'll take it one day at a time. That's all we can do."

Yeah, Mark thought, it was one day at a time. Maybe it was not even that. It was one hour or even one minute at a time.

His butt already rebelled against the wood plank serving as a seat on the wagon, and wasn't even halfway to the ranch. The time he spent loading the wagon would be a break, but then came the long drive to Arapahoe. They might hassle him in Oxford or elsewhere, if he ran into Vince's posse members. If it gave him a break from the road, that might almost be something to look forward to.

Lyle said he didn't have to go that soon, but Mark felt a need to prove himself, and the phrase that pays was 'the sooner the better.' He had to prove himself to Ellen, as well. A corner of his mind observed Mark needed to prove himself to Mark. Yeah, maybe that was so. Maybe the real judge was the face in the mirror Lyle talked about.

What did he need to do to prove himself? How long would Ellen wait for him to do it? How about Lyle?

"Forget them," his inner voice said. "How long will you wait before you believe in yourself or give up on yourself?"

That is a point, Mark had to admit. He wasn't sure he had ever really believed in himself.

The voice continued its lecture.

"At that point," said the voice, "you'll know what to do or it won't matter."

Great, Mark thought. Now he was hearing voices. At least it was company.

There was no activity at Harlan Ranch. Everything seemed in decent order, though. Mark filled the wagon with small bales of hay. Then, he walked to the silent house. He peered through the window, and knocked on the door before going inside. No one had been there since Ellen left last time. He got all his warm clothes. There was no telling what kind of weather he'd run into. Mark also took cans and jars of food, following the dictum from Lyle.

He stowed his gear with the tack, checked the horse he was leading was securely tied, and got on the road. He had breakfast before leaving the Lillard place. Lyle had assured Mark nobody would hassle him for rolling through the county without an escort, but he was very familiar with people not getting the word. Rolling past the guard post at Oxford, the guys just waved, so maybe the word did get out.

It was a really long road to the ranch. Getting to Oxford took forever. Every moment took him farther from Ellen until time no longer had meaning. He floated in a blank universe. Was the horizon inviting? The hills south of the Republican River stared back at him, more foreboding than an invitation. The terrorists came from that way, after all. The high ground to the north was just bleak. Tom was right. Wherever he looked, there was only more mud, and it got worse the farther he looked.

Tom, Tom, the sniper's son nailed Mark behind the arena with no weapon but his mouth. Were Tom and Sammie still at Arapahoe? If they were, maybe he could get more information. At the same time, Tom and Sammie would try to get more information from Mark. That might be a problem. Mark wondered if what Lyle said about letting people into Harlan was for publication.

Lyle didn't say not to spread the word. He didn't say to announce it, either. Mark concluded that when Lyle wanted to let them know, he'd do it on his own schedule, and in his own way.

After an eternity of dark thoughts and gloomy outlooks, Mark got to Arapahoe. The two Peepul taking care of livestock and wagons, opened the service door. Looking around the service area for bikes and horses, Mark saw the McCook bunch was not around.

"They left this morning," one guy said. "They talked about going home." He took a second look at Mark's load. "Is the hay for here or for somewhere else?"

Mark smiled. It felt strange to smile. "It is all for here. I need to check in with Jimmy before I unload."

"Don't worry about it. We will take care of it."

Mark didn't argue. He grabbed his bedroll and personal gear. Inside, Jimmy took one look and steered Mark into a guest room. When he came out, Jimmy had a cup of coffee waiting for him.

As Mark sipped, Jimmy brought Mark up to date about Sammie and Tom. On seeing that the roads were melting and the western sky was clear, they decided to travel while things were in their favor. Mark thought the weather was in his favor, too, keeping them from picking his brain. When he got to McCook, he could stick to the facts. He passed the word, and the ball was in Lyle Lillard's court.

Jimmy got to the next point, which Mark thought he left behind. "It sounds like Mr. Lillard is still your boss. After everything that you and Ellen have been through, it's too bad she couldn't come along."

Mark considered Jimmy put that delicately. He wasn't sure he could reply as nicely. "Mr. Lillard wanted me to do this job quickly, and with a minimum of fuss. Meanwhile, Ellen is staying with them."

Mark didn't know if he should have blabbed that much. Jimmy took it in stride.

"That's really nice of them to let your wife stay. It will give everybody some company."

Mark checked on the horses and wagon. Everything was in good shape. The two Peepul working with the stock were still there, so he asked them about hay. One recalled seeing a lot of hay in small square bales, like what Mark brought, and described the place. Mark wondered if they would ride with him the next day to get the hay, and the two men had no problem. They even seemed enthusiastic about the project.

Later, Mark thought he'd see what Jimmy learned from the dark lady and her ghosts. "Now that they are married, it's too bad they didn't come to Harlan and say hello."

Jimmy nodded. "I asked them that. Sammie looked straight at me and said, 'I don't think so, Jimmy.' I asked why not, and she said, 'It feels like we're under continual surveillance when we're there. Everyone in Harlan thinks we have ulterior motives for what we do.' I thought that was strange."

Mark nodded. "If they had no ulterior motives, then everything they did was for the hell of it. Considering what I know they have done, that would make them devils, indeed."

Jimmy shrugged. "That was what I thought, too. I told her everyone has a private agenda. Tom stared at me like I was the wall, and said, 'We were in an impossible position. Nothing we could hope to do had a chance of being even remotely right.' When he said that, I realized they might be as screwed up as me."

Mark nodded. "When they were in Harlan, before you ever saw them, they had at least two choices. They took the option that let them avoid personal pain, as opposed to finding a way to save lives."

Mark took a sip of coffee and asked, "Did Tom happen to explain that statement, by any chance?"

"Yeah, he did. He said, 'Our main decision was whether to follow orders.' That kind of statement burned its way into my brain, if you know what I mean."

Mark considered how he hit home with their situation, both at the schoolhouse and when teaching Sammie to ride. Ellen commented how he had made himself the judge of the dark lady and her ghosts during those riding lessons. Sometimes a person's first impressions are correct, even before thinking about them.

Mark steepled his fingers. "I'll tell you something that needs to stay just between us. A mission took them to St. Louis but made it impossible for them to stay. Soon after leaving, their superiors advised they were not in the military any more. In spite of that, they gave the team additional orders, calling for them to witness the deaths of innocent people. I was just a lowly enlisted swine, but those simply aren't legal orders."

Jimmy looked at Mark. "I know Tom and his buddies are snipers. Yeah, I'll keep it to myself. I wouldn't jump into Stanley's cook pot and I won't bring up things that could put me into that team's crosshairs."

Jimmy nervously glanced around as if he was afraid either the sniper team or Stanley might have heard him. He licked his lips, and embarked on a new subject. "If you want a bath, we can rig a curtain near the cook stove, and heat water for you."

"I'll be okay for tonight. Thanks for thinking about it."

Jimmy went back into the kitchen. Mark found himself with nothing constructive to do, and paced up and down in the public area. Jimmy kept glancing at him. Mark finally got the message and headed into his room.

He found little sleep even after Jimmy turned out the lights. Even in Afghanistan, guys could keep in contact with their wives on a daily basis. At least, they did until the solar flares knocked out the satellites. Even then, they got letters. In his unit, letters had a bad habit of being of the 'Dear John' category. Their wife or girl friend wrote telling them not to try reaching them any longer.

Even letters were soon out of the question. That started while he was overseas. They couldn't deliver mail. The military declared them all missing and presumed dead. Even if delivery was possible, any letters would have stopped cold. Mark's previous relationship was over before he went to Afghanistan. Now, the military which declared him dead had itself turned to dust.

The ride to Arapahoe took forever, but didn't hold a candle to that long, lonely night without Ellen. He lay there, waiting for the dawn. He finally got some sleep, thinking about what would be involved with a new mail system. Personal letters could ride piggy-back with official missions between Harlan and McCook.

After breakfast, Mark collected the two Peepul and went after hay. It turned out all Mark had to do was drive the wagon. The two guys took him to the hay and bucked the bales into the wagon. Back with the hay, Mark found something like a party in the garage. Okay, it was more like a situation.

Jimmy stood by the door going into the Inn, staring toward scuffling sounds by the corral. As Mark's eyes adjusted to the dimly lit area, he saw five figures in a clump by the corral fence. The members of the group seemed more fearful than hostile. The outside passage door opened, and the over-sized figure of Stanley stepped in. He carried a large object, but set it down as he assessed the situation. Then he strode over between Jimmy and the group.

Stanley looked at Jimmy. "I brought people to keep the place clean and cook the food. Could you have Vickie come out here, please?"

Jimmy went back into the Inn without a word. Mark and his crew went past the group into the service area and unloaded the hay. Mark saw his helpers knew the people Stanley brought, but got the impression there wasn't much love lost between them. Jimmy was soon back with Vickie.

"Vickie," Stanley said, "you remember these Peepul. You worked with them at the castle."

"Yes, I remember them."

"Good," Stanley nodded. "They will not work with you now. They work for you. Do you know the difference?"

Vickie looked uncertain, but replied, "I think so."

"Maybe you'll get it when I say something to your new help."

Stanley turned to the five. Mark now recalled a couple of them from the castle. All still looked very uncertain about the situation.

"You five did what the dark lady said at the castle. Vickie is now your dark lady. You will do what she says. You see that man with her. His name is Jimmy. He is like the four ghosts at the castle. You will do what Jimmy says."

The five nodded their heads. Mark looked at Jimmy, and saw a bit of enthusiasm. He glanced at the five tribe members, and thought the fear dissipated. Vickie looked at Stanley, then at the five, and finally at Jimmy. She stood there momentarily. Mark watched the still life while his two guys bucked bales. It ended when one of the women took a couple of small steps forward.

"What do you want us to do, Vickie, ma'am?"

It wouldn't be hard for Vickie to divide the tasks. The ladies from Harlan already divided the work. There were two men who could do cleaning and check on things around the Inn.

Vickie straightened. "Come with me," she told them. "I have things for all of you to do." She turned back into the Inn. The five formed a line and followed her, like orphaned ducklings following whatever passed for a surrogate mother.

Stanley stood there, as though waiting for somebody to congratulate him. Jimmy did look at Stanley, but he just shook his head.

"Every time I figure out something I can do, somebody tells me I'm unemployed. Anyway, thanks for all the help. Maybe it will keep Vickie happy and satisfied."

Stanley seemed to instantly switch gears, finding the left-handed thanks sufficient. He grinned at Jimmy. "Don't worry what you'll do. I'm sure Vickie will find tasks fitting your many abilities. Vickie has come a long way in a few weeks. Being with you has been a good thing for her. I think it's been good for you, as well."

Just then, the two guys who normally cut wood staggered in. They were maneuvering a cast iron stove on an improvised dolly. His two hay guys had just finished stacking hay, and they went to help take the stove into the back room where they lived.

Stanley nodded to both Jimmy and Mark. "That is the result of my morning's scrounge. Don Rowley took a lot of good stuff, but he didn't get it all. The only room available to house the Inn's employees is this one, and it needs heat. I also brought insulation. Jimmy, you and Vickie are nice neighbors, but you two make too much noise for me to get any sleep."

Stanley took off then. Jimmy just blinked, and checked the water tank. He turned on the water and went back into the Inn. Mark's crew came back, wondering how they could get hay if Mark wasn't there. Mark suggested they use hand trucks. They might look around for hand carts or wagons around town that might work.

He could head for the castle the next day. This turned into an easy project. Not only that, he might even get credit for it. Lyle might even smile, but there was no purpose in pushing the fantasy too far.

There was a crash from the room behind the corral where the stove went. Going over, Mark saw the sections of smokestack fell apart when they tried to get it through a small window. It appeared the sections hadn't been pushed together properly. Stanley was showing them how to correct it by the time he got there.

Soon, Stanley went back to placing the insulation along the wall. Mark recalled do-it-yourself shows back when there was still television and electricity. Stanley looked like a featured presenter. Mark tried to compare Stanley with the big dummy he saw in the cannibal camp, but couldn't match the images.

Inside, the new Peepul crew already moved like a well-oiled machine. Jimmy stood and stared, a lot like his first day. Once again, his assistance was not required and barely tolerated. Jimmy gave up, inviting Mark to a table where they had coffee. Watching the work swirl around them made Jimmy nervous and Mark uneasy, as well.

After a while, the two newly unemployed men gave up and made a joint expedition to the back, to see how Stanley's folks were doing. There was a fire in the stove, and Mark could feel the heat at the door. Not only that, Stanley's insulation job was nearly complete.

Chapter 18
More Terrorists

Mark suddenly saw a problem with all the creature comforts in the room. Just to his right, all the meat hung from cables strung from wall to wall. Aging meat needed a cool room. The worst possible thing was for it to sit at room temperature.

Across the room, Stanley declared the insulation job done, so Mark called to him. When Stanley looked his way, Mark just pointed at the meat. Stanley immediately got the point and nodded. Jimmy joined them as they went in search of a solution. They found it only a few feet outside the building. Mark smiled at how obvious it was while Jimmy stood there and gawked at the thing.

"I remember seeing them around farms. Is that a grain cart?" Jimmy wondered.

Mark nodded. Something called a grain cart always brought to his mind a little two-wheel contraption with a box on it that a person could push or a pony could pull. Like his vision, this had two wheels, but there the comparison ended. The grain cart was ten feet high and twenty feet long. Mark thought it would have to be a long way off to even vaguely remind anybody of a pioneer's hand cart. It had a ladder and a large bin to receive combine loads of corn and other crops.

It had a metal bottom and a tarp cover that rolled across the top. They couldn't find any place critters could get in, so it could protect their food. By running poles across the interior and setting them on a lip just under the cover, they could hang all the meat. It had a window in the front to inspect the contents.

Moving all that meat was a lot of work. Mark pitched in and Jimmy did what he could. In addition, Stanley rousted the four resting workers. Once the workers understood the situation, they set to work willingly.

The wood cutters knew of poles of sufficient length and strength, and took the other two to get them. That was the easy part. Hauling large cuts of meat to the grain cart took a great deal of effort. Even worse was getting them up and over the lip of the thing. Then, they had to be arranged inside the cart. Even with all the help, the job took the rest of the morning. They finished not long before one of the household workers came out to announce that lunch was ready.

Mark didn't feel like he was competing for Stanley's admiration, but Jimmy apparently felt threatened by the situation. He suddenly blurted out, "Hey, Stanley, come on in and eat with us."

Stanley stared at Jimmy. "Are you sure?"

Jimmy nodded enthusiastically. "Absolutely. Oh, so you can get some rest when you're in town, why don't you sleep in a guest room?"

Stanley studied Jimmy, "They never invited me to eat in the castle, other than during the dust and rain. Just for showing up, you invite me to eat here. You make me think I might someday be accepted as human."

Jimmy grinned. "You made me an honorary member of the Peepul tribe. You're the head of it. It's the least I could do."

"What if travelers show up?"

Jimmy wasn't concerned. "We'll work that out when the time comes."

Mark followed them inside, where he watched the newly arrived help swiftly reorganize tables to include Stanley. They just sat down when one of the new men apologetically slid up to the table, nervously looking at Stanley.

"Excuse me, Mr. Peepul, sir. One of the outside men is asking to see you. He's at the door."

Stanley walked over and talked briefly to one of the wood cutters. Stanley then beckoned both Mark and Jimmy.

"A group of hunters is over by the tree line. It would take something extraordinary for them to poke their noses out of the trees."

The three, with Stanley leading, went to check out the hunters, who looked very uneasy. Mark figured they must be even more concerned about something else.

The leader of the hunting party glanced at Mark and Jimmy, but focused on Stanley, "Yesterday, hunting toward the west, we picked up the spoor of the dust people. They got into McCook. We found them at the highway. They suddenly took cover, and a minute later, the dark lady and her ghosts came through."

"Did the dust people attack the dark lady?"

"No, they didn't. We got into position to defend the dark lady, but it never happened. They seemed worried by the ghosts' rifles, and that the ghosts rode bicycles. They seemed impressed by the dark lady being on horseback."

"What happened then?" Stanley wanted to know.

"After the dark lady and her ghosts turned toward the castle, the dust people chattered in a foreign language. Then they crossed the highway and went into a store. They posted sentries, and stayed all night. The next day, they started walking this way. They went down the middle of the highway."

Stanley appeared puzzled. "You're here. Why aren't they?"

The leader of the hunters seemed to understand.

"They do not act normal, like a group of people exploring a new area. They do not act like hunters, either, but just trudge along as though it is punishment. Everybody except for the leader stares straight ahead. A couple of times, one of them looked around a little. The leader came back and yelled at that person a long time. Then they started trudging again, chanting something in that foreign language, everybody looking straight ahead."

"The first group of dust people did that as well. Won't they get here today?"

"They made camp on the road. There were many good campsites beside the road, but they made a cold camp in the road. They didn't carry much food. Another hunting party is keeping watch so we could tell you about it. We think they'll be here about noon tomorrow."

"Did you bring extra spears?"

"Yes, we did."

"You did well," Stanley assured them, and then stopped to think what should happen next.

He finally instructed the man, "Bring me the extra spears. Two of your fastest people must go to Oxford and let the rest of our people know. You should also tell the Harlan people. The rest of you make camp. We will greet these dust people tomorrow."

"Where will we take them? You said we had to stay in the tree line except for McCook and Oxford."

Stanley nodded. "We can come out of the tree line in Arapahoe, but only on this side of the highway. We will stop these dust people before they get this far tomorrow. We do not want their stench near the Inn."

Mark wondered what Stanley had in mind. As everybody scattered, he realized that if he had a letter for Ellen, one of Stanley's hunters could have taken it.

Stanley had a plan. Mark couldn't imagine how he came up with it so quickly, but it sounded like it could work. Even his back-up plan would handle it, although it could be messy. They spent the afternoon being certain everybody knew their part.

The next day, they brought a chair and table in front of the old motel. Those went on a flat spot at the edge of the road, with the chair on the shoulder facing the centerline of the highway. Meanwhile, the hunting party found hiding places on either side of the highway. Mark had his Army rifle locked and loaded.

A member of the hunting party following the terrorists, showed up to let them know their visitors were close. Jimmy looked back at the Inn and waved his arm. Then he sat down as their help hustled up with a napkin and flatware. Right behind came pork stew, cornbread, and coffee. Just as the got out of sight, the terrorists came shuffling down the highway. They all looked like they'd gone too far for too long on too little.

Mark made sure he was out of sight. He could just see Jimmy, who savored each bite of the stew as the terrorists approached. A breeze came to him from them, and Jimmy nearly choked. Without turning his head, Jimmy muttered, "They absolutely stink. The smell is of death and corruption."

Jimmy suddenly got some of Stanley's abilities. Stanley's voice softly came from behind another tree nearby. "Don't choke. Be sure to greet the distinguished guests. Be happy. Enjoy your meal."

Jimmy did that, acting like everything was dandy. Jimmy whispered that he recognized the terrorist who spoke for their leader. This must have been the same guys he met back in McCook. Mark snuck a peek, and it looked like the entire bunch coveted Jimmy's stew.

Jimmy pretended to taste a morsel of stew, followed by a nibble of cornbread and a sip of coffee. Then, he dabbed his lips with a napkin. Only then did he appear to realize they were there. He looked at them for a moment and then nodded.

"If I'm not mistaken, you are the same fine folks I met in McCook," Jimmy observed.

The spokesman nodded, "We talked in the empty town. You were helpful then. Perhaps you can help us now. Do you know anything about the soldiers on bicycles?"

Jimmy dripped sincerity. "Yes, I can tell you about them. They are very dangerous. They kill everything they see."

"When we last talked, you spoke of cannibals. Are they still north of McCook?"

"A few may be there. Most have moved."

The man chewed on his bearded lip and then asked, "We have friends and comrades, all holy warriors. They may have come this way. Did you see them?"

"Would they have been a group like yours?"

"Yes, they would have looked much like us," the man said, hopefully.

"No, I'm afraid I didn't see them." Jimmy watched the man paste on a crestfallen look before he continued. "I heard about them, though."

"Really? What did you hear?"

"I heard the cannibals got them."

The man shivered and licked his lips. Then, he translated for his leader. Mark, who spoke Pashto, listened to the exchange. He thought the translation conveyed the sense of the conversation. Finally, he turned back to Jimmy.

"Do you have any extra food?" he asked. "That smells delicious. What is it?"

Jimmy smiled innocently. "Yes, the stew is really excellent. I would be happy to get you some." Then he added as an afterthought, "Oh, by the way, it is pork stew."

The man backed up, his hands in front of his face as though trying to fend off a rapist, he gasped, "We can't touch that. It's unclean."

The gang of terrorists were hypnotized by the food, and none of them understood the conversation. By now, the Peepul had two hunting groups arrayed behind the terrorists. Other hunters hid behind Jimmy with Stanley. They wouldn't give the terrorists any chance to use or even think about the weapons they carried. Mark was there to ensure nothing got out of hand.

Jimmy put down the napkin and flatware. "This pork is quite clean. It's definitely cleaner than you bunch of jokers."

The stage was set for act two of the play. Jimmy sat back and slowly surveyed the group.

Finally, he attempted another smile, but even the terrorists could see he was only showing his teeth. "By the way," he continued, "you didn't ask where the cannibals moved."

Jimmy slowly and carefully stood up, and moved a half-step to clear the chair. The terrorists didn't know whether to watch Jimmy or the food now.

With a somber face, Jimmy continued, "There are specific members of the tribe you should really concern yourselves with. They are right behind you."

The translator glanced back at his leader to say something. It brought both the hunters and their spears into view. The translator's sudden wide-eyed look of terror didn't need translation. The hunters moved in unison, and a few seconds later, thirteen deceased terrorists were on the pavement.

"The smell of those people," Jimmy commented, "is awful. All I want to do is throw up."

Stanley walked up beside Jimmy. "It's not just me smelling the dust and the people who spread it. Would you have any problem detecting any nearby?"

Jimmy shook his head. "My only problem would be trying not to get sick. Mark, are these clowns enjoying their seventy-two virgins?"

That brought a low chuckle from Stanley.

Mark moved out a step. "All the so-called martyrs, taken by dust, rain, and other misadventures, are ahead of them. By now, anything resembling a virgin will never be anything but a virgin."

That hit Jimmy's funny bone, but when he started to laugh, he also choked. "Oh, please, it's hard enough to keep my breakfast down. I've got to get some distance from this."

Mark felt the ground vibrate and heard the unmistakeable sound of multiple horses coming at a rapid pace. A moment later he saw them pounding up the road. Josh, Mr. Lillard, and Kevin were among a large number of mounted men and women. All had rifles at the ready, and drew up a little way from the scene.

"We didn't quite get here in time for the fun, I see," Mr. Lillard commented.

Jimmy looked up. "You didn't miss much. Stanley didn't want them stinking up the Inn, so we had a small reception out here."

Mr. Lillard listened to Jimmy's description. At the end, Lyle shook his head. "They marched up the road and found you eating a hot meal at a table beside the road. They didn't think that was odd?"

Jimmy grinned. "That should have been a weak point in the plan. We knew they were neither carrying much food or anything else. Stanley figured their hunger would overwhelm any good sense. He has a very low opinion of any group marching through unfamiliar areas, whose leaders forbid their members to check around for problems."

Stanley and Mark were off to the side. Mark stayed put as Stanley walked over next to Jimmy.

Lyle Lillard looked at him. "Stanley, we have to thank you again for taking care of terrorists or dust people."

The new household help were all outside staring at the horses. Jimmy beckoned them to remove the food, table, and chair. He then grinned at Stanley and offered his hand. Stanley returned the smile, shook hands, and looked at Lyle.

"I appreciate the gratitude, but this was for me and mine. They were looking for the first ones we took care of. Mark and I had a short chat about it one time, but I need more information. How many of these creatures are there?"

Josh leaned forward in his saddle. "An informant reported fifty like these and six hundred slaves. The first fireteam you destroyed made his information doubtful. With this lot, he is clearly lying. A total of six hundred might be real." He turned to Lyle. "We don't need to tell our source about this, do we?"

Lyle nodded. "I always had doubts about his story. He first claimed to be a slave. He is now a snake in the kitchen."

He then turned to Vince. "Find our guest full occupation as far from the rest of us as possible. Let him know Stanley's folks find his presence extremely offensive. Don't say how you know this."

Mark saw all the horses were lathered. He took a couple of steps. "You know, Jimmy, those horses could use some rest and water."

Jimmy picked right up on it. "Might I offer the hospitality of the Arapahoe Inn? I'm sure your horses would like the break."

"Excellent idea," Lyle said. "We left in such a hurry that nobody brought anything but weapons. I don't think very many even brought bedrolls. I know I didn't."

"We can handle some of that," Jimmy replied. "If Stanley's people could cross the highway here, I think his people could gather linen and blankets. We should have a stock on hand anyway."

"That would be fine, Jimmy. Stanley, you already have the Furnas County side of Oxford. You should have the same freedom here, as long as nobody gets in the way of traffic on the highway."

Stanley looked at Lyle, mildly surprised. "That works for me. I have a favor to ask. Could your people could drag these filthy dust people away? My tribe can't stand to be near them."

Mark nodded. "I can saddle up."

Josh looked at Mark. "By the time you get saddled, we'll have it done. Kevin, Vince, limber up your lassos. We can take out the trash. The tribe has the river side and the town. Let's drag them up the hill beyond the houses."

Mark stood with Jimmy as the corpses departed. At that point, he joined Jimmy in hand wringing while he tried to figure out what his function might be. Tomorrow, he could head for McCook. The rest of this day would be to celebrate Stanley and Jimmy defeating another group of terrorists. It would no doubt become the stuff of legend.

Stanley commented the spears they used to take out the dust people would have to be purified in fire to get rid of the stench. The procedure would make the spears lose their temper. At times the McCook farmers were able to get them back in shape. Very often the only alternative was to replace the spearhead. There seemed to be no way to wash off the smell.

Jimmy suddenly took off and was everywhere, directing staff and guests. The Arapahoe Inn looked like a going concern, taking care of people nobody could have predicted even two days earlier.

Mark now realized that Sammie, Tom, and the sniper team, trying to manipulate and control the situation, only isolated themselves from the centers of power they tried to influence. Alex and Cordelia Thomas, with their neighbors, would be part of the new order. The castle was a dead end, with no way to include them. Mark himself was the only link to the dark lady and her ghosts.

Mark's internal dialogue was interrupted a minute later when Ellen rode up.

"You kept your foot off the fence rail," she quipped, smiling.

He hadn't even thought about that. "I didn't have time, setting this place up as a way station for an express rider system. The next step was to get the castle a supply of hay, but before I could do anything, we heard about the terrorists coming. Taking on those jokers with the farm wagon didn't seem smart."

"You did a good thing," she said, dismounting and rewarding him with a kiss.

Ellen said she volunteered for the cavalry. Adeline offered a horse. Mark helped her unsaddle. Then they wandered until it got cold, when they joined the festivities. It surprised Mark when everyone insisted they keep the room he had the night before.

At dinner, Lyle came up to Mark. "Could you separate from your new-found siamese twin for a few minutes?"

While Mark had to agree to the request, he couldn't help wondering what new test of his resolve to expect. All the information he got was that there was a project, and Lyle wanted his assistance. After collecting Josh, Lyle gave the two of them the task of keeping Jimmy in place. Meanwhile, Lyle grabbed Stanley. After some finagling, they were able to find something approaching a private spot. Lyle got eye contact with everyone, and cleared his throat.

"Stanley, all of us need to know the number of terrorists, or dust people. More than the numbers is the threat. Your people are now the front line, so you absolutely need to know what you are facing." Lyle shrugged apologetically. "We only know their intention to kill all of us. Harry Dover is both connected to them, and number one on their list to wipe out."

Stanley considered that. "I hope they never come in any larger groups. My people — your front line — consists of four hunting parties spread over eighty miles. This one group took two hunting parties. It wouldn't take many more before a significant number would get past us. That's even though we can smell them a long way off. What are the weapons they carry?"

Josh spoke up. "This lot all carried AK-47s, with little ammunition. Nobody had more than one extra clip of thirty-round magazines. That is nearly eight hundred rounds between them. You'd suppose that would be more than enough against the two hundred of us they know about. This is where theory is nowhere close to reality."

Stanley grunted. "The only weapons I ever saw them use was the dust. We got two in the solar buggy in that encounter. Since then, we got another twenty-eight. They killed fifty of my people. They owe me twenty more before the count is even. However, from what you tell me, settling accounts isn't an option."

Lyle nodded. "Should we engage the terrorists?"

"You saw the results when they poked at us blindly. How would we do better against them?"

"They are based in the NORAD bunker in Cheyenne Mountain, near Colorado Springs. We were able to verify that much," Lyle replied. "We do need to find out what they are up to. Only two people, Mark and Josh, are capable of such a mission."

Stanley agreed, but had a second thought. "There are the four ghosts. They can be as sneaky as anyone I've ever seen."

Josh and Mark exchanged looks. "Sneaky and intelligence gathering are both in their job descriptions," Mark admitted. "On the other hand, Vince gathered them up like vagrants. How can we take them seriously? In addition, you knew they were watching you in Harlan."

Stanley smiled. "Willy just had me sit there. It was easy to notice when anything in my little world changed. I believe the four of them are quite capable of doing whatever might be needed to get information."

Jimmy looked up then. "I don't know anything about what you're saying. On the other hand, they let slip enough for me to believe they're very real. They got into the military camp taking care of survivors in St. Louis. They were supposed to take out somebody important. Maybe it was the commander. They followed Stanley out of town."

"Willy told me the guy who told us to leave St. Louis was called a general," Stanley commented. "I remember the conversation you had with the ghosts. They got really nervous when you asked about it."

Lyle considered that. "These guys are not field troops but can be sneaky. Also, to qualify as snipers, they must hit what they're aiming at. That could be useful."

Josh and Mark agreed, but Mark wasn't enthused. The idea of the team tagging along on reconnaissance didn't do much for him.

Mark asked Stanley. "What do you know of the country west of McCook?"

"The rain ends a few miles west of McCook. I've explored some of the area beyond. The first thing is a belt of dense fog, for another ten miles. The fog lifts just before the next rains come in. After that, it's been dry since the great rain. The rain band at McCook separates this area from what is becoming a desert farther west."

Mark already knew the answer, but needed to have Stanley tell about it in front of Lyle. It took him to his next point, dealing with the logistics. "We cannot count on water going to Colorado Springs," he said. "The terrorists must know of water, but there's no guarantee we can find it, or that it will be enough for us and our horses. We will need riding horses and pack horses."

Lyle agreed. "We need to train five riding horses, suitable for novice riders. Then there's training six pack horses."

"That will be a full time job for Kevin. It will really slow up the training program."

"Kevin needs to continue training. You can do it when you're not honeymooning."

Josh looked at Lyle. "You're dead set on taking the snipers — novices — on a combat mission that is 350 miles one way."

Lyle grinned. "They're Marines. That means they are tough. Right?"

"They claim a version of 'cowboy up' in the Marines. That mostly translates to a bunch of trail-sore hombres who don't dare whine about it too much," Josh snorted. He looked at Mark. "How long would that training would take?"

"It would take at least a month per horse. A trainer can work with multiple horses each day. It'll still be winter, working with them full time."

"That sounds right," Lyle replied. "Even if you did it all in a month, we're nearly into winter, now. This will be next spring. I don't see the terrorists doing much either." The meeting broke up then. It had been a long day and the Harlan people wanted an early start in the morning. Mark wandered back over to Ellen.

"The express rider project is at a standstill. We can send a message to McCook, but they can't send one to us, as it stands. Lyle tells me I need to concentrate on training horses. I can't do that unless we're at home."

Ellen's eyebrows rose. "He told you that? Just that way?"

Her question should have been a tip-off. He was about to get nailed again. Still, it had been a long, tough day. "No, but that's the only way we could do it. Why?"

"He's right behind you, and doesn't look happy with what you said. That's why."

Mark turned to see Lyle, and as usual, Ellen had it right. He did look disappointed. "What will it take to keep the thinking side of your brain turned on, Mark?"

"What do you mean? You just described a full-time job through the winter. If the weather gets much worse, an express rider would have no way to get to McCook from here. What part of the story did I miss?"

Lyle shook his head. "Process the information some more. Get the larger picture. What is our first need? I mean, before the horses?"

Ellen snorted. "Come on, Mark. It's right in front of you."

"We need riders."

Lyle nodded. "Where are these riders, pray tell?"

The light finally dawned. "The riders are at the castle. Do I need to take a message to Sammie and her sniper pals?"

"Do more than take a message. Sell the point. If this winter kills them, those snipers will be of no use next spring."

"How do you want me to do it?"

"You can tell them that everyone from McCook is welcome to the town of Orleans. Nobody is in the area, and there is lots of room. Some of the farms are pretty nice."

"Sammie and Tom won't even visit Harlan." Mark glanced at Ellen for confirmation, and she nodded.

Lyle rubbed his chin. "They might be more comfortable staying in Arapahoe. It may be touch and go to keep this place supplied. Sell it any way you can, Mark. I'll let Ellen stay here. However, she cannot go any farther. The horse she rode will give you a spare going to McCook. Meanwhile, I'll get Don and his people to help with the evacuation. That's what it is, Mark. It's an evacuation."

"What happens with Stanley's tribe?"

"That's a good point. I'll speak with him in a minute. Now, you two need to go have some private time."

Lyle went after Stanley, who, at well over six feet tall, was not hard to find. He was heading out into the service area just then. At least, that's what he was trying to do. Jimmy stood in the door, blocking him. It was a unique sight, and immensely foolhardy on Jimmy's part.

"Where are you going, Stanley?" Jimmy looked up at him.

Stanley shook his head. "We agreed I could stay here when you didn't have guests. They're here. It's no big deal."

Jimmy looked around and raised his voice. "Stanley got rid of the dust people without a shot fired or any of our people hurt. After that, does he have to stay out in the cold?"

"Hell, no!" came the response from all around.

"There you go, Stanley. Your guests just voted. Go back to your room. You paid for it twice, and you're entitled to it forever. What do you say, folks?"

Agreement came from all sides. Stanley finally accepted the honor, looking embarrassed. He hauled his kit back into the room. Lyle was right behind him, leaning against the door frame. Mark couldn't hear, but Stanley was not one to use lots of words when a few would do. A couple of minutes later, Lyle nodded, gave a partial salute, and walked away.

Ellen let Mark watch the show and then drew him into their room. As the door closed, Ellen looked at him. "How is it with you and the horizon?"

"The only horizon in my mind's eye has your face."

"Oh, now you are the sweet talking devil. What you're saying is that events haven't gotten bad yet."

"I can't argue that. Everything's better than I had a plan for or right to expect. I'm sorry you're losing another horse."

Ellen smiled. "You're a sweet talker and considerate, too. I've been the lady of leisure at the Lillard place. I'm all practiced up. All these folks can serve me, hand and foot. Vickie has them pretty well trained."

A knock came on the door. It was Jimmy. "I check the weather every day. It looks like the storms will stay toward McCook, at least for a day."

"That sounds great, Jimmy. Is there anything else?"

"If you want coffee, you'd better get it now. Everybody is finding a spot for the night. It will be tough finding your way to the counter. I'm trying to keep a path open to the bathroom."

"A cup of coffee sounds good. Would you like one, Ellen?"

Mark followed Jimmy to the kitchen. Jimmy leaned on the counter. The new help filed past, heading to their home in the room behind the corral. Each one thanked him as they went past.

Jimmy went from town joke to lord of the manor in an astonishingly short time. Vickie soon went into their room and turned the light on. Jimmy said that meant it was time to call it a day. Mark took the two cups of coffee back to his room. The public room lights went off as he went inside.

Chapter 19
Message to McCook

Mark kissed Ellen after an early breakfast. Lyle saw it and walked over. "It looks like you're off to the office, Mark."

"I am. Your message won't deliver itself. Nobody knows how the weather will be, but it's clear to me that it is only getting worse."

"I understand that. Ride safe, Mark. We need you back here."

Mark saddled one horse and put the other on lead. The two Peepul opened the door for Mark, promising to go out soon to bring back hay. The cold air slapped Mark in the face as the overhead door went up. He pulled his hat down further, hiked his collar, and got moving. The sky was clear. Mark considered he should make as much time as possible while he could.

As much as he needed speed, Mark stayed at a trot going through town. The last thing he wanted was to run over one of Stanley's tribe. The only things in the road were small dark stains marking where the terrorists met their end.

The intervention was just outside Arapahoe, and rather than reflect, Mark increased the pace to a lope, enabling the horses to cover the most ground with the least effort. It didn't stop him from flashing back to the day, however.

Where he stopped the carriage for the Lillard intervention felt like a very long time ago. Mark was amazed, realizing it was only a week. At that time, they were looking at a first frost. He'd already gone through a pretty good snow storm. The trees in the area skipped fall colors, their leaves just curling up, turning dark, and dropping without ceremony.

He'd heard claims that a Quarter Horse could lope all day. Mark wouldn't make either horse try. Any horses doing it would have to be in top condition to begin with. Most of these horses just got healthy and could not perform at extreme levels. He was doing close to ten miles per hour, and planned to switch horses after an hour and a half.

A little more than halfway, his mount started to labor. He brought the horse to a walk for several minutes. The air hadn't warmed, staying below freezing. On top of it, clouds were gathering. Mark dismounted after allowing the horse to cool off, and found a place to tie both horses.

Nobody timed him, but Mark felt he switched tack as fast as when he was at the Rowley place. That was when the Peepul charged across the field at him. This weather made the thought of charging tribal members almost seem a nicer choice.

Just as he finished, scattered snow and sleet began. The footing would not let him to keep it up for long, but Mark got back to a lope. At the same time, he kept a close eye on road conditions, like he was back in the days of automobiles, and concerned about black ice. The snow soon covered the grass, but the dark pavement stayed warm enough to keep his path clear for a while.

Mark let the horses walk coming into McCook. In town, the snow was now accumulating on the concrete. It was starting to stick on the pavement. As he turned onto the ridge road, Mark found himself going into the wind, which was about as bad a situation as he could imagine.

Mark and the horses soon became much alike. None of them knew anything beyond the need to keep moving. There was no longer either past or future. There was only an endless effort as the snow got deeper. The wind suddenly switched around and blew on his back. That seemed favorable but didn't answer the question: would the ride ever end?

Structures resolved out of the swirling snow. The castle was dimly visible and soon the stable and arena appeared. Stopping at the main door, Mark dismounted. Slogging through several feet of snow, he bulled his way through a passage door. After the white outside, the area inside seemed completely black. Mark was perfectly aware that this was the arena. Wavering yellow spots registered at first. Finally, his eyes began to adjust, and the yellow lights transformed into campfires. Members of the Peepul stared at him, their mouths agape.

Mark's brain started to work again, and soon after, he made his mouth function. "I have two horses outside the big door. Could you help me get them in?"

Several jumped up. "When you came in, covered with snow, we thought you were a ghost."

"I was beginning to feel like one. Do you have hay and water for my horses?"

"Yes, we got all we could. When the dark lady came back with a horse, we figured the four ghosts would eventually have horses, as well. Stanley sent a message two days ago that we needed to be ready."

"You guys thought that out pretty well. What will it take to get over to the castle?"

"We have to clear a path. There is a shift change soon. Can you wait that long?"

"I could wait quite a while if I can share your fire. You wouldn't have any coffee, would you?"

A few minutes later, by the warmth of the fire, and his hands wrapped around a coffee cup, Mark began feeling human again. As he recovered, the tribal members took care of the horses.

"Have you had many storms like this?" Mark asked the guy next to him.

"This is the worst by far," he replied. "We have solar power in here, but they shut it down until after the storm. I don't know what we'll do if it gets worse. They say the weather is better toward Arapahoe and Harlan."

Mark nodded. "That is true. If it looked like this at Arapahoe, I wouldn't have stepped outside, much less tried this ride."

It wasn't long before tribal members grabbed tools, and started to dig a path to the castle. Mark tried to help, but they told him to take a load off. Working in pairs, they relieved each other every few minutes. Mark was impressed. The pathway got punched across to the front door of the castle faster than he believed possible. Bedroll in hand, he followed the work crew to the castle in a trench with snow up to his waist.

As a messenger, Mark should have waited at the door until invited in. After that ride, he didn't feel like it. Mark went just inside the door. The incoming shift could advise Tom and Sammie of their unexpected visitor.

True to form, Tom soon appeared at the balcony overlooking the front door. If Mark interrupted anything, Tom did not let it show.

"I don't see Ellen. Tell me you aren't running away again."

"If Ellen was with me, she'd have beat sense into me and we'd have turned around at the first snowflake."

Mark paused to see if his attempt to parry Tom's wit worked. Tom leaned against the railing, waiting, so Mark switched to straight mode. "Ellen is in Arapahoe. I'm just a messenger."

"Mark, you may have a message, but I'm sure that you are more than 'just' a messenger. Any information coming through that storm is more than 'just' a message. Come on upstairs. Your room is vacant. Get warm and clean up."

Sammie showed up, insinuating herself tightly against Tom. She looked at Mark and shook her head. "We'll send some fresh clothes. I'll have Dora send up food so you don't perish before supper. We'll let you know when it is ready. You sure aren't heading back right away."

The snow that remained on him was puddling around him on the tile floor. The suggestion to get warm and dry sounded inviting, indeed. Household staff were at hand to mop up the melt water, and he had no doubt they would follow his trail up the stairs.

The choice of room was unfortunate. Everything reminded him of Ellen. He hadn't felt the separation until then. Worse was the knowledge that he wouldn't be able to head back right away. The snow storm hadn't been nearly so painful.

He got warm and clean in the bathtub. When he came out, clean clothes and a light meal waited. As far as creature comforts went, it was a damn nice way to live. Then there was his current mission front and center in his mind. He was here to talk Sammie, Tom, and the team into leaving it all behind.

What was his best case scenario? He'd relate the message that Lyle had given him. His audience only had to look at the early snow to get his point, and everyone would agree. They could hardly disagree, having proposed the idea in the first place. That made it sound easy. Hell, it even made sense, but Mark didn't think it would happen. If it was that easy,

Lyle could have given Stanley a note to take on his next trip. The idea, as Lyle put it, made perfect sense.

Still, Lyle saw a need to sell the idea. That meant Mark had to play salesman. That was as close to a joke as he'd heard in a while. There were those who could sell ice to Eskimos. Mark wasn't sure he could give away a second chance to a condemned man. Thinking about the situation, that was precisely what he'd come to offer. Not only was he offering a second chance, it was all free. That meant it would never work.

He got a bit of a nap, in spite of himself, sitting up suddenly when a rap came on the door. It must be meal time. Mark hoped he wasn't playing Christian martyr to the local den of lions. Whatever positive thinking sales people were supposed to do, that was all Mark found. At least he was warm and dry.

Downstairs, it was a top-heavy table, with both Tom and Sammie at the head. Tom's team of ghosts sat on the near side. They indicated for him to sit on Sammie's right. That, in theory, qualified as a favored spot. Of course, they hadn't heard Lyle's offer. It was still snowing, which could be part of Mark's presentation.

It wasn't until they finished eating that Sammie give Tom a sign, and saw Tom nod. Turning to Mark, Tom asked, "Okay, I think we can hear the message you've brought. Whatever it is, everyone here can hear it."

Mark took a deep breath. "Lyle Lillard and Harlan County welcome everyone from this area. The town of Orleans and the area around it will be for all McCook people. Stanley Peepul has a separate deal."

"You make it sound like that includes the five of us."

"It specifically includes you. Lyle didn't get more specific. I'd guess that would be so you could maintain your current situation. It would be nice if some McCook people volunteered to help defend the area. We don't think that would not involve much over this winter. Orleans has nothing like the castle, but there are some nice homes. Don Rowley might help put solar and other conveniences wherever you wanted to stay."

Mark hoped he hadn't put his foot too far into his mouth, promising something approaching autonomy. This was supposed to be a temporary solution, so maybe it would fly with Lyle. Tom acted as though he was absorbing what Mark said. At the same time, Mark was sure Tom and Sammie already had well-defined answers to anything he said. In any case, there was nothing like surprise or shock on any face at the table.

Tom finally replied, "Our request was for the farm families to take refuge in Harlan. Staying together will help them, and I'm sure they'll pitch in however they can. We are comfortable, and don't intend to go anywhere. Why would we even consider it?"

Mark was prepared for that. "You had severe problems charging your batteries during the big rain. How will you deal with several feet of snow on your solar panels? Consider Stanley's situation. Will he endanger the lives of his tribe for your comfort?"

"Are you Stanley's spokesman too? If there's a problem like that, we'll take care of it directly."

Mark suddenly noticed there was a large figure in the doorway. "You are correct. Mark is not my spokesman. I speak for myself and for my tribe."

Mark was astonished. "How did you get here, Stanley?"

"On foot, as always. I arrived shortly after you came to the castle. I gathered the tribe, and we discussed the situation."

Tom looked over at Stanley, then turned to glare accusingly at Mark. "It looks like you are ganging up on me."

Mark shook his head. "The notion of two of us ganging up on five of you doesn't make any sense. Lyle said he would talk to Stanley. That's all I knew. What they said was never passed along to me. What Stanley did was all on his own. Having ridden through that snow storm, I'm at least as astonished as you at the fact that he's here."

"It is as I told you," Stanley replied flatly. "Dark lady, Tom, Ghosts, I never lied to you. I never stretched the truth. I never manipulated the situation. The five of you manipulate the soul. Every one of you would know if I used your methods or approaches."

Tom flinched and Sammie blanched. Mark recalled people called spin doctors, who could put a favorable light on anything but the truth. Evidently that was what Stanley talked about here. Adeline's comment that delving through an onion's layers didn't accomplish anything, since an onion was nothing but layers also came to him at that point. Tom and Sammie didn't say anything, but both sat stiffly.

Stanley merely nodded, and stepped into the dining room, lightly leaning against the back of a chair beside the last sniper. "What Mark said was true. Lyle did not say anything about Mark. I did not know until

I got here that Mark came on his own errand. What I tell you is that each of the tribe will make their own decision to stay or go. Some will stay for as long as you five. Others will leave in any case. It appears five will stay as long as you do."

Mark considered Stanley really cornered Tom. Glancing at Tom, Mark saw he wasn't the only one who thought so.

Tom licked his lips briefly. "You're laying the responsibility for these members of your tribe on us."

Stanley neither blinked nor changed expression. "Yes," was all he said.

With that, Stanley turned and left the room.

Mark knew Stanley's upbringing didn't include many social niceties. He was nearly beyond blunt that time, showing a different side of his personality than he'd used with Lyle or even Jimmy. It seemed Stanley didn't consider the fact of Sammie and Tom educating him worthy of eternal gratitude and undying devotion. Of course, Mark only heard how the savage Stanley got civilized from the dark lady.

Come to think of it, her part in his transformation had come across as rather heroic. Mark thought it would be interesting to get Stanley's point of view about that. He let his eyes rest on the doorway, now empty. Then he brought his gaze back around to his hosts. What Mark had to say would not be words of comfort for his hosts.

"How does your comfort look now, Tom? Stanley didn't say which five would stay."

"It stretches us pretty thin," Tom allowed. "You have me over a barrel. We'll only evacuate after everyone else. Also, we will only go as far as Arapahoe."

"Lyle thought you might say that. Jimmy isn't comfortable around you. Lyle might allow Jimmy and Vickie in either Oxford or Orleans. Whether Don Rowley leaves any of his equipment in place in Arapahoe, is between you and him."

"We might live with that. We are aware that this rescue mission is not out of the goodness of your Harlan hearts."

Mark leaned back. He knew the conversation would get here sooner or later. His best bet was to follow Stanley's example, and simply lay it out. He was really pushing the limits of their hospitality. Then again, if he ended up in the arena with the tribe, so be it. It was better than living outdoors.

"Next spring, we will reconnoiter the terrorists. We need to know their strength, composition, and intentions. Lyle wants to include some or all of your team with our party. That would be difficult if this winter kills you. Personally, if we all had the same boss in the military, it would be a nice touch for us to combine forces. We could camp together this time."

Tom seemed puzzled. "What's the urgency with the terrorists?"

"A group, about fire team strength, got to McCook at the same time you guys returned from Arapahoe. They watched you go by. Stanley's hunters took them out at Arapahoe. Stanley says they stink like the Omega dust. The terrorists say the only way there will be peace is when we're dead. We need to know if they will hit us in force."

Tom nodded. "They just won't leave us alone, will they? Still, their only way here is on foot. That takes them through several hundred miles of desert followed by a perpetual blizzard, at least until warm weather. That gives us the winter to figure out what we want to do. With any luck, this area of snow will shield us from them until the weather warms up again."

Mark smiled grimly. "That requires a double-dose of luck. The first is that the terrorists will have enough good sense to not probe us. The second is that the weather will remember to warm up again."

He saw no future in debating the unknown and decided to try for a summary and close to their session. "I understand you guys will hang on here until we get all the farm families out. After that, you'll evacuate to Arapahoe."

Tom looked at Sammie, sitting between them. She pursed her lips and gave a brief nod. Tom then looked at Mark. "We agree that is how it should happen. The terrorists are another situation. If we can't come back here to the castle, Arapahoe will be the tip of the spear. It is a logical place for a military unit. For a family starting out, it sucks."

"Ellen is in Arapahoe. The weather being the only shield between her and the bad guys, I can only hope for lots of blizzards, whatever it means for getting everybody out of here."

"I'm glad to know that Ellen's on your mind. We'll hope the terrorists decide to take the winter off, and make life more bearable for everybody. Switching to survival mode for the winter is something they knew about in Afghanistan. Shall we toast our agreement?"

"Since I don't have to drive home, that's a great idea."

Outside, snow still came down but seemed lighter. It also looked like the wind was blowing more strongly up the ridge. Mark hoped that meant something positive. A breath of warm air would be nice.

Mark had a long and miserable night, not that he expected anything else. He stewed about what the dark lady and her ghosts would do. That was in addition to the black hole where Ellen should be. It was beyond understanding. He took her for granted for so long, and then wrote her off so easily. Now, he missed her so much after just a few days of real wedlock.

Soon after first light, Mark looked out at clear skies. There was a rumble above him, followed by an avalanche of snow past the window. Toward the stable and arena, Stanley's people were outside without the heavy winter gear from yesterday. Maybe he could get out sooner rather than later. The main points of his message were delivered and accepted. Still, he was dead in the water until the roads cleared enough to get back to Ellen.

The only place he was going for now was the dining room, where, as expected, the dark lady and ghosts hadn't appeared. The four snipers had left behind the military discipline of being up at 'Oh-Dark-Thirty.' Mark did not believe the dark lady ever cultivated such nasty habits in the Air Force. Dora and her crew were up and working. She took his breakfast order personally.

"Stanley says you all talked about the weather situation, Dora. What are you going to do?"

Dora was noncommittal. "Stanley told us that each of us has to make up our own mind. For me, that means staying here and doing my job as long as I can. If things get too bad, but the dark lady stays, I would leave anyway. It wouldn't be until the last wagon, though."

"Stanley talked like some were loyal to the dark lady, and others were not. You would abandon them to their fate?"

Dora stopped for a moment. "I heard what he said. He said the truth, but not all of it. Many of us had lives before the tribe and before Willy. We are true to the job we do. It's all we have left. Stanley earned some loyalty. He saved us several times. The dark lady and her ghosts earned nothing. Stanley told us to come here and do what we're doing. It beats being out there. Some of the tribe were on drugs as children, and after, only knew Willy's abominable sacrament. Now, Stanley has to be their leader and parent."

"Nothing is simple when it comes to people, is it?"

Dora grinned. "Genius is simple. People are complicated." She cocked her head. "I have breakfast business coming. I'd best get busy."

Mark considered Dora's job now must be a lot like whatever she did before all the catastrophes. He had heard nothing, but maybe she had a second sense for customers like he did for predators hunting him. Her senses were on time. Tom and Sammie paraded in the door moments later, the three snipers close behind. Mark raised his coffee cup in salute. Tom and Sammie nodded in response.

Dora didn't have to take their breakfast orders. An assistant came out with coffee just after they sat down. Dora brought their food soon after. Mark would have considered it spooky if he hadn't seen so many other things just as strange in the past several months.

"You guys are up early," Mark observed.

"We couldn't sleep with the snow sliding off the roof," Tom returned. "The storm is over. Maybe the roads will clear enough for you to get home tomorrow."

"Yeah, that's what I was thinking."

Tom leaned back in his chair and relaxed a moment. "When you go, we have a message for you to take."

Mark stiffened. Did they decide to turn down the proposal?

"We agree with what you offered. Our group will be the last out. Our message is not a counter-proposal. It's more of an addition to what we talked about yesterday."

Mark blinked and took a sip of coffee. What could they possibly add? "Okay," Mark replied carefully.

"Arapahoe will be the tip of the spear. When the terrorists come, that's the way they go. There is no way we'll go into Harlan, so that leaves us Arapahoe. Mark, we want you and Ellen there in Arapahoe with us. You can train horses, and you can train us to ride."

Mark was astounded. He couldn't think of anything to say, but had to say something. "Arapahoe will be the end of a bridge to nowhere."

Sammie came in then. "Think of it. There are five rooms. That's one for you and Ellen, one for Tom and I, and each team member will have a room. It works out perfectly."

Mark didn't think Ellen would agree. The word 'perfect' might be in Ellen's response, but it would be paired with a word like 'disaster.' How would Lyle respond? Did he expect something like this? Mark gathered his scattered thoughts.

"You put a good deal of thought into this. I can only tell you what I did last time. I'll give your message to Lyle. He'll make the decision and let you know what he decides."

Tom raised his eyebrows. "What I'm hearing doesn't sound like a vote of confidence."

Mark shrugged. "Among other things, it's not how Ellen envisions life. I do see your point about having somebody from Harlan."

"If you want us on this long-range recon patrol, we have to learn how to get along. I think we all agree it is a long way to Colorado Springs, especially on horseback."

That was a point Mark couldn't argue, and didn't try.

Mark prepared to go. The snow level quickly dropped, hastened by rain storms. He had his bedroll and was near the stairs when Sammie and Tom came out.

"Thanks for the hospitality. Just in case Lyle Lillard asks, the farmers do know about our discussions, don't they?"

Tom nodded. "We got everybody together when we first asked you. They agree it's the only sensible thing. Have a safe ride."

Mark rode out, his second horse on lead. It was a clear morning. The road was paved, keeping it from being a foot deep in mud. Mark set a fast pace, like he started, and at first featured a fair amount of water splashing up on him from the wet roadway. The pavement began to dry as he continued on.

It was a fast ride, compared to the other way. Mark still had lots of time to think, but there was not enough time in the world to find a way to break it to Ellen. In Arapahoe, Ellen ran up to him.

"If you have as much to tell me as I have to tell you, we'll be chatting the night away," she told him.

"What's to tell?" Mark replied. "It was one hell of a storm. I barely got to the castle. Tom and Sammie agreed with most of Lyle's proposal. They had an exception. They called it an addition."

"Can I know about it?"

"Yeah, Tom and Sammie want to be our roommates."

Ellen was flabbergasted. "They want to move onto the ranch?"

"They want us to be their roommates in Arapahoe."

"How can you train horses and people here?"

Mark shrugged. "Facilities don't train horses. People do. What about you being up close and personal with Sammie Moore? I know what you think of her."

"The prospect of being trapped with her over the winter could make me ill. What will Lyle say?"

"We'll find out. The message is for him, not us. Lyle has to decide. I think you also had quite a bit to tell me."

Ellen nodded. "Jimmy asked Stanley about plans for getting cargo to Arapahoe if Don Rowley quit making runs. Stanley got really irritated. After he settled down, Stanley talked about how his life had consisted of following somebody else's plan until a short time ago."

Mark nodded. "That's what we saw in Harlan."

"The first person with a plan was his father. That plan was to stay away from everybody, since all people were both stupid and crazy. That included his mother. He would slap or hit her, yelling she was stupid and crazy. All she ever gave him was somebody stupid and crazy, just like her."

"His father included Stanley, then."

"Funny, that's just what Jimmy said, and Stanley agreed. To survive, Stanley had to know nothing and do nothing. Acting retarded became his entire persona, and was no longer a conscious act. Stanley learned cannibalism from his father. When his mother died, they ate her, and buried the bones."

Mark shook his head. "Is that where the sacrament business came from?"

Ellen nodded. "Later the same year, during a bad storm, a large hail stone killed his father. Stanley did his father like his mother. Stanley then torched the place and walked to the city."

Mark nodded. "That does sound like where we dumped the vial of Omega bugs."

"Stanley took off for the castle then. Did he really get there through all the snow?"

Mark chuckled. "I think he had an easier time than I did. How was the snow here?"

"We got a good dose, but not like what you went through. Jimmy cut off nearly all lights to keep the batteries up. The next morning, Jimmy had a get-acquainted session with the people Stanley brought. He was mostly fishing for more about Stanley. The tribe was Willy's deal. He called it by Stanley's name so when the cops busted them, Stanley would take the fall, and Willy would just be another victim."

"That agrees with what we'd heard."

"Veronica, who took over the kitchen, said Willy was a low-level drug pusher. The cops picked him up now and then. They used him to find his suppliers. Stanley wasn't a client. Willy ran into him in jail. That was before the quakes. Veronica wasn't a client, either. She found her way to a refugee camp, run by a guy calling himself a general. He had a pot belly, strutted around, gave orders, and kept all the supplies for himself. One day, he put out cases of bottled water, and lined up soldiers between the supplies and the camp."

"He was trying to stir something up."

Ellen nodded. "One guy, who lost everything but his child, stomped out the gate, demanding water. The general ordered his uniformed thugs to fix bayonets, and yelled forward march. Leon, one of the two guys, spoke up. He was just inside the wire when they did the bayonet charge. The so-called general said one guy pleading for water was a riot. They killed him and wounded several more. Everyone hid in their tents. The thugs grabbed people they claimed were known criminals. They took Veronica, but left him."

"Enter Sammie and the team of snipers."

Ellen nodded. "Veronica said the thugs herded them up a hill outside the camp, and gave them to Willy. Willy said he had a secure camp and something to eat. The streets were dangerous, but he knew a safe path. Later, they had the choice to be a cannibal or dinner."

"Damned whatever they did. How did Leon join up?"

"On Christmas Day, he helped set up a tent and wire enclosure just outside the regular military camp. The general moved in. Leon's bunch was told to wait while he conducted business. A dark-haired woman sat in the shelter of a bit of ruin with a small fire, while Leon's group huddled together. A Humvee drove up. Two big guys drug a small fellow into the tent. He was soon out of the tent, walking by himself northwest. The woman put out the fire, and went to the tent, after exchanging looks with the two big guys. The two guys went in opposite directions. She was soon out, going a third direction from the first two."

"That would be the dark lady and her ghosts."

Ellen nodded. "Leon had a front row seat. The general strolled out of the tent, and looked around. Leon heard the crack of a large caliber weapon. A red spot appeared between the general's eyes. He collapsed. All hell broke loose, and Leon snuck off, following the little guy, who you no doubt guessed was Willy."

Chapter 20
Decisions & Preparation

"What are you doing?"

Ellen leaned against the service door frame, her arms folded. Mark glanced at her as he checked a cinch.

He shook his head, puzzled. "We're headed back to Harlan. We'll leave a horse and tack here. The tribal people have the hay covered, so we take the ranch wagon. I saddled your horse. There's no use in you having to put up with the wagon seat."

"That is very considerate, Mark. You know what happened our last trip to Harlan. There's no telling what fool's errand Lyle will send you on next. I'll sit next to my husband unless you have an objection."

"After the welcome you gave me last night, I won't argue. I'll get the tack off your horse."

"That's quite all right. I'll take care of it."

Just then, Stanley came in and checked them out. "You are heading to Harlan. The dark lady and Tom agreed, I presume."

"They agreed, but tacked provisions onto it. I'll pass them along and see what Lyle Lillard has to say."

Stanley smiled. "I see their counter-proposal was not to your liking." He looked at Ellen. "How is Vickie? That's the main reason I stopped."

Ellen nodded. "Vickie says she is fine now, but I'm not sure I agree. Yesterday morning, Vickie could barely walk, much less do anything. You could ask Veronica. I have no idea what the problem is."

Stanley nodded. "The degree to which her mind and body were abused is beyond imagining. It's a miracle she's alive. I'm astounded how normal she acts. Jimmy's influence has been positive and gratifying."

Stanley looked at Mark. "I suppose Arapahoe will be a way station for everyone evacuating McCook."

"That's the only way it can work. We can do one or two families at a time. That gives me an idea. We could run the farm wagon between here and Harlan. Don Rowley could take care of the route to McCook with his larger wagon. We could use the corral to store household goods and personal effects. Do you think the farmers will be able to move back, Stanley? I can't see any way they could work their fields with those daily downpours."

"I agree but think we don't need to share them too widely. It might be best to start like we believed it is just for the winter. If you and I agree, there will be less friction."

"Stanley, the farmers have no illusions about the situation. Still, but rubbing their faces in it won't make anybody happy."

"You and I see eye-to-eye about that."

Something about Stanley's hunting area struck Mark. "Stanley, how is hunting between Arapahoe and McCook?"

"We harvested most of the available large game near McCook. I'm glad Mr. Lillard let us expand. Being able to hunt around the lake has helped a lot."

"What if I suggest to Lyle that you extend north and east from Oxford toward Holdrege? That would give you game, and Harlan more defense."

"Oxford is working out well. Harlan folks bring cattle to our meat plant. It's been very peaceful. Of course, it's only been a short while, and you know that if it is possible for trouble to start, it will."

"That is a fact. I caused a fair amount myself," Mark reflected. "The problem will be whether we can keep Arapahoe going over the winter. Most of your tribe is toughened to the weather. Some like Vickie will need as much shelter as we can find. Lyle is fine with the farmers being in Orleans, I'm not sure about tribal members actually in the county."

Mark was surprised to see Stanley smile and nod. "There are limits to tolerance. Still, Jimmy handled the situation better than I expected.

For that matter, your Harlan people and my tribe worked together with no problems."

"Most of that cooperative spirit was your doing, Stanley. We need to get on the road. I suspect we'll see each other sooner rather than later."

Stanley waved at them and headed inside.

Ellen pulled off her saddle and manhandled it into the wagon. "You handled Stanley well, Mark. Somebody might mistake you for a person with sense."

"I hope I didn't make him think my wild ideas might actually fly in Harlan."

"Those were just talking points. I believe Stanley is quite aware of the situation. He knows a lot more than he lets on."

Mark did a last check of the rigging. "That's certainly been the case, hasn't it? I don't know if he is that way all the time, but I have yet to see anything get by him."

Ellen climbed onto the seat, and Mark led the horse toward the door. Before he took more than a couple of steps, two tribal members appeared out of nowhere to open the door. Mark grinned and waved at them as he got up onto the wagon after checking one last time that Ellen's horse was secure.

Ellen slid over next to him, making it one of the famous narrow seats Mark recalled the old folks talk about.

"All of a sudden, this seat is a whole lot more comfortable than I ever remember."

Ellen leaned her head on Mark's shoulder. "It makes you wonder why anybody ever bought cars with bucket seats back in the old days."

Mark wondered if Ellen had a psychic streak.

It was a smooth if chilly ride on the same wooden plank Mark couldn't tolerate before. Now, it felt good but there was no mystery as to why. Ellen was beside him. Halfway to Oxford, Ellen grabbed his arm.

"Stop the wagon. Now!"

Remembering her session of morning sickness in the carriage, Mark immediately complied. Instead of jumping off the wagon, Ellen spun around and got into the cargo box. She spread her bedroll, got inside, and wiggled around. After a moment, she looked at Mark.

"We need a rest stop. Tie the horse. You can only drive when you are well-rested. Anyway, I'm cold, and you need to warm me. Hurry."

Mark secured the horse to a nearby highway sign. Adding his bedroll to Ellen's and crawling inside, he discovered why she was cold. Ellen had removed her clothes. The second he was in with her, she stripped him. Things quickly warmed up. Afterward, Mark shook his head.

"Wow! That was really something. Not complaining or anything, but what brought all this on, Ellen?"

She looked like a teacher explaining a basic concept to a slow learner. Ellen brought one hand out from between them, and laid an index finger on the tip of his nose.

"We'll be back in Harlan all too soon. Who knows what strange errand Lyle has for you? Staying with Mr. and Mrs. Lillard, I expected lectures about married life. All I heard was how happy they were to be together in spite of everything. So if I can keep you happy, maybe your foot won't go over the rail, whatever is on the horizon."

Mark didn't know how to take that, and changed the subject. "There is no mystery about the next big job. It will be to evacuate McCook."

Ellen found a slightly different position, where they were in even more contact than before. "Veronica says the weather got strange in St. Louis last fall. After the big quakes, the Mississippi River began getting wider. The water didn't smell right. It was brackish, like sea water. They said the country unzipped straight up the river, across the Great Lakes, and up to Hudson Bay. The Mississippi is now a sea, pivoting on a spot near New Orleans. The eastern half of the country is headed for Europe."

Mark blinked. "I don't see what that has to do with the weather."

"The weather we're seeing now comes from the arctic instead of the Gulf of Mexico. St. Louis started having intense cold waves, alternating with abrupt warm spells. When they started west, the weather got more stable. That meant cold all the time, but not the really frigid times they had seen."

Mark tried to both think and enjoy the physical contact. "We haven't seen that so far, it is a lot like that. Whatever caused it there is doing it here, now. According to Stanley, the weather changes totally just beyond McCook. There is a belt of fog. Beyond is desert."

Ellen stroked Mark's cheek. "We need to tell Lyle all this."

A deep voice boomed, "Hello the wagon."

"Hello, Stanley. You didn't stay long in Arapahoe."

Stanley looked over the side of the wagon. "I stayed long enough to do what I could for Vickie. I'm headed for Oxford."

"Ellen needed a rest stop."

Stanley's face appeared over the side and his nose wrinkled. "There wasn't much resting going on. Either get moving or build a house."

"You always tell it straight, Stanley. We should let you be about your business, as well."

Ellen grabbed Mark's groin under the covers, making Mark grunt. Stanley laughed and left. Mark and Ellen pulled their clothes on and picked up the pace. Mark kept an eye toward the tree line, but never saw Stanley. On the tribe's side of Oxford, there was Stanley, chatting with some of his people. Mark couldn't imagine how he could move like that, although he recalled how far and how fast he went with Josh before they got out of the Army.

They waited at the bridge for some steers coming across, bound for Stanley's processing plant. The guards at the bridge were more relaxed. When the traffic jam cleared and they crossed the bridge, Mark looked at them.

"Is there anything we need to know?"

"Not that anyone told us, Mark."

"I'm glad, especially after our reception the last time."

"There's nothing today. Are you headed for Harlan Ranch?"

"We'll head to the Lillard place. It remains to be seen where we spend the night."

Both guards shook their heads sympathetically. At least, that's how Mark took it. Ellen ignored it.

There was little activity as they passed Harlan Ranch. One guy was close to the bunkhouse, and waved as they passed. Mark's decision to go to the Lillard place first was well-advised, from the reception they got. A couple of Lyle's people took the wagon and horses. Adeline had them take their bedrolls to the guest bedroom. The feeling was a lot warmer than the last time.

They joined Lyle and Adeline in the kitchen over cups of coffee. Lyle didn't seem to be in a hurry for the news, and Mark waited for a clear sign. In the meantime, he sent the conversation in another direction.

"Did Doctor Dover stick around? There was some talk he and his buddies might start a school for the kids."

Lyle chuckled. "When he heard the terrorists were still coming at us, he thanked us for our hospitality and left. Doctor Dover didn't say where they were going and we didn't ask. I wouldn't be surprised if they are back where you found them in Lincoln. If they didn't go there, it is no longer a concern of ours. I didn't realize you liked him so much."

"I don't care about him, one way or the other. The man was silent nearly the entire time coming back from Lincoln. Since he thought I had good questions when he first came into Harlan, I expected at least a little conversation. He spends a lot of time looking down his nose at everyone."

"You didn't want me to consider you another Harry Dover while you waited for me to declare it show and tell time."

Lyle could connect totally unrelated things. Maybe they were related. "Something like that, yeah."

"So, show and tell, already."

Mark started with the high points. Lyle soon wanted details, so Mark expanded where required. Lyle went further with things Mark thought insignificant. Mark speculated that he was checking to see if the previous attempt to smooth over the Vickie and Jimmy episode might happen again.

To ensure Lyle got no such impression, Mark carefully related their encounter with Stanley earlier in the day. Ellen gave him a look, and Mark was happy Lyle didn't question the need for a rest stop along with not getting any rest. Adeline then asked Ellen to help her with the meal, and asked Mark, "Is there anything you'd like?"

Mark shook his head. "Anything that's not pork stew will be just fine."

That drew grins all around. "I believe we can manage that. Why don't you gentlemen go to the parlor? You'll just be in the way here."

After relocating, Mark inquired, "What is the difference between a parlor and a living room?"

Lyle shrugged. "Adeline says this is a parlor, so that's what it is."

After a pause, Lyle pursued the real question. "As it happened, you didn't worry about your situation."

"That is true enough. Did I promise them anything I shouldn't have or say more than I should?"

"You did well and you've told me what happened. We need to get down to it. What do you think should happen?"

That sounded more like Lyle's side, but he took a stab anyway. "It makes sense for Stanley to hunt Oxford to Holdrege. Tom has a point about Ellen and me moving to Arapahoe with them. I don't like it. We might have to train at Arapahoe if they won't come into Harlan."

Lyle nodded, but leaned forward and raised a finger. "That bunch cruised all over Harlan when they thought nobody knew. Now when they have to come openly, they think we suspect their intentions. We have every right."

Lyle leaned back, steepled his fingers, and looked directly at Mark. "Let me rephrase the question. Assuming you ran Harlan, how would you respond? Tom made a formless threat. If we don't do what they want, they'll go sulk."

Mark thought about that. "If I ran Harlan, there would be no way to go along with it. I couldn't run Harlan if I wasn't here."

"What would you tell them?"

The light suddenly dawned. "I wouldn't tell them anything. The weather is forcing our hand. We agreed about moving the farmers and their families. I didn't talk to the locals, but Tom claims they don't object. What Tom actually told the farmers may be open to question."

Lyle nodded but waited for more, so Mark continued. "Don Rowley and his folks could get a family to Arapahoe every trip. I could run the farm wagon between Arapahoe and Orleans, and send updates through the guards at Oxford. When we get to where the only ones left are the bunch at the castle, Don can do a final run. Some of the tribe said they will leave on the last wagon."

"If the five go out on the last wagon, you will still be hauling people and goods. What will you tell them?"

"My place is in Harlan. When we get horses trained enough to get them started, we'll make arrangements."

"What if they stay at the castle?"

"When my foot was on the rail, nobody stopped me from going. They relied on me being able to figure out what I needed to do. We're reaching a hand out to them. If they want to kill themselves, they'll do it anyway."

"Are you trying to convince me that you've turned a new leaf?"

Mark shook his head. "No, I know better than that. When events go south, and I can think about it, I won't predict what I'd do."

Lyle grinned. "I need to keep you too busy to worry about such things. We can handle that. You just gave yourself plenty to do over the near future. It's too bad the express rider idea didn't pan out, but getting the McCook people to a safer place has to be our first priority."

Mark sat back and reflected about it. Then he leaned forward, quietly commenting, "If the dark lady and her snipers have a tendency toward self-destruction, they're the last people I'd want on a mission."

"You're exactly right. There would be no way you could rely on them to watch your back."

"Josh thought you were in the same end of the military that we were. You wouldn't have run into a guy named Gutierrez, would you?"

"The name strikes a bell. It's been a long time, Mark. When I got out, I made every effort to bury all of that. It keeps coming back anyway. What brought that name up?"

"That's who gave the orders to the snipers and Sammie Moore. He also ran our higher headquarters."

Mostly through breakfast, Lyle leaned back and smiled at them. "What are you two doing today?" he asked.

Mark was puzzled and suspicious. "Do? We figured there'd be any number of missions to accomplish."

"Don Rowley knows about the rescue mission. He won't be on the road until tomorrow, at the earliest. Two days to McCook, a day to load; another day back to Arapahoe. Everyone will need to rest overnight at Arapahoe, so it will be four days before you need to leave."

"And?" came from Adeline.

"I realized you two have not been home since you got married."

"I helped Lyle with that," Adeline added.

"Home?" Mark mused. "I figured we'd bunk wherever there was a spare room."

"Your sarcasm precedes you," Lyle grinned. "We considered setting you up in Ragan or Huntley, but there's a shortage of decent places. There is the wedding night house, or maybe you could rough it at the Harlan ranch house for now."

Mark tried to act like he was considering the idea. "It's either Harlan Ranch or a room at Arapahoe, and Arapahoe will be sold out for the next several weeks. Yeah, we could do that for now."

"I'm glad that's settled. Ellen, can you make sure Mark doesn't jump the fence? We'll need him to ferry folks back here."

"I'll nail his foot to the floor if I have to."

Lyle shook his head. "By the way, Mark, we brought back your duffel bag. We parked it at your house."

"You brought back my duffel bag?" Mark was really astonished. They expected him to come back for it. "I completely forgot about it. Thank you."

The Lillard's help had saddled Ellen's horse, but she tied it on the back of the farm wagon and rode with Mark. As they rode away from the Lillard place, he glanced at her.

"Will we need any rest stops?" he quietly asked with something of a leer.

She looked at him for a minute. "I believe your lust will get us to the house. I don't see much wanderlust at the moment."

Mark spent the drive thinking of all the lovemaking coming. Ellen had other ideas, immediately rearranging things to suit her sense of how their happy home should be. He found himself getting domestic, to his dismay.

Grouchy old Don Rowley come rumbling in after lunch, but Mark took his arrival as a gift. It was an opportunity to get out of the house. Several workers were with him along with a load in the wagon. "I've got supplies, and Lyle insisted I give you these," he said pointing at a couple of refrigerators.

"If you'd known about this treasure a while back, this place would still be the Rowley Ranch," Mark observed.

"I expect so. The second set-up is for the bunkhouse. I've got solar panels, batteries, wire, and the guys to install them."

"I'll just stay out of your way, but if you need extra muscle, just let me know. It might get me out of furniture moving for a minute. That is a hint, by the way."

Don smirked. "I thought Ellen already had everything where she wanted it, after being the housekeeper all this time."

"How she arranged things as a housekeeper was one thing. Ellen has a different role now. I don't suppose you noticed any change in how your wife acted before and after you got married. I know it was a day or two ago."

"You're making me exercise my memory. She lived at home until we got married. I only saw her room at home after we were married and I was hauling her stuff out. It was definitely a girl's room. She rearranged the house, but not with the vengeance I see right now. You realize when you haul anything into the house, she's got your ass again."

"Maybe I could haul something to the bunkhouse."

"There you go. You're getting smarter by the minute. Grab one side of the refrigerator."

The helpers took the other refrigerator into the house, where they negotiated its location with Ellen. Don and Mark drug pieces and parts to the bunkhouse. Mark had no idea why all the gear was going into the bunkhouse, of all places.

"Do you know something I don't about this bunkhouse? Is Ellen sending me out here to live?"

"Not that I know of," Don laughed. "I have a bone to pick with you, now that we've got privacy."

"What's that?"

"It's not bad enough I'm supposed to get along with you. Now I'm supposed to take orders from you," Don growled.

"Who told you that?"

"That old snake Lyle did."

"Any orders you get from me will only be what Lyle tells me to pass along. In any case, we'll only see each other in passing. You'll have the bigger job of getting people out of McCook."

"Lyle said it's your show." Don had to shake that rat another time.

"Did he say that? What he meant to say is that you get the credit, and I get the blame. How do you like those apples?"

"Mark, you're turning into one strange dude. I thought you'd have been tickled pink to be able to lord it over me."

"If I tried to tell you what to do, you'd do exactly the opposite. It's too much aggravation, and I'm not going to bother with it. You know what we have to do. You know your people and equipment better than anyone. The way the storms are coming in, McCook may have snow as high as an elephant's ass. The only thing I could require is to know whether you can do it."

Don rubbed the stubble on his chin. Finally, "Yeah, I can do it. It'll be hard on the horses, equipment, and people, but I can do it. Are you happy now?"

Mark snorted. "I'll be happy when Lyle pats me on the head and tells me I did okay. That won't happen, so we can both be grouchy. When will you be able to go?"

"Lyle wants tomorrow, but it won't happen. Clay Williams is putting rims on a couple of wheels. The day after tomorrow is the best I can do. Can you pass that along to Lyle and save me having to argue with him about it?"

"I can do that, Don. Thanks for letting me know. That means I'll see you in Arapahoe in about five days."

"We hope."

Don had no sooner disappeared when Kevin showed up with an apprentice. Each led a couple of horses. Clinging to the horses behind Kevin were two more guys. Kevin stopped in front of Mark, and did an astonishing flourish with his hat. It resembled a salute.

"Hail, oh great one. I just passed Don Rowley. The man almost looked happy. Damnedest thing I have ever seen. Other things remain the same. Mr. Lillard tells me I'm in charge of all the horses. Then he says I have to bring you four of my best. Ranch management is the same, except I now see what you were talking about."

"So what are these bang tails the best of?"

"One is for saddle. The other two are for pulling. The apprentice next to me volunteered to help with the driving. There was something about evacuating everyone from McCook. Is that right?"

Mark considered Lyle did miracles. "That is the idea. Don Rowley has the heavy lifting out of McCook. I'll make a million trips in the farm wagon from Arapahoe to Orleans. He'll also bring people in the carriage, while I do double duty with both people and cargo."

It looked like Kevin fit a couple more puzzle pieces together. "That explains why you need all the horsepower. Oh, this is Rick Forbes. He's decent with horses. He has no experience driving."

"Thanks for letting me know. Who are the other two?"

"They are working their way up the list to become apprentices. They'll stay out in the bunkhouse and take care of this place until I bring replacements."

"The bunkhouse just got upgraded with supplies, a refrigerator, and some solar panels."

Kevin nodded. "I saw the solar panels." He looked at the three. "Okay, don't bother Mark and his bride about meals. You know the drill. Now get with it."

Rick led the two candidates to the bunkhouse. Mark turned to Kevin. "How are things with you and Susie? I wouldn't ask but Ellen will need all the sordid details."

Kevin's jaw tightened. "Her parents invited me to stay away."

"I'm sorry to hear that. How much fun did you have while the rest of us escorted the last vial to Red Cloud?"

"Maybe too much, considering."

"Do her parents know?"

Kevin's voice dropped to a whisper, as though Susie's parents might hear. "They don't know yet."

"Damn. What happened?"

"Mr. Maguire said we crossed the line. He never said what line. I swear I never knew there was a line."

"What did Susie say?"

"They didn't give her a chance. They just hustled her into the house and slammed the door."

Mark shook his head. "That's not right. A lot of people could give you good advice. Anything I told you would be wrong. Ellen tells me that if I studied women like I did warfare and ranching, I would be in a lot better shape. Your studies should have included their parents, too."

"I think you're right." Kevin's face brightened up and he chuckled. "If there was a scandal sheet in Harlan, you and Ellen would make the front page on a regular basis. Everybody knows about you guys, to hear them talk. By the way, that was why I chose Rick. He keeps his mouth shut."

"Whatever he knows about you and Susie, he keeps to himself."

Kevin shrugged. "He doesn't say a hell of a lot about anything. He's no natural horseman. He's not much of anything. He listens and follows directions. Once you tell him something or show him something, Rick never forgets. He knows how to work."

"Knowing how to work is a rare commodity. At least that's what Lyle and Don tell me. So far, you haven't dropped any bombs on my head."

Kevin shook his head. "If I had any, I'd have done it right away so I could back away as fast as possible. I came here hoping that Lyle didn't give you any birds of ill omen with my name tattooed on their butts."

"The horses you brought represent most of a month's work. That's very strange, considering how short a time you've had them."

"Most already had substantial training. Once this bunch of horses got healthy, the training was easy. Somebody else already did it."

"That's very considerate to give credit elsewhere. My ears still ring from the bragging you have been doing."

Kevin's face reddened. "Everybody already knew. I don't want to look like a complete idiot."

Mark grinned. "If you want advice from Ellen, we could spare a cup of coffee. It might keep me from rearranging furniture for the tenth time."

"I'd like to, but I need to get back to the other place. By the way, use the two candidates for anything. Their real pay will consist of any and all recommendations they can get. That includes moving furniture. I hope Rick does a good job. If he messes up, a long line of guys are willing and eager to take his place."

Ellen came out of the house. "I'm making supper. Can you stay, Kevin?"

"No, ma'am, I sure can't. By the way, my guys have strict orders not to bother you for meals. They have their grub with them."

"Is that right? Are you ordering me not to feed them?"

Kevin was already mounted and laughed nervously. "I don't know any man who could give you orders. Well, Alex Thomas might."

"Kevin, for a snot-nosed kid, you got pretty smart. Susie had better watch her step around you."

"Susie's folks threw me out and said not to come back."

Ellen just laughed. "From what I heard about the ride to Red Cloud, Susie may have already solved that one."

Kevin's face turned a bright red. "That may be so. I've got to go."

Chapter 21
Evacuation

As they watched Kevin leave, the new guy, Rick Forbes, came out of the bunkhouse. Mark got the impression he had waited for Kevin to leave. As Rick approached, he nervously took his hat off.

"Excuse me, Mr. Tahner, what did you want me to do this afternoon?"

Mark was impressed and shocked. "We're working together, so call me Mark. I'm not royalty, so leave your hat on. Today, we want to get the stock settled in. We'll do some driving tomorrow. Kevin tells me the new guys may need supervision, so you can ride herd on them this evening and tomorrow morning."

Rick seemed relieved. "Yes, sir, Mr. ... er, Mark. I can certainly do that."

Rick quickly turned around headed back to the bunkhouse. Ellen regarded Mark quizzically. "I figured you'd use any excuse to get out of rearranging furniture. I saw how fast you got out of the house when Don Rowley came. I also saw how you found ways to stay away."

Mark thought a moment and nodded. "It was an excuse for a change of pace. Being with you is great, but I'll never be an interior decorator. I have never worried about the precise placement of furniture. I can't complain about what you did with the place, even if I don't have the wit to appreciate it like I should."

"That almost sounded like a compliment, Mr. Tahner. Have you been studying women lately?"

"I'm working on an unbreakable cipher called Ellen. Without a clue about the specifics of the message you bring, I think the horizon I see in you is what I was looking for all along."

"Well, that was a romantic thing to say." Ellen sighed. "The house is arranged how I want it. Let's go practice being married for a while. How does that grab you?"

"It grabs me in a place I'd best not ignore. Did I mention lately that I love you, Mrs. Tahner?"

"Not since you moved furniture. I love you, too. If we work at it, we might get the pheromone level up enough to impress Stanley."

"Even Stanley couldn't sense our pheromones outside the county."

Ellen grabbed him by the hand and towed him back to the house. "We'll need to kick up a real cloud of those little buggers, won't we?" she said over her shoulder.

Mark started to look around to see if anyone was watching, but then decided he was now married and it didn't matter.

The next day, Mark wandered outside and saw chores were nearly done. He had nothing to do but watch Rick supervise the new guys. In turn, the new guys were doing well enough that Rick just watched them. Soon, Mark nodded to Rick, and headed back into the house.

"How do you like supervising the supervisor?" Ellen wondered.

"It feels different. We need to find you a supervisory housekeeper over maids and cooks. Then you could get a feel for it, too."

Ellen shook a knife at him. "You'd just chase the maids."

Mark raised his hands. "Not when you make the point with that blade. You're the only girl I could see anyway."

"That wasn't bad. We'll see what you learned, but that will be after you get ready for the evacuation."

It was just as well that Ellen didn't put Mark to the test right away. Don Rowley pulled up with his double wagon, with the carriage right behind. He had outriders and extra labor in the wagon.

"Will you be at Arapahoe on the fourteenth, Mark?"

"I'll be there, Don. Good luck to you. Do you have enough cold and inclement weather gear with you?"

"I believe so. We'll see you in a few days, then."

"Godspeed, Don."

Mark worked with Rick and the horses. The horses knew far more than Rick. On the other hand, Rick picked it up quickly. Soon, he drove the farm wagon on the road. That afternoon, Rick backed the wagon and used all the horses. Rick didn't say much, but listened carefully and followed directions precisely. That forced Mark to think what he was saying, since Rick did what Mark did say instead of what Mark thought he said.

After a full day, Rick headed for the bunkhouse, and Mark stumbled into the house. Ellen looked at him. "I'd ask how your day went, but I watched a good amount of it. You had an interesting time, trying to communicate with Rick."

Mark shook his head. "That is the understatement of the week. How's the furniture?"

"Now that's frustration I hear. The furniture is fine. Rick was getting it by the time you quit. What will you do tomorrow?"

That stopped Mark. "Rick and I can find one of the driving horses a home in Orleans tomorrow, but we need a source of hay."

"The feed lot isn't far from Orleans. They've got hay. Maybe they could share some."

"That is a good idea. I'm glad you're on my side."

Ellen smiled. "They say I'm pretty smart for a girl."

"Girls are smarter than boys. That means you're exceptional. I knew that already, though."

"You're coming up with all these great lines. Hold me up. All this will make me swoon."

"Swoon. That's another old-fashioned thing you like. Should I be on your left side or your right side, to catch you properly?"

"Screw the swooning. Come here and give us a kiss."

Finding a place for the horse was easy. Orleans was the location of the county fairgrounds, which Mark had forgotten. They selected a large metal barn with livestock pens. They even found hay inside. It was also the obvious destination for the evacuees. On a whim, Mark directed Rick to the feedlot. George Jergenson, the owner, was standing to the side, keeping an eye on things.

"Hey, George, did you hear we're bringing folks from McCook into Orleans for the winter?"

"Yeah, Don Rowley was beating his chest about the heroic thing he's doing."

"He's got the equipment for the heavy end of the job. I'll bring them in from Arapahoe. I need a place for a spare driving horse. Would you be able to handle an extra?"

George immediately nodded. "I'd be glad to. When you drop your people and belongings in Orleans, come over here. We'll switch horses. With the tribe processing beef, we've reduced the number of cattle, so Conrad is not that busy. He'll get you on your way quickly. Is this your spare driver?"

"Yes, he is Rick Forbes. He is working out well."

A little later, Rick commented, "Thanks for the vote of confidence, Mark."

"It was the least I could do. Kevin said you're a good hand, and he's right. I appreciate everything you're doing."

Rick shook his head. "Everything is so different from what I wanted and trained to do."

"Not many people do what they plan. When they do, it isn't what they thought it would be. Now, everything is different. I don't know if it's harder, but it sure is different. We all had to learn new skills. What did you want to do?"

"I trained to be a computer programmer. I was on my way to a job on the East Coast when some guys hijacked my car. They dumped me here. The guys who jumped me all died. Sometimes being a victim is the best revenge."

Mark nodded. "I'm sorry about your misfortune but I'm glad you're here. Your education explains your following instructions literally. I will have to think more carefully what I saying."

Rick smiled absently. "I needed to work on fuzzy logic and neural networks."

"You're dealing with Mark Tahner's fuzzy logic just fine, and you manage the neural networks called horses as well as anybody."

Mark watched Rick take care of the horse and wagon before heading into the house. Ellen was waiting for him on the porch. They saw clouds just over the western horizon.

"I'm glad, the snow hasn't come here," Mark commented. "Don may be dealing more snow than he wants. I told Don he could crow about his part in this evacuation. He may earn all the chest pounding he wants."

"I can't imagine how Don's wife copes with it," Ellen replied. "Make sure you stay safe."

The next day, while they got ready, one of the posse members rode in from Oxford about mid-day.

"One of Stanley's hunters brought a message," he told Mark. "Don Rowley left Arapahoe for McCook. Stanley thinks the snow will be too deep for his wagons."

Mark visualized those wagons in waist-deep snow, and considered the horses trying to pull those wagons. He agreed with the message. "What do they want to do?"

"Somebody suggested putting skis on the wagons. I'm supposed to have Clay make skis for a freight wagon and the carriage. Can you delay until Clay does that? Clay may need to go with you."

"We need Lyle Lillard in this conversation. From what you say, Clay has to go. He's the only one who could adjust and fabricate anything else they dream up."

The guard grinned as they went to the corral. "We figured that. It doesn't sound like Don will be back as soon as he thought. The snow might be a couple of feet deep around McCook."

"That would mean it is no deeper than when I was there."

Lyle immediately agreed with the plan, and joined them riding into Ragan. Clay had considered building skis, but put it off with no snow in Harlan. It would be a full day's work, and Clay not only agreed to go, he stated flatly that was how it would be.

The following evening, Mark tested Rick, sending him after Clay by himself. An hour and a half later, Rick and Clay were back. The farm wagon was filled with just the skis. They had to re-think what they were taking, and how they'd haul it. Mark would ride and carry a few things. They'd delay taking most things, knowing there would be many trips.

Clay started for the bunkhouse, but Ellen wouldn't hear of it. She dragged him to the house, installing him in the spare bedroom. Over dinner, Clay told about keeping Don's wagons on the road, and said he needed an apprentice. So far, it was too much like work for the young studs.

Mark replied, "Stanley would be your man, except he already has a job. Nobody would be comfortable with him in the middle of Harlan."

"I need somebody, and I'm getting less particular, if you must know," was Clay's reply.

Their rollout was not as impressive as Don's earlier departure, but with any luck, he had what Don needed to make the evacuation happen. Mark felt good being back in the saddle instead of sitting on the wagon seat. Rick was slender, which helped since Clay Williams was compact and powerful. Mark delved into Clay's ideas.

"How did you get the idea for making the skis, Clay?"

"I saw some a long time ago. They used these when horses were the only horsepower."

"The old times are new again, Clay."

Clay chuckled. "I guess they are. The trouble is that I don't know all the details separating an attempt from one that works. I hope I can find enough parts and pieces in Arapahoe to finish the job."

"I guess you have other things going on, as well."

"Yeah, Don's horses will need better traction on ice. That's why I brought my farrier gear."

Mark suddenly remembered something. "You know, Clay, where the tribe bunks still has parts and pieces for a machine shop. Maybe we could use them."

Rick spoke up. "Arapahoe has solar power. That means a twelve volt supply. Automotive starters are just twelve-volt motors. They can run equipment well enough to do a job."

Clay turned to Mark, "I don't know where you found him, but if you get tired of him, I'll take him."

"A few days ago, Jimmy barely had power to keep his refrigerators and water running. That's one hell of an idea in any case. Rick, while we're at Arapahoe, check the electrical. I'm amazed Don Rowley didn't grab you."

Rick grunted. "I tried working for him, but we didn't hit it off very well. Mr. Rowley owns the only point of view that will ever be heard. Mr. Williams, I know you're tight with Mr. Rowley, but he never made a secret of what he thought of me."

Clay rumbled deep in his throat, a strange laugh. "The folks in Ragan offered Don a building. The back room of the livery stable was perfect for my trade, since it was a blacksmith shop. I do what he needs and can get nowhere else. At the same time, he finds supplies I need. We get along. Don't confuse that with any notion of us being tight."

Mark suddenly remembered something from Orleans. "Near the Harlan fairgrounds in Orleans is a building where they demonstrated the art of the blacksmith and farrier. If you moved there, everyone would bring their work to you instead of being Don's neighbor."

"I know that shop, and it would do the job. It might help me find an apprentice, too. I'm the closest thing to high tech around here, even if it involves a lot from my buddy, Mr. Armstrong."

Mark caught the joke but Rick puzzled about it a while. Finally, he brightened. "Oh, Armstrong. Strong arm. I speak fluent computer, but I'm still getting up to speed with rural talk."

"Computer is a dead language, like Sanskrit or Latin, isn't it?"

"If we get enough solar power, computers might come back," Rick pointed out.

Mark snorted. "If we ever find people to build computers, we know where to find a programmer. Until then, save your Dixie cups, boys. The South's going to rise again."

Clay joined in with, "Yeehaw!"

They pushed through slush, arriving mid-afternoon. The snow was staying away today. In spite of all that, Mark entertained visions of Don already being there. If that happened, he would certainly give him a full dose of grief about being a lay-about. Clay and the skis were Mark's only way to distract that situation.

He didn't have to worry. Don and his freight line were nowhere in sight. Stanley was there. He just got back from checking down the line, and gave them an update. The situation in McCook was nasty and got worse toward the castle.

Don Rowley and his party staggered in with only a little light left. Don was not in a good mood. His draft horses were exhausted. Behind him, the carriage was more than full. Each outrider pulled a travois piled with goods. Don's mood finally lightened when he saw the skis. Jimmy even turned on lights to let everyone get settled. The horses would need at least a full day to recover. It would take at least that long to exchange the wheels for skis. Mark looked at the people Don brought, wondering if anyone could make the run into Harlan the next day.

Alex and Cordelia were not with the group, which Mark knew would disappoint Josh and Alicia. They were still at the castle with Tom and Sammie and the rest of the people. Everyone congregated at the castle. It had been the only safe place during the dust and rain. Now, Mark thought, the castle might be the worst place to stay. The only positive thing was that Don only needed to go to one place to find them.

Another positive thing was how quickly Stanley put his people at Clay's disposal to take off wagon wheels and install skis. Harlan folks and Stanley's Peepul could work together. For the big negative issue, Mark was in Arapahoe and Ellen was in Harlan. Figuring out how to get everyone to Harlan occupied him sufficiently that he didn't dwell on the situation.

Mark was one of the first up, showing how bad the trip had been along with the conditions at the castle. He carefully picked his way through the mass of bodies toward the kitchen where coffee was brewing. Clay soon joined him. Mark was surprised when Don Rowley showed up just after Clay.

Don described the situation. "Conditions were bad and only got worse. There were several feet of snow on the ground in McCook. The wind got stronger as we went up the ridge. The team barely got through with empty wagons. Thankfully, the snow never got much deeper. We went to the castle and found out that's where everybody was. The snow started again, and we were stuck in the stable. Stanley's people got food to us."

Clay wanted to know, "Will my skis help? You talk like it is pretty slushy."

"If we don't put much of a load in the wagons, it might be okay. If we haven't already broken through, it's all the team can do to get themselves through it. Forget about pulling anything. I don't see getting much out besides the folks themselves. Their possessions have to wait until spring. The carriage has to follow where my big team breaks a path."

Jimmy refilled their coffee, but came back when Clay had a thought.

"I read that in the old days they didn't plow the roads. They ran a roller to compact the snow, making it easier for the horses to walk and pull a sleigh."

"That makes sense. Would you come on the next run? You'd know how to adjust the skis. Alex Thomas can do some metal working at his place."

"Of course I'm going. Have I ever done only half of a job?"

Jimmy leaned against the other side of the counter. Mark saw a cloud of concern crossing his face. He walked to the window and stared. Then he turned to Don and Clay. "You gentlemen may want skis sooner rather than later. There's already a line of clouds to the west. The last time that happened was also the last snow."

"When will it get here, Jimmy?" Don asked.

"It will be a couple of hours." Jimmy chuckled. "That supposes we have a clue about the time. If this is like the last storm, you'll see snowfall and lunch the same time."

Mark's plan of action came into focus and he nodded to Jimmy. "The first McCook people up go to Harlan this morning. I'd appreciate it if you could feed them as quickly as possible."

Don was astonished. "Are you sure, Mark? I promised they'd have a day or two, anyway."

"Look around. This place is a zoo. They can rest all winter in Harlan. We don't have a moment to spare, getting the rest of those folks out. Rick and I will be back tomorrow if the weather holds. This is my part of the evacuation. We'll haul until everybody is in Harlan or until nobody can go anywhere. I hope you have good luck, Don. Actually, I'll be hoping for a miracle or two. Clay, I hope the skis and snow packing work."

Rick joined them and Mark told him the situation. Rick nodded, grabbed a cup of coffee, and headed out to get the spare horse hooked up.

"How do you stand him, Mark?" Don wanted to know. "He never has a damn thing to say."

"Kevin described him that way, too, Don. The way he told it, that was one of his best characteristics. As I understood the situation, he couldn't see trying to compete with you in the mouth department."

Don growled, and Mark laughed. Then he took another look around the public area. "My lucky ticket holders are up. I need to let them know about their prize."

They didn't take much from McCook, and nearly all of that stayed in Arapahoe. As they left the Inn, it was not snowing, but clouds were building. Mark took the reins and Rick rode shotgun. Their passengers huddled in the box, trying to survive one more day.

Mark kept the horse moving, and except for a brief skiff of snow, managed to avoid the weather altogether. An hour into the run, they got out from under the clouds and the temperature started to rise.

The guards whooped and cheered as they crossed the bridge. Mark saw riders heading out of town at a gallup. One went up the bluff and the other straight ahead. They proceeded at a walk. Mark pointed out places, and the people on board seemed interested in what he had to say.

In Orleans, George Jergenson and Kevin were on hand, along with several ladies from Huntley. They had a barbecue going, and helped the newcomers off the wagon. George also had the spare driving horse, and helped change horses. Mark and Rick started to help the people they brought. George pushed them back to the wagon.

"You two head on to Harlan Ranch. We've got it here," George told them. "We watched that bank of clouds coming at us and were glad it stopped. Both of you will earn your keep and then some. Take advantage of a soft bed while you can."

At home, Ellen had dinner ready. The one rider let her know of their arrival. Rick offered to find his own dinner, but Ellen sat him down with them. She did not object when Rick excused himself just after eating, and went to the bunkhouse.

That was when Ellen showed Mark what she prepared for him alone. Mark later considered Ellen could have been a teacher. He was certainly learning a great deal with her method.

Mark and Rick were almost ready when Don Rowley's people showed up with a pile of supplies. Mark shook his head.

"It will take four or five trips to get all this to Arapahoe."

The guy running the show grinned widely. "That's what we thought, too. We didn't want Mr. Rowley to think we didn't keep him supplied."

"He's a Mister Rowley, is he? Okay, transfer what needs to go right away to the wagon. The rest goes in the covered area by the bunkhouse."

"Is it as bad as they say? People talk about deep snow."

Mark nodded. "It's bad enough. If you get to Orleans, ask the folks we brought. They can tell you."

"It's hard to imagine conditions changing so much over such a short distance. We could use some snow here. We have been kind of dry."

Mark automatically gave the old proverb. "Be careful what you wish for. You might get it. Let's get this transferred. We should have been on the road half an hour ago."

The guy chuckled. "You damn near sound like Mr. Rowley."

Mark favored him with a hard stare. "You know those are fighting words. It's a good thing you were smiling."

They did load quickly, and rolled out after a mandatory goodbye kiss to Ellen. Mark hoped for a smooth run. The sky was clear now, but the storm almost followed them to Harlan. They got into slush a few miles west of Oxford. Mark wished Don Rowley's man could see this. It was interesting, although the ice the horse kicked back at them wasn't fun.

The slush got deeper, and by the time they got halfway to Arapahoe, the horse struggled to get through. They stopped several times to rest the animal.

"The rate we're going, it'll be dark before we get to Arapahoe," Mark grumbled. Rick agreed.

Ready to move again, the horse's ears perked up, hearing something ahead of them on the road. Mark pointed it out to Rick, commenting that a horse's hearing was far better than a person's. He suggested they make sure their weapons were ready. Whatever was ahead might be friendly. Then again, it might not be. Preparation could be very helpful.

Watching Rick handle the rifle, Mark hoped whatever it was wouldn't need two riflemen. Rick was obviously uncomfortable with the weapon. When it came to weapons, Rick and Kevin were on a par. At the same time, Mark sensed friction between them.

Mark looked for a good defensive position, visualizing meeting another gang of terrorists. He couldn't imagine the terrorists getting through the snow and past Arapahoe. If they got this far, Mark knew the two of them were toast.

After a while, he could heard men's voices and horses snorting. The voices sounded American. Finally he saw what was coming. They were two of Don Rowley's outriders. They had their horses hitched to a wheeled frame with a blade suspended below. A roller followed. They plowed the road, only clearing the loose mushy stuff on top, leaving a solid surface for horses and wagons.

Approaching the wagon, the blade operators waved and grinned. One straddled one of the two horses. The other rode on the blade, and manipulated the depth and angle. Mark recalled the conversation, but seeing the real thing seemed a wonder to Mark.

"When did you come up with this?"

"One of the Peepul told us about it. We got it working this morning. We came this way to see how it works."

"It looks like it's working just fine."

"We pretty much have it figured out now. We'll scrape around you, and you can follow us back."

"That suits me."

"You've got quite a load."

"We said we'd bring supplies, right?"

With the road plowed and the snowplow guys cheering them on, the rest of the run was far easier. On top of it, the mob at Arapahoe treated Mark and Rick like conquering heroes, bringing supplies and for the promise of more people heading to Orleans. Mark and Rick told how it went for their first group of evacuees.

"They had a barbecue ready for them?" one of the McCook people asked in amazement.

"They did, indeed. It smelled good, too. Just so you know, George cooks a mean brisket. We'd have joined them, but we had to get to Harlan Ranch."

"You had newlywed duties, Mark. What did Rick have to do?" Don asked.

"If Rick wants to tell you, he can tell it himself," Mark replied. That drew general whoops of laughter.

"At least you didn't lose your wit out there on the road."

"I hope not. When my horse's ears focused forward, I didn't know what was coming. I was more than happy to see snowplows instead of terrorists."

"Seeing the supplies, I am happy, too." Don suddenly got a suspicious look in his eyes. "Speaking of which, all of that didn't come out of your pantry."

"A fellow showed up this morning. I didn't catch his name, but he grinned a lot and said he needed to keep somebody named Mr. Rowley supplied."

Don shook his head. "He's a kiss-ass of the first water. What's worse, he's supplying me out of my own warehouse."

Mark swallowed his reply in the interest of keeping things peaceful. "How are the skis?"

"They work fine," Clay commented. "With them, Don's team can pull the double-header, but any kind of load would be a killer. We'd need at least four and preferably six horses to do it right. The snowplow guys will start west tomorrow."

"This way, your team can rest for a day or two, Don."

Don agreed. "Clay will stay with me to adjust the skis. Are you going back tomorrow?"

"Not with the horse that brought us today. It's a good thing I left a spare. It could be interesting since that horse is trained for riding instead of pulling."

Mark got serious as he looked around the room. "You need to decide who goes tomorrow. I'm doing people first and then your treasures. You know the size of my wagon."

Chapter 22
Snowplows

With all the coughing, sneezing, and people moving around through the night, Mark didn't get much rest. Rick didn't say anything, but it was clear that he didn't have a good night either. At least they could swap off the driving.

Before they could go anywhere, Mark had to give the horse a short course in pulling the farm wagon. He thought he started early enough, but it took a while. Don Rowley came out and lent a hand. Of course, the horse would haul Don's stuff, so maybe he had a vested interest.

Once the horse got the idea of pulling the wagon, he already knew the way home. In addition, the road was easier to drive, with the snow melting. It was like the last Harlan run, although they weren't racing the weather now. On the other hand, they needed to keep moving. The weather would be back, and everybody knew it.

There was no barbecue when they arrived, but their current group was greeted warmly by their friends and neighbors. George showed up with the relief horse, commenting that if this kept up, they would need more horses so the current ones could rest a little more.

At Harlan Ranch, four guys waited for them. All were mounted, and wanted to help with the evacuation. Mark eyed their mounts with envy, but had an idea what those horses and their riders could do.

"Don Rowley can use you. Rick will show you what to load into the wagon. After that, he'll show you the bunkhouse."

Rick didn't complain, and Mark headed for the house. Maybe this place was home. It was so long since he had anything deserving the name. The very concept seemed novel. Mark kept those thoughts to himself and just enjoyed being with Ellen. He only hoped she got half the enjoyment out the two of them being together that he did.

Lyle and Adeline Lillard arrived. Lyle commented that Stanley didn't waste time sending hunting parties to Holdrege. Vince gave him reports every day.

"Vince knew the tribe was okay from Oxford to Holdrege. Then his people saw evidence of hunting parties east of Holdrege, and Vince became concerned," Lyle recalled. "I asked if he'd rather have terrorist sightings. He got my point. At least he hasn't emphasized the situation since then."

"That leaves our east unprotected," Mark responded. "Stanley doesn't have the manpower to cover more area. I'm surprised he went beyond Holdrege. There's lots of hunting in the area you gave him."

"Our people in Oxford say Stanley's tribe hauls in a lot of meat. It's to the point they delay processing cattle to handle the deer, feral pigs, and other game."

"I won't complain if I have to get by on venison. Okay, you want my angle on the evacuation. Here's what I know right now ..."

Mark and Lyle talked for a while, and Mark discovered Adeline and Ellen were not just chatting in the kitchen. The four soon had dinner. Mark thought it felt comfortable. Afterward, Lyle asked, "Have we kept you busy enough, Mark?"

That caught him off guard. "Yeah, you're keeping me more than busy enough. I hadn't even thought about that lately. I'd have to completely lose my mind to think of wandering off through deep snow."

Lyle looked at Ellen. "If our boy loses his mind, would you please help him find it?"

"I'll do what I can. If it drops into a gopher hole or down an ant hill, we may be out of luck."

Everybody laughed. Lyle glanced at Mark. "Why is your face so red, Mark?"

"The coffee must be too hot," Mark muttered, drawing more laughter.

It was an uneventful run to Arapahoe the next morning. There was no slush until near Arapahoe, and Mark got the wagon, two drivers, and four outriders there not long after noon. Jimmy took Mark aside.

"The snowplow guys cleared seven miles of road. Don Rowley took them lunch. They drug it back last night, and are resting today. Clay is checking the equipment. Mr. Rowley talks of setting his wagon up like a chuck wagon and taking cooks with him. They plan to camp instead of coming back."

Mark was impressed. "I brought four guys who want to help. It sounds like the snowplow guys need help. That should make it sooner than if the two guys did it on their own."

Jimmy nodded. "You brought another load of supplies. We aren't short, but we'll put them to good use."

"I'm sure Don Rowley will be happy to hear that. By the way, are you going to tough it out here for the winter?"

"If it was just me, I might. Vickie says she feels better, but if anything bad happened, I couldn't get her any help. We could go to Orleans, if they'd have us. Most likely, we'll stay in Oxford on the Furnas side."

"Why would there be a problem with you being in Orleans?"

"Everybody in McCook hates me and Vickie is a tribal member. I wouldn't be welcome in Orleans, and Vickie couldn't stay anywhere in Harlan."

"The Peepul work with Harlan folks just fine. The McCook farmers haven't given you grief here, have they?"

Jimmy shook his head. "Everybody is in a strange situation. I shouldn't push it, that's all."

"You got awfully smart lately," Mark observed.

"I can't get the stench of those dust people, or terrorists, out of my nose. I think how I was when I first ran into them. It made me think about things, that's all."

"You changed a lot before they arrived, Jimmy. Vickie has been a good influence."

"With Stanley breathing down my neck, good behavior goes with the territory. If you don't mind me saying so, you've changed quite a bit, too."

"You say that even though I don't think the terrorists stink worse than any other goat herder."

The two men laughed, and went into the Inn.

It took two more trips to get the first batch of refugees to Orleans. They speculated how the snowplows and Don Rowley were doing. It had been four days, after all. Their next trip would be to get the evacuees' personal possessions.

A new snow storm blew in just after they got to Arapahoe for the personal possessions. Standing at the massive front window of the Inn, Mark couldn't see the road. Unless they got a notable warm front, they couldn't get out of Arapahoe. This one probably got to Harlan and that guard in Oxford would be wishing for something beside snow.

It cleared a day and a half later. Jimmy and his people tried to keep the solar panels clear, but finally, everyone just hunkered down. They didn't even use the stoves, since they couldn't get out the door for more wood. With all the refugees in Orleans, Mark and Rick both had rooms, which was a definite improvement.

The weather cleared, and the solar panels were able to charge the batteries. They turned on the well again. Water pumped into the tanks and lights came back on. The batteries kept the refrigerators going, but Jimmy was concerned how long they could go on the battery power they had. Mark got the impression it wouldn't have been much more.

Jimmy put out the word that the water tanks had to be full at all times. Additional supplies of firewood came into the service area. With the firewood, bugs came as well, but it was a trade-off they could live with. Mark scouted around, looking for additional batteries to connect to the array. He expanded the Inn's ability to survive by a bit, anyway.

After thinking about it, Mark elected to stay in Arapahoe rather than go with personal possessions. There was no way he could know the most important items. The best alternative was to wait for Don and ferry live refugees instead of wearing out the horses on dead weight.

The weather stayed clear for five days and Don got back. His rig was a sight, overloaded with people. Sammie, Tom, and the ghosts were with them. Sammie was mounted and carrying two children. Mark thought that was a nice touch. Nobody wanted to talk to Mark, and Don Rowley was even more abrasive than normal. None of the snow plows, horses, or men were going anywhere for a while.

Later, Mark recognized one of the guys who had ridden with him to Arapahoe. "I get the impression you guys had quite an adventure."

"Adventure?" he fairly spat the word back. "Can you spell that with a four-letter word? It started out okay. The two of us rode the horses, while other guys ran the snowplows. They thought we made pretty good time. Mr. Rowley grumbled the whole way, of course. The second night found us in McCook where we sheltered out of the weather. The next day, we got halfway to the castle, and stayed in a barn. Everybody was looking forward to electric lights and hot water, so we pushed on at first light, and got there about mid-day."

"What did you think of the castle?"

"It looks impressive. We never got inside. Hell, we never got to the front door."

Mark was puzzled. "Why is that?"

"Their solar power went to hell. They had a separate system for the arena. Everybody was in there, including the four guys and gal who run the place. They were glad to see us, but snarling, too. The farmers were just glad we got there. It was quite a mob, with all the horses. Another storm moved in just after we arrived. We were stuck. Mr. Rowley and the bunch who said they ran the place chewed on each other."

"What was the problem?"

"The one guy, Tom, refused to go anywhere unless there was some agreement. Mr. Rowley said there were two points. First, he neither knew nor cared about any agreement. Second, he pushed his animals and equipment as far as he was about to. There would not be any more rescue missions after this. The tribe listened to it, and jumped into the argument, saying if this was the last stage out of Dodge, they'd all be on it. Stanley said that's how it would be."

"What happened then?"

"The five run the place, but the tribal people make it run. Everybody retired to separate areas, periodically growling at one another. All of us working the snowplows got to know the local farmers. They're nice folks. It seemed we stayed in the barn of the leader, a guy named Alex Thomas. He knew you and your wife, Ellen."

Mark nodded. "Alicia, Josh's bride, is his daughter. Ellen and Alicia grew up together. It is obvious that you all survived. What happened then?"

"When the storm quit, it was obvious that we'd have to plow the road again. The five were back trying to cut a deal with Mr. Rowley. In turn, he became more aggravated by the minute. The tribal members had a meeting of their own, and finally walked over to Mr. Rowley. They said they'd do whatever he said. The farmers were already in the wagon, and Mr. Rowley told them to grab the five, throw them in the wagon, and sit on them if they had to. The tribal members took him literally. He also said to get the gal's horse and put kids on it."

"I don't imagine Sammie and Tom were silent."

He pursed his lips. Mark thought it might have been an effort to keep from snickering. "No, they weren't, but we had the plows out on the road by then, and quit listening. I did hear Tom ask Mr. Rowley if he knew who the tribal people were. Mr. Rowley told him he knew damn well since their former leader worked for him. I guess you know more about that than me."

Mark laughed. "That was Willy the rat. Oh, yeah, I know about that."

Mark and Rick slept in the public area, giving the refugee families a little privacy. The next morning, Mark hunted up the snowplow crews.

"Your horses cannot do any more. The driving horse I used to get here is well-rested. There's an extra driving horse plus a riding horse. Both are fresh. You could run one plow. We could follow and get some folks to Harlan today. What do you think?"

The opportunity to get away from the mob at Arapahoe appealed to the snowplow crew and they quickly went out to sort out equipment and animals. Inside, the question was how many volunteers could fit in the farm wagon.

Alex and Cordelia Thomas could have gone, but they stayed. Alex insisted another family go instead. Even with the plow, it was a slow trip. There was ice and snow all the way to Oxford. In Oxford, Mark saw that several riders went out in front of them, with a third heading up the bluff to spread the news. There might be secrets in Harlan, but their arrival was not going to be one of them.

In Orleans, those who Mark brought earlier were on hand with a welcome, food, and comfort for their neighbors. That was good, but even better was that George and Conrad arrived just after they got unloaded, bringing a fresh horse for the wagon. The snowplow drivers stayed in Orleans looking for fresh horses. On the way to Harlan Ranch, Mark and

Rick talked about what they should do, and decided it would be nice to have a down day, but getting everybody to Harlan came first.

Lyle and Adeline Lillard were waiting for them. Mark wondered if he made the right choice when Lyle invited Rick into the house for their discussion. Mark related what he'd seen as well as the story from the snowplow driver.

"If Tom, Sammie, and the other three stay in Arapahoe, they'll do it on their own," Lyle observed.

"That's the bottom line. Sammie and her ghosts haven't talked to me. In fact, they avoided me. That puzzles me, given how hard they tried to sell their proposal earlier."

Lyle studied Mark. "Does it matter to you?"

That was an easy question. "What's important is to get the rest of the farmers to Orleans. Rick and I talked about it, and want to head back to Arapahoe tomorrow. The big problem is the condition of the horses. We used all our relief stock to get back today."

Lyle and Adeline glanced at each other, and Lyle nodded, looking back at Mark. "I agree with you. Still, we may be able to do something about the situation. Do us a favor and wait a while tomorrow morning. Kevin may have extra stock."

"I wiped him out. George Jergenson is checking for extra horses, too."

"Hang on until we get back to you, okay?"

Lyle and Adeline took off, leaving Mark wondering what was going on. Mark knew the numbers, health, and training of the stock. There just weren't enough horses to make it work. Rick went to the bunkhouse, and Mark settled in with Ellen for the evening. He was happy to know Lyle thought he was doing a good job, but damn it was good to be home.

The next morning, Lyle and Adeline showed up, leading the horse Mark knew Kevin had been training.

"Here you are," Lyle told Mark. "Use these three horses. Adeline and I will bunk with your bride until you get back. If you keep track of such things, today is Halloween. Consider the use of these horses as your treat. Please don't do us any tricks. We have one particular requirement along with this. You will rest all of the horses a day in Arapahoe before you start back."

Adeline also had something to say. "I want to see every one of the horses as you bring them back into Harlan. That includes all the stock you have down at the feedlot and in Orleans. I told the vet to be over here two days from now as well. We cannot afford to push our horses too far. We just got them healthy, and they are all we have. You get me?"

Mark and Rick were soon on their way with additional supplies and leading two horses. It was remarkable. In Orleans, the snowplow crew took the two horses gratefully, understanding they were the personal mounts of Lyle and Adeline.

The snow had a good crust, letting the plowing move fairly rapidly, widening the way, and packing the snow. Arriving in good time, Mark's biggest challenge was explaining why they couldn't turn and burn the next morning.

Mark was prepared for the bedroll on the floor routine. Another challenge was the fact that there was a single toilet. He discovered they had reestablished a path to the outhouse, marked by a wide path. The girls used the indoor toilet, and the guys went to the outhouse. Yellow snow and wet streaks on the sides of the outhouse showed how they shared the facility.

Sammie, Tom, and the ghosts kept their distance from Mark, like he had a communicable disease. There was discussion between them, and he seemed a large part of it. It reminded him of when Ellen was making her point to Lyle and Adeline not so long ago. At the same time, they were at the bottom of his list of things to worry about.

At the moment, he was glad so many aspects of the evacuation went so well. Lyle seemed happy, and every time he could get home, Ellen greeted him with open arms and warm lips. What could Sammie, Tom, and company do? The refugees were in Harlan or on their way. Stanley's tribe dealt directly with Lyle. Sammie and Tom were out of the game.

Mark had breakfast at the counter, enjoying the bacon and eggs. Having stew for all three meals never seemed right. He could get picky about how the eggs were prepared, but that was minor.

His pleasant thoughts were interrupted as the prickly feeling in his neck kicked off. Mark had no doubt about who it was. Tom and Sammie headed his way, with the three snipers right behind.

Tom favored Mark with a drill instructor glare. "You didn't respond to our proposal."

Mark slid his plates out of the way, turned around and leaned back, both elbows on the counter. "Your proposal was to my boss, Lyle Lillard.

Mr. Lillard observed to me that the weather outranked him. The snow decided the issue. I see you came anyway."

"We had no choice. The Peepul grabbed us and threw us into the wagon. Then they sat on us. They literally sat on us." Tom spat the words.

Tom seemed intent on getting Mark to react. He would have to try harder. Mark relaxed even more as he looked at them. "If you were intent on death, the castle was still there. You could stage the place. Somebody exploring in the future could reflect on your heroic last poses."

"You're not here with Ellen," Tom growled.

Mark reached for his cup of coffee, and took a sip. "What do they say about a command of the obvious? Ellen is playing hostess for Lyle and Adeline Lillard at Harlan Ranch. They lent me their personal mounts, and decided not to walk home. This is a down day, at their orders, to keep the horses in good shape. We will head back tomorrow."

The reactions all seemed to be coming from Tom at the moment. After a moment, he asked, "Will you be back here?"

"Rick and I plan to return. First, our horses have to be checked and cleared by Adeline Lillard and the vet. We'll come as long as our stock holds up and people want to get to Harlan. I understand Jimmy will be on the last wagon. Vickie may go sooner since her health is an issue. The Peepul tribe can ride or walk. I'll work with them either way."

Sammie was aghast. "You're abandoning Arapahoe, after all this work?"

Mark went cowboy then. He took a sip of coffee and pushed up his hat brim slightly. "Yep," was all he said.

"What can we do? Where can we go?" Sammie seemed terrified.

Mark considered that. "I remember the parade from Harlan to the castle. We stayed here at Arapahoe overnight. You wandered off when everybody else stayed here. That didn't bother you."

Mark knew Sammie did not want to think about that. "For company, there is Orleans and the McCook group. They're doing fine. Nobody in Harlan spies on them. Everybody is too busy working on how to survive over the coming winter to waste their time spying on you. You could squat with the Peepul tribe on the Furnas side of Oxford."

Mark saw increasing desperation in Sammie's eyes. "What about our special relationship?" she asked.

Now that was funny and Mark didn't even worry about smiling. He waited for wrongness of her statement to soak in.

Finally, he said softly, "Our special relationship, where I run Harlan behind Lyle Lillard's back? I already told you how that didn't work."

"There is no way we could stay here," Tom commented.

"That is true, Tom. There are the places I mentioned. In addition, there are other abandoned towns around here. Don Rowley and his people would be your only visitors. He's pretty well stripped every place around here."

"Isn't there anything you can do for us?"

"I owe you big time for getting me together with Ellen. I suppose we could expand the bunkhouse at Harlan Ranch. Lyle has me going six ways from Sunday. You wouldn't see much of me."

The exchange attracted spectators, but the five standing in front of Mark didn't seem to know anybody else was there. It was like he was a king holding court. "For your proposal that we stay here with you, Lyle says that won't happen. We can't control the weather, which forced the decision in the first place. What you do and where you go is up to you."

They stood there, Tom and Sammie both shifting uncomfortably from one foot to another. Mark noticed Stanley was watching with great interest. Super. No pressure here. Suddenly a realization struck Mark, and he smiled softly.

"You completed the mission Gutierrez gave you, so you invented a mission, but it didn't fly. Now you want me to give you a mission. Okay, Stanley's tribe does their meat processing in Oxford. In addition to pork and game, they also do beef. There are complaints they don't do enough beef. Here's your new mission: Move to Oxford near the meat processing plant. Ensure an appropriate mix of products. The Peepul have shown they can easily hunt out an area, so you need to watch that, too. We'll find more, but this will get you started."

The five blinked and looked at each other. After a moment, Tom nodded. "Sure, we can do that."

Stanley gave Mark a thumbs-up and disappeared. Jimmy tapped on Mark's shoulder. "Do you want any more breakfast, Mark?"

"A refill on the coffee would be great."

Mark and Rick had a load of people, as well as a string of horses, and a snowplow team when they went back to Harlan. Adeline started inspecting horses the moment they arrived. The vet was there, and they triaged the bunch he brought. Since he brought the ones in the most distress, the outcome didn't surprise him. Adeline and Lyle took back their personal mounts and pronounced three other horses fit for duty, with reservations.

Mark finally got permission to proceed at a much slower pace. One stipulation was to rest the horses overnight at each end. It didn't start immediately, as that afternoon, Harlan got its first significant snowfall, and they put off the run for a day.

A strong southerly wind melted most of the snow. The snowplows came along in case they were needed going back. As it was, they had a clear road, and Mark's only complaint was the continuous banging of the roller behind the blade on the pavement.

Don Rowley came back with Mark after putting the wheels back on his freight wagons. His team was not doing well, and he took very little. That disappointed the folks waiting for a ride, but they appreciated the situation and didn't complain too loudly. Tom and Sammie stayed in the background, which Mark found gratifying.

Mark managed two runs before the snow forced him to stop. On his last run, he brought Vickie, a couple of the Arapahoe Inn staff, and a farm family. Sammie, Tom, and the ghosts were still there. Jimmy swore to Vickie that he would join her the second he was able to close things at Arapahoe. In addition, Alex and Cordelia Thomas were still there. They'd go with the last of their friends.

One condition Alex and Cordelia made was that Vickie and the staff members all go to Orleans. They had become quite protective of Vickie, and wouldn't do it any other way. That surprised Mark, but he didn't say anything about it. Alex and Cordelia were godparents again.

A week later, Adeline and the vet released Don Rowley's team to do one run to Arapahoe to complete the evacuation. Then the team was to rest for as long as it took to get them back in shape. By this time, the only way to Arapahoe was a single wagon with skis. The full complement of snowplow people went.

As the snow brought everything to a halt, Lyle and Adeline moved to Harlan Ranch. Adeline said the ranch, now that it was duly equipped with solar panels and other conveniences, was just as comfortable as their place. Besides, all the action was there, nursing the horses back to health. Mark thought Lyle and Adeline also kept an eye on him, seeing how he would act.

After Don made the final run, he came by the house for the required horse inspection. Adeline said she was satisfied, and then said, "Take your team and wagon to Ragan. Then you have a new job. Come back with Nancy. Tomorrow is Thanksgiving, and getting everybody safely to Harlan is certainly a reason to give thanks. Anyway, you always had Thanksgiving in this house. I see no reason for that to change now."

Over the next several days, Don talked about that final run. He went into excruciating detail. The snow depth at Arapahoe was like what Mark found at the castle on his last ride. Fortunately, that trip was between storms. When they left, the tribal members rode the wagon. All of them, except for the Arapahoe Inn staff, got off in Oxford. Sammie, Tom, and the ghosts got off there too. Don took the remainder to Orleans.

"What happened when Jimmy showed up?" Mark wondered.

Don actually smiled then. "Jimmy made a bee line to Vickie's side, with the rest of the staff right behind him. She tried to act healthy, but everybody saw she had gone a long way downhill since Jimmy made her go. Everybody in Orleans adopted her as a community daughter, and she's the focus of everything. Seeing the Peepul tribal members taking care of her made them accepted as well. Everybody thought Jimmy was the best medicine Vickie could have."

"Where are Vickie and Jimmy staying?" was Mark's next question.

"For the moment, they are in that building where you took everyone. They asked me about extra solar panels and refrigerators. It sounded like they want everyone in the old school building. The idea of running water and electricity appeals to them."

"What did you tell them?"

"What could I tell them? I'd see what I could do."

Mark laughed. "You've got warehouses full of them. Share the wealth, man."

"It wasn't supposed to work this way," Don growled.

Everybody laughed, including Don's wife, Nancy.

When Thanksgiving ended after three days of feasting, Don and Nancy went back to Ragan. After seeing them off, the four went back into the house. Later, Mark stared out at the early evening gloom.

"Are you staring at the horizon, Mark?" Lyle wondered behind him.

"I never stopped staring at the horizon, Lyle," Mark replied. Turning around he got eye contact. "Lately, I've started to look at it differently. Tom has his problems, but he was right. There will always be mud where we are. Still, if we work at it together, maybe we can find a horizon we all want to move toward."

Lyle seemed amused. "I'm with you on that, Mark. Welcome to the club."

The End

www.ingramcontent.com/pod-product-compliance
Lightning Source LLC
Chambersburg PA
CBHW060541180626
46817CB00002B/672

* 9 7 8 0 9 9 1 4 6 2 7 2 8 *